*Enter the unique ...
A place of high adv...
and unforgettable characters.*

"This action-packed book will delight
epic fantasy enthusiasts."
—*Library Journal*
on *Death's Mistress*

"Goodkind's world-building abilities are
outdone only by his striking character
development, resulting in an adventure that
is remarkably impactful."
—*RT Book Reviews* (Top Pick)
on *Death's Mistress*

"Wonderfully creative, seamless, and stirring."
—*Kirkus Reviews*
on *Wizard's First Rule*

"Outstanding . . . Characters who actually
behave like adults. Highly recommended."
—*The San Diego Union-Tribune*
on *Temple of the Winds*

BY TERRY GOODKIND

TERRY GOODKIND

HEART OF BLACK ICE

SISTER OF DARKNESS

The Nicci Chronicles, Volume IV

TOR

Tor Publishing Group
New York

This is a work of fiction. All of the characters, organizations, and events portrayed in this novel are either products of the author's imagination or are used fictitiously.

HEART OF BLACK ICE

Copyright © 2019 by Terry Goodkind

All rights reserved.

A Tor Book
Published by Tom Doherty Associates/Tor Publishing Group
120 Broadway
New York, NY 10271

www.tor-forge.com

Tor® is a registered trademark of Macmillan Publishing Group, LLC.

ISBN 978-1-250-19480-0

Our books may be purchased in bulk for promotional, educational, or business use. Please contact your local bookseller or the Macmillan Corporate and Premium Sales Department at 1-800-221-7945, ext. 5442, or by email at MacmillanSpecialMarkets @macmillan.com.

First Edition: January 2020
First Mass Market Edition: December 2020

Printed in the United States of America

13 12 11 10 9 8 7 6 5 4

HEART
OF
BLACK ICE

CHAPTER 1

Hidden in the forested hills, Nathan spied on the vast army of General Utros. The bedraggled wizard stood among scrub oaks and spindly pines, camouflaged by crosshatched shadows. The white robes he wore over his black pants and fine shirt were stained and scorched from fighting against the impossible, ancient enemy.

But he would keep fighting. Though the city of Ildakar was gone, he and his rebels were still alive.

A hundred and fifty thousand reawakened warriors filled the valley below, ready to march across the Old World. Fifteen centuries ago, the legendary General Utros had laid siege to Ildakar, with its shining buildings, high walls, and beautiful gardens. Using a remarkable petrification spell, the city's wizards had turned the army to stone, filling the plain with statues, but now the spell had worn off, and the invincible army renewed its attack. Desperate to save their fabled city, the remaining wizards had hidden Ildakar behind the shroud of eternity . . . which stranded Nathan and his compatriots outside. Now they were the only defenders left against an army large enough to conquer the continent.

"Dear spirits . . ." He plucked dry grass from his long

white hair. The immense military force reminded him of when Jagang's Imperial Order had filled the Azrith Plain beneath the People's Palace. Nathan took heart in knowing that Jagang's army had been defeated, although back then Richard Rahl had fought at their side. And Nicci . . .

Prelate Verna adjusted her skirts and sat on a lichen-stained boulder nearby. "When my party left Cliffwall, we didn't expect to find an entire army blocking our way. We were just hoping to find Ildakar."

"Ildakar is gone," groaned the wizard Renn, crunching through the underbrush as he came up to them. He wrapped his hand around a gnarled pine branch and looked past the camped army to where his glorious city had been not long ago. With a distracted frown, he wiped a smear of sticky sap on the frayed fabric of his maroon robe. "The wizards hid Ildakar from time itself. They didn't give a thought to those of us outside." His jowls sagged into deep lines. "At least they're safe now . . . I suppose."

"We've got to make the most of our situation out here," Nathan said. He felt more abandoned than the others, because he had lost more than just the city. The scorched swath across the battlefield below was a poignant reminder of how dear Elsa had sacrificed herself in an inferno of transference magic. In doing so, she had wiped out thousands of General Utros's soldiers. Tactically speaking, it was a victory, but at such a tremendous price. He felt dark sadness in his new heart, rather than triumph.

Escaping into the hills as the enemy army reeled, Nathan and his companions had unexpectedly encountered an expedition from Cliffwall—Prelate Verna, several Sisters of the Light, numerous scholars, and a party of D'Haran soldiers led by General Zimmer. Their combined forces, though, were just a handful against a titanic army.

Nathan had been fighting so hard and so long that he'd barely had a chance to think about all they had lost. "How will Nicci get back to us now? If Ildakar has vanished, where will she go? Where will the sliph take her when she returns from Serrimundi?"

Traveling through the sliph network, Nicci had rushed off to the coastal city to warn about the threat facing the Old World. With Ildakar gone, she would be cut off on the other side of the land.

"We could certainly use Nicci's help," Verna admitted. "But we are not powerless. Don't forget that."

Nathan stroked his chin. "I will not, my dear prelate, but the sorceress isn't the only one we have lost." He didn't know what had happened to Bannon either, who had been fighting inside Ildakar when the city disappeared. Nathan hoped the eager young swordsman was safe beneath the shroud. He sat beside Verna on the large boulder. "This is not the sort of reunion I anticipated having with you. I spent centuries trying to get my freedom from the Sisters of the Light, and now here we are together again."

"Yes, here we are again." The prelate's smile was tired, and she tucked a lock of gray-brown hair behind her left ear. "But we need to get moving again."

"But where will we go?" Renn asked, pacing among the pines. "Do we just run? We can't expect to defeat General Utros all by ourselves."

Lord Oron stepped up to them, looking haughty, his blond hair in a thick braid over one shoulder. His narrow face was speckled with fresh blood from the recent battle. "What is our best course of action? We cannot be just a bunch of rabble. Shall we form our own council of the gifted to fight General Utros?"

"It would be a small enough council," Renn said sourly.

"You forget how many gifted we have among us," Verna said. "Don't underestimate my other Sisters of the Light and the Cliffwall scholars."

Lady Olgya joined Oron, her body wrapped in special camouflaged silks, tough fabric that her silkworms had produced back in Ildakar. "Don't underestimate any of us. But we can't just hide in the bushes and watch that army bustle about. What plan should we pursue?"

Nathan realized they were all looking to him. "Am I your leader now? Will you call me wizard commander?" He found it ironic, since he had been unable to use his gift at all only a short time ago. "I never asked for the job."

Uncomplaining, the former slave Rendell distributed rations of dried food to the group. "This is the best meal I can provide, since we don't dare light cook fires." The older man had fought for his city along with other freed slaves. He had risked his life so Elsa could mark her deadly transference rune on the ground. Now Rendell, too, was stranded outside of Ildakar.

Oron frowned at the meager fare the former slave offered, being accustomed to fine banquets in the nobles' district. Nathan, though, chewed on the dried fruit and meat without complaining. He said, "I enjoy fancy meals as well as anyone, not to mention clean clothes and a soft bed, but I will endure a bit of hardship under the circumstances."

"Shall we develop a bold plan to defeat that gigantic army?" asked Leo, one of the other wizards who had been cut off from Ildakar. His eyes were bright but his grin looked forced. "Where do we start?"

"Lani would have had some unexpected ideas." Renn stared longingly at where the great city had been. He sighed. "I'll never see her again. When I left, she was a statue, petrified by Sovrena Thora as punishment, but the spell would have worn off. I miss her. . . ." The long hard journey had made the portly wizard lose weight. His face was thinner now, and his skin hung loose. "I wish I could have talked with her again. It's been so many centuries." He drew a hopeful breath. "Maybe if we can get back through the shroud of eternity—"

"Lani is dead, killed by the general's twin sorceresses," Oron said with offhanded bluntness. "Didn't anyone tell you?"

Renn paled until his skin resembled white stone. "Dead?" It was as if Oron had spoken to him in a different language. He turned to Nathan. "What does he mean?"

Nathan wanted to ignite Oron's hair for his heartless comment. "I'm sorry, Renn. I'm afraid she was killed. . . ." He cleared his throat and tried to sound as soothing as he could. "Lani used a pool of water to spy on the general's camp, but Ava and Ruva turned the magic back on her. They . . . drowned her." He shook his head. "Elsa and I fought to save her, but there was nothing we could do."

Renn placed his face in his hands. "That was the only thread of hope I still had." His shoulders shook as he sobbed. "I waited for her. I protected her. I mourned for her. . . . She . . ." He struggled to find the right word. "She mattered a great deal to me."

"I'm sorry you didn't get to see her again," Nathan

said. "She was brave and strong. I'll never forget what she did."

Olgya sounded grim and impatient. "No time for mourning any one person. Countless people have been lost, and we have suffered. Think of my son Brock, Oron's son Jed, the thousands of fighters. They all mattered to someone."

Renn glowered at her. "It still hurts."

"It still hurts, my friend," Nathan agreed, thinking of Elsa and what she had begun to mean to him. "And we need to hurt the enemy."

Sudden shouts came from the forest nearby, and Nathan lurched to his feet, reaching for the sword at his side. General Zimmer's soldiers in the scattered camp grabbed their weapons and formed ranks for mutual defense. Figures sprinted out of the forest.

"Get ready! Here they come!" Zimmer's voice held a hard edge of anticipation.

Three people burst through the underbrush, running at full speed. Oliver and Peretta, two young scholars from Cliffwall, dashed forward, along with Amber, a novice Sister of the Light. "They're right behind us!"

"We brought them here," Peretta called to her startled companions. "Now it's your turn!" Despite the flush on her narrow face, mischief sparkled in her eyes.

More crashing sounds echoed through the sparse forest, followed by gruff shouts. Lured onward by the trio of runners, twenty enemy soldiers blundered into the camp, hacking branches out of the way. They wore ancient-styled leather armor bearing the distinctive flame symbol of Emperor Kurgan. Oliver, Peretta, and Amber scampered ahead, taunting their pursuers into the trap.

One of the enemy soldiers bellowed, "There's more of them!" He held up a curved sword. "Wipe them out."

In a blur, two fierce women rushed in from opposite sides, letting out high-pitched yells. They had been waiting to strike. Each morazeth wore a black leather band around her chest and waist, and their skin was mottled with branded symbols.

"We will let you kill a few of them," Thorn called out to Nathan and the others. "But not every one." She held a short sword in one hand and a dagger in the other. She plunged her sword into the stomach of the nearest soldier and laughed as he crumpled. "That's one!"

Not to be outdone, her companion Lyesse snapped a barbed whip, which wrapped around an opponent's thick neck. She yanked it hard, ripping open his throat. "And one for me!"

Thrusting out his hand, Nathan threw a burst of wizard's fire that struck an enemy in the chest. The man's leather and plate armor was like paper against the deadly fire that burned through his torso.

Howling a war cry, Zimmer's soldiers threw themselves into the fight. The enemy scouts clashed with the D'Haran soldiers in a clatter of blades, grunts of pain, and shouts of anger.

With the fighters milling together, Nathan could not risk more wizard's fire. Prelate Verna used her gift to dislodge a heavy bough from the trees above and dropped it directly onto a soldier. Oron, Olgya, Leo, and Renn summoned a raging wind to slam more armored men into tree trunks.

Finding themselves in a real fight, the enemy soldiers fell back on their rigid military training. The pair of wild morazeth attacked as if they themselves were an army, and the D'Haran soldiers tried to keep up with the women, kill for kill.

As the enemies fell bleeding, Nathan noticed something he had not expected. Previously, General Utros's soldiers had been partially stone, their skin hard and chalky, but now they were *real flesh* again! He caught his breath. And if the enemy was fully human again, that would make them easier to kill. The D'Haran steel cut through the armor, hacked skin and bone, and the ancient enemies now died like normal men.

The gifted fighters Leo and Perri used magic to knock soldiers off their feet, impaling them on sharp branches. Even the slave Rendell jumped in with a knife, pulling off the helmet of a stunned soldier and slitting his throat. Nathan spotted an outlying man and used wizard's fire to burn his head entirely off his shoulders like a grisly lantern.

In short order, all twenty of the ancient scouts lay dead in the underbrush. Thorn and Lyesse stood grinning, their bronzed skin covered with blood. "Three!" said Lyesse.

"Three for me as well," Thorn responded.

"And that's twenty more dead," Nathan said. "Twenty fighters erased from the enemy forces."

"The army will not even notice those losses," Verna said. "Alas."

"General Utros hasn't finished counting his dead from our last attack," said Oron.

"Dead men are dead men," Renn said with grim satisfaction.

The D'Haran soldiers wiped bloodstains from their swords and armor. Zimmer nodded to each man, complimenting them. "Until we have a better plan, we will cut that army down little by little."

"If that's the way it must be," Lady Olgya said.

Nathan sheathed his sword, which he had not needed after all. He still reveled in using magic after being without his gift for so long. "At least it's a start."

CHAPTER 2

The empty city towered around Nicci, silent and mysterious. She turned to get her bearings and assessed the dark buildings, the imposing stone walls, the thick pillars and ornate carvings . . . the utter bleakness. This was not Ildakar, not at all.

The moon spilled silver light over the ruins, but she saw no cheerful lanterns or torches lighting any of the stone structures. All the windows and doors were black and vacant, like the eyes of dead men. The thin air held an underlying chill. She could see the silhouettes of black crags that ringed the city, and she realized she must be high in the mountains.

Nicci stepped away from the sliph well, angry and confused. Her body ached, as if the abortive journey had wrung her like a washrag. "Sliph!" she shouted, but the quiet was so deep and intense that it buzzed in her ears.

The spiteful silver creature had dumped her here and abandoned her.

In the middle of a central plaza, a waist-high stone barrier surrounded the enigmatic well. The sliph had simply retreated down into the depths after lashing out at Nicci, leaving her alone. She had no idea where she was.

As Nicci caught her breath and her balance, she felt uncharacteristically weak, disconnected. She had never felt like this when traveling in the sliph before. She called to the deep, empty well. "Come back! This is not my destination. I wish to travel."

Her words resonated in the deep black gullet and whispered back at her from the high stone buildings, but no other sound came. The silvery creature refused to respond. This particular sliph, a determined adherent of Emperor Sulachan's long-lost cause, had finally realized that Nicci did not, in fact, serve the same master. When Nicci had revealed that Sulachan was dead, defeated not once but twice, the silvery woman had broken her bonds of duty and stranded Nicci in this forsaken place.

"Sliph! Where am I?" Nicci's voice vanished into infinity below. She could do nothing to help fight General Utros if she was trapped . . . here.

As her head rang and throbbed, Nicci wondered how much damage she had suffered in the dangerous passage. She remembered that the sliph had said one other intriguing thing before leaving: "Ildakar is gone. Ildakar is no more. I cannot take you there." Clearly, the sliph had also been damaged when she tried to reach her destination, and failed.

How could Ildakar be "no more"? Maybe the sliph well in the lower levels of the legendary city had been destroyed or sealed somehow. What else could prevent the sliph from traveling there?

Then Nicci recalled something else. Before she'd killed Kor, the Norukai captain, he revealed that King Grieve had launched a massive attack against Ildakar. How could the great city defend itself against the invincible army of General Utros as well as a second threat from the Norukai? Was it possible that the wizards' duma had raised the shroud of eternity as their only recourse? Would they have left the rest of the world to face the scourge alone? Yes, the wizards of Ildakar would have done exactly that.

And if that were the case, Nicci would be on her own.

First, she had to find out where she was. Her close-cropped blond hair was dusty from hard travel. She still had blood on her skin and black dress from fighting the Norukai in Serrimundi Harbor. Her body felt shaky and sore, an aftereffect of the sliph passage. Her gift was weak.

Exploring her new surroundings, Nicci studied the massive pillars and stone buildings, huge monuments, temples, or governmental halls. As she moved across the plaza, her feet whispered on the uneven flagstones. The city was littered with looming stone towers and fallen arches, long-dry fountains, intricate decorations weathered into indeterminate lumps.

The structures were immense and ostentatious, designed to inspire awe. The imposing grandeur reminded her of Emperor Jagang's palace in Altur'Rang or the Wizard's Keep in Aydindril. This place had once been a large population center, a capital, or at least a major trading hub. But all the doorways and windows were sealed or bricked up, like crypts. This was a city of the dead.

She heard a rustling sound and saw a pair of wild deer wandering through the empty park, eating the shrubs and flowers. Startled to see Nicci, the deer skittered off, but halted not far away and went back to grazing.

In another magnificent square, Nicci came upon the enormous statue of a man, which now lay broken on the flagstones. The raised marble base was the size of a building's foundation, and originally the titan must have towered three stories high, but only the sturdy boots remained attached to the base. Someone had smashed the legs, intentionally toppling the statue.

She absorbed the scene and felt an undertone of violence and destruction here. The stone arms had broken off, and now the remnants lay overgrown with vines.

She stepped up to the toppled statue and regarded it, ignoring the moss and dust. The man's haughty face had a heavy brow and hooked nose, and his hair hung in snakelike braids beneath a blocky crown. The carved mouth was open in a weathered smile, showing one prominent pointed tooth, clearly an affectation.

With growing suspicion, Nicci walked around the toppled statue to the front of the base, where engraved letters were worn down but still readable.

EMPEROR KURGAN

Nicci turned back to the head of the fallen statue. The pointed tooth must be the iron fang Kurgan had worn to intimidate those in his presence. He had been a violent and capricious emperor who skinned his wife alive and fed her to flesh beetles when he learned of her affair with General Utros. Outraged at what he had done, Iron Fang's own people had overthrown him and dragged his body through the streets. They had even smashed his statue.

Even now, after fifteen centuries, Nicci took grim satisfaction at seeing this evidence of his demise. Given the broken figure of the despised emperor, as well as the immense buildings and monuments, Nicci had a good idea of where she was. This city must be Orogang, capital of Kurgan's vast empire, which had collapsed after his downfall.

She turned slowly as the pieces fell into place, but she still didn't understand why the city itself was a graveyard. Even with Kurgan dead and the empire torn apart by political turmoil, why would such an important metropolis have been abandoned? Why would the population have left these impressive buildings to the rats and spiders? Where would the people have gone? Had a plague wiped them out? A famine or drought?

And why were the doors sealed and the windows bricked shut, as if to seal something inside?

She passed a sunken amphitheater, a deep round bowl with circular tiers of seats leading down to a central stage at the bottom. Kurgan must have addressed the people from there, his voice resounding up the walls of the deep bowl. The seats were empty now, many of them crumbled, the stage overgrown with weeds.

Beyond the amphitheater, Nicci found a second towering statue, but this one looked barely weathered, as if someone had maintained it over the centuries. The figure was a muscular, broad-chested warrior wearing a helmet and ornate armor once emblazoned with Kurgan's stylized flame, though the symbol had been defaced, leaving only a white scar on the stone. The handsome, broad face beneath the helmet's scooped cheek guards had a firm jaw, piercing eyes, strong cheekbones, a regal-looking nose.

Nicci knew this man, had faced him on the battlefield. *General Utros*—Iron Fang's greatest military commander, who had been dispatched from Orogang to conquer the Old World in the name of his emperor. Utros had accepted the mission without questioning the worthiness of his leader, because Utros was a man who didn't question orders.

Judging by the condition of the sculpture, the people of Orogang had revered the general. It seemed odd to her that the Utros monument was even now clean of debris and stains, not dilapidated like the rest of this empty city. She froze when she spotted fresh flowers strewn on one corner of the base.

Someone had been here, and recently.

Suddenly wary, she looked around. The buildings remained silent, some of them collapsing, but others deceptively intact. Maybe some hermit or devotee had placed a flower at the statue of his hero. No one here would possibly guess that Utros could still be alive after fifteen hundred years.

Nicci sensed something more than the loneliness of this place, but a presence, eyes watching her. Orogang might not be as abandoned and desolate as she had thought. Staring into the shadows cast by the moon, she heard a rustle of movement. At first she thought it might just be the wandering deer, then realized it was a different kind of furtive sound. Footsteps.

Nicci spun, reaching out with her gift, though she still felt weak and strange. "Who is there?"

The hush fell again after her words faded. She turned toward the largest structure that dominated the main plaza, a massive building with tall fluted columns at the grand entryway. The doors were now open, though they revealed only darkness within. Beyond the Utros statue, she saw more movement, a shadow darting into deeper shadows, multiple gray-clad human figures melting into the murk.

Nicci turned cautiously, alert. "Reveal yourselves!

Come out and face me." Her voice sounded as loud as a gong in the empty city. She touched the daggers at each hip and prepared to defend herself.

At last, she was able to discern human silhouettes as they emerged from hiding places, darkened doorways, narrow alleys. The strangers moved with trepidation, whispering among themselves. They refused to answer her.

"Who are you?" Nicci turned in a slow circle and realized the figures were all around her, but she could barely sense them, as if they were only spirits. She saw many more people than she expected.

Looking beyond the city, she saw a faint glow of dawn outlining the mountain crags and revealing more figures scuttling out of their stone-walled lairs and converging on her.

Nicci let her hands rest threateningly on the daggers. "I don't want to attack you, but I will."

The brightening dawn seemed to agitate them, and she heard urgent voices rising, but the few snatches of words made no sense to her. Nicci backed toward the base of the Utros statue and stared up at the stone face that merely gazed ahead.

Then, as if they heard a silent signal, the shadowy people lunged forward to surround her.

CHAPTER 3

After the wave of fire had incinerated thousands of his brave soldiers, General Utros saw how the battlefield was devastated. The sour smoke of burned grass and roasted flesh lingered in the air for days, and he doubted he would ever get the taste and stink from the back of his throat. The loss of so many loyal men felt like a hot knife through his heart.

Elsa's transference magic was far more powerful than he had ever imagined. Too late, Ava and Ruva had realized that the defenders were marking boundary runes to unleash terrible magic. Too late, Utros had seen the individual strike forces encompass part of the valley around his army. Too late, he had watched the gifted Elsa lay down the anchor rune at the center of camp and trigger her devastating spell. The twins had barely shielded him in time.

His thousands of soldiers hadn't had a chance.

Even with the breathtaking losses, though, his army was still more than a hundred thousand strong. His warriors were incensed, ready for blood, hungry to conquer the land from horizon to horizon, and he would lead them to victory. That was what he had vowed to Emperor Kurgan, even if his emperor was long dead.

In the late afternoon of a troublesome day, Utros adjusted the golden mask that covered half of his face. His helmet bore the horns of an enormous bull, an Ildakaran monster that he himself had killed. He stood outside the pavilion his soldiers had erected, a replacement for his burned-down command headquarters. The fabric was a patchwork of salvaged pieces, and the wooden posts were roughly hewn from charred trees, but General Utros did not require the ostentatious trappings Iron Fang would have demanded. The tent provided shelter and shade, which was what he needed.

Standing out in the open, he smelled ashes in the wind. Ava and Ruva stood close, stroking his heavily muscled arms, the copper wristbands. "We are ready to receive the Norukai king, beloved Utros," said Ava.

"And we are ready to conquer the world," replied her twin sister.

The identical sorceresses were beautiful in their blue gowns. They had shaved and scraped every trace of hair from their bodies, then painted their skin with swooping curves and angular designs that invoked arcane powers. Instead of their usual multicolored pigments, Ava and Ruva now marked themselves with black soot and dried blood, which was more powerful than paint.

"We will impress our new allies with the strength of our army," Ava said, "but our hospitality is sorely lacking."

Her sister added, "We cannot offer King Grieve a feast."

Utros clenched his jaw, knowing their situation was far more serious than that. Once Ildakar had disappeared in front of them, his army no longer had hope of raiding the city for food and matériel. He had counted on that for their very survival.

He looked toward where the plain abruptly dropped down to the Killraven River and the extensive morass of swamps below. "King Grieve will bring provisions from his raiding fleet. It will be enough for now." Utros did not manage to convince himself. "Keeper and spirits," he whispered under his breath.

From the river drop-off he watched a party of the Norukai raiders trudging forward as if they meant to conquer the valley. He knew this was only a small delegation from the serpent ships on the river. The big raiders were hideously scarred, clad in vests of sharkskin leather or reptilian hides. Even from a distance he recognized King Grieve and his prancing albino shaman, the gangly scarred man known as Chalk.

Behind them came a group carrying crates, barrels, and sacks—enough supplies to feed a small army. Unfortunately, Utros had a *large* army, and now that the stone spell had entirely worn off, they were a hungry army.

Just after Ildakar vanished beneath the shroud, the lingering remnants of the stone spell had suddenly and inexplicably faded from his troops, and they became entirely human again, flesh, blood, and bone. At first, the army had rejoiced at being able to *feel* again, but Utros quickly realized that their restored humanity also brought them vulnerabilities. When they were still half petrified, the numerous regiments had experienced no hunger or thirst; now, though, they all felt the needs of the flesh. He had a hundred thousand mouths to feed, out here in the middle of a vast valley with no city to raid and no supply train.

First Commander Enoch arrived at the command pavilion, grim-faced with his report. Utros wanted his majordomo to join the discussions regarding their new alliance. The veteran pressed a fist against his heart and then looked at the supplies carried by the Norukai. With only a glance, he made his assessment. "That stockpile will be enough to feed the officers down to the squad commanders. We can ration carefully."

"It won't be enough for all of us," Utros said, keeping his voice low.

King Grieve, Chalk, and six more raider captains approached the pavilion, trudging across the burned grass. Facing the general, Grieve clacked his jaws together. His cheeks were slashed all the way back to the hinge of the jaw and sewn up again. Tattoos covered his face, symbolic scales of his serpent god. The king's chest was enormously broad, as if he had an extra set of lungs so he could dive deep and wrestle sharks. Implanted bone spurs protruded from his shoulders. Instead of a belt, an iron chain encircled his waist.

"We brought food, as you requested. Let us have a celebration feast!" Grieve gestured to the downtrodden slaves who served as beasts of burden. The slaves piled the supply crates, sacks, and barrels outside the pavilion, near large cook fires that had already been lit.

"My hunters also provided three deer they killed in the hills," Utros offered. "We will roast them as part of the meal."

"You can have all the fish," Grieve grumbled. "I am sick of fish. I'll take the venison."

"Fish, fish!" Chalk capered about. "Suck the bones and chew the heads. I like how the eyeballs pop." He bent his elbows at odd angles as he hopped from one foot to the other. "My Grieve, King Grieve! They'll all grieve!" He wore only a loincloth of sewn-together fish skins, leaving his skin bare, as if he wanted to show off the bite marks that covered his body, thousands of pocked holes from tiny fanged mouths. His mangled lip made his grin horribly twisted.

Ava and Ruva regarded the shaman with displeasure. In unison they lifted their chins, haughty and beautiful, as if to emphasize the inferiority of Grieve's companion.

"Today is more than just a celebration feast." Utros tried to sound diplomatic as he led the Norukai party under the stretched fabric of the pavilion. He used his best skills of diplomacy, because he needed this large fighting force and their ships. "We must plan our war, together. My army needs to move, since we have many mouths to feed." He gestured out to where the soldiers had set up rough tents and bedding in the blackened valley. "Our numbers may be unwieldy, but we are invincible. My army will conquer any lands we encounter."

Grieve chuffed out a loud laugh. "You mean, any lands the Norukai leave for you!"

Utros spoke firmly. "The Old World is ours."

"Yes, ours. Mine and yours."

Utros remained firm, businesslike. "Together, we have to contemplate strategy. We can't simply rampage across the continent. We must conquer and use it."

The Norukai king was impatient. "As you wish, but we can break the continent just a little. I need the exercise."

Ava and Ruva watched Grieve and his albino with intent gazes. The Norukai king openly leered at the two women, but they did not respond. Utros knew the twins didn't need protection. The sorceresses could kill anyone who bothered them.

As the deer carcasses roasted over the fire and the fish cooked on smaller spits, First Commander Enoch oversaw the distribution of Norukai supplies among the army, stretching the food as far as possible.

Later, while he gnawed on bloody meat from a joint, King Grieve frowned at the emptying crates. "That is the rest of our supplies from our ships." He did not sound upset. Rather, his voice had an insulting undertone. "You worry too much about food."

"My soldiers must eat," Utros said. "My challenge is managing the supplies and stockpiles."

"Then your soldiers are weak." The Norukai king reached inside his wide mouth and used a fingertip to dig a morsel of meat from his back molar. "We don't worry about supplies. We raid to take what we need, then we move on."

"They'll all grieve!" Chalk said.

"We will have to follow your example," the general conceded, though the empty foothills and the great valley offered few resources.

King Grieve leaned forward, studying the general's half mask. "I may want one of those myself. I like the way it looks."

Utros peeled off the golden covering to reveal his flayed face. By now the wound had healed, the dark muscle scabbed and hardened over the skull. "It was not my choice. It was necessary for a spell."

The Norukai nodded appreciatively and fingered the mouth scars on his own cheeks. "Sometimes we do what is necessary." He planted his elbows on the rough wooden table. "So tell me your plan to conquer the world."

Utros gazed beyond the pavilion toward his huge army. "I have many thousands of fighters, armed and ready to march. Are any of your ships still intact after being crushed in the river ice?"

Chalk squirmed at the rough-hewn table. "Ships and

fish, ice and fire, great serpent ships." He grinned. "Serpent ships! Splintered ships now!"

"Not splinters!" Grieve roughly knocked the albino in the shoulder, then apologized by sweeping his arm around Chalk, squeezing the scrawny man. He faced Utros. "When the river froze, a hundred ships were anchored in the river, many up against the docks so we could climb the bluffs and invade Ildakar. The ice crushed some hulls, snapped the keels." He pounded a heavy fist on the table. His knuckles, augmented with small iron plates, made the wood ring loudly from the blow. "But we will repair them. The Norukai are great shipbuilders." Grieve glanced behind him toward where the land dropped abruptly to the river. "The swamps provide all the wood we need. We have tools. We have slaves."

The general took him at his word. "We will need your vessels and your Norukai fighters for the war. You said you have many more ships back at your islands? We require your navy and your fighters, along with my entire army." He grew more serious. "Your ships will move faster down the river out to sea. Even at a hard pace, my army will take longer to travel overland to the coast."

"Some of my serpent ships are nearly repaired, and I am anxious to move, too," Grieve said. "I will sail back to our Norukai islands, where I expect another hundred ships will be completed by now. My raiders are thirsty for victory and plunder. While we wait for your marching soldiers, we will attack cities on the coast, like a storm of steel and blood."

In his calculating mind, Utros manipulated the pieces, saw the large tactical picture. "If the Norukai raiders attack the coast, and my army sweeps overland, we will form a pincer across the Old World."

Grieve bit down on the bone from which he had stripped the deer meat. "We will crush the land like a grape between two fingers. It is a good plan."

"Once our fighting forces unite," Utros added, "we will march together and subjugate Tanimura, Altur'Rang, and then move on to the New World."

"King Grieve!" Chalk cried. "They'll all grieve."

"Yes, they'll all grieve," said General Utros.

The Norukai weren't much for small talk. After they finished their feast, the raiders were anxious to get back to their ships. Like General Utros, they had expected to conquer Ildakar, but now that the city itself was gone, neither army had a reason to remain here in this empty place. King Grieve departed as if the two commanders had planned the entire war in detail, and Utros realized that the Norukai were not much for planning. They simply attacked, moved on, then returned whenever they felt like it.

He suspected Grieve would be an even worse leader than Iron Fang had been, but Utros would worry about the brute later, when it became an issue. He would use these violent Norukai to accomplish his aims. He had sworn to grind the entire continent under his boot heel—out of loyalty to his emperor and secretly out of love for Majel. Now all of that had broken inside him, and so Utros would have to do it for himself and no other reason.

The Norukai returned to the bluffs above the river and climbed back down to their damaged ships. When the ugly raiders were gone, First Commander Enoch approached Utros, deeply concerned. "All the supplies were distributed, General. They did not go far."

"I did not expect them to," Utros said. "There was truth in what the Norukai king said. Recently, our scouts mapped out some nearby settlements. We know where there are supplies for the taking—at least a few—and we must have them. Disperse raiding parties in all directions. Find every town and strip them of every scrap of food." He lowered his head. "It's the only way our army can survive."

CHAPTER 4

As the following dawn spilled across the river flatlands, Norukai taskmasters pounded on drums to rouse the groaning slaves, kicking the ones who didn't move swiftly enough.

"Time to work!" bellowed Gara, a muscular female shipwright with gray braids dangling like drowned vipers from her patchy scalp. "Work until your fingers bleed." She opened her scarred mouth and snapped her teeth back together.

Tied on the tilted deck of a damaged Norukai ship, Bannon squirmed to avoid a vicious kick. A raider cut his bonds so he could join the others at work.

The captives set about their repairs in the faint dawn light. Gara used a mallet to pound boards and pegs into place, but Bannon had seen the ugly woman employ the bulky tool to bash the skull of a slave who worked too slowly.

As Bannon rubbed his raw wrists where the rope had chafed him during the night, the ghostly pale shaman crept up and grasped his shoulders with spidery fingers. "Time to hammer, or time to be a nail!"

Bannon shook him off, uneasy about the strange behavior of the scarred albino. At least he understood the uncouth Norukai, but Chalk was deeply unsettling. For some reason, the shaman found him fascinating.

After days of captivity, Bannon's body was battered and sore. He still had healing cuts, torn fingers, and massive bruises from fighting the Norukai invaders on the bluffs below Ildakar. He had nearly killed Chalk and King Grieve before they all tumbled down the cliff-side to crash in a heap of bodies and weapons.

But rather than dying then, Bannon had been taken as a slave. Being captured by the Norukai was one of his greatest nightmares, ever since the slavers tried to seize him as a boy on Chiriya Island. Back then, his best friend, Ian, had been seized in his stead while Bannon got away, and he had regretted that moment of cowardice ever since. Now, many years later, he found himself a slave after all.

Chalk shook him by the shoulders again, and Bannon lashed out instinctively, remembering what they had done to Ian. "Don't touch me, filthy Norukai!"

The albino cackled, delighted by Bannon's reaction. In the brightening daylight, King Grieve saw him rebuff his pale friend, and the big man strode forward, his expression like an angry storm rolling across the sea. "Show respect or die, slave!" Grieve grabbed Bannon by the neck and yanked him off the deck. "Are you worth the air you breathe? Are you worth the water you piss?"

Bannon struggled, ready to fight back even though he knew he'd be severely beaten or killed. He was not a coward, but he would not be an example for these monsters.

Scowling, shipwright Gara stepped up to intervene. "Break him later, my king. We need the workers if you want these ships repaired. Lost three men yesterday, and we're not getting any more workers from the city." The shipwright glanced at the bluffs rising above the river. The top of the cliff above, where Ildakar had been, looked like a cleanly sheared tree stump, the city simply swept away. "We need to use the ones we have, at least until we're done."

Grieve released his hold and let Bannon drop unceremoniously to the slanted deck. He raised a heavy battle-axe in his hand, threatening, and that provoked a delighted reaction from Chalk. He crowed, "The axe cleaves the wood! The sword cleaves the bone!"

Bannon didn't know what the shaman meant, but his jabbering often made no sense. Chalk looked at Bannon and nodded, as if he expected the young man to agree with him. "The axe cleaves the wood! The sword cleaves the bone!"

Grieve dismissed his odd friend. "My axe can cleave bone just as well, and it will take off this one's head as soon as the ship repairs are done."

"Not yet, my Grieve. Not yet." Chalk stroked Bannon's long ginger hair, which made his skin crawl. "Not this one."

Slave crews got to work among the numerous damaged vessels. The Norukai fleet had consisted of a hundred serpent ships sailing up the Killraven River and closing on Ildakar. The raiders had intended to climb the bluffs and overwhelm the city's defenses, but they didn't know anything about the besieging army of General Utros on the other side of the city. Bannon and his morazeth partner Lila had fought with hundreds of other defenders on the cliffs, hurling down projectiles, battling with spears and swords to drive the raiders away, but the Norukai had overwhelmed them.

He had fallen from the cliff, been knocked unconscious and taken captive. Bannon didn't know what had happened to Lila since then, and even if he managed to escape from the countless hundreds of watchful Norukai all around him, he did not know how he could reunite with his friends. Nathan had been leading a huge raid against General Utros when the city vanished beneath the shroud of eternity, and Nicci had gone on another mission, to warn Serrimundi. Bannon had no hope of meeting up with any of them ever again, so he would have to fend for himself. If he ever got away.

When Elsa's transference magic had frozen the entire river, the ice-locked ships were structurally damaged. The angry Norukai now worked like ants, making repairs and forcing their captives to do the hardest labor, cutting down trees in the swamps, dragging the logs back, and sawing the wood into lumber.

Some of the serpent ships had sunk to the silty river bottom. Those wrecks were stripped of ropes, which were used to repair the rigging of other ships. Sheets of midnight-blue sailcloth were moved to the intact ships and mounted as sails. Workers sawed the masts from the scuttled ships and installed them on other vessels; salvaged wood provided new hull boards where needed. Expert Norukai shipwrights like Gara moved from vessel to vessel directing the repairs, commanding slave teams.

Always looking for his chance to escape, Bannon reluctantly hauled lengths of rope from one deck to another, carrying tools and supplies. During the hot, endless work, he considered using the mallets and pry bars as weapons. He knew he could harm several of the slavers, but it would be an impotent gesture against thousands of ruthless Norukai, and he would just end up dead. He wrestled with what to do.

The day before, one of the Ildakar slaves attempted to fight back and succeeded in injuring one Norukai, who was taken by surprise with his back turned. Though Bannon applauded the man's effort, it was poorly planned, and the Norukai instantly subdued the rebellious slave. They were not quick about killing him. They forced Bannon and the other captives to watch as they broke the bones in the slave's arms one at a time, then his legs. They piled heavy weight stones on his chest, one after another with a long pause in between, until his ribs cracked, his eyes hemorrhaged, and blood spouted from his mouth. When the poor man gasped for mercy, one of the Norukai simply stepped on the weights, slowly pressing until his sternum cracked.

Though Bannon wanted to murder these tormentors, he wouldn't waste his life to no purpose. He watched and waited, knowing an opportunity would arise, and he hoped he could help the other captives as well as himself.

Sullen slaves dismantled a sunken wreck, using pry bars to detach the hull boards for patching holes in other vessels. The exhausted workers were fed little and allowed no rest. They had only the greenish river water to drink.

King Grieve bellowed from the prow of one of the nearly finished ships. "I want to sail soon. Finish these ships so we can head back to the Norukai islands and launch our war."

Bannon muttered, "Since so many Norukai were killed here, you'll need fewer ships going home." The shipwright reached over and slapped Bannon hard on the face, bloodying his lip and leaving a bright red mark on his cheek.

Chalk laughed as if the young swordsman's remark was the funniest thing he had ever heard. He squatted in front of Bannon and nodded, grinning. Unfortunately, the king also heard the comment. Grieve grabbed him again, ready to kill him, but Gara hissed her warning again. "We need him to work!"

The king lifted Bannon and tossed him over the side of the ship and into the river. "He can work at the waterline, soaking up mud and slime."

With a yelp, Bannon fell, plunging into the river. Spluttering, he struggled for something to hold on to. He trod water and looked up, his reddish hair hanging in muddy strands like weeds. Grieve leaned over the rail and growled from above. "Next time I'll put weights on your ankles! Then you can repair the bottom of the boat until you drown."

Chalk peered over the rail, staring down at Bannon with incomprehensible concern.

Gara threw a mallet down to him, which splashed in the water. Four other slaves were tied to the listing ship alongside spare boards and wooden buckets filled with nails. The river sounds hummed in the oppressive humid air around them. Norukai guards passed close in landing boats, ferrying equipment and people from one serpent vessel to the next, while also keeping watch on the slaves working at the waterline.

Bannon realized that further resistance—today—would accomplish nothing more, so he grudgingly took the floating mallet and followed instructions. For now. Picking up one of the patch boards, he reached into a bucket of nails that hung on a rope and joined the other slaves in pounding the wood into place, overlapping hull boards. Another slave dug his hands into a pot of warm pitch and slathered a waterproof seal across the wood.

A nearby slave commiserated, "Terrible duty, but better than bilge work."

Bannon had seen other slaves going into the dark and stuffy lower decks of the damaged ships, hauling out buckets of water so the vessels could float higher. "I guess we can always think of something worse." Optimism had often been Bannon's saving grace, and he clung to hope that frequently turned out to be foolish. But it was the core of his personality. He would find a way to escape these disgusting captors, and he would make things better. He wouldn't give up.

The slave beside him let out a bitter chuckle. "This is much better than the bilge—" Suddenly, his face twisted in an expression of pain and terror. He flailed at the rope holding him, but something yanked his body beneath the water before he could scream. The rope stretched tight, then snapped, and blood blossomed in the water.

Bannon instinctively reached out to save the man, but the victim was snatched away. The other slaves scrambled to get out of the river as the knobby reptilian back of a swamp predator broke the surface and swam briskly away with the poor man's broken body in its scissorlike jaws. The swamp dragon dove under the water, taking its meal.

The slaves in the water screamed, pulling on their ropes as they tried to lift themselves to safety. Bannon grabbed the snapped cable that had held the victim and used it to climb the hull, reaching down to help the others. Norukai rushed to the rails with boat hooks and spears. They jabbed downward, knocking the slaves away. "Back in the water. Back to work!"

"Monsters in the river!" one of the slaves cried. "We'll be killed."

"You should be more afraid of us than anything down there," Gara said.

Bannon still held his wooden mallet, wishing he had his faithful sword, Sturdy. He wanted to kill these hideous people, but as he looked up at the forest of jagged spear points, the curved swords and the angry scarred faces, he realized he would just be throwing his life away. Chalk was watching him, shaking his head and wagging his finger, as if warning Bannon.

Despising the Norukai more than ever, Bannon let himself slip back into the river, alert for ripples in the water and the scaly backs of swamp monsters. Soon he knew he was going to have to kill something.

Lila kept to the thickets on the riverbank, hidden but close enough that she could have thrown a spear and killed a Norukai warrior, right out in the open. But right now that would have wasted her element of surprise to no good purpose. She had already quietly killed nine of them under cover of darkness and fed their bodies to predators, and that satisfied her for a while. Now, though, she lurked in her camouflage, watching and waiting for her chance.

Bannon needed her.

When Ildakar had disappeared in the middle of the battle, she, too, had fallen from the bluff. Despite what should have been a fatal plunge, she had tumbled into shallow water and soft river mud. Stunned, Lila had drifted down the current until her body caught in the tangled bushes, where she pulled herself to shore. The Norukai hadn't seen her.

Now, days later, her short brown hair was caked with mud, and her face was sunburned. She wore only scant black leather. The branded runes on her skin protected her from magic, but did nothing to ward off insect bites or dangerous thorns. She had a dagger, but she had lost her short sword in the fall. Since she was a morazeth, though, her entire body was a weapon. She relied on her muscles and reflexes. She would bide her time and do whatever damage she could, any time she caught one of the Norukai alone. . . .

Lila and her morazeth sisters had sworn to defend Ildakar, which was now gone, but she had also accepted personal responsibility for Bannon, promising to protect him. She had trained the boy in the combat pits, challenged him with her harshest exercises. She had even occasionally taken him as a lover to reward him when he did well, and as time went by, she found more and more excuses to reward him in such a way. Lila didn't understand why the young swordsman failed to appreciate all that she had taught him. Her hard lessons had certainly saved his life more than once.

At one point, during an assault on the army of General Utros, Bannon had been taken prisoner and nearly killed. That incident had shown her that she didn't want to lose him. She realized it wasn't just a matter of pride for her. Bannon was cocky, believing he was a good fighter—which he was—but Lila was better. The two of them fought well together, but she doubted he could survive without her.

When he had plunged down the bluffside with King Grieve and Chalk, Lila thought he was dead, but after she survived her own fall and worked her way close enough to spy on the slaves the Norukai had taken, she caught a glimpse of Bannon, unmistakable with his long ginger hair, his familiar body. Thus, she knew he was still alive, knew she still had a chance.

For days after the city vanished, Lila prowled through the thickets, staying hidden as she climbed over knobby roots and dangling vines, always watching the Norukai. She couldn't fight thousands of them, no matter how much she might enjoy it. She would have to be clever.

Throughout the day, she crouched among the thorny shrubs as the sluggish river lapped along the muddy shore. Bloodthirsty biting insects buzzed around her face. Even after the damage their navy had suffered, Lila could see that with all their furious work, the raiders would have several serpent ships repaired soon. She would have to think bigger.

Lila worked her way to the base of the bluffs, where she found the ruins of the Ildakaran docks, splintered boards, anchoring posts, all of which had been smashed when the Norukai warships arrived. Overhead, she saw only the remnants of sheared-off tunnels in the cliffs that now went nowhere.

She caught a glint of sunlight on steel among the dock boards and broken branches against the rocks. She hunched in the shadows until she was sure of her camouflage, then slipped forward to see what the object might be.

It was a plain, leather-wrapped hilt. She moved the broken dock boards aside, careful to make no noise, and found a sword, an unimpressive blade that had fallen from the cliffs above. She pulled it loose from the mud, splashed water on the blade and cross guard to reveal the discolored metal. This was not an ornate sword, but it was serviceable. She recognized the weapon—Bannon's sword, Sturdy.

The edge was still sharp, and she knew that this was a better blade than any she could have wished for—and appropriate, too. Now she was armed, and she would find a way to save Bannon, even if she had to take on the entire Norukai fleet.

CHAPTER 5

W izard Commander Maxim looked beautiful. Adessa held up his head, wrapped her fingers in his spiky dark hair. His dead face sparked a thrill of satisfaction that flowed through Adessa like warm honey.

Maxim's decapitated body lay sprawled in the dirt in front of the cottage. Ribs poked out like broken twigs from his smashed chest. Wind rushed through the boughs of the surrounding dark spruce trees like whispered cheers. The morazeth leader raised the head in front of her face in the moonlight.

The wizard commander had been so handsome once, the haughty leader of Ildakar, but now his face was slack, his lids like loose fleshy flaps covering his eyes. His mouth hung open, and blood dribbled down into his goatee. Gore glistened on the stump of his neck.

After she sprang her trap, the man would have perished soon enough from his smashed chest, but Adessa didn't want Maxim to die on his own. The Keeper would have him one way or the other, so she had hacked through his neck and lifted up the head in triumph.

"My mission is complete." Adessa's voice was a hard whisper, muffled by the stirring spruce trees around the cottage. "I always knew I would kill you, but you were too arrogant to believe it yourself."

The dead wizard commander did not respond, but his slack cheek muscle twitched, startling her with the unexpected movement. Maxim's mouth fell open wider as his jaw muscles relaxed in death.

Adessa drew a deep breath. She had done as Sovrena Thora commanded. Finally, she could go home to Ildakar.

Wizard Commander Maxim had betrayed Ildakar by creating unrest among the lower classes, provoking a revolt—just because he was bored! Such betrayal was unthinkable to Adessa. She and her fellow morazeth were utterly loyal to their city and to the wizards' duma.

On the night of the uprising, when mobs killed their masters and destroyed thousands of years of the sovrena's perfect society, Maxim had fled the city laughing. As the chaos continued to build, Thora had sent Adessa after the wizard commander with instructions to hunt him down and bring back his head as a trophy. For many days, weeks, she had tracked the man through the swamps, down the Killraven River, until finally trapping him here at this isolated cottage. She recalled the delicious impact of her sword against his neck, the crunch as she cut through his spine. A shiver went down her back as she thought of it now.

With her highly attuned reflexes, she whirled at the sound of a crackle like melting ice. Pale statues stood just at the edge of the cottage's garden: a broad-chested man in patched clothes, and his wife with her hair bound in a scarf, her wide hips covered by a patchwork skirt. Three children were by them: a young girl of about five, a boy of eight, and an older boy of eleven or twelve. The petrified figures began to move sluggishly, inhaling deep breaths as they came alive again. Confused, the family bent their arms in wonder.

Adessa relaxed. She should have expected this would happen once she killed Maxim. The Farrier family lived in this cottage in the forested hills above the river town. Apparently, the kindly people had welcomed the wizard commander and offered him shelter, but when they tried to flee, he had turned them all into statues. Now that the wizard commander was dead, his petrification spell had worn off.

Their skin softened and flushed with color again. In the minds of these terrified people, they had been running into the night, terrorized by Maxim, when their existence had suddenly *stopped*. Now, like a snapped string, it was a different night sometime in the future, and everything had changed. They didn't even know how many days had passed or what had happened in the world.

And there was a bloody woman standing before them with a severed head in her hand.

The little girl screamed. The disoriented mother grabbed her youngest children. The father stood next to his older son, ready to defend his family.

Adessa realized that she must look a horrific sight, a muscular woman clad only in black leather, her skin covered with branded runes. She lowered the head and spoke in raspy words: "You no longer need to fear the wizard commander. He is dead." She looked down at the head she clutched in her left hand. "You are safe now."

The family stared at her with wide eyes, then looked at the headless body sprawled on the ground among the dry spruce needles.

She said, "I am Adessa, the morazeth leader from

Ildakar. I was sent to kill Maxim, and I succeeded in my task."

The parents and children clung together, afraid to move, though they clearly wanted to run like skittish deer. Adessa made no threatening gestures. "I am no danger to you. The wizard commander can no longer hurt you." She turned to the little girl, saw the fearful face soften into fascination as she fixated on the dripping head. "I need to take my trophy back to Ildakar."

Though the father was still wary, his shoulders relaxed. He put his arm around his wife. "If you killed that awful man, then you saved us."

"What happened to us?" the wife asked. Her face was lined with wrinkles, though she seemed rather young. "We slipped out of the house at night, hoping to get our children to safety while Maxim was sleeping. We were going to run to the river town and beg for help."

"He turned you to stone," Adessa said. "You had no chance against his spell."

The eleven-year-old boy said, "I remember running. I turned around and saw him come out of the cottage. I tried to shout a warning, but—" He swallowed hard.

"We were statues?" the father asked. "Just stone figures standing out here under the trees?"

"And now you are whole again," Adessa said. "You can live your normal lives."

Unceremoniously, she kicked the headless body at her feet. "I tracked him here. I set a trap." She turned to look at the heavy tree trunk still dangling on ropes; it had swung down like a murderous pendulum to smash him in the chest. "I used a bent sapling, that fallen log, some rope. He focused on me because he thought *I* alone was the threat. . . ." Her stiff face fostered a grim smile. "Now you are safe."

The Farrier family moved uncertainly around the headless body, running back to their cottage. The father hurried his children ahead of him. The mother said, "We should thank you. Is there anything we can do for you?"

Adessa stood with her feet planted in place. "I have a long journey back to Ildakar so that I can deliver the trophy, as I promised."

Standing at the cottage doorway, the husband said, "Come in and eat with us. We'll provide a meal so you will be strong for the journey."

The mother said in a harsh whisper to her husband, "Your naive heart and hospitality caused us enough trouble already!"

"It'll be fine," he whispered back. "She killed the bad man."

Adessa just wanted to be on her way, but she realized she was in no hurry now. Maxim was dead. Suddenly she felt weary. Hunting the wizard commander had given her a clear purpose, and she had endured so many hardships to achieve that goal. Now her guiding light had winked out. But her mission wasn't finished until she delivered his head to the sovrena. She would be foolish to refuse the offer of sustenance, which would help her run farther and faster. "Yes, I accept your food."

Still carrying the repugnant head, she followed the family into the cottage.

"Must you bring that inside?" asked the mother, horrified.

"Yes. I must."

While the children looked uneasily at Adessa, the father lit candles and built a fire in the stone-lined hearth. Soon, the interior was bathed in warm, comforting light.

The younger children ran to their beds, huddling together. The older brother stood uncertainly beside his father, while the mother moved about the kitchen, opening the larder to see what they had left to eat. She sighed in dismay. "That man ate most of our supplies. I have part of a ham, smoked catfish, and some cheese." She scrutinized a rock-hard heel of bread. "This is old and stale."

"I will eat it," Adessa said. "I don't know how long Wizard Commander Maxim lived here alone, but he would never deign to bake his own bread."

"I might find a chicken in the yard, wring its neck," the father suggested. "We'll have a proper feast, if you're willing to wait."

Adessa considered, but shook her head. "I need to be on my way."

Though he had felt obligated to make the offer, the man seemed relieved when she declined.

The mother set out whatever food she could scrounge and called the children from their beds to the wooden table. Adessa set the severed head on the corner next to where she would eat.

The father regarded her awkwardly. "I have water from the cistern. You can wash before you eat. You have . . . blood on you."

Adessa looked at her bare skin, at the scarred designs that had been burned by hot irons as she earned each rune of protection. Maxim's blood covered her arms and abdomen, and rusty red flecks caked the black leather band around her chest. The speckles made mysterious patterns, drying to form a meaning, a message that she couldn't understand. "The blood of my victim is a mark of honor. Why would I wash it off?"

The mother quickly sliced the ham, fish, and cheese,

and they shared cups of water, though the conversation was awkward. Adessa ate ravenously, paying little attention to the taste as she absorbed the nourishment she required. Now that the wizard commander was dead, she tried to feel the remnants of the blood magic inside her, but she had used it all. Her unborn child had given her the magical strength she needed to kill a powerful wizard, and now she was back to her normal self—and her normal self was powerful indeed.

The family ate in nervous silence, unable to look away from the gruesome head resting on the corner of their table. The neck stump left a rusty stain on the wood. From now on, whenever they looked at the mark, the Farrier family would remember her.

"You can bury his body out in the yard," she said after finishing the stale lump of bread she had promised to eat.

The father stared at her, then nodded. "We will get rid of it."

The younger children whimpered.

Adessa wolfed down her food. "I must be moving now." She gulped the last of the water in her cup. "I have many miles to travel upriver."

"We'll help you be on your way," the father blurted out a little too quickly, though it was still many hours before dawn. "Can we give you supplies? What do you need for your journey?"

The mother offered, "There's more in Gant's Ford. Down in the town you can stock up on any provisions you require."

"I need little." Adessa checked her weapons, the dagger and short sword she had brought from Ildakar, the morazeth agile knife clipped to her side, which could bring such intense pain with just a touch. As she lifted

Maxim's head by the hair, she reconsidered. "There is one thing you could give me. I need a sack."

The mother scurried about the kitchen until she produced an empty burlap sack that had been filled with millet. Adessa thanked her and stuffed Maxim's head inside, twisted the end around her wrist, and turned to the door of the cottage. "I will be on my way."

CHAPTER 6

The strange, shadowy people in Orogang closed around Nicci with outstretched hands, as if they intended to overwhelm her by sheer force of numbers. They rustled as they moved, unnaturally quiet.

When she reached out for her gift, she struggled with a wave of unsettling nausea that lingered inside her from the abortive sliph journey. The silvery creature had damaged her somehow, maybe accidentally, maybe intentionally. Where was the sliph? Nicci needed to go!

As the strange, muttering people closed in, she drew her two daggers and held them out in a threatening gesture. "I have no quarrel with you, but I will defend myself." She backed to the base of the towering Utros statue. "I don't want to kill you."

One of the hooded figures cried out in gibberish, some dialect Nicci didn't understand. More voices joined in, sounding frantic. Another spoke in slurred, deeply accented words that sounded like, "Take her! Not much time." The people carried no weapons, no swords or knives, not even sticks or clubs, but their numbers had doubled into an alarming force in just a few moments. They closed in on her.

A third voice was more agitated. "Sun is rising! Hide."

Facing them, Nicci slashed the air with her daggers to ward them off. As dawn brightened over the mountain crags, the strange people grew desperate. Several more of the shadowy people emerged, waving antique-looking swords. They howled, a sound of deep alarm. As Death's Mistress, Nicci would have had no qualms simply incinerating them all with a wash of wizard's fire, but these gaunt, scuttling figures were obviously frightened of something. Right now her command of magic seemed uncertain, yet it was her best way to drive away so many without massacring them.

She thrust one dagger back into its sheath and extended her arm, palm outward. Despite the throbbing in her head, she called up her gift and formed a wall of air as a defense. The invisible battering ram knocked aside five encroaching strangers, and they tumbled back into their fellows, but the crowd closed in from opposite directions. Their voices became more understandable, though it remained a distorted dialect.

"Take her! Inside the buildings!"

"Hurry! The sunlight!"

Though she reeled, weak and dizzy, Nicci found enough strength to blast with air again, shoving more of the people away from her. Hands grabbed her shoulders from behind. Four of the silent strangers had climbed over the base of the Utros statue to attack her from an unexpected side. They jumped on her, tried to drag her down. The drab people fell upon her like wolves on a wounded deer.

She spun, used her gift to form a circular whirlwind that shoved them all away. "Stay back!" Lashing out, she stabbed her dagger between the ribs of a gaunt woman, who collapsed, bleeding onto the statue general's feet. Others immediately whisked the injured victim away and took her to one of the buildings. The dark, open doorways looked like toothless mouths.

Her eyes flashed from target to target as the mob hesitated but pressed in, looking for any opening. Why did they want her so badly? Nicci decided the time for patience was over, and she couldn't allow herself softness or sympathy. She concentrated on the hardness inside her, the heart of black ice that was Nicci's strength when emotions were a vulnerability. It was her shield against love, although Richard had taught her that love itself could be a different kind of strength. Through him, Nicci had learned a new respect for helping people and fighting for a greater good, but she couldn't forget her other strengths.

As the desperate hands reached out to grab her, she called up her gift, ready to release more destructive magic. "Leave me alone, or you will all die."

"All die!" shouted a man in the crowd. "The zhiss can't have her!" They pushed forward as if it were a rallying cry.

Nicci called a band of lightning from the sky to blast the flagstones of the plaza, a clear warning. It shattered a long furrow and hurled four of the gray-robed people aside. She whirled in her black dress, ready for the next foolish challenger. She would drive them all away. As the daylight brightened, she could see their expressions, which were oddly fearful and yearning, not bloodthirsty. That gave her pause again. Did she really need to kill them?

"Take her!" shouted one woman. "Hurry."

The people surged forward as if they'd already forgotten the powers Nicci had just demonstrated, and she was forced to blast another dozen with a second bolt of lightning. But the hooded people didn't seem to care; they only wanted to capture her.

Several surprised her by throwing a crudely woven net over her from behind. Weighted with stones, the net drove Nicci to her knees, but she hunched her back and released a burst of heat that incinerated the tangled strands. She rose back to her feet, brushing off strings of ashes.

Striking out with greater power, Nicci made the ground tremble, loosening the flagstones and shifting the earth. An ornamental pillar on the other side of the square toppled. She flung out her hand and pushed a wall of wind into the crowd, but they came at her from different sides. There were so many people. So many!

When Nicci had fought Sulachan's swarms of half people, with their blank, bloodthirsty eyes, she never once felt a flicker of doubt, never saw them as anything but inhuman. But these gray-robed strangers had a different emotion in their eyes. It was not a hunger, but rather a need, a sadness.

"I don't want to kill you. Why are you doing this?" She held her bloody dagger in one hand, her other palm outstretched as she called up more of her gift. She still had plenty of fight left within her, but she was definitely feeling weaker. She needed to rest and recuperate after the disruptive journey through the sliph.

A man tackled her from behind, but Nicci reached out to crush the man's throat with her gift, then cast his heavy body aside. She could no longer use a velvet touch if they were attacking her. More and more of them swarmed all around her and crowded in, unafraid. Growing more angry, Nicci blasted them, hurling bodies in all directions. She had warned them many times, but it was as effective as standing on the seashore kicking at the waves.

Someone seized her wrist, making her drop the dagger. "We have to take you!" the shrouded man urged. "Stop fighting!"

Another attacker struck Nicci on the back of the head, and a red blur flashed through her skull. She heard shouts and excited whispers, terrified groans. Dozens of hands grabbed her arms, her legs, picking her up and carrying her away. Stunned, Nicci realized they were taking her toward the towering palace that loomed over the great plaza.

She struggled for consciousness, tried to reach for her gift, but her ears were ringing. With a cry, Nicci unleashed an instinctive, barely controlled surge of magic and seared two of her handlers. They stumbled back, their hands smoking, but others kept whisking her along. Nicci thrashed.

"The sun's cleared the horizon," someone yelled. "Hurry!"

Outside in the open square, as dawn washed away the gloom, the frenetic people disappeared like beetles scattering from beneath an overturned rock. They rushed to different buildings and ducked inside the dark interiors. As she fought to break free, she heard doors slam around the plaza, the heavy thunk of crossbars sealing them inside. The attacking mob dissipated like smoke in a heavy wind.

The grip on her arms and legs was like iron as her captors rushed her through the arched doorway into the building. She was engulfed by shadows. Forging her anger into strength, Nicci fought with renewed vigor, scratching, punching. "Don't make me kill you!"

"Come with us!"

Feeling wet blood in her hair from where she'd been struck on the head, Nicci could no longer afford mercy. She crashed the people away with a surge of magic, and dropped to the floor in the enclosed foyer, free. Lurching to her feet, she called a more powerful weapon, a sphere of wizard's fire, which she tossed into the crowded corridor just inside the entrance. She had to get these people away from her. Deadly flames carved through eight attackers, and she smelled roasting flesh and burning hair. The charred corpses slammed against the wall and crumpled onto the floor. Fires from burning bodies illuminated the shadows inside the palace entry.

Nicci tore herself free from the last clinging hands and turned to rush back into the open plaza, but one old woman in a gray robe scuttled forward, blocking her way. Her wrinkled face held a beseeching expression. Her words were heavily accented, but understandable. "Stop! We're trying to save you!" Nicci's blue eyes flared with angry questions, but the woman urged, "Don't go out there. You'll die. We'll all die. Please!"

Outside, a golden sunrise lit the city of Orogang. Razor-edged shadows spread across the ground, and the distorted silhouette of the General Utros statue stretched over the flagstones. The ancient city again looked entirely abandoned. Nicci knew that if she got outside, these people couldn't pursue her. For some reason, they were terrified of the sun.

She faced them by the door, breathing hard from the effort she had expended. "I don't know who you are or what you mean to do. Why did you attack me?"

"We were saving you!" The old woman clutched her hands together. "It was for your own protection."

Other drab figures staggered forward, ignoring the

still-burning corpses of their fallen comrades. "The zhiss are coming! You have to stay inside."

"We'll kill you before we let them have you."

"Who am I to you?" Nicci demanded. "What are you talking about?"

The old woman approached more guardedly. "Watch from the safe shadows, but we must bolt the door. If we let the zhiss have you, if we let them feed on fresh blood . . ." Her words trailed off, as if completing her sentence was too terrifying to imagine.

The pale people fell into quiet muttering, covered by a blanket of fear. Nicci realized they were not afraid of her, and she found that quite disturbing. She turned to face the brightening day, saw the empty city.

Outside, following the golden morning light as if summoned by the rising sun, an ominous black mist rolled in like a living thing. Hugging the ground, it was made of thousands of flecks, tiny shards of darkness, like a swarm of ebony locusts. The black miasma flickered and sparkled with inky shadows, extending tendrils and exploring as it crept into the ruins of Orogang.

Nicci felt an evil danger that vibrated to her bones. "By the Keeper, what is that?"

"The zhiss," said the old woman.

The expanding black cloud crawled into Orogang like a deadly plague, and the hidden people shuddered in terror.

CHAPTER 7

"We can do only so much," Nathan said, "but, dear spirits, we can do *something*."

The group had retreated deeper into the forest, where they continued to monitor the enormous enemy army.

Sitting on a moss-covered log, Prelate Verna looked determined, as if she had worked a spell on herself. Her blouse and travel skirts were frayed and dirty after her long journey. She turned to the Sisters of the Light and the Cliffwall scholars who accompanied them. "When the enemy looks too large, focus on small victories, and we will defeat General Utros one step at a time."

The two morazeth flashed each other a determined grin. Thorn said, "Each skirmish is an opportunity for us to pick off more of them."

Lyesse nodded. "A hundred at a time, then another hundred, then a thousand. Eventually we will make a difference."

"I applaud your confidence, ladies," Nathan said. "You are as deadly as you are attractive."

"We work hard at both," Thorn said with a sniff. She had short black hair, heavy eyebrows, and rich brown eyes. Nathan saw very little softness about her, not that he expected to.

He brushed a fly from his silk sleeve, then looked at the band of defenders. "You all saw it. The soldiers we killed were *fully human,* not half stone. If the petrification spell has worn off, they will be easier for us to kill."

"And, they will be *hungry,*" General Zimmer pointed out. "With Ildakar gone, they cannot raid the city for supplies. More than a hundred thousand soldiers, entirely cut off. Therefore, they will have to raid every village and town they can find."

"We can't leave those places defenseless!" Amber said in alarm.

"We have to seek out and warn any nearby villages, prepare them for what's coming." Nathan raised his chin and gestured to the group. "We can move faster than any scouting expeditions."

The wizard Renn came up to them, fidgeting. "From old records we, uh, have a basic idea of the towns in the area, though few gifted nobles ever explored beyond the city walls." After so many days out in the wilderness, he looked like a horse that had been left out in the rain without being tended. "We didn't pay much attention to poor, primitive villages when we had all of Ildakar."

"Utros will want whatever towns he can find," Zimmer said. "He will strip them bare. It is the obvious move."

Captain Trevor glanced at his remaining city guards, who stood together under the tall, dark pines. Their uniforms were tattered and frayed, but they remained loyal to a city that no longer existed. "Once the shroud of eternity came down years ago, Wizard Commander

Maxim dispatched scouting parties. He wanted to know about the outside world. I remember reviewing the reports. I can recall some of the nearest towns, so we can find them before Utros does." Trevor bent to scrape forest mulch from a patch of flat dirt, then used the point of his belt dagger to sketch out the general landforms around Ildakar, marking where the prominent towns would be.

Zimmer stood over the map, getting his bearings. "We should split up into several parties in order to spread the word as swiftly as possible."

Verna added, "Utros has thousands of mouths to feed and no resources. Starvation might kill more of them than swords would."

"I like killing them with my blade," Thorn said, touching the hilt of her short sword.

"You'll have ample opportunity, my dear," Nathan replied. "Don't worry."

Once the separate groups chose which settlements to track down, the defenders split up and departed from their hiding place in the forest. Renn asked to accompany Nathan, and the two gifted wizards set out in search of a town called Hanavir.

Beneath his gold-trimmed white robe, Nathan still wore black travel pants, a white ruffled shirt, and black leather boots. He considered himself both a wizard and an adventurer. He carried his ornate sword, should he find himself in a more traditional battle.

Renn walked beside him through the forests and over the hills. He had shaggy brown hair that he had once kept in well-maintained ringlets; his chin was covered with stubble and his eyes were red. Despite the harrowing retreat from Ildakar, Nathan still made a point of maintaining his own appearance, using a sharp knife to shave his chin and taking advantage of his gift, or just stream water, to scrub stains from his silk robes. Renn, though, was broken and weary, no longer interested in how he looked. Sadness had knocked him off his feet.

"I wanted a chance to talk to you," Renn said as they followed a game path. Nathan lifted a low branch, and the other wizard ducked under it without noticing. "When I left Ildakar to find Cliffwall, Lani was still just a statue." He heaved a deep breath, looking down at the ground. "She was so beautiful, even in stone. I would come into the ruling tower when it was empty just so I could look at her." He held out his hand, wistfully studying it. "Sometimes I'd stroke her cold, hard face and remember kissing her."

Nathan had been impressed by Lani, too, for the brief time he had known her. "I know she loved you. I recall how determined she was."

Renn let out a sigh. "I wish I'd been there at her brave end. I could have protected her."

Nathan placed a hand on the other wizard's shoulder. "I know you think that, my friend, but I was there, as were Quentin and dear Elsa. Ava and Ruva turned the scrying magic against Lani so fast that she was dead before we could do anything."

Tears brimmed in Renn's bloodshot eyes. "I still should have been there. At least I could have held her one last time."

Nathan felt a lump in his throat, feeling a similar pain. "Elsa used her last magic to fling me and the rest of us to a safe distance before she activated her spell. I couldn't save her either." He set his shoulders. "But there's one thing we can do to make up for it. We can do our part to save the rest of the world."

After hours of moving through the trackless hills, they stumbled upon a wagon road. With a lighter step, the two wizards picked up their pace. Soon, they saw outlying dwellings, grazing sheep, old apple orchards. A larger cluster of homes, barns, and shops formed a bustling town. Nathan spotted grain silos, storage sheds, smokehouses. People tended gardens in the yards; a man rode in a mule-drawn wagon.

"That must be Hanavir," Renn said.

The townspeople greeted them, not at all shy about strangers. Nathan called out, "We come to deliver a warning. This town is a target. A great army is coming to strip you of all your supplies, possibly kill your people. You need to prepare."

An old man came forward, walking with a limp. He had a square face and thick gray hair matched by a thick gray beard. "That is quite an odd way to introduce yourselves, gentlemen. I am the mayor of Hanavir."

"We, uh, thought you'd appreciate the warning," Renn said. "The army of General Utros has awakened. Hundreds of thousands of soldiers are about to sweep across the Old World."

"And they need supplies," Nathan continued. "They've dispatched raiding parties, and they will find Hanavir. They'll take everything you have."

"But we have very little." The mayor looked more confused than alarmed.

Nathan snorted. "With full bellies and quiet lives, you may not realize how much you have. This town has plenty to plunder."

"But we've never been troubled before," said a cartwright who stood in front of his shop.

"There's always a first time," Nathan said.

The mayor politely suggested they gather for a large meal to discuss the matter further. Though his mouth watered at the thought of well-prepared food, Nathan felt impatient with the casual attitude. He looked around, noting the granaries, the storehouses, the butcher shop, the smokehouse. "We need to get started right away. Take your supplies to caches in caves or bury them in the forest where no one can find them. Move your sheep from the meadows. Otherwise the raiders will take everything."

The mayor clucked his tongue as he hobbled along. "We need to call a meeting so we can discuss this disruption. Do you have any proof that this great army is coming here? We shouldn't be too hasty."

Exasperated, Renn held his hands up in the air. "By the Keeper's beard, Ildakar is gone, and General Utros is on the move! That's why we came to warn you."

Nathan saw that Hanavir had been complacent for too long, never expecting any crisis. Unfortunately, he didn't have time to convince the people before hoof-beats pounded along the wagon road leading into town. A raiding party of several hundred soldiers came forward, raising a cloud of dust. They were clad in antique armor that bore the flame symbol of Emperor Kurgan. As the raiders galloped into town, the mayor and his people let out a chorus of alarm. Panicked parents grabbed their children and ran to lock themselves in their houses, while others hurried to seize any weapon.

Nathan recognized First Commander Enoch leading the soldiers. The old veteran sat tall in his saddle, and one of the twin sorceresses rode on a bay mare beside him, her body covered with swirls of black and crimson paint. She was exotic, beautiful, and deadly.

As the fearful townspeople watched, Enoch raised his voice. "In the name of General Utros, we require your food and supplies. We will confiscate your grain, your flocks, your meat, your bread. We will take your wagons for transport."

"We'll starve!" cried the mayor.

"And we will not," Enoch said. "Our soldiers need it more than you do."

Beside him the sorceress curled her lips in a thin smile.

The two wizards worked their way through the crowded townspeople, coming into view. Nathan felt his gift rising inside, ready to be released. "I'm afraid we'll have to stop you, First Commander."

Enoch recognized the wizard from their very first parley with General Utros. Next to him, with a look of delight and hunger, the sorceress laughed out loud. "I know you, old man. Nathan, isn't it?"

"I may have lived a thousand years, but I am not old," he retorted. "Which one are you, Ava or Ruva? I thought you twins were inseparable."

"We were separated by a knife when we were young," she said, unconsciously touching a long scar on the outside of her bare leg, "but we are still connected. I am Ruva."

Renn's face twisted in anger as he called on his gift. "You killed Lani!" He stretched out his fingers and hurled a lightning bolt at the sorceress. The jagged lance of energy made a searing pop, but Ruva deflected the bolt with a shield, and the whistling explosion struck the ground near her mare's front hooves. The horse reared, but the woman knotted her fingers in the mane to hold on.

She retaliated with a rippling wave of hot air, and Nathan barely raised his own shield in time. Her attack was ragged, and scattered fringes of heat knocked down the limping old mayor and several townspeople. Five hundred soldiers rode into the town behind Enoch, and outriders chased the surprised villagers, who screamed and fled. The situation quickly got out of hand.

Renn hurled walls of air against the ancient soldiers, but Nathan focused on his main opponent, the sorceress. He crafted a ball of wizard's fire and raised it to hurl at Ruva.

First Commander Enoch sat tall in his saddle and bellowed, "Stop, Wizard—I command you!"

Nathan shifted the ball of wizard's fire and turned to the scarred veteran. "Since I can incinerate you in an instant, it is time for you to surrender. Tell your soldiers to back off."

Enoch didn't flinch. "On the contrary, you will cease your resistance." He raised his voice even louder and skewered Nathan with his steely eyes. "Or I will have my soldiers kill every last one of these villagers, and then we'll take the supplies anyway. I have five hundred soldiers. You can fight us, even kill many of us, but I'm confident we can slay every family in this town before you stop us all—and you know I can do it." His tone changed, sounding more reasonable. "Right now, we only want the supplies, but it could easily turn into a massacre, if you force my hand."

The sounds of screams accompanied galloping hooves as the soldiers spread out among the buildings, riding down the narrow streets. When the two wizards hesitated, looking at each other, Enoch shouted orders: "Men! Show them we mean business!"

The remorseless soldiers rode down mothers and their children, trampling them, hacking at shopkeepers and craftsmen who tried to defend their town. The people of Hanavir were not fighters, and the blood-shed was immediate and dramatic.

Reacting together, Nathan and Renn bowled down the ancient warriors with waves of wind, blocking part of the attack, but despite their efforts the widespread slaughter continued across the town. Lightning strikes blasted five or six soldiers each time, but the raiders just rode harder, increased their mayhem. Hanavir was infested with enemies ransacking countless buildings. Two wizards couldn't possibly fight against five hundred bloodthirsty warriors dispersed among the civilian population.

"Halt!" Nathan cried, calling more wizard's fire into his hand to threaten Enoch directly. "I'll incinerate you, First Commander."

The veteran just laughed at him from the saddle. "Then who will stop my men from wreaking havoc throughout the town? Or, I can call them off now—if you capitulate." His words were quieter than the screams and the clashing blades. Several homes and shops were already on fire as the raiders cast torches. He reiterated in a hard but reasonable voice, "All we want is the food. The people don't need to die. But if you force us to burn the village to the ground, that guilt is on your shoulders."

Nathan struggled to find some other solution, and a dozen more people died during his brief pause. A wailing young girl ran to her mother just before a soldier killed them both, and they died in each other's arms.

"Stop!" Renn wailed. "Please stop!"

Ruva returned his poisonous gaze. "I can fight both of you if you like. I'd love to pull the bones one by one from your skin."

Though he ached to save Hanavir, Nathan couldn't

battle the entire army on such a widespread front. How many villagers would die in the meantime?

The soldiers had rounded up a hundred panicked men and women, including the old mayor, all of whom raised their hands in surrender. The soldiers lifted their swords for a mass execution, and Enoch turned to Nathan and Renn, raising his hand, ready to give a signal.

"Stop!" Nathan groaned. "Don't kill any more of them."

"Then cease your resistance," Enoch said. "Now."

"Give the order," Renn cried as the screams continued. "Tell them to stop killing!"

The first commander waved his hand, and shouts went up and down the line. "Enough bloodshed for now! We need workers to load the supplies." He snorted. "Do not make this any more difficult than it has to be."

Furious, feeling like a failure, Nathan struggled to contain his gift, knowing that if he unleashed his magic, Enoch would retaliate with a vengeful massacre. He wanted to incinerate the old veteran the moment he saw an opportunity that wouldn't result in countless more deaths.

"Take the wizards back with us," Ruva said, sitting proudly on her mare. "General Utros will love having them as prisoners. My sister and I can dissect them to find the magic inside."

Renn shouted, "I'll kill both you and your sister. For Lani!"

Nathan thought strategically, though. He whispered to Renn, "We don't dare let them capture us."

From the streets of Hanavir, he summoned the wind, manipulating it like a weaver with fine silken threads. He pulled smoke from the burning buildings, dragged it closer to them like thick and acrid curtains. Before

Enoch could issue a command, Nathan whipped the whirlwind of smoke around them, twirling it like poisonous veils to camouflage himself and Renn. He grabbed the other man's maroon sleeve. "Come, we have to run!"

They darted through the streets as the smoke thickened, covering their retreat and leaving behind Ruva's screams of rage at being cheated.

Nathan's heart was heavy because they had failed to save Hanavir. The two wizards themselves had barely escaped.

He hoped the other parties were more successful.

CHAPTER 8

After he endured another day of exhausting work on the river, seeing no chance to escape, Bannon collapsed on the open deck near the bow of King Grieve's ship. As night fell, stars began to sparkle overhead, but the new constellations seemed very far away and unable to help him. Nevertheless, Bannon would fend for himself and save as many of these people as he could. That was what he held on to.

The other fifty or so slaves from Ildakar groaned and whimpered as they were tied or chained securely to the decks. In darkness, the swamp sounds grew louder as predators emerged from the muddy banks and thick underbrush.

Though Bannon didn't bemoan his circumstance, he felt determined and angry. His beaten body was bruised, his muscles sore. Hunger clawed like a beast inside his stomach. He knew the other slaves were in as much misery.

After days of intense activity, many damaged ships had been partially repaired. The ruined hulks had been stripped bare, leaving only skeletons of wood. Masts and yardarms were replaced, rigging ropes restrung, broken hulls patched, bilges pumped dry. Bannon had looked for opportunities to sabotage the repairs, and he had left flaws in some of the vessels, but not enough to cause the disaster he needed to inflict.

Seven slaves had died so far during the work, and Bannon could tell that many others were ready to perish from sheer exhaustion. But he was in better shape than these others. While held in the combat pits in Ildakar, Bannon had been trained and toughened to fight; the rest of the Ildakar captives, though, had led soft and prosperous lives. They wouldn't last much longer as slaves of the Norukai.

Impatient to launch his war, King Grieve took out his ire on his own people. That afternoon, he roared at Gara and two other shipwrights. "Faster! I need ships now. We must sail back to the Norukai islands."

"Four will be ready and provisioned tonight, my king, my Grieve," said Gara, cringing deferentially. Her braids flopped from side to side. "I promise."

Now, Bannon crouched on the deck with his wrists tied and ankles chained to an anchor bolt. Repairing the serpent ships was horrific work, but he knew his situation would be worse once the raiding fleet set off down the river, taking him and the other captives. After the serpent ships sailed away, Bannon could never find his way back to the site of Ildakar.

His heart ached over the loss of the city, as well as his friends. Despite its dark flaws and ugly secrets, Ildakar had great potential. With the overthrow of Sovrena Thora, it could have been a magnificent city again. Lila had wanted Bannon to stay, but now she was gone, and his heart ached even more. He realized he didn't just miss the young woman's company as a protector and fighter. She had cared for him, guarded him at first out of a sense of duty, but it had become more than that.

Nathan was gone, too, but Bannon hoped the wizard was still alive. Now that his gift was restored, no one would trifle with Nathan Rahl. And Nicci . . . she had been cut off somewhere when Ildakar vanished.

Bannon doubted he would see any of them again. He was trapped here alone, chained to the deck of a Norukai ship. "Sweet Sea Mother," he mumbled. But he would not surrender his optimism. There must be a way he could survive and help defeat the hated Norukai.

As the deceptively soothing swamp noises grew louder, Bannon's stomach growled. The slaves had to drink dirty river water from buckets. When some of them spewed the water back up, the gruff Norukai would splash another bucket over their faces to wash away the vomit and keep the stink from lingering on the deck.

In the thickening darkness, Bannon saw lanterns lit on the decks of the many ships lashed together in the current. Grieve's ship and three others were anchored together near the shore, ready to depart, and the king did not intend to wait. He would leave the rest of his fleet behind.

Two Norukai men walked along the torchlit deck carrying a wooden tub between them. They stopped at the first group of bound slaves and set down the heavy tub. One man lifted a ladle that dripped a slurry of fish guts and river water. "Dinner!"

The first slave turned his head away in disgust, but the Norukai dumped the contents on the bound man's face anyway. Wet entrails ran down his chin, and when the slave realized this was all the food he would get, he tried to slurp some of the entrails. Learning the lesson, the next slave braced himself and opened his mouth, so the Norukai ladled the nauseating mess onto his face.

Prancing behind the two men, Chalk hopped from one foot to the other. "Dinnertime, dinnertime! My fish, your fish!" He scooped a long-fingered hand into the wooden tub and rewarded himself with a fish head, which he tossed in the air and caught with his mouth like a trained dog. Crunching down on the scales, he came closer to Bannon. "Fishes tried to eat me, and now I eat them!" In the light of the rising moon the puckered scars were prominent on his albino skin. Bannon wondered what had happened to him, what the shaman had endured, what ordeal had created those scars and driven him to the edge of madness. "They didn't eat enough of you," Bannon said under his breath.

Chalk hopped over to him and squatted down. "They ate just enough. Razorfish nibbled my arms, nibbled my legs, and nibbled between them." He clamped a palm against his loincloth-covered crotch. "They took much away, but they gave me something, too." He leaned so close to Bannon that the young man could smell the rotting fish in his mouth. "That gave me my power! I see things. I know the future, the fire in the towns, the blood on the swords, so many screams. But good screams, I think."

"Are they the screams of dying Norukai?" Bannon asked, but the shaman seemed oblivious to his vitriol.

Chalk cocked his head as if listening to whispered voices. "Yes, some of them are Norukai screams." He sounded as if he was imparting a secret.

The shaman seemed to find Bannon fascinating, as if he recognized that the young man was different from the other Ildakaran captives. The two Norukai men set their stinking wooden tub on the deck, and Bannon steeled himself. He raised his head to accept the food, vowing to keep his strength for when he really needed it, but he nearly choked as they poured fish guts onto his face. He made himself swallow.

Squirming next to him, imitating Bannon, Chalk also turned his head up like a baby bird begging for a worm. The Norukai splashed the fish-gut soup across the shaman's face, which satisfied him. He plucked a small fish head and held it between his thumb and forefinger. "You didn't get a fish head. A special treat."

Before the young man could protest, Chalk popped the head between Bannon's lips. He took it into his mouth, wincing as he swallowed the horrible morsel. Why was the albino paying so much attention to him?

Drumbeats echoed from the stern of the serpent ship, and King Grieve stepped out into the lantern light. All the people fell silent, slaves and Norukai. Grieve's voice boomed out to all the nearby vessels. "These four serpent ships are ready to sail, and four is enough to spark terror as we proceed downriver. Tonight, we will head back to the Bastion so we can begin this war."

Chalk leaped to his feet. "My Grieve, King Grieve! They'll all grieve."

The king raised his heavy wooden baton and pounded the oar master's drum again, louder than before. Guttural cheers resounded from hundreds of Norukai aboard the other ships, which were in various states of repair.

"We will raid villages as we make our way to the estuary and the open sea. The rest of our fleet is already gathering at the Norukai islands, and I must be their king and warlord." Offhandedly Grieve shouted across the water to the other vessels. "Finish repairs to the rest of the ships and sail back to us." He raised his iron-knuckled hand. The chain around his waist jingled as he spun about and gave the order to raise the anchor. "These first ships will set off. Now!"

Norukai sailors raised the midnight-blue sails on the four repaired ships, striking the ropes that lashed the hulls together.

Bannon felt sick, knowing that once they sailed away from Ildakar with him and this small group of slaves aboard, he would likely never escape. He gazed longingly at the dense vegetation on the bank as he strained against his ropes and chains. He could think of no way to get off the ship, but he would keep looking.

From her hiding place among the thorny reeds, Lila spied on the raider ships, knowing that some—including Bannon's—were repaired and ready to depart. In the darkness, she heard the drumbeats accompanied by distant gruff shouts, a voice she recognized as King Grieve's.

Lying in wait for days as the repairs continued, she had made her plans and created a booby trap. With all of the vines and trees along the river, she fashioned her tools, working quietly in the shadowy blanket of night. Her greatest advantage was that the Norukai didn't know she was here.

She had dismissed dozens of different plans because they would surely end in failure. Lila could not let herself fail. If this were just for her sake, she would have thrown caution to the wind and charged in with her weapons, confident she could kill a dozen or more Norukai before she died. But she had a greater calling now. She needed to free Bannon.

When the four repaired ships prepared to depart down the river, Lila vowed to stop them. Fortunately, she had worked for days, laying her trap. She used vines to pull down the supple swamp trees, staging them, forming makeshift catapults. Her surreptitious work left her vulnerable to swamp dragons, large coiled snakes, and hunting spiders the size of rats. Lila killed many of them, avoided others. Now everything was ready as she lay in wait.

With the anchors raised and the dark sails set, the four serpent ships moved off into the night. Lila knew she had only one chance.

She wasn't sure of her aim, since she'd been unable to test her crude catapults, so she had to rely on her guesses and her hope. Bannon was aboard King Grieve's ship, and she had to make sure she didn't accidently kill him in her attack.

With three resilient saplings tied down, Lila had gathered bunches of dry twigs and dead vines into flammable bales that could fly like projectiles. The bent trees were quivering and ready to launch, loaded with all the dry material. When the ships began to move out, Lila struck her dagger against the flint she carried in a pouch, lit a spark to ignite the first bale. As the flames caught, she ignited the bundle in the second catapult, then the third. She could smell the sour odor of green wood burning.

When her makeshift catapults held their blazing clumps, she slashed the rope holding the first bent tree in place. With a groan, it sprang upright and released the bale of fiery wood, throwing a burning comet toward the Norukai ships. Lila cut the second rope to launch the next projectile. The ball of fire raged across the sky as the first bale struck one of the four ships—not

Bannon's, she saw with some relief. The Norukai crew scrambled to extinguish the blaze before the ship could catch fire.

The second bale whistled over the top of the next vessel, missing it and plunging into the river, where the flames spat as they were extinguished.

The third projectile, though, crashed into the vessel just behind the flagship, and the flames spread as kindling scattered across the deck and caught in the rigging. The Norukai rushed about to extinguish the flames, but the blaze quickly got out of control. The vessel was engulfed in fire, a torch on the Killraven River.

Fleeing the blaze before it could spread, the other three ships sailed away from the burning ship, while King Grieve and the Norukai shouted insults at their unseen attacker on the riverbank.

Lila emerged from the underbrush on the muddy shore to watch the mayhem she had caused. She smiled before ducking back into the shelter of the trees. The other three ships pulled away.

Neither King Grieve nor his crew could save the fiery wreck, so the flagship raced away, gaining distance from the spreading sparks.

Tied and chained onto the deck, Bannon could barely contain his joy as he watched Norukai diving overboard to flee the burning vessel. He wondered who had launched the catapults of fire that soared overhead like shooting stars. Someone else was fighting back! Someone else was still free out there! On the deck, several slaves laughed and cheered at this unexpected victory until their Norukai masters cuffed them into senselessness.

As they sailed away from the bluffs, Bannon kept watching the thickets, and he thought he saw a flash of skin, a lithe young woman. Could it be? Lila! Even as the serpent ship sailed away, Bannon felt great joy just to know she was out there.

CHAPTER 9

From the sheltered stone doorway of the palace, Nicci watched the black cloud creep into Orogang. "The zhiss . . ." said the old woman next to her, and a deep shiver lurked in her voice. The other shrouded people crowded together, more afraid of whatever was out there than they were of Nicci. Some of them peeked out into the daylight, while others retreated into the gloom of the windowless passageways.

The sentient cloud swirled like a thunderstorm that had been shattered into obsidian fragments. Each fleck was only the size of a biting black fly, and together they swirled in a shapeless predatory mass. A buzzing simmered in the air like a thousand beehives, and the sound grew louder as the mass drifted among the abandoned buildings.

"What are they?" Nicci whispered.

"Death," said the old woman. Behind her, in the gloom of the shuttered palace, the other people remained utterly silent.

Tendrils of the black mass extended, probing, hunting. The zhiss had a purpose.

From the doorway, Nicci spotted movement in the overgrown shrubs in the empty square. As the daylight brightened, the two foraging deer cropped tender green vegetation. The doe pricked her ears and raised her head, while the young buck with short velvety antlers continued to munch flowers, until he also sensed the buzzing cloud.

The zhiss moved toward the animals. Black specks tumbled, rotated, extended in an ill-defined tentacle that advanced like candle wax pouring down a slanted surface. The uneasy animals skittered, but they didn't understand the threat.

From her sheltered overhang, Nicci wanted to shout at the deer and make them run, but the old woman squeezed her shoulder like a vise. "Remain silent! We don't dare call attention to ourselves."

The black cloud buzzed forward, expanding, then swooping down around the deer. Too late, the animals tried to bolt away, but one extension of the zhiss blanketed them like countless bloodthirsty mosquitoes. Smothered, the deer collapsed on the flagstones. The poor animals twitched and thrashed, but eventually lay still.

Before long, individual specks rose up like drunken bumblebees and drifted away from their victims. Now, the tiny flecks were swollen globules the size of grapes, purplish red instead of black, engorged with blood. The rest of the cloud drifted and kept expanding, still hungry, still probing through the ancient city for prey.

Sickened by what she had seen, Nicci turned to the old woman, realizing what these strange people had done by capturing her. "You did save me." She had killed so many of them! "You knew what was coming. If I had been out there when the sun rose . . ."

"We saved you, and perhaps we saved the world," the woman replied. "We could not let them have you. The blood of a gifted sorceress is incredibly potent."

Nicci was frustrated that they had been unclear, that their muddled old dialect and their urgency had led to such tragedy, but they had been desperate to keep her away from the black cloud. Now their voices were loud in the silence, and the zhiss detected the sound even from outside. Part of the swarm poured toward the towering palace in which Nicci and the others hid. The furtive people let out a collective gasp and retreated deeper into the shadows. The old woman pushed the thick door shut, assisted by others. Nicci added the last nudge to slam the barrier in place just as the buzzing, swirling zhiss struck the blocky structure. Through the stone-hard wood, she could hear a vibrating hum as the angry force vented its frustration.

With the door sealed, Nicci waited for her eyes to adjust to the light of intermittent torches mounted on the stone walls. The people had covered every crack and cranny, allowing no outside light and no speck of predatory blackness to enter.

The building was huge, an imposing palace with vaulted ceilings and enormous chambers larger than the torches could effectively illuminate. Hundreds of the pale people were crowded inside, far more than Nicci had expected. They all wore gray, unobtrusive garments. Although they seemed healthy enough, the people looked haunted.

The clamor of questions became too loud in her mind. "Explain what is happening here," she demanded. "What are the zhiss and who are you?"

As the people muttered, the old woman pulled back her hood to reveal gray hair with a few streaks of brown. Her skin was pale to the point of translucency, showing the faint lines of blood vessels. "I am Cora. We call ourselves the Hidden People, for that is what we do—we hide."

"What do you accomplish by hiding? I rarely find that a useful strategy."

"We control the zhiss," Cora replied. "We keep Orogang safe. We keep the world safe."

The people with her muttered more loudly. Nicci was glad to confirm her suspicion. "So this is Orogang, the capital of Emperor Kurgan's empire."

"What is left of it," Cora said.

A square-jawed man with a grim expression said, "Emperor Kurgan is long dead, destroyed by his vengeful people, but General Utros will return. That is what the old prophet said." Nicci was surprised to hear the statement, but did not point out that the man's desire might actually come true, though not in the ways he expected. The man introduced himself as Cyrus.

The old woman explained, "The city fell many centuries ago, after the people overthrew Iron Fang. The populace longed to anoint General Utros as their next emperor, and back then a crazed prophet insisted that Utros would come back to Orogang. But years passed, and he never returned. The empire fell into a civil war. The people were busy fighting under different flags, breaking into factions, paying little attention to anything but their own conflict." She drew a deep breath. "Then the zhiss came."

"Utros will return!" Cyrus insisted.

"I think we've waited long enough," said a brown-haired young woman with a huff, drawing an annoyed glance from Cyrus.

"What are the zhiss?" Nicci asked, interested in the true danger. "Where did they come from?"

The Hidden People stirred uneasily at hearing their own history, but let the old woman continue the tale. "A fiery star fell from the heavens and struck the mountains. Inside, it carried the zhiss, like an egg sac filled with spiders." A frown settled into her deeply lined face. "They fed on the population. The zhiss were just a black wisp at first, but each time they consumed a human, the swarm multiplied. The things used our blood to breed, and the cloud doubled and doubled again. Some of us learned how to hide." Cora closed her eyes, and in the dim torchlight Nicci could see tears glittering.

Nicci considered. "But Kurgan fell fifteen hundred years ago. You cannot be that old." She remembered the preservation spells woven through the Palace of the Prophets that prevented aging. Nicci herself was over one hundred and eighty years old. "Or are you?"

Cora shook her head. "No, that was generations ago, but we have stayed because we know our duty. We need to keep the zhiss here. If we leave, the cloud will seek out other villages, towns, cities, and then the zhiss will be unstoppable."

The young woman who had scoffed at Cyrus came closer, even managing a smile. "The swarm only comes out in daylight, so we are safe as long as we remain sealed in our buildings until dark." The girl would have been pretty, a heartthrob for any young man, if she hadn't been so pallid. "I am Asha. We go out at night to hunt and gather. We have stockpiles of food throughout the city, enough to last for decades, but we dare not leave Orogang."

"We wait," Cyrus said. "We have our purpose."

"But the zhiss fed on those two deer," Nicci said. "Won't the swarm reproduce now?"

Cora shook her head. "The zhiss sustain themselves

with the blood of animals, but there is some quality in human blood that lets them reproduce." The old woman lowered her voice. "And gifted blood is the most powerful of all."

Nicci realized the significance of how vulnerable she had been out in the ruins. "When you first saw me at night, how did you know I was a sorceress?"

"We didn't," Cora said. "We just tried to save you, but when you fought back using your gift, we knew it was imperative to get you inside, away from the zhiss, even if it cost the lives of many of our people. If the black cloud had fed on you . . ." She let her words trail off, shuddering visibly.

Nicci wondered if her gift would have been able to deflect the hungry black swarm. She didn't count on it.

Old Cora continued her explanation. "And so we remain here and feed the swarm just enough to keep it under control. It doesn't wander away, but we cannot leave. Not ever."

"Unless we stop it somehow," Asha interjected.

Looking around inside the expansive foyer of the palace, Nicci frowned at the burned bodies of those she had killed with wizard's fire while trying to avoid capture.

"I'm sorry I caused you so much harm," she said again, tasting the regret in her throat. "I didn't understand what you were doing."

"We were not only doing it to save you," Cyrus scoffed. "If the zhiss had fed on your blood, our situation would have grown far worse." He added an edge to his voice. "If we could not bring you inside the shelter in time, we would have killed you."

Nicci faced him in the flickering torchlight. "You might have tried."

CHAPTER 10

Creeping through the trees, Verna and her companions searched for a small mountain village, hoping to find it before the enemy raiders did. The fresh-faced novice Amber accompanied her, as well as the morazeth Lyesse and five of Zimmer's D'Haran soldiers.

Lord Oron stalked beside the prelate, hard-faced and unhappy with his circumstances. "I was once a respected member of the wizards' duma, as well as the head of the skinners' guild. Now I am wandering through a trackless forest hoping to find a few hovels."

Ahead, they heard bleating sheep, and the trees opened up to reveal an expansive meadow. A terrified flock was being driven down the grassy slope by thirty armored soldiers.

Verna shot a glance at the powerful wizard from Ildakar. "And I was once the prelate of the Sisters of the Light. Now it appears we will both be shepherds."

Lyesse was already sprinting forward. "That is enough meat to feed many enemy soldiers. We cannot let them have the animals. Come, let's stop them."

As Verna watched the aloof soldiers herding the sheep along, her voice came out in a low, husky growl. "At least we will make them pay for what they did to that poor shepherd's family."

Only an hour earlier, they had smelled smoke and come upon a burning cottage in a high meadow, where they found the bodies of a woman and her daughter, both with their throats cut. The cottage had been stripped of supplies, all the food eaten. Farther out in the grazing fields, they found a tent that held the shepherd and his teenage son, both also dead, along with their dog. The tent had been set on fire, and the corpses were half burned. Now the ancient raiders were driving the whole flock back to the main army.

"It is only thirty soldiers," said Lyesse, pausing to watch from the edge of the trees. "Our swords will make quick work of them. I'd kill them all myself, but then Thorn might not believe my score." Her lips quirked in a smile as she looked at the other D'Haran soldiers. "I will let my comrades have a turn as well."

"The prelate and I also have a respectable amount of magic," Oron pointed out. "We'll take care of a few ourselves."

Out in the open meadow, the soldiers banged their swords on their flame-embossed shields to keep the sheep moving across the sloped grasses. They had no idea they were being watched.

The D'Haran soldiers drew their weapons and crouched, hiding in the forest camouflage. A breeze stirred the branches, rustled the leaves. Lyesse gripped her short sword and looked over her shoulder at her companions. She raised her heavy dark eyebrows. "What are we waiting for?"

Oron raised his hand and called upon his gift. "I'm not waiting." The sky darkened over the meadow, and a sharp wind began to blow harder. The marauders looked up, grumbling at the sudden afternoon thunder-storm. A single black cloud unleashed a downpour that fell only over the meadow, drenching them. The bleating sheep kept moving.

With a smile, Oron twisted his fingers, and a thin lightning bolt speared down into the middle of the enemy soldiers, killing two and scattering the others. In terror, the sheep bolted in all directions.

Prelate Verna and the others needed no further encouragement. Smiling, Amber used her own gift to summon a whirling whip of air that lashed out and caught one of the enemy soldiers, knocking him over. He yelped in surprise.

The D'Haran soldiers charged out of the forest, with the lean morazeth bounding ahead of them. In the pelting rain and howling winds, the ancient soldiers didn't realize how few were attacking them.

Thunder boomed from Oron's black cloud. Another bolt of lightning shattered one of the enemy warriors into chunks of charred flesh. Fleet as a jaguar, Lyesse leaped in among the startled soldiers. Swinging her short sword, she decapitated one of the men, then gutted a second with her backstroke. "Two!" she cried, and fell upon more victims.

Yelling, Verna ran after them. Amber followed her. "I'm at your side, Prelate."

Though Verna felt old and weary from the long journey, she was tough. She had trained many young wizards in the Palace of the Prophets, had even been able to enforce her will on Richard Rahl. She was a scholar, a leader, and powerfully gifted.

And she had been to war before.

Verna called up a pocket of air above the milling, frightened sheep, then collapsed it, pressing her palms together. The snap of compressed air made an explosion of sound, a harmless boom that sent the panicked sheep bolting into the trees.

She looked at Oron. "The raiders will never catch those sheep now."

The wizard gave a small nod. "Effective, Prelate, though I would rather kill the enemies, not just startle them." He raised both hands, twisted his wrists, and changed the magic he had released. The pouring rain froze into a wave of long, sharp ice projectiles that were like pointed arrowheads pelting the drenched soldiers. Then the D'Haran soldiers fell upon them.

Utros's raiding party had expected little resistance when they harassed undefended villages and an isolated shepherd's family. Surprised, they were easy targets, and all of them were quickly and methodically dispatched.

True to her word, Lyesse accounted for six of the enemy soldiers herself. Three D'Haran soldiers had been injured in the fray, and they all sat together under now clear skies and bound each other's wounds. Verna and Oron used their gift to heal the worst of their cuts.

Before sunset, they made camp outside the damaged cottage. Two of the men retrieved the bodies of the shepherd and his son from their burned tent and brought them back so the entire family could lie at rest next to one another. Verna and her companions took the time to give the poor victims a proper burial, which seemed fitting.

"The Keeper took them too soon," she said. "But at least they will all be a family in the underworld."

In a hard voice Oron said, "The Keeper didn't take the rest of the ancient army soon enough. I'd like to send them all to the underworld."

It seemed fitting to leave the bodies of the ancient warriors to rot on the hillside.

As night fell and the party built a fire outside to brighten the darkness, Lyesse trudged back across the meadow with one of the sheep over her shoulders, killed and gutted.

"The rest of the flock is scattered," she said. "This one will be enough for us, and Utros will get none of them." She dropped the carcass near the fire, then used her dagger to cut chunks of the richest meat for them to roast. "It has been a good day."

"A good enough one," Verna said. Though they had killed thirty of the enemy, she knew there were countless more soldiers, and that thought weighed on her. Was this merely an exercise?

But when she looked at Amber's satisfied smile, she decided to let the novice enjoy the victory. Verna promised herself that the war was not, in fact, insurmountable. There would be many defeats and setbacks before all was said and done, but they had won this day, at least. . . .

CHAPTER 11

The great army of General Utros consisted of as many tactical details as there were soldiers. As the general planned the conquest of the Old World, his greatest challenges were administrative.

In the late afternoon, he stood outside his pavilion and stared across the sweeping encampment, deep in thought as the sun lowered behind the mountains to the west. His tactical mind was a complex series of turning wheels, one thought changing another as he considered the consequences of his actions. He touched the gold mask that covered the left half of his face, a price he had been forced to pay. Consequences . . .

Although he understood his army's dire situation better than any of his soldiers did, he refused to let desperation press him into making another brash choice. He would plan his next move carefully, using his insights, experience, and strategic knowledge. He listened to the camp sounds as his hungry troops settled for the night. They gathered around communal bonfires to tell stories of their lost loved ones or to play ancient gambling games.

After the devastating setbacks—the mayhem of the titanic Ixax warriors, the return of the gray dragon, the fiery transference magic—his subcommanders had reported the actual tally of losses only to Utros. He could not let the masses understand just how terrible a blow they had suffered, because his army must never learn that true defeat was possible.

The bodies of the fallen were swiftly burned in funeral pyres to disguise the vast numbers of corpses. Also, so they would not feel the constant reminder of their fallen comrades, Utros reorganized his entire fighting force, reassigning the surviving soldiers into new companies under new subcommanders, so they would not immediately see how many comrades they had lost.

The greatest blow, though, was the loss of Ildakar itself.

Utros turned toward the end of the valley and the sheer drop-off to the river lowlands. The whole city was gone, as if it had never existed. His explicit purpose, burned into him by Emperor Kurgan so long ago, had been to conquer Ildakar. That was the reason he and his vast army had marched through the mountains down from Orogang, and now their primary goal had been snatched away.

Utros knew he had little time. He pressed his mask against the hard scar of his cheek. The pain in the stripped side of his face sent twinges into his skull. For now, his men still had faith in him. They trusted their general, swore deeper loyalty to him than they had ever felt toward Iron Fang. Utros would not let them down, but he had to give them something to hold on to, some new hope, an attainable goal. He would rally them, fire their determination.

Ava stepped out from the pavilion's shade. She had applied black soot and dark red paint in incomprehensible designs over her breasts and flat stomach, then donned her filmy blue gown. She was breathtakingly beautiful, like her twin, and she was equally terrifying. She reached out to stroke his thick biceps. "My sister is returning, beloved Utros." Her touch lingered on the embossed design on his copper armband. "I sense her."

His gaze was drawn to the scar that ran along her outer thigh where her leg had been fused with her sister's at birth, before their father had hacked them apart as babies. Though they were physically separated, their Han remained connected.

Ava gestured with her chin toward where a large party trotted out of the northern hills through the scorched grasses. Several hundred mounted soldiers led a train of wagons and pack mules loaded with sacks of grain and casks of ale, and they also drove sheep, cattle, goats, and a few yaxen. Even from a distance, Utros recognized First Commander Enoch and the pale, painted figure of Ruva at the front of the party.

Groups at separate campfires let out cheers when they saw the supplies. Throughout the day, dozens of scattered raiding parties had returned with whatever provisions they could liberate from villages or isolated homes in the hills. The trickle of food was enough to reassure the army, for now.

Utros was confident none of his soldiers could complete the calculations of just how many sacks of grain, how many cattle, sheep, goats, chickens, deer, or boar, were needed to feed more than a hundred thousand mouths. He had to find a solution before his army understood the magnitude of the problem.

Utros retrieved his imposing helmet adorned with two curved horns from an abominable bull that the fleshmancers of Ildakar had sent against his army in the early days.

As the returning party rode through the cheering camp, Ava slipped her arm through the general's and strolled at his side, protecting him with her beauty as well as her powerful gift. Enoch and Ruva rode up to report to the general. His veteran subcommander had a grizzled, craggy face adorned with numerous battle scars that gave him character. Enoch removed his helmet and wiped a palm over his bristly gray hair. "Our mission was a success, General."

"I can see that." Utros watched the wagons move among the camped troops, distributing the commandeered supplies and meat animals to the companies. Utros lowered his voice. "The animals should all be slaughtered tonight. We don't have the means to feed and keep them. Give everyone a full meal."

Enoch looked grim. "This food won't last long, sir."

"I'm aware of that. Did you have any difficulty?"

Ruva answered with a strangely malicious smile. "No."

When Utros gave his first commander a curious look, Enoch explained, "The town of Hanavir had many supplies, but we encountered unexpected resistance."

"The townspeople fought back? Against five hundred armed warriors?"

The old veteran shook his head. "No, there were two stray wizards. You remember the one with white hair known as Nathan Rahl?"

Utros pressed his lips together. "Yes, he fancied himself a historian and informed me that my name is legend." He tasted the bitter sarcasm in his throat. "Nathan is also the one who told me of the fall of Emperor Kurgan. It was he who told me what really happened to my dear Majel." Bile rose in his throat every time he thought of that sweet woman, how her own husband had skinned her alive to get his revenge.

The gold mask felt heavy on his face, and Utros adjusted it against his cheekbone. "But Nathan's gift was gone, was it not? He seemed impotent as a wizard. How did he fight you?"

"His gift is back," Ruva said. "He and one other wizard from Ildakar, a man named Renn, attempted to protect the town. But we defeated them."

Utros was pleased but perplexed. "You defeated two wizards? How?"

"Compassion was their weakness," Enoch said. "We couldn't fight their gift directly, but we slew some innocent townspeople and threatened to kill them all if they did not relent. The two wizards escaped, and we took all the supplies."

With a haughty sniff, Ruva said, "We should have killed the townspeople anyway, just to punish them."

"Those were not my orders," Enoch responded with a hint of anger. "My priority was to commandeer supplies to feed our troops, not to secure some petty revenge."

"It wouldn't have taken long," the sorceress said flippantly, but she deferred.

They watched the carts being unloaded, so many soldiers dividing up the supplies. Second Commanders Halders and Arros directed the activity.

"The soldiers will follow orders until the hunger in their bellies convinces them otherwise." Utros shook his head. "We can't just stay encamped in this worthless valley. Ildakar is gone, as are all its supplies. There is no reason to remain. Our army has to move, and soon."

"We have a continent to conquer," Ava said.

"We dare not let King Grieve have it all," Ruva said.

The thought made Utros ill. He looked across the valley. "We break camp at dawn and march westward at a swift, even brutal, pace. Our food will run out before long." He lowered his voice. "When we were partly stone, our bellies were quiet. We did not appreciate the blessing that went hand in hand with that curse. Now this army must hold itself together long enough to cross over the mountains."

"*You* will hold the army together," Ruva said.

Utros couldn't drive away the cold knot in his chest. In the past month he had already dispatched dozens of expeditionary armies with thousands of men to plant the banner of Utros across the landscape. Now he would have to strip every resource they could find just to keep the huge army moving.

But he looked forward to the march.

CHAPTER 12

As Adessa moved up the riverbank on her long journey back to Ildakar, her only company was Maxim's severed head, which she carried in a bloody sack at her side. She traveled at a steady pace, without urgency, since the hunt was over. She had killed her prey, but her quest was not finished. She still had to bring the trophy back home.

Home. Adessa rarely let herself think such thoughts. As a morazeth, she gave her body and her skills entirely to Ildakar. Adessa had no joys, no doubts, only service. She would fight and defeat any opponent in the combat arena; she would kill any enemies of the city, even the wizard commander himself. She did not count the cost in blood, nor did she celebrate the amount she spilled.

Before she had killed Maxim, he'd taunted her that Ildakar might be under siege by a Norukai war fleet. He also claimed to have broken the petrification spell and intentionally unleashed the gigantic army of General Utros. Adessa had no reason to believe this was true, since she also knew that the wizard commander had a habit of lying. Once she got back to the city, she would see the truth for herself, and fight if necessary.

As she moved mile after mile, Adessa anticipated seeing the glorious city, the arbor-lined streets, the ruling tower and the sacrificial pyramid, the combat arena soaked with blood and glory. Adessa had trained so many fighters, and some, like Ian, even became champions, a rare honor. She had also allowed Ian to become her lover, to impregnate her with her most recent child. Even though Adessa had killed Ian when he betrayed Ildakar, she could not deny the fondness she'd felt for him. If only he had not been corrupted. . . .

At Gant's Ford, after leaving the Farrier family, she considered finding a riverboat pilot who would take her upriver to Ildakar, but Adessa was in no mood for company. She could travel swiftly enough alone, and she had been by herself ever since the sovrena sent her on this hunt. By now the uprising in Ildakar would have been subdued, Thora and the wizards' duma would have reestablished their rule and punished the criminals. Adessa would come home triumphant.

She followed a dirt road alongside the Killraven River, but as she went farther from the town, the path degenerated into a faint trail among the trees. The dangerous swamps far to the north would be much more of a challenge.

After a day of hard traveling, she ate dried meat and fruit from her pack and eventually stopped to make camp. Adessa gathered dry wood in a clearing and sat on a fallen tree whose bark had rotted away. The campfire of dry willow wood, grasses, and oak twigs cracked and popped, exhaling a ribbon of smoke. She drank from her waterskin and made a small meal of more preserved food. In a few days, she would have to hunt, but tonight she would just rest and then move on as soon as the sun rose.

The nearby river curled along the banks with a whispering sound. Night birds chirped and insects muttered as they stirred in the comforting darkness.

Adessa picked up the sack with its grisly burden and set Maxim's head on a stump across from the campfire. She pushed the fabric down to expose the discolored, swollen skin. The wizard commander's eyes were puffy and half open, a gelatinous milky white. His mouth hung slack as the lips drooped to expose his teeth. He had once possessed a capricious trickster smile filled with more poison than humor. Now his skin held an oily greenish cast of decay, and rusty brown stains covered the stump of his neck.

Trying to balance the head upright, she pressed down to squish the soft tissue. "You will be my company for the evening," Adessa said. "But you were not good company in life. Sovrena Thora despised you. Now you will at least be silent and respectful."

With his dead face across from her, Adessa squatted on the log and contemplated as she finished her meal. Ravens squawked in the trees above the river and burst into flight. She looked up, wondering what had disturbed them.

Then a taunting voice sent splinters of ice down her spine. "You think you have won."

Her hand flashed to the short sword at her side and she rose from her seat. The campfire snapped again. She looked around.

"You won't win," the voice said, and she turned toward Maxim's head. Though bloated and discolored with decomposition, his eyes were now open, with the whites focused on her. "Ildakar has already fallen."

"By the Keeper!" she cried.

"Yes, by the Keeper." Maxim's lips spread apart and

cracked as pus leaked through them. His swollen tongue protruded from his teeth as the jaws moved to form words. "You haven't finished the job, morazeth."

Sure that she was imagining this nonsense, Adessa stared. "Be silent!"

When Maxim laughed, his head wobbled on the stump. "The veil is frayed, the boundaries slippery. Many souls moved through the cracks." The head chuckled again. "And I am slippery indeed."

"Be silent!"

Gripping her short sword, she strode around the fire to loom over the severed head. The eyes blinked at her in mocking innocence.

"I hacked your head from your body," Adessa said. "I shattered your chest with a tree and burst your heart. You are dead."

"Maybe I can't be killed so easily." He laughed again.

"I will cleave your head in two, and then I will chop those pieces into more pieces."

He merely scoffed at her. "You think that by removing this receptacle you can destroy my spirit? You are welcome to try." His lips curled in a sneer. His rotting eyes squinched shut and he opened them again so that runny liquid oozed out of his eyeballs. "Did you not promise my dear Thora you would bring her my head? If you hack me to bits, how will you explain your failure?"

Adessa wavered, glaring down at him.

The eerie voice continued, "Come, we will be companions on the long journey back to Ildakar! But I assure you, nothing remains of the city." He snickered again. "How would you know? You've been gone so long."

"You're lying."

"I see things as a spirit."

"You know nothing. You're my victim. You're dead."

"I am," Maxim replied. "And yet I am still here."

Frustrated and disgusted, she yanked the burlap sack over the severed head, wrapping it up and tying it tightly. Now his voice was just a whisper, but still there. She set her burden on the other side of the fallen tree. Adessa had no further appetite, nor could she sleep throughout the long and noisy night.

CHAPTER 13

Throughout the bright daylight hours, the Hidden People busied themselves inside the gloomy buildings of Orogang. They had plugged every chink, sealed every crack so that no hint of sunshine could penetrate their sanctuary. The pallid men and women struck sparks to torches, lanterns, and candles to illuminate the corridors of the palace. Even safe and sheltered within the blocky walls, they still moved furtively.

Nicci looked up to the high arches where the stone pillars vanished into shadows overhead. Old Cora led her through great, dim chambers where the cool stone walls were covered with patches of moss. "Why did you come to us?" the old woman asked. "Orogang sees almost no travelers. What brought you here?"

Tagging along, young Asha added, "Did you come over the mountain road? We keep it guarded, but our night hunting parties didn't see you."

Several others walked close, their gray garments rustling as they followed, listening. They spoke in low voices, as if their language were composed entirely of rumors.

"I did not come by road," Nicci said. "The sliph

carried me. If you have lived in this city for so long, surely you know of her well?"

The Hidden People muttered nervously. Cora considered. "We have heard stories of the silvery woman in the well, but no one has seen her in our memory. It is said she fell dormant more than a thousand years before Emperor Kurgan."

"The sliph was created to transport spies and saboteurs for Emperor Sulachan, long before Iron Fang was born." Nicci straightened. "I awakened her. I wanted her to take me to Ildakar, but instead she abandoned me here. Something strange happened during our journey. She thinks I betrayed her." Her heart felt heavy with the knowledge that she might not ever summon the creature again. The sliph was gone. "But I have to get back to my friends. There is a terrible war, and I can't stay here."

Cora paused as she led Nicci along. "Another terrible war. There is always a terrible war."

They entered a cavernous chamber with a domed ceiling supported by gigantic marble pillars. Nicci paused to take in the size, assuming this must have been a grand throne room. Iron Fang's?

"Ildakar is many days' ride from here." Cyrus sounded dubious as he accompanied them. "And the sliph brought you all that way?"

"The sliph carried me to Serrimundi on the coast and Tanimura before that. Those places are much farther away than Ildakar. Distance is not the same for such a creature." Nicci paused. "But if I cannot summon her again, then I have no way to get to where I need to be—not in time. Ildakar is under siege, and it may already have fallen."

"Our people cannot leave Orogang, or we would

help you," Cora said. "Because of the zhiss, we are honor-bound to remain here and keep the rest of the world safe."

Nicci looked around at the shadowy people, who slipped in and out of corridors and disappeared into dark passageways. "How many of you are there?" Hundreds had swarmed into the city square when they attempted to capture her, and she had seen many more silhouettes hovering in the doorways and arches of the sealed buildings. Were they a significant fighting force?

"Many," Cora said. "Our people live inside the buildings and in the catacombs that connect the largest structures, others in caves in the mountains. We are everywhere in Orogang, but we don't allow ourselves to be seen."

The torches burned like fiery eyes filling the large chambers. Emperor Kurgan's ancient palace held innumerable wings and chambers, as well as underground levels, but shadows disguised the magnitude of the place. The ancient capital city had many imposing structures. Iron Fang had built them all with heavy taxes and forced labor as he crushed citizens to prove his power. Though he had been murdered by his own people, Kurgan's monuments had endured for fifteen centuries.

The Hidden People went about their daily business. In large communal chambers, Nicci heard the clack of looms, the rasp of files, the rough biting sound of small saws. Craftsmen were shaping wood to make chairs, building tables, creating common amenities. Others wove fabric or spun yarn, while seamstresses sewed garments. The interior of the city had a hushed quality, but Nicci also sensed a certain contentment rather than fear.

"How do you feed so many people?" she asked. "I saw storehouses and granaries in the streets. Do you really farm at night?"

"We plant crops," Cora explained. "The daylight cares for its own and the zhiss do not bother the plants. At night we till and harvest. Our hunters bring back meat." Her smile showed genuine satisfaction. "We produce enough to care for ourselves."

Asha pulled ahead, excited. "But there's more! Our most important crop is underground. Come, let me show you." The girl reached an arched doorway above a descending stone staircase. She trotted down the steps with a patter of feet, leading them to a dark lower level beneath the palace.

Nicci followed Asha down claustrophobic and confined stairs into an underground chamber with rough rock walls. The room was illuminated by an eerie silver-blue light emanating from fleshy growths that covered the walls. Nicci smelled a lingering swampy odor in the air that was not entirely unpleasant.

Ten Hidden People, including some younger children, worked among the bulbous growths. They carried baskets and harvested the gray-white fungus, while others distributed brown mulch from baskets to fertilize the growths. Asha tore a piece of the shapeless mass from the wall and popped it into her mouth, obviously relishing the taste.

As stern Cyrus stood at Cora's shoulder, the old woman spoke with a hint of awe. "We cultivate and nurture this substance, making it our greatest weapon against the zhiss. This is why the swarm has not swelled across the land."

Two of the children harvested the mushrooms, stuffing their baskets while snitching a bite or two.

Cyrus also took a mouthful, as if it were his duty. "We consume the special fungus every day so that it permeates our flesh. It . . . helps our work."

Nicci realized how hungry she was after her ordeals, and she reached out to take a sample, but Cora violently yanked her hand away. "Not for you, Sorceress! Not for you."

Nicci backed away. "I do not understand you or your people."

The old woman seemed conciliatory. "We will explain everything. It is important." She picked one of the misshapen mushrooms and crushed it in her palm, showing the mess to Nicci, who inhaled a deeper breath. With her gift and her heightened senses, she found an ominous undertone to the slightly savory smell, a foul chemical that she had not noticed before. Cora said, "The fungus is deadly to all who are not accustomed to it, a poison as strong as the deathrise flower. It would kill you if you ate even a mouthful."

As they stood in the lambent glow of the chamber, Nicci watched other people arrive for their daily rations, plucking the fast-growing mushrooms and eating them as they walked back out.

"This fungus makes us deadly to the zhiss," Cora continued. "We have bred ourselves to endure it. We accustom our bodies to the poison from the time we are mere infants. We expose our bodies to the chemical, building up our resistance until our blood, our skin, every bit of us is filled with the poison."

Cyrus frowned at Nicci. "You could not survive it, Sorceress, no matter how great your gift is."

Nicci had endured poisons before, but she did not wish to test this, especially when she was already weak after her ordeal in the sliph. "I need to regain my strength, not diminish it. If the sliph does not respond to my summons, then I will have an arduous journey ahead of me . . . if I can find my way back."

"We know where Ildakar is," Cora said. "We can show you the mountains and the passes and how to get there. I am even familiar with these cities on the coast that you call Serrimundi and Tanimura, though our records are ancient."

"How can you know about the coast if you have never left this city?" Nicci asked. "Orogang has been cut off for centuries."

The old woman gave a mysterious smile. "That doesn't mean we have forgotten."

Leaving the fungus chamber, Cora led her and the others into an enclosed wing aboveground that connected to another grand building. They entered a speaking chamber with tiers of empty benches and a great open area for lectures on the floor. It was a place where Nicci could imagine shouting sessions and political debates.

On the floor stood a solid table on legs as wide as tree trunks. The table held a large, immaculately detailed relief map of the Old World sculpted out of clay and painted with natural colors. It was as if someone had shrunk down the actual mountains, valleys, and rivers of the Old World to fit there.

Bright lanterns rested on the four corners of the massive table, like suns shining down on the terrain. Previously, Nicci had seen only small swatches of the Old World marked on maps, but this three-dimensional representation encompassed the entirety of the Old World, from the coastline to the mountains and beyond.

Cora stretched out her arm and touched a bowl in the craggy mountains surrounded by difficult passes but connected by the fine lines of well-traveled imperial roads. "This is Orogang, the center of Iron Fang's great empire."

The old woman traced her fingertips along mountain ridges, following the roads south, plunging down into drainages and wider valleys as converging streams formed the headwaters of the Killraven River, which led south to another prominent city, Ildakar. From there, the river rolled along until it reached a widening estuary that spilled into the sea. Finding Ildakar, Nicci retraced the path that she, Nathan, and Bannon had traveled over the high pass of Kol Adair, back to the desert canyons that hid Cliffwall, and westward over more ridges to the sea and Renda Bay. She followed the coastline to the north, saw numerous shoreline cities all the way up to Serrimundi and Tanimura.

"This map was created long ago by order of Emperor Kurgan. He wanted to know the whole world, because he commanded General Utros to conquer the whole world."

"And General Utros will return someday," said Cyrus, who stood utterly confident, his pale chin thrust forward. "Remember the old prophecy! We have been waiting for so long, though he is surely long dead. . . ."

Nicci surprised them. "Oh, General Utros still lives. He and his giant army were turned to stone for centuries by the wizards of Ildakar, but now they have awakened." Cyrus looked astonished by the news, but she cautioned him, "Hear me, he is no savior. Even though Iron Fang is long dead, Utros means to conquer the Old World for himself. Do not expect him to be your hero."

"We have had legends for generation after generation." Cyrus stiffened, squared his shoulders. "He is a great man. The prophecy tells us he is coming back for us."

"You might have legends, but I have confronted the man myself. I know how much destruction his army will cause, how many people will die because of his ambition. You should fear him, not hope for his return."

Cyrus scoffed, "I will believe what I wish to believe."

Beside Nicci, Cora adjusted her gray cloak. "I would not put too much stock in legends or supposed prophecies, Cyrus. Your people have held on to a vain hope for too long. Remember, we also know silly tales about Iron Fang, myths that portray Kurgan as a brave and noble emperor, and he was certainly not worthy of legends or hope. How do you know General Utros is worthy?"

"Because I know," Cyrus said with rising defiance. His gray eyes showed no interest in the truth. "I believe the prophecy."

Nicci had seen the same blank and intolerant expression many times in the followers of the Imperial Order. She, too, had believed in their teachings and refused to consider that she herself might have been deluded, that she might have been wrong. Not until Richard . . .

"I know the truth as well," Nicci said, "whether or not you believe it."

CHAPTER 14

The huge army moved out, more than a hundred thousand soldiers along with countless cooks, carpenters, leatherworkers, swordsmiths, horse handlers, and craftsmen. Each man was responsible for his own armor, his own weapons, his own boots. He had to mend his cloak, build a fire, chop wood, dig latrines. The military force was an enormous city on the move in search of conquest.

The first divisions moved out at sunrise. They marched across the valley away from the blank space that had been Ildakar, heading toward the foothills and the mountains farther west. Second Commanders Halders and Arros mounted their warhorses and rode at the head of large companies that fell naturally into ranks.

General Utros watched from his command pavilion with Ava and Ruva hovering beside him. He was pleased that the war had actually begun again. "My army is like a great boulder on a hillside. It needs a push to start it rolling, but then it will crash downhill, unstoppable, destroying everything in its way." The golden mask hid half of his smile. "I will be the unstoppable force that crushes the Old World into submission."

Ava looked up at him as if she were entranced by a glamour spell. "What about King Grieve? Will you not share the land with the Norukai?"

"They are barely more than animals. Let us see how many Norukai survive after the war is won."

With a rumble of hoofbeats, boots, and creaking wagon wheels, the army moved west toward the foothills, raising clouds of dust and ash across the burned valley floor. The soldiers had eaten all the confiscated supplies, so each man went to bed with food in his belly and few questions. They would march until General Utros told them otherwise.

He had dispatched six more expeditionary armies, each with two thousand men, to head off in different directions, seeking cities to plunder and stockpiles to raid in his name. Thus, Utros increased the size of his invasion and also decreased the number of mouths he had to feed by twelve thousand. Meanwhile, his primary force headed relentlessly over the mountains.

Knowing the situation, First Commander Enoch sat grimly in his saddle as he rode up. He looked down at General Utros and the two sorceresses, who stood together outside the command pavilion. As the remaining companies formed ranks to move out, the pavilion would be broken down and packed into supply wagons. Utros and the twins would mount up and follow the main army.

"Your soldiers are determined now, General, and they will focus on the march," Enoch said. "But before long they will think about their sore feet and the discomfort of a rough camp. The day after that, they will think only about how hungry they are and worse, how hungry they are going to get." He scratched a thin white scar on his cheek. "They revere you, sir, I have no doubt of that, but the pang of an empty belly for long enough may break even the greatest loyalty."

"I know the costs of loyalty." Utros thought of what Iron Fang had told him after discovering his affair with Empress Majel. *Loyalty is greater than love.* After her grisly execution in the real world, sweet Majel's spirit had been tortured for centuries in the underworld, browbeaten and broken by her abusive husband's dominant spirit.

Loyalty is greater than love.

"I will raid any town and dispense all supplies to my soldiers," Utros said. "I don't know any other way to feed them."

Ruva spoke in a whisper as they watched the army plod toward the foothills. "My sister and I have a way to sustain them, beloved Utros. A dangerous spell. We will have to do it in secret, because the men will not like it, now that they've been restored to flesh and blood. But without our help, your army will crumble and the soldiers will die."

A breeze stirred the heavy fabric of the pavilion, blowing dust past them. "How will you do it?" Utros asked.

Ava said, "My sister and I know a spell that can reduce the body's need, slow and numb their appetites, change their metabolism so they will keep going, although it will not last. They will be digesting themselves."

"The spell will also work on the functioning of their bodies," Ruva added. "They will be able to eat anything, digest anything—grasses, trees, bones, whatever nourishment they find. The army will be like a swarm of locusts, stripping the land bare."

"But surviving," Ava pointed out.

When Enoch's brow furrowed, his many scars looked like twitching worms. "It sounds like a demeaning thing."

"If they starve and drop dead, they are no good to my war," the general said.

"If they do collapse and fall dead on the march," Ava said with a smile, "then thanks to this spell, the others can eat their bodies and gain even more strength."

Utros did not need to hear more. "They will live and they will keep fighting for me. Tonight in camp, after we have crossed the first foothills, I want you to work your spell." He sighed. "I will take the credit and the blame, if need be, once the soldiers discover what has been done to them. I promised to keep my men alive, and in this manner they will live." He looked to the twin sorceresses. "Save them by any means necessary."

The army trudged into full darkness, trampling the grassy hills and rising into thickening forests. Behind them, the ground was pounded hard by countless boots, flattened and lifeless.

After so many years of experience, the soldiers knew how to set up and break down camp with quick efficiency. Scouting parties dispersed to cut down trees and build bonfires. Second Commanders Halders and Arros distributed meager rations, promising the ranks that they would have more to eat as soon as they raided a city. The soldiers believed them, for now.

Each man found some patch of ground for his blanket where he could lie down to sleep and look up at the stars while he and his comrades remembered being human and all they had lost. They were fifteen centuries overdue to meet the Keeper.

In front of the command pavilion as darkness settled

in, Ava and Ruva laid the foundations of their spell. The largest bonfire was a beacon of crackling flames and smoke from the burning green wood. Utros sat outside the newly erected pavilion where he could watch his camp and listen to the activity. Curious, First Commander Enoch joined the general as the twins made their preparations for the dark spell.

Ava and Ruva had filled small clay pots with different powders, dried blood mixed with salt, the ashes of bones, powdered roots, flower petals and berries they had collected.

When the women proclaimed themselves to be ready, both were naked, their blue gowns discarded, all hair cleanly shaved from their skin, scalp, eyebrows, armpits, even the thatch between their legs. With their bodies painted with whirling patterns of deep red, intense black, and bursts of white, Utros barely noticed their nakedness. Each woman cradled a small pot of powder against her flat stomach. "We will begin, beloved Utros."

Ava dipped into one of the pots and held up a finger covered with a greasy yellow substance like tallow mixed with honey and sulfur. She dabbed a mark at the center of the general's forehead at the edge of his golden half mask.

"What is this for?" he asked.

"To protect you."

"Is your magic dangerous? Are my men at risk?"

"It will save you," Ruva replied.

Ava smeared a dab of the substance on her own forehead, then did the same to her sister. "This will nullify the spell. The magic won't change you. You will stay human."

Concerned, Enoch rose to his feet. "If we are asking

the soldiers to make this sacrifice, should we not do the same?"

"There was a time I would have said yes," Utros said, "but so much is uncertain. We need to lead them, First Commander." He gestured toward Enoch. "Give him the mark as well."

When Ava stepped forward with the pot, Enoch raised his arm to ward her off. "I don't want it." But when Utros gave him a steely glare, the veteran lowered his arm with a sigh. "If you must." As Ava marked his forehead, he asked, "Is this spell reversible? Once you have placed it on all these soldiers, can you change them back? After we achieve our victory and have all the supplies we need, can they be normal again?"

The twin sorceresses replied with noncommittal shrugs. "It's what we have to do."

The soldiers bedded down around their fires, exchanging stories, comparing dreams, and boasting about how wealthy they would be from the spoils of war, how many enemies they would kill.

Ava and Ruva circled the largest bonfire, throwing powders into the embers. Sparks flared and the smoke thickened, changed color, and spread like a miasma across the camp. Near their own campfires, the other soldiers didn't notice the mysterious smoke.

The sorceresses began a low chanting. They threw blood powder, bone ashes, flammable mineral dust, dried mushrooms, and ground-up tubers. The heady smoke dispersed among the scattered soldiers, changing them, tightening their stomachs, altering their blood flow.

"I need for them to survive until we reach the big cities, and there we will take enough supplies to feed them all again," Utros said.

"Your army will carve a swath over the mountains all the way to the coast, General," Enoch said. "Nothing can stop them."

"Good." Utros crossed his muscular arms over his chest and surprised the others as he announced his unexpected decision. "For the next several days, the army is in your hands, First Commander. You will lead the continuing march, while I need to depart for another destination." He had been considering his next move in great detail, but there was something else he had to do first. "I will take a thousand mounted soldiers and ride hard to the north. Ava and Ruva will go with me."

Alarmed, Enoch wiped the smear of greasy yellow off his forehead now that the spell had been cast. "You leave the army under my command? Where are you going, sir? The soldiers will want to know."

Utros nodded slowly. "Emperor Kurgan is long dead, but surely some remnant of the empire must remain. I serve the empire." He looked through the darkness, seeing the shadowed silhouettes of hills that blocked the vault of sky. "We will make the long ride to the capital city of Orogang so that I can report to whoever is left there."

CHAPTER 15

The defenders straggled in from their separate missions and met at a sandstone outcropping in the forest. Some looked frightened, while some were giddy with excitement. Nathan did a rough tally, guessing that several hundred ancient warriors had been killed, all told, but four D'Haran soldiers had fallen in the various skirmishes. Most battlefield commanders would consider those acceptable losses, but losing even four members of their ragtag band was a serious blow.

The last group to return included Captain Trevor and the wizard Leo. Leo was a skinny man with a narrow face, shaggy gray-black hair, and a dark goatee. He had managed two yaxen slaughterhouses in Ildakar, but those days were gone. He seemed terrified as he sat among the others beneath the sandstone overhang. His hands were covered with drying blood. "I killed people. I used my gift, and I . . . I tore them to pieces. I watched them die."

"They were our enemies," Zimmer said. "It is what they deserved. You already killed many on the battlefield while you were helping Elsa lay down her transference magic."

Leo nodded, though he still looked shaken.

"That is how we survive," Verna explained to him in a calm voice. "And there will need to be much more killing."

Oliver and Peretta returned to the camp with water from a nearby stream, while Amber and several Sisters of the Light foraged for berries and wild vegetables. Since they couldn't risk building fires, Nathan used his gift to heat a flat slab of rock, which served as a stove, and Rendell made a decent meal by boiling dried beans along with some wild onions. They shared stories as they ate.

As he listened to Renn talk about Hanavir, Nathan absently rubbed the scar on his chest. Although his new heart beat steadily, he felt a dark vengeance trying to gain hold of his thoughts. A foreign part of his mind, some stain of Chief Handler Ivan that still dwelled inside the heart, chastised him about what he had done when faced with the terrible decision. Ivan's sour presence complained that Nathan and Renn should have shown no mercy, that the weak townspeople of Hanavir were a necessary sacrifice to stop the raiding party. They deserved it. How many more people would die, now that General Utros could feed his army? Nathan gritted his teeth. His heart—Ivan's heart—beat like a loud primal drum inside his chest.

Trying to drown out the unwelcome thoughts, he lurched to his feet, startling the others as he breathed hard and heavy to drive back the pain. "Hanavir could have gone a different way," he said, interrupting Renn and ignoring the alarmed expressions around him, "but then there would have been more bloodshed. We have to save people where we can and when we can!" His pulse calmed as he exerted control over his rebellious heart. He sat back down, insisting he was all right, and quietly ate his beans.

Thorn, who had accompanied General Zimmer's group, proudly told of how they had defeated a hundred and twenty armed soldiers outside of a mining village. She and her sister morazeth Lyesse compared notes about their victims. Nathan found their discussion an odd mixture of boasting and technical advice on killing the enemy.

With a concerned look, Verna offered him a handful of berries that Amber had gathered. "Is this our life now, Nathan? Hiding in the forest, harassing the fringes of an overwhelming army, and then running again?"

Lyesse heard the comment and made a defensive reply. "We're more nimble than the army is. Our small group can strike and run, strike and run. Given several years, we will decimate them."

"Dear spirits . . ." Nathan shook his head. "I don't doubt your claim, but fools can be confident as well— and we can't afford to be fools."

Zimmer squatted on a rock across from them, wolfing down his meal. As a military commander he had eaten camp food for much of his life. "General Utros is now on the move. We saw them break camp and depart yesterday, marching across the valley into the foothills. It's our job to stop them."

Nathan pondered the great distances that he, Nicci, and Bannon had already traveled across the Old World. He didn't downplay the tremendous dangers they had faced in their journeys—the Lifedrinker, the sorceress Victoria, the deadly secrets of Ildakar itself—but the unstoppable army of General Utros might be the greatest threat. "We can't just endlessly strike and run. We may hurt them, or we may just annoy them. We need a better plan."

Oron cracked his knuckles and said sarcastically, "Yes, why not find an invincible weapon or gather our own huge army? How do you suggest we do that, Nathan?"

"I do not appreciate your attitude." He had washed his face, cleaned his garments, and actually felt presentable. That made him feel like a wizard again. "As a matter of fact, I do have an idea. We can obviously move much faster than the huge army, and our path will take us back to Cliffwall. The scholars there can help us find powerful magical defenses inside the archive. It may be our best chance. We'll get there well ahead of General Utros."

Peretta nudged Oliver, who sat next to her. "Yes! At Cliffwall, we can also train all those gifted scholars to fight."

Prelate Verna had the same thought. "And once we're hidden at Cliffwall, we'll be safe from the army, at least for a time. Utros will never even know to go there."

"It's decided then," Zimmer said. "We will move at our best pace back to Cliffwall."

Lyesse and Thorn looked at each other, and then in an oddly synchronized gesture they removed their daggers and began to sharpen the edges on a nearby rock. "But we will still harass them and kill as many as possible on the way."

"Yes," Thorn agreed. "It only makes sense."

CHAPTER 16

After a day sealed inside the ancient buildings, Nicci felt restless. She understood the plight of the Hidden People against the bloodthirsty zhiss, but her greatest concern was General Utros's army and the threat to the entire continent. He might be marching *now*! She couldn't hide inside the safety of shadows when those soldiers might be battering down the walls of Ildakar. Or Ildakar itself might be gone, if she understood the cryptic comment the sliph had made before vanishing.

The ambitious general would not rest on one victory or one failure. Conquest was his mind-set, and Nicci had to help stop him. She had left Nathan and Bannon behind, as well as the gifted members of the wizards' duma. She needed to find a way to go back.

Recovering from her strange weakness after her last sliph journey, Nicci rested in former guest quarters in the emperor's palace. Most furnishings had long since been removed, and the remaining tapestries and curtains were faded. The Hidden People lived a drab existence devoid of sunlight, color, and joy.

Young Asha brought her water, bread, and meat, and Nicci tried to rebuild her energy, but sleep refused to come. Too many priorities and frustrations consumed her.

Her sensitive ears picked up soft footsteps in the corridor, and Cora appeared in the open doorway. The old woman said, "The sun has gone down, and it is safe for us to venture out into the darkness. If you want to go into the city streets, now is the time for you to do so."

"I'm not your prisoner then?" Nicci asked.

Cora was startled. "Not at all. We tried to keep you safe, not hold you captive! You are a powerful sorceress. If you wanted to fight your way free, we could not stop you."

"No, you could not. It is good that you won't try."

Backlit by the hall torches, Cora adjusted her gray garments. "We hope you understand the danger now. The sun is down, the city is dark, and the zhiss have returned to their lair. You can go where you wish. If you decide you must leave Orogang, make sure you are far from the city by dawn, or the zhiss will find you."

Nicci had crossed a continent with Nathan and Bannon, and long before that, when she had kidnapped Richard, the two of them traveled from Westland all the way to Altur'Rang. She had seen the sculpted map in the speaking chamber and knew generally how she could travel south out of the mountains back to Ildakar. Such a trek would take planning, though, and Nicci reconsidered. "I'm not ready for that yet. I must try another means of travel first." Maybe she could get the sliph to listen. . . .

She followed Cora through the winding corridors of the imposing palace to where the main wooden doors swung wide to the night. Nicci breathed deeply, letting the cool air bathe her face. A faint breeze ruffled her ragged blond hair. Trellises held sweet-smelling vine flowers, and fluttering moths swooped around, drinking nectar from the white blossoms.

Outside, the Hidden People scoured the nearby hills. Some were already returning with cartloads of wood, while others moved supplies from isolated storage buildings. Silent men and women worked in garden plots or tended orchards. Except for the constant danger of the zhiss, this city seemed almost peaceful.

While Cora joined a team harvesting vegetables from gardens, Nicci walked through the streets of Orogang, always aware that she had to get back to shelter by sunrise. She remembered how the black cloud had swarmed around the two hapless deer and drained them dry.

She explored, walking among the fallen columns, collapsed archways, and the huge sunken amphitheater. She passed the towering statue of General Utros, where the dour Cyrus bowed reverently to his long-lost military hero. Others of his faction had draped offerings of night-blooming lilies around the granite base. The delicate pale flowers would shrivel in the next day's sunlight, but the Hidden People who revered the ancient general would add fresh flowers, night after night. Though she didn't accept the deluded prophecy that their great hero would return, Nicci did not disturb them. She had other business. She made her way to the empty sliph well.

The toppled statue of Emperor Kurgan sprawled in the square, the head broken off, the stone arm snapped just above the elbow. The emperor's face retained a haughty expression. Even if she had known nothing about Iron Fang's violent history, she would have disliked him just from the stone sneer.

Nicci had little interest in a forgotten tyrant, though. Right now the sliph was the most important thing . . . the sliph who had served Emperor Sulachan and despised anyone who did not follow that evil man's cause.

During the great war three millennia ago, this sliph had been created with terrible magic, a zealous volunteer transformed into a liquid-metal creature. That fiercely dedicated young woman had given up her life to become an inhuman being with the power to transport clients through a secret network. Nicci did not know the woman's original name, only that she considered her duty to Emperor Sulachan to be greater than her own happiness, her own family, her own loves, her own life.

Now, Nicci stepped up to the waist-high wall that encircled a bottomless pit. The stones had been mortared together, fitted so well that she could barely see the cracks. A dank smell wafted up from the depths.

She had traveled by sliph many times before, engulfed in the amorphous silvery substance and hurtled along the unseen passageways. The sliph had brought her here to Orogang because she said Ildakar was gone. They had both been damaged by the unexpected deflection from their goal.

Worse, Nicci had unwittingly revealed to the sliph the failure of Sulachan's cause, telling her that the ancient emperor was long dead. The petulant creature had fled, vowing never to help her.

Leaning over the low wall, Nicci felt the resounding silence in that deep well. "Sliph! I wish to travel."

Her words echoed in the well, bouncing down like dropped stones that never hit bottom. Not expecting an immediate answer, she listened but did not hear the frothy sound of the approaching creature. Nicci peered into the depths and thought of the blackness she had held in her own heart. She was stronger than that now, better than that.

"Sliph!" she called again. "I command you. I wish to travel. You were made to carry passengers, and you have carried me before. Take me back to Serrimundi." She raised her voice. "Take me back! Now!"

Her words were just hollow ricochets down into the emptiness. She gripped the edge of the low wall, pressing her hands hard into the cool stone. She reached out with magic, shouting with more than just words. She touched the Subtractive side of her gift, the darkness that had once served the Keeper, and she also pulled with Additive Magic, stretching out to summon the sliph with the full spectrum of her abilities. Only those with both sides of the gift could summon a sliph, and now Nicci beseeched her.

The silvery woman ignored her.

If she could not persuade the sliph to grant her passage to one of the great cities, Nicci would have to set off on foot. But if Ildakar had disappeared, that journey across the continent might take months or longer. Where would she go? All the way back to Serrimundi?

"Sliph!" she shouted with greater desperation. Nicci had no way to force the creature, no means to bribe her, if she could even guess what the sliph might want.

Then Nicci realized that she did have something to offer! She had made the sliph distraught by telling her that Sulachan was gone, but she had explained nothing more. This woman had surrendered her humanity because she was so dedicated to an ancient cause. The sliph would want to know the answers about her sacred leader, and Nicci was her only possible source for information.

It was a gamble, but she thought it might work, the most tantalizing carrot she could dangle before the sliph. Nicci leaned over the well. "If you take me back to Serrimundi, then I will tell you what happened to Sulachan. All of it. Every detail. I'll reveal the history of how he was defeated in his original war, but Sulachan came back from the dead to lead his armies again—and that was only a year ago. Can you exist without knowing? I will tell you about your cause." After a pause, she spoke louder. "After three thousand years Sulachan returned as the spirit king and almost conquered the world again—while you slept. I will tell you how you could have helped him. Don't you want to know?"

She hunched over the well and waited, listening. Surely the temptation would be great? She heard nothing but the Hidden People stirring in the dark city.

Nicci called down even louder. "This is your *cause,* sliph, and I am the only one who has the answers! I can tell you. If we cannot go to Ildakar, then take me back to Serrimundi. I have much to reveal to you. Don't you want to know?" She felt certain that the sliph had heard her, but no response came. "Don't you *need* to know?"

Throughout the night, the moon moved overhead in a slow arc across the heavens. Nicci remained there for hours, cajoling the sliph, enticing her, but to no effect. As the night ended, the Hidden People moved back toward their shadowy sanctuaries. Nicci was sure she had failed. She was stuck in the heart of an empire that no longer existed.

CHAPTER 17

The swamp dragon's jaws were as strong as the winches on the main gates of Ildakar. Lila strained against the monster in the midafternoon sunlight. She could feel sharp teeth against her skin as the monster tried to bite off her arm. The smell of decaying meat in the uneven rows of teeth made her gag.

She pitted her muscles against the creature. The underbrush crashed as the scaly beast dug its clawed feet into the mud to find purchase, but Lila pushed it back. The armored tail thrashed. They were matched in strength, but the swamp dragon was a primitive, stupid brute, and she was a *morazeth*.

Lila shoved with an extra burst of energy, yanked her arm free of its jaws, and spun as it recoiled in surprise. She lunged with her dagger when the beast opened its jaws wide. She drove her arm into the open mouth, and the dagger pierced the pink flesh of its gullet. She thrust into the back of its throat until she severed its spine from the inside.

The swamp dragon continued to twitch and snap, already dead but still deadly as its wild nerves kept firing. Panting and exhausted, Lila dragged herself out of the fang-filled mouth and rolled on her back into the muddy sawgrass. The swamp dragon let out a belching exhalation as it quivered in death. Lila got to her feet again, covered in blood, slime, and mud. She kicked the armored body with the hard sole of her sandal, shoving the large beast into the muck.

Tributaries and side currents curled like snakes through the vegetation. The dead reptile floated along in the shallow water, drifting as the current tugged it. Already, Lila could hear splashes and ripples as more swamp dragons prowled toward the disturbance. Though eager to feast on human flesh, the scaly predators were just as happy to devour the carcass of one of their own. Meat was meat in the deadly Killraven swamps.

Lila would have preferred to rest and eat her own meal, but she couldn't afford the time. The swamp dragon had already delayed her enough. She sprinted off through the grasses, splashing in the shallow mud and ducking under dangling vines and mosses. Her struggle had made a great deal of noise, and Lila didn't want any Norukai scouts to investigate, though she was confident she could kill them all. And she would, when the time was right.

Lila kept moving at a steady pace, jogging downriver. The three serpent ships had already sailed out of sight, and Lila had to keep up with them. Fortunately, the raiders dropped anchor at night, so as not to crash into river hazards in the dark. She didn't fear the swamp predators as much as she feared losing Bannon.

For years she had fought combat beasts in the arena. As a young woman, when she first trained as a morazeth, Lila had defeated any opponent, honed her skills, and received the protective runes that her trainers burned into her smooth skin. Combat came to her as instinctively as breathing and eating. She had single-handedly killed spiny wolves and a razor-tusked boar with nothing more than a short knife. Her back still bore long scars from when a combat bear had mauled her, but although her skin hung in tatters, Lila had killed it.

When she'd become a full morazeth, Lila began to train combat slaves, some of whom accepted their chance to achieve glory while others resented her for it. Lila had no sympathy for any of them. Her job was to turn the trainees into skilled warriors, whether or not they liked it. She was proud of what she had achieved.

Bannon had been one of the most difficult trainees, and she was especially pleased with him. That was why she protected the young man, why she rewarded him with her body, and why she felt affection for him against her better judgment. Bannon was earnest and dedicated, unlike any other slave she had seen in Ildakar. His eagerness gave him a naiveté that seemed absurd, yet his optimistic façade covered a deep darkness inside, scars from unspeakable pain in his life. Lila had helped him find balance so that he could become the best fighter, the best killer.

At one time, her job had been to create arena fighters merely for the entertainment of the Ildakaran nobles, but now she realized there were so many more important things she and Bannon could do together. First, though, she had to free him.

She still had his sword, which was a sufficient weapon for what she needed to do. Bannon had used Sturdy to fight against her in the training pits, so she knew the blade was solid and sharp. She used it to hack a thorny vine out of her way.

She ran into a marshy clearing at a bend in the river. On the wide channel ahead, she saw the Norukai ships as specks in the distance, but she knew where they were going. Lila just kept running. Biting gnats flew around her face, attracted to her sweat, smelling her blood, and she swatted them away.

The perils of the swamp were merely an inconvenience. She had to catch the serpent ships, and she refused to lose hope. They would not get away from her.

King Grieve and his raiding ships sailed down the river, and the small riverside village was in their path. Lila knew the Norukai could not resist fresh victims and spoils.

She ran through the afternoon and into the sunset. Ahead in the deepening darkness, she could see burning huts, smashed piers, a scatter of bodies. Even above the buzz of the swamp, she heard faint shouts and screams. She put on a burst of speed, but by the time she arrived at the village, there were few of them left alive.

The three serpent ships had dropped anchor in the channel, and the ugly raiders rowed to shore in landing boats to fall upon the fishing settlement. As she ran closer, sure she was too late, Lila looked at the aftermath, inhaled the bitter, smoky air. Twenty reed-and-willow huts had been built along the bank, with rickety docks extending out into the water. Other homes were farther from the river, in the trees. Several of their canoes had been smashed, sunk, or set adrift. Storehouses stood on higher ground above the bank. All were burning. The Norukai had been pillaging the place for hours already.

Lila approached stealthily, keeping to the underbrush. She could hear guttural shouts from the raiders, groaning and whimpering from captives. Several outlying homes were ablaze, and she could hear the screams of people trapped inside. Sprinting past the flickering fires, she came upon sprawled corpses, villagers hacked to pieces—old women and children who would have been considered useless, while the stronger men and women must have been dragged back to the serpent ships to be sold as slaves.

Set back from the riverbank, a shack had been set on fire, and she heard the wails of children inside. An overturned cart had been jammed up against the door by the cruel Norukai, intentionally preventing anyone from escaping. A man with a splintered boat hook still clenched in his hand lay dead outside the door, gutted. Lila understood the story with just a glance. A father had tried to defend his children, his home, but the Norukai had killed him, then locked the young victims inside and set the walls on fire. She imagined the raiders laughing as they did so.

The screams grew more urgent, more despairing. Terrified screams continued from deeper in the village, but Lila couldn't save them all. In her mind, though, Lila could hear Bannon's voice, insisting that she try to help people however she could, that she save as many as possible. Without thinking, she bounded to the overturned cart that barricaded the shack. She kicked the side of the cart, shoved it away, then yanked the rickety door open.

Inside, three red-faced girls were covered with soot, fallen to their knees, coughing. Waves of smoke curled out with the gush of fresh air. The oldest girl emerged to stare at the sprawled body of her father lying facedown in front of the shack, but Lila grabbed her arm, swung her in the other direction, and pushed her and her two sisters away from the burning home. "To the forest!" she hissed. "Run and hide in the trees." She had caught glimpses of other figures who had fled the village. "You'll find others out there. Stay with them."

Before the three girls could run, a big Norukai emerged from one of the nearby storage sheds. He spotted the girls, saw Lila, and his scarred face twisted in a hungry grin.

"Go!" she urged the girls, and they bolted, running for the trees. She remained to face the thug. Lila pulled Sturdy free, gripped the leather-wrapped hilt, and sprang forward, surprising the raider. His slashed mouth dropped open in a roar of challenge, but before he knew what had happened, Lila had hacked sideways to slit open his belly. The Norukai man gurgled as his intestines squirmed out like a basket of escaped snakes.

Lila would have liked to let him die slowly from the awful wound, but he was making too much noise. Impatient, she struck off his head and prowled forward, glad she had saved the three girls, but wanting to do more.

She saw four landing boats rowing back to the anchored vessels. Some of them carried huddled prisoners, while others were loaded with sacks of grain, stacks of smoked river fish, casks of supplies stolen from the town. Lila squeezed the sword's hilt, wanting to kill more of the Norukai.

Fortunately for her, a few raiders were still ransacking homes, starting more fires. They were stragglers simply having fun, and so she would have fun, too. One male taunted a growling dog tied to a post before he finally lost patience and lopped off the dog's head. Two other scarred men held down and raped a sobbing middle-aged woman. With a flare of fury, Lila threw caution aside and ran toward them.

As one Norukai man finished with the woman, he grunted with displeasure because she had gone limp. Petulant, he stabbed the naked woman in the heart and yanked his knife free before readjusting his sharkskin girdle. Her dying sigh sounded like a blessing.

It all happened before Lila could get there. She did not scream a challenge, because that would be wasted breath. Instead, she bounded ahead with Bannon's sword raised. She could not let the man live after what he had done. As the rapist turned his hideous face toward her, showing off his lips cut all the way back to the hinge of his jaw, Lila slashed his throat so viciously she nearly severed his head. He dropped gurgling on top of his victim.

The second raider holding down the now-dead woman let out a surprised shout. He lurched backward, grabbed his battle hatchet, and drew back his arm, but his waist girdle had been undone so he could take his turn, and it tangled around his legs. He stumbled.

Lila didn't let emotion color her need. She stabbed him in the gut and slashed sideways, as she had done with the man at the burning shack. As he fell, the man reached out for her with one hand. She kicked him down in a tangle of his own entrails. "I will let you die at your own speed."

The shacks continued to burn, and Lila heard moans and panicked cries from another barricaded home. She tore loose the barrier, freeing the people inside. She kept running, letting the people stagger out, gasping and choking.

As she made her way through the village, she took stock of the bloody bodies scattered about. One old man lay near the ruins of a fish-drying rack. He had been stabbed deep in his side. He reached out to Lila as she knelt beside him, but from her time in the combat arena, she knew it was a mortal wound.

She gazed deep into the dark forest beyond the river, the low trees, the willow thickets. She saw more figures running deeper into the forest, surviving families taking desperate shelter. Good, maybe even more of them had survived.

"Norukai," the man said, twitching his fingers.

She clutched his hand, because that was what he seemed to need from her. "I know who they are. I will kill as many as I can." She had already made up her mind, but it was what he wanted to hear.

"Kill them all," the man said, then died.

"I will." She set off.

A landing boat remained tied to the only intact pier. A Norukai man stood at the prow, impatient to shove off. The other landing boats had already rowed back to the serpent ships. "Finish up!" he growled to his unseen companions in the burning village. "King Grieve won't wait for us, and I don't want to be stuck here with these vermin."

Lila walked out of the smoke onto the dock as the man looked up at her in disbelief. Even though she held a bloody sword and carried a dagger at her hip, the raider seemed to think she was a gift, not a threat. He stepped out of the long landing boat and stood on the pier. "Did they send you to me?"

"The Keeper sent me to you. Now I send you to him." Using both hands, she swept Sturdy sideways.

The startled man recoiled, barely avoiding the sharp tip. He lost his balance on the dock and fell into the river. He bellowed and splashed, grabbing on to the boards to haul himself up, cursing her. Lila struck down and lopped off both of his hands at the wrists. As he let out a deep-throated scream and flailed his stumps spouting blood, she thrust Sturdy through his neck. His body slid into the shallow water and floated away in the current.

Out in the middle of the channel, the three serpent ships raised anchor and set their dark sails. She wasn't surprised that King Grieve would take his spoils and depart without even waiting for his last few men.

She stood at the end of the pier and watched the ships move. She intended to do exactly what the nameless dying man had demanded of her. She would kill them, and she would free Bannon.

CHAPTER 18

As the enemy army pressed through the foothills behind Nathan and his companions, they did not follow single file but spread out, trampling everything in their wake. The mass of warriors camped for only a few hours each night and moved again as soon as dawn suffused the sky.

Nathan's band pressed on, but they had not gained a great deal of ground from the relentless march of the vast army.

"We've already killed so many of them, and they keep coming," Renn said in uneasy awe. The two wizards stood together.

Nathan thought of his own loss rather than the enemy's. "Elsa's transference magic incinerated thousands on the battlefield, but even so, they didn't pay a high enough price." He shook his head, flushing with anger. "She was worth more than that whole damned army."

The other wizard's eyes were red-rimmed, and his mouth sagged in a frown. "And Lani? Did she at least fight well before she died?"

Nathan brightened. "Oh, yes! Dear spirits, during our first sortie against General Utros, Lani made the ground shake with her gift. All by herself she flattened entire enemy companies. She impressed me very much."

The bedraggled wizard sighed. "Yes, my Lani was a good fighter. I wish I'd been at her side."

Thorn and Lyesse frequently disappeared from the group, flitting back to prey upon more enemy scouts and stragglers. The morazeth women kept careful score of the enemies they killed. Though such losses did little to weaken the multitudes, the bodies discovered every morning caused great agitation in the large army.

General Zimmer did not have enough horses for all of them to ride, so many doubled up as the group made their way toward the hidden archive. He dispatched one messenger ahead to ride with all possible speed, so Cliffwall could prepare, although the scholars should already have known about the threat of General Utros; Zimmer had already sent word weeks ago, after they had wiped out an expeditionary army in an avalanche below Kol Adair. By now, Nathan hoped, the imaginative scholars might have found additional defenses to suggest. . . .

For his own part, Nathan had hard memories of the archive, the damage done by the Lifedrinker and the sorceress Victoria, but also the tragic loss of the dear girl Thistle. Nathan knew how much powerful magical lore was stored in Cliffwall, and he was sure that some of it could be turned against General Utros, but he also knew how easy it was for that power to grow out of control. He vowed to be vigilant when they searched the dusty library for defensive spells. What could their band of defenders do against an army that had withstood all the wizards of Ildakar?

Because Cliffwall was so cleverly hidden, the ancient

army might simply march past without any scouts discovering the isolated canyons and the archive. He could only hope.

Crossing one forested ridge after another, they could see the rugged, snow-streaked mountains in front of them, beyond which were the canyons of the western slope. Zimmer and Prelate Verna rode ahead to climb into a sweeping meadow, a lush hanging valley amid the thick forests. Before them, the wide meadow was filled with a splash of flowers, as if some ambitious painter had used the high valley as an enormous palette. The plants had swordlike leaves and fleshy green stems; the deep violet flowers were shot through with crimson veins.

As the party emerged from the forest into the flower-filled meadow, Amber let out a cry of delight and slid down from her horse. "They're beautiful!"

Oliver and Peretta joined her. "I've never seen so many blooms," Peretta said.

Verna moved into the meadow. "They are indeed beautiful." General Zimmer stared ahead as if searching for a path through the sea of blossoms.

"We should bring some specimens with us to Cliffwall," suggested Oliver.

Out of breath, Nathan and Renn trudged up on foot as the troops milled in place before the great meadow. Nathan could smell the perfume of flowers in the air. Considering so many open blossoms, he expected to hear a buzz of bees, see a flurry of butterflies, but the meadow seemed oddly silent.

Laughing at the beauty, Amber and Peretta ran together toward the meadow, like children about to plunge into the ocean. Nathan felt a cold twist in his gut, and he shouted, "Stop! Dear spirits, don't go there!"

But the sounds of the horses, the muttering soldiers, the rustle of armor drowned out his words. Urgent, he drew a deep breath and shouted out with his gift as well as his voice, making a boom of thunder in the air. "*Stop!*"

The blow of the word was enough to bring the young people to a halt. Nathan pushed through the soldiers to reach the edge of the meadow and looked at all the blooms, aghast. "I know these flowers. They are *death-rise flowers,* the greatest poison ever discovered. A single blossom is deadly enough to kill a dozen full-grown men. I'm glad I stopped you in time!"

The soldiers pulled their horses back. Amber and Peretta retreated, and no one else ventured closer. Tossing his long white hair, Nathan cautiously approached the meadow, and Renn followed him, curious. "I have never heard of deathrise flowers."

Oron rode up to them, tall in his saddle. He sniffed sarcastically. "We lived inside a walled city for fifteen hundred years, Renn. How much wild plant life would you expect us to know?"

Zimmer frowned in his saddle as he looked across the meadow. "It will take a long time to ride entirely around those flowers."

Like a man approaching a poisonous spider, Nathan bent close to the nearest blossoms, studied their petals without touching them, the intense purple, the slash of deep red, the golden stamens. The mere touch of any one of these flowers would cause an agonizing death. "Emperor Jagang would grow fields of these flowers and then test the poison on his prisoners. Even the smallest touch is enough to bring rashes and blisters, horrible boils. A little more will kill you."

Renn scratched the stubble on his cheek. "There must be thousands of blossoms."

Nathan hung his head, remembering the girl Thistle with her large dark eyes and her positive attitude. Thistle had eaten one of the deathrise flowers, and thereby forced Nicci to kill her to stop the agony. It had been one of the most terrible choices Nathan had ever witnessed.

"Keep the horses away," Zimmer said, and gestured toward the edge of the meadow. "Follow the trees to the opposite side until you reach the stream, then keep to the forest." He shook his head. "Thanks to you, Nathan, we dodged a dangerous thing. We would all have been dead before we crossed the field."

The morazeth trotted up, wondering why the group had stopped. The two women were not impressed with the pretty flowers, but became much more interested when they learned about the deadly poison in the blossoms.

Nathan kept staring at the meadow, stroking thumb and forefinger along his chin as he pondered. "This is the obvious route through the hills. At least part of General Utros's army will surely come this way." He gave Renn an intense smile. "With a little provocation, we could lure the enemy soldiers right across this meadow."

CHAPTER 19

As she stayed among the Hidden People, contemplating her plans, Nicci recovered from the unsettling side effects of her journey through the sliph, and at last her gift felt strong again. Trapped inside during daylight hours, she explored the gloomy passageways that echoed with whispered footsteps. The silent population seemed as much in a trance as the ancient city was.

Asha, Cora, and other Hidden People offered only vague answers to her questions about their history in Orogang and how they had watched over the zhiss. As the old woman arranged drooping night lilies in a vase to add a splash of white in the torchlit gloom, Nicci asked, "Is this all you do every day? You just wait and hide? Do you do nothing else?"

"What else can we do?" Cora asked. "We don't dare leave, or the zhiss will spread far and wide. We have to contain them, and they stay here because of us. That is our purpose."

Agitated, Nicci brushed the soft stems of the lilies. "Is that enough after so many centuries? Will it ever change?"

"It will not change until the zhiss are destroyed."

"And will that ever happen?"

Cora hung her head. "I do not know, and my grand-mothers before me did not know. We can only hope that someday one of our children will rid the world of this scourge."

"I can't wait that long," Nicci said. "I have other things I need to accomplish."

Cora continued arranging flowers as pointless decoration. Frustrated with the woman, Nicci returned to her room and lay back, planning how to leave this isolated city without depending on the sliph. If Ildakar had hidden itself again beneath the shroud of eternity, then nothing would keep General Utros from sweeping across the continent. Meanwhile, Nicci was here locked in a building, hiding from daylight. . . .

She didn't realize she had dozed off until she found herself among powerful, feral thoughts. In her dream state, her body shifted to become a tawny feline shape. She prowled along, seeing the world through a predator's senses. Smells became a different language. Mrra!

Part of the sand panther's mind, Nicci loped along, constantly moving, but she panted with exhaustion, and her large padded paws were sore and raw. She had covered countless miles, racing across the landscape toward a destination that was so clear in her mind: Mrra needed to find her sister panther.

Nicci had been separated from the sand panther when she traveled through the sliph to Serrimundi, but through the spell bond the two remained connected. It had been so long since she'd felt a clear contact that she'd feared Mrra had broken the bond. The big cat had been an excellent spy, roaming around the perimeter of the giant army, feeding information to Nicci through her feline eyes.

Now, Nicci expressed her joy through the spell bond. She felt a growing awe as she realized that Mrra had run overland, tracking her down over the mountains. The connection was faint, but she knew that the panther was not far away. Mrra could taste her presence in her mind.

"Come to me, sister panther!" Nicci whispered in her sleep.

The big cat growled as she bounded through the forest. With her enhanced senses, Nicci realized that other cats were accompanying Mrra. Long ago, when the sand panther had been raised by the handlers of Ildakar, she was trained to fight and kill in the combat arena. From the time she was just a cub, Mrra had been bonded with a pair of sand panthers, her *troka,* who fought together, moved together with shared hearts. But when the other two cats had been killed by Nicci and her companions, Mrra was bereft and mortally wounded, until Nicci became her sister.

In her lonely sojourn across the landscape, Mrra had encountered other big cats and brought them along as her new pride. Though the sand panther did not understand numbers, Nicci sensed there were at least six or seven cats loping along beside her across the mountainous terrain.

"Come to me," Nicci murmured in the halfway land of sleep, and Mrra let out a roar in her mind. The other sand panthers roared as well, and Nicci fell into a deeper sleep, content that they would soon be reunited. . . .

When she awoke hours later, still groggy and stiff, Nicci went to the speaking chamber to study the relief map and plan her best route over the mountains to where Ildakar had been, or back to Serrimundi or

Tanimura. She had tried to coax the sliph with the promise of information about Emperor Sulachan. Had the silver creature even heard her? There had been no response whatsoever.

As Nicci ran her hands over the sculpted map, finding possible routes, one of the gray-robed men entered the speaking chamber—dour Cyrus, who believed too much in the legend of General Utros. His expression shifted between anger and hope when he saw her. "Though you spoke ill of Utros, we are reassured to know that he is alive. He will come for us, just as the prophecy foretold."

"You believe too easily in things," Nicci said. "If you had seen the general attack Ildakar, you wouldn't revere him so much."

"Emperor Kurgan commanded him to attack Ildakar. What else would he do?" A scowl crossed Cyrus's face beneath the fold of his gray hood. "Even if he chose the wrong leader to follow, Utros is a great military commander. Iron Fang is long dead, and Utros can be the true ruler that we have always needed. Our people will be part of his new army. He needs us! The Hidden People are a great army. We have waited so long for him."

"Utros has more soldiers than you can imagine," Nicci said. "How will you help him? Many mobs consider themselves armies until they face a real enemy."

Cyrus looked at her defiantly. "Follow me. I will show you."

Leaving the speaking chamber, Cyrus glided through the stone corridors until he paused before a sealed storeroom. Cyrus took a deep anticipatory breath and tugged on the door. The dark wood was so old it looked petrified, and the hinges creaked as they reluctantly swung open.

When the torchlight chased away the shadows, Nicci saw a vast chamber filled with gleaming swords in storage racks, enough weapons for an army of thousands. Spears stood in the corners like corn shocks. Curved helmets were piled on shelves. Stacked shields all bore Kurgan's flame symbol.

Cyrus lifted one of the swords. "We keep these sharpened and oiled, ready to be used the moment General Utros calls us to war. We train at night, practicing our swordplay in front of his statue." He looked eager. "We have waited long to be called to our duty, but it will happen. We know it will happen! Considering the stories of General Utros, we have no doubt."

"You should have doubts," Nicci scolded. Despite her skepticism about the man's blind faith, she admired the blades and armor. "There is much you don't know about your hero."

Cyrus cut her off. "I know all I need to know, and we are ready for him."

After showing her the weapons, he ushered her out and closed the door behind them. She heard the Hidden People stirring inside the dim corridors of the shuttered buildings, their conversations building. Outside, the sun had gone down, and once again the people had the freedom to roam the city.

CHAPTER 20

Inside the enclosed hold of the Norukai serpent ship, the air stank of sweat, fish, and fear. Bannon hunched on the wooden bench, feeling the manacles like jaws around his wrists. The jangle of the heavy chains was softer than the groans of pain and anxiety from the nearby slaves. But he made himself stay strong. He had survived this long.

The oars creaked as the slaves strained to row, driving the serpent ship downriver. The dull heartbeat of the pace drum echoed inside the hold, where the captives struggled to keep up with the rhythm. They worked hard to avoid the whip of the oar master, who was all too anxious to start the day by making an example of someone.

Open hatches in the hull were designed to let in sunshine and air, but provided little of either. Instead, the reminder of daylight and freedom was merely another aspect of the Norukai torture. Gripping the sweat-slick oars, Bannon's hands were covered with blisters. His voice was only a dry croak as he groaned. He couldn't guess how long it would be before the hourly bucket of river water was passed around again, a ladleful splashed into their mouths.

Bannon's muscles throbbed from his biceps to his bones. The current of the Killraven River would pull them along, and the dark sails caught breezes, but King Grieve insisted on greater speed, forcing the captives to sweat and bleed and die if necessary. While others begged, Bannon didn't give the scarred raiders that satisfaction. The drumbeat pounded harder, and he strained to keep up.

The oar master was a surly man named Bosko, prone to flatulence, which only increased the stink in the confined space belowdecks. Tattoos and scars covered his face, but Bosko would have been ugly even without the mutilation.

Sitting under the open hatch up to the main deck, he bellowed, "Harder, you worms! Lazy men will be hungry men. If you want your feast at noon, you'd better work up an appetite." He laughed, flinging his scarred mouth wide.

Bannon's stomach recoiled at the thought of the rancid fish guts they would shove into his mouth. He had been starving for so many days, and he would force himself to swallow the nourishment, no matter the awful taste.

The big miserable man chained next to him whimpered. His shoulders hunched and shook, and his hands were loose on the oar. Bannon whispered, "Please row—help me. If they think you're lazy, they'll chop off your hands, and I don't want that to happen to you." The man flinched as if Bannon's words were as sharp as a Norukai whip. "Trust me, stick with me. We'll get through this."

Sullen, the big man gripped the oar shaft and pulled, though he couldn't articulate words.

The man, Erik, was one of the new captives taken

two nights ago when the serpent ships had raided a small peaceful village. When the raid had launched, Chalk remained behind on deck, bouncing with excitement as he watched King Grieve swing his war axe and lead his fighters. "The axe cleaves the wood! The sword cleaves the bone!" the albino called out. He had looked at Bannon as if the words had special meaning. From the deck of the main ship, Bannon had watched the ruthless Norukai ransack and burn. He wished he had Sturdy, or even a stick, to smash Chalk's face, or King Grieve, or the shipwright Gara, or the oar master Bosko. Any Norukai would do.

They had pillaged the settlement, seizing supplies, burning homes, slaughtering children, raping women. They had also captured a handful of strong, healthy people, including Erik, to press into slavery. After the serpent ships set off again, Bannon was glad to learn that several of the Norukai had not come back, so the villagers must have put up unexpected resistance.

Now, Bannon and Erik were chained together on this bench, though they had few opportunities to talk. The big man was drowning in grief. "You've got to work so they don't kill you," Bannon urged him. "I know it's terrible, and I can only guess at what you've lost, but don't give up. Keep watching for your chance to escape. You'll know when the time comes."

Still sobbing, Erik nodded. "They're all dead. . . ."

Bannon tried to think of a way to give the poor man strength. "Getting killed won't bring your family back. The Norukai won't tolerate insubordination. We're no more than a haul of fish to them."

"I hate them." Erik had shaggy brown hair and a beard, a square face, broad shoulders. The raiders had killed his wife and two children, but captured him because he looked like a strong worker. "I hate them," he repeated.

"We have that much in common. Sweet Sea Mother, we will find some way out of this. Stick with me, and don't give up."

A looming shadow appeared at the hatch above, and King Grieve shouted down into the hold. The oar master stopped drumming so the king's words could be heard. "You are beaten. You are slaves. You serve the Norukai. Your lives are ours, and we can take your lives whenever we like, if you don't work."

The chained men slumped on the benches. Bannon held his silence, though a flare of anger made his skin feel hot. Erik tried to stifle his weeping. Bannon wanted to comfort the man, but he could only offer empty hope and his own optimism. He comforted himself with the promise that he would kill as many of the Norukai as he could.

Bosko lifted a ladle of clean water from a wooden bucket at his side and slurped a drink for himself as he eyed the captives who looked desperately at the liquid. Without the least bit of embarrassment, he passed gas in a loud burst.

Grieve glared at the oar master from the deck above. "Why did you stop drumming? Keep the ship moving."

Bosko pounded out the beat again at an even faster pace than before.

After Grieve retreated from the upper hatch, a spidery shape dropped down on the wooden ladder, peering into the smelly place. Chalk scuttled into the hold, where his bare feet splashed in the puddles of bilge that collected there.

"Row, row, row! Down the river we go. You'll all grieve!" He stopped abruptly when he saw Bannon chained to the bench. With mincing footsteps, he came to torment the young man, though he seemed to consider it conversation. "You like to row? Off we go!"

"I hate to row," Bannon said, then thought of Ian as well as Erik's family, all of the victims the raiders had left in their wake. "I hate the Norukai. Can you understand why?"

With a grave expression, Chalk bobbed his head on his bony neck. "Some Norukai are not nice."

Erik shrank away from the scrawny albino, but Chalk's attention remained entirely on Bannon. He took a seat on a sharp edge of the adjacent bench, squirming to find a comfortable spot, as if this were merely an afternoon in the park and they were two friends chatting.

"I want all Norukai to die," Bannon said.

"Even me?" Chalk said. "I'm your friend."

He paused in his rowing. "Friend? I'm chained here as a slave!"

"I give you fish," Chalk said.

"You give me fish guts."

"Moist and tender fish guts." He licked his lips. "They are good! They are what I eat."

"Leave me alone." Bannon bent to his rowing because that was better than the albino's taunting. Next to him, Erik groaned and sniffled.

As if jilted, Chalk frowned. "If you don't like my fish guts, then I'll give your portion to *him*." He looked indignantly at the new captive. The thought only made Erik moan even more.

"Why do you keep pestering me?" Bannon asked. Was this creature some kind of strange ally? "You don't see how cruel King Grieve is, how cruel you all are, the pain you've caused."

Erik found the courage to echo the words, "I hate you all." The other slaves muttered as well, all of them listening.

Chalk was surprised and curious, as if he honestly hadn't considered the idea. "Why? Why do you hate?" From the expression on the albino's face, he seemed to be expecting an answer.

Bannon was surprised. "You honestly don't know? You can't see the terrible things you've done?"

"Terrible? We are Norukai. This is what we do." He scratched his hideously scarred chest. "Would you have us be different?"

"Yes!" Bannon wasn't sure how he could get through to the odd man. "The Norukai tried to capture me when I was a boy, but I got away. They took my friend Ian instead, sold him to Ildakar as a slave for the combat arena. He spent all his life being tortured and trained."

"Ah, a champion," Chalk said.

"A slave!"

The shaman remained perplexed. "If he was captured, why do you feel sorry for him? That means he was weak. If he fought in a combat arena, he must have had a glorious life. I know about Ildakar. Yes, yes, Ildakar! Gone now." He frowned, tugged on his scarred lip. "What did your friend expect?"

"Ian expected a life!"

Chalk scratched his straggly white hair. "A life? If he was a champion, what better life is there? Maybe he could have been a Norukai warrior instead. Would that have been a better life?"

"No! He could have lived on Chiriya Island. He could have married, had a wife, children, a nice home." Bannon sighed with the sadness of lost hopes for his friend.

Chalk made a rude noise. "Weak. Sounds weak. I think he must have been strong."

"If he had stayed home, he would have been loved," Bannon said. "I loved him. He was my friend, and the Norukai took all that away. He would have had a much better life."

"Love . . ." Chalk frowned. "Not everyone has love. Not poor Chalk. Do we all deserve love?"

"Yes, we all deserve love," Bannon said, "even if someone else takes it away."

"I have never known love. I don't understand it."

"You don't understand a lot of things."

The shaman found that hilariously funny and said in a singsong voice, "Love, love! Grieve, Grieve! You'll all grieve. No love for me, I've seen it. No love for me."

Chalk seemed entirely convinced, and Bannon felt an odd moment of twisted sympathy. The countless bite marks and rough scars on the smooth white skin made the shaman repulsive. In frustration, Bannon asked, "Why do you keep bothering me? Why am I special?"

"The axe cleaves the wood. The sword cleaves the bone!" Chalk tapped his temple. "Because you're in my head and maybe by talking to you I can get you out." He paused to consider. "You'll all grieve. Sailing, sailing, sailing!" As if he heard some hidden whistle, Chalk bounced off the bench. "Talk later. For now, row, row, row! Soon, we'll be out on the shining sea again."

Leaving Bannon baffled, the albino scrambled along the underdeck, ducking low even though he was much shorter than the beams. He climbed the ladder to the open air, while the slaves looked longingly after him.

CHAPTER 21

As Adessa continued north along the river, the channel widened to create a maze of marshes, tall reeds interspersed with sluggish rivulets and stagnant pools.

Carrying her stained sack, she splashed along, stepping on grassy hummocks or sliding into loose muck. Once, she sank up to her waist in a slurry of silt, but she hauled herself out, disappointed in her clumsiness. If she wasn't careful, she might lose her trophy. She had carried the wizard commander's head for many miles and many days. Adessa was eager to see the expression of warm gratitude on Thora's face when she opened the sack and pulled out the rotting horror.

As she made her way through the marsh, she felt the bloated burden at her hip. By now, Maxim's head was growing softer, squishier. The marsh was full of unpleasant odors, but the sweet nauseating stench of decay hung like a cloud. She skirted several fishing towns at bends in the river, not wanting questions or company. The closer she got to Ildakar, the more threatening the swamps would be, the deadlier the predators. For now, she wanted to make good time.

She pressed her fingers against the sack to feel her

victim's clumped hair, the oozing skin. Liquid seeped through the fabric, making a new stain of pus and spoiled blood.

"Do you remember these marshes?" she asked aloud. "That town where you thought you were safe? Tarada, I think it was called. I killed your followers there, and you ran." She paused, expecting his mouth to move and speak. "What? No reply?"

Sure that she had not imagined it the first time, she kept trying to provoke the wizard commander's spirit to come again. She knew for certain that Maxim's eyes had opened, that he had truly spoken to her. Since then, she had kept the head tied inside the sack to stifle his reanimation.

But Maxim could not speak to her because he was *dead*! It must have been her imagination. And even if the wizard commander did utter words, he was defeated. He had nothing to say to her.

That night Adessa made a solitary camp on a hummock of brown grass and peat, where she could sleep. Setting the sack in the matted grass, she found a dead swamp oak with wood rotten enough that she could break off the branches. She piled the twigs and dry grasses to start a fire. The orange flames were the only light for as far as she could see. Adessa heard the constant buzzing of marsh insects, night birds, and slithering creatures that hunted in the darkness. She sat cross-legged on a mossy rock that was solid, if not comfortable. Adessa needed no comfort.

She peeled thick reeds and roasted the bland but edible pulp. She had found berries during the day, even killed a small marsh hare with a thrown knife, which she now skinned and roasted. It was enough to satisfy.

Maxim's head remained wrapped in the sack, but she

couldn't tear her eyes from it. She saw only the lumpy outline inside the fabric, but she knew that he was staring at her with jellied eyes. His puffy purplish lips would be twisted in a mocking smile.

She heard a whispered voice above the undertone of swamp sounds. "You can't hide from me by keeping me in this sack."

"You cannot speak."

"Then why are you answering me?"

"You're dead."

"I don't dispute that fact."

"Then stop talking to me!" She bit into the roasted rabbit leg so viciously that she broke the bone between her teeth. She spat out the hard shards.

"I am still the wizard commander." Maxim's voice was muffled by the sack. "You tricked me, surprised me. That was the only way you were able to kill me, but I still have great powers you can't understand."

Adessa lurched over to yank open the sack. She pulled out the head. "Be quiet!"

His blackened skin sagged in all the wrong places, and his oozing eyes came bright and alive, turning toward her. "I merely thought you might like some conversation. No need to be rude. It's lonely out here in the swamps, and you don't have any company." His gruesome face grinned at her. One of his loose teeth fell from his gums and dropped into the grass. "My many lovers have told me I'm very good company."

"I don't want your conversation."

"I know what you fear, dear Adessa. You're afraid that you might be going mad."

"I'm not mad!"

Maxim's lips parted. "Would a sane woman talk to a rotting head in the middle of a swamp?" His smile broadened so that the decaying skin cracked and yellowish pus ran down into his goatee. "Would a sane woman hear him answer?"

She carried her grisly trophy to a stagnant eddy at the edge of the hummock and submerged the head. "Now I don't have to hear you." She stood up, smug.

Through the still water she could see Maxim's eyes looking up at her, but his mouth made no sound.

Satisfied, she went back to her meal, finished the rabbit with a handful of berries, but she couldn't stop thinking about her trophy. She worried about the decomposing head under the water. What if the current was stronger than she expected? What if he drifted away?

She knelt on the edge of the grasses to check on the head. She was alarmed to see half a dozen brown fingerlings nibbling on the decaying face. The little fish darted in to peck at the open eyes, to eat flakes of putrid flesh. If the fish devoured what was left of the wizard commander, Adessa would have nothing more than a skull to show Sovrena Thora!

In disgust she plunged her hand into the water, and the fish scattered to hide in the reeds. Grasping his hair, she lifted the head back onto the grass. Some of the stains had rinsed off, but Maxim was no more attractive.

Once out of the water again, he opened his mouth and continued the conversation as if he'd never been interrupted. "You will not make it back to Ildakar."

She snorted. "You said I would never kill you either, yet I succeeded in that."

"This is different. I told you before, by now Ildakar has fallen. The wizards raised the shroud of eternity, and the city is gone. You have no home."

"I will still go there. I don't believe you."

Maxim continued to taunt. "Even if you complete your journey, you will never find Thora. Alas, my dear wife is already dead. Her spirit is in the underworld—I have seen her myself. The Keeper is quite happy to have her. I think he has a lot in common with the unpleasant bitch."

"You lie!" The thought of the sovrena being dead hurt Adessa more than any of his other statements. "You lie!"

"Poor Adessa, am I not in a position to know? After all, I'm dead, too—as you yourself reminded me."

"Then stay dead. Stop speaking."

"The dead are not the same as they were, and I have drifted back and forth through the veil. We arrogant wizards of Ildakar caused our own damage to the order of the universe by turning General Utros and his army to stone. We stole all those souls from the Keeper, held them away for centuries. The shroud of eternity also kept our nobles out of the stream of time. But the Keeper is patient. He will claim what he is owed. He will come for you too, Adessa."

"The Keeper always does," she said. "You don't frighten me."

"Maybe I'll stay here to keep you company after all. Or maybe I can call the Keeper's attention and have him come for you now."

"Be quiet!"

Maxim laughed.

Her voice rose to a shout, or maybe it was a scream. "Stop laughing!" Thoughts echoed inside her head, and a dark inner doubt made her wonder about her sanity. The wizard commander and his insidious taunts would be enough to drive any morazeth insane.

The campfire crackled and popped as the flames hit a loose knot of wet wood. Trembling with anger, Adessa stuffed the head back into its sack, hoping that would shut the man's mouth. "There, you can rot in the dark."

She heard a rustle in the underbrush nearby, a splash in the water, something large approaching. Wary, Adessa grabbed her short sword and stood by the campfire. The movement didn't sound like a marsh deer or a bear. She had thought the campfire would keep large predators away. She crouched, holding her silence, her ears attuned to any sound.

A lean mud-spattered woman stepped forward into the circle of firelight as if she feared nothing. Adessa was astonished to recognize the scant black leather outfit, the protective runes on the skin just like her own, the pale brown hair.

"I didn't expect to find you," Lila said, "but I need your help."

CHAPTER 22

After darkness fell like a protective blanket over the ruins of Orogang, the palace doors opened again. The Hidden People performed the same tasks they had undertaken for countless generations, and they were no closer to defeating the zhiss.

Nicci explored the streets, looking for something she could use. She understood the danger of the blood-thirsty cloud, but she could not stay here. Unlike the Hidden People, Nicci was not satisfied with just waiting. Since the sliph refused to answer, she needed to take supplies and head out on her own, though the journey would take many days or weeks. But it was her only option if she had any hope of intercepting General Utros and his army.

In front of the statue, a group of twenty men and women practiced with swords from the armory vault. Nicci watched them with a skeptical eye. They had sparred with one another for so long, using the same skills and moves, but they had never battled a real opponent. She realized that if Cyrus and his zealous followers actually joined Utros somehow, then they would become *her* enemy. They didn't understand their own legends.

Nicci spent the night searching the wide streets and plazas, the empty passageways and alleys. The sliph well remained silent. The bowl-shaped amphitheater was like a deep crater in the middle of the city, and Nicci stood on the outer rim, looking down. She imagined Kurgan down there skinning Majel alive and then planting flesh beetles in her wounds. No wonder the people had risen up and overthrown him, pulled down and smashed his towering statue.

Suddenly, she sensed another presence nearby, powerful and dangerous. She snatched one of the daggers from her waist as a tan shadow leaped over a collapsed marble column. The big cat bounded toward her, and Nicci gasped, opening her arms wide. The sand panther drove her backward with momentum and exuberance, then licked her face with a raspy tongue. Laughing, Nicci wrapped her arms around Mrra's neck. Pulling away, the cat paced around her, rubbing her fur against Nicci's black dress, nearly knocking her over again. An ominous purr rumbled through her chest.

"Mrra, you're back!" Nicci held the big predator tight. She had lost so much, been through such ordeals, that just having her sister panther gave her great reassurance. "Oh, Mrra! I can't imagine how far you've come." She pressed her cheek against the soft fur.

When she saw more movement at the edge of the plaza, she realized that other cats had entered the city, a dozen or more. Their glowing eyes gleamed in the shadows of the ruins, but they did not venture closer, even though Mrra had convinced them to join her pride.

"The people in this city are my friends, Mrra," Nicci explained. "Allies. Your sand panthers must not harm them. They are not prey." She concentrated hard, hoping that Mrra could communicate the warning to the other panthers.

Across the city Nicci heard the Hidden People raising their voices, and she saw a faint glow outlining the eastern mountains. Daybreak. Recalling what had happened to the two hapless deer, she felt sudden alarm. "Mrra, we have to get inside. You can shelter in the palace with me and my friends." She tugged on the panther's neck. "You need to tell the others to hide, though." She summoned an image in her mind of the deadly zhiss swarm that would appear with the sunrise. Under normal circumstances, sand panthers would bed down in a dark protected area during the day, but she felt a great sense of urgency. "Tell them, Mrra! This is important."

When her sister panther roared, the other cats twitched their tails, flashed a last feline glance at Nicci, and bounded off into the ruins in search of a shadowy lair. Nicci hurried with Mrra back to the palace entrance. Cora and the Hidden People looked at the predator with alarm, drawing back as Nicci led Mrra inside. "She is mine. She won't hurt you."

The drab people withdrew as she took Mrra inside the sheltered corridors before the sun spilled over the mountains. Throughout the ruined city, barricades slammed into place, entryways sealed to hide from the sun. In a rush, the Hidden People pulled shut the palace doors.

In a last glimpse, Nicci saw the swirling black cloud flowing into Orogang like a million wasps.

Mrra growled, and Nicci held her sister panther as the Hidden People barred the door.

* * *

The wild cat did not like being trapped inside the stone walls. Mrra was haunted by horrific memories of being tortured and trained by Chief Handler Ivan. Through her spell bond, Nicci saw memory flashes of the young cub clawing and biting the iron bars of her cage. Back then, the only freedom Mrra and her sister panthers had experienced was when they were turned loose onto the bloody arena sands. Now, she longed to be outside.

But Nicci knew what the zhiss would do to any living creature they encountered. She stroked the panther's tan fur, running her fingertips along the branded rune scars. "I need to keep you safe. Trust me."

Today, the Hidden People seemed tense and fearful, but it had nothing to do with the big panther locked inside with them. They were preparing to do something Nicci had not seen before. A group of the muttering people moved to the barricaded entrance. Young Asha caught Nicci's eye and hurried in among the nervous gray-robed men and women.

Intrigued, Nicci followed them to the closed main door, where one middle-aged man stood alone, facing the rest of them. He had a worn expression and sad brown eyes. He braced himself and ate a mouthful of the fleshy, poisonous mushrooms as if for extra energy.

The Hidden People looked at him with reverence. Several touched him on the arm. "Thank you, Cal."

"We appreciate you, Cal," said another.

A drab woman kissed him on the cheek. "Oh, Cal . . ." She couldn't form any other words.

Nicci didn't understand what was happening. Cal swallowed the poison fungus and turned to the barricade, as if in a trance. Two men lifted the crossbar as he stood at the door, trembling.

Nicci realized they were going to let this man out into the sun. Mrra's tail thrashed, and a low growl filled her throat, but Nicci rested a hand on the furred shoulders to calm her. "What is he doing?" Nicci asked Cora. "You're letting him out? What about the zhiss?"

The old woman turned to her, and Nicci saw tears filling the wrinkle tracks in her cheeks. "We've had to do this every month. It is the only way we keep the zhiss under control."

The men pulled hard on the heavy doors and opened them to let an axe blade of sunlight spill into the gloom. Cal turned to the gathered people. "Farewell. I—" His voice cracked. He dashed into the bright morning, pulling the hood over his head like a man darting into a downpour. The Hidden People pressed closer to watch.

Once away from the great building, Cal paused out in the open sunshine, filled with wonder. Turning slowly, he pulled down his hood and lifted his face to the sky. He squinted in the blinding sun, but reveled in the warm light.

"What is that man doing? Why is he sacrificing himself?" Nicci fought back the urge to push past these people and rush out to rescue him. "What will he accomplish? The zhiss will feed on him."

Cora narrowed her eyes. "We are counting on it."

The man walked placidly to the middle of the plaza near the toppled statue of Kurgan, where he stripped off his gray robe and tossed the garment away. His pale skin was milky, translucent, his face filled with rapture. He spread his arms, felt the sunlight, touched his bare chest. "This is my payment! Oh, what glory the sun is!"

Inside, the muttering people fell into a hush as Nicci heard a buzzing sound that grated her teeth, her spine. Mrra's growl grew louder, and her ears flattened.

Flowing among the high buildings like a shapeless predator, the black swarm approached, thousands of black specks. Cal kept his eyes closed, refusing to look at the deadly cloud as he drank in the sun. The swarm swirled and knotted, then rolled forward, picking up speed.

"They'll drain him dry," Nicci said. "You said that if the zhiss feed on human blood, their numbers will increase dramatically."

"Not with our blood." Cora gestured outside. "Watch."

Obviously agitated, the black cloud was ravenous as it closed in on its victim. Cal faced it and knotted his hands into fists. He howled in defiance as the zhiss swarmed over him, covering his body like a thousand biting black flies, coalescing as they had done around the two unfortunate deer. Within moments, the man was just a vaguely human shape cloaked in black.

Flailing about, Cal dropped to his knees and then collapsed face-first onto the flagstones. More zhiss pounced in to drink deep of the blood. The buzzing grew louder, like a brewing thunderstorm.

Once they had gorged themselves, the individual specks rose up from the body like fat raindrops. The dark red globules wavered, a cloud heavy with Cal's blood. But instead of drifting off, as they had done after draining the deer, they became discolored. The crimson from Cal's blood turned a sick brownish purple. Hundreds, thousands of the floating zhiss swelled, wobbled like drifting pustules, and burst in the air, splattering dark stains across the plaza. Every one of the zhiss that had fed upon Cal suffered, swelled up, and died.

"Because we spend our lives eating the poison fungus, our flesh and blood is deadly to them," Cora explained. "Individually, the zhiss have no minds, only instinct. This is how we keep the swarm in check. Cal just destroyed a good part of them. We choose a new sacrifice every month to curtail the growth of the cloud." The old woman continued to stare longingly into the sunshine. "The zhiss learn their lesson for a time, and then they forget."

Nicci watched the flickering black cloud disperse, the surviving zhiss aimlessly flying away from the desiccated body.

"All of our generations have been a sacrifice," Cora continued. "Someday, I will draw the marked token, and I'll go out to surrender my life just as Cal did. We only hope there will be enough of us in Orogang to keep the zhiss from prowling elsewhere."

When part of the black cloud wandered toward the palace, the Hidden People swung shut the door and lowered the crossbar into place.

Asha came up, her eyes sparkling. "It is our sworn duty, even if no one else knows what we do."

"*I* know what you do," Nicci said. "But you don't know how to destroy them. If you're all committed to destroying them, why don't you send fifty people out there in a single sacrifice? If you each destroy as many of the zhiss as Cal did, then surely that would eradicate the whole swarm."

"We've tried that, many times," the old woman said, shaking her head. "Some of the zhiss are fooled, but the others flit away. Many of us died, and still the black cloud returns."

Asha pulled on Nicci's arm, pleading. Her pale cheeks were streaked with drying tracks of tears. "You are a great sorceress, Nicci. Can you help us? Can you find a way to destroy the zhiss?" She hung her head. "Or will you just leave us?"

After growing impatient with these sullen, passive people, Nicci had almost made up her mind to set off on foot. She could not ignore the threat that General Utros posed, but now she also had a different perspective on the danger posed by the zhiss. If the deadly black cloud ever left this ruined city and swarmed overland to engulf other human settlements, doubling in size each time, the entire world could be covered in a black, blood-drinking shroud.

Nicci recalled what the witch woman Red had written in Nathan's life book, long ago: *And the Sorceress must save the world.* She had accepted that mission for her own reasons. After Richard showed her a different way to live, a different role to play, her heart of black ice had melted enough to allow love and duty.

And the Sorceress must save the world.

Nicci saw the tentative hope on their faces. "I will find a way." She let no doubt creep into her voice or into her heart. When Nicci made up her mind to do the impossible, she usually succeeded. "I will find a way."

CHAPTER 23

With an escort of a thousand mounted soldiers, General Utros headed north in search of his lost capital. At the front of the expedition, he rode an imposing black stallion fitted with a black saddle of embossed leather with polished brass studs.

Utros maintained a brisk pace, searching for old imperial roads, which had weathered away over time. They had crossed this terrain fifteen centuries before, but the details of the landscape were fresh in his mind.

"It seems like only months ago, beloved Utros." Ava rode a bay mare beside him. The painted, hairless sorceress sat high in her saddle, her fingers woven into the horse's mane. Her loose blue gown rippled in the breezes.

Ruva rode an identical bay mare on his other side. "But now the roads are overgrown, and forests cover the lands that we once dominated."

"We will conquer them again." Utros ran a finger under the gold mask to wipe away sweat. He nudged the stallion with his heels. "And this time, I will do it for myself, not for Iron Fang."

Fifteen centuries ago, with the entire army behind

him, he had led a slow march across the continent, sub-jugating town after town. Some foolish leaders re-sisted, and they all died. More importantly, the vanquished rulers served as a lesson. Utros made sure they were executed in the most hideous and painful ways, slowly eviscerating the upstarts, burning them alive over low fires until they were smoked like veni-son sausages hung for the winter. The tales of the atroc-ities spread swiftly, which extinguished defiance among those who might consider resisting.

It was a careful strategic calculation. Unlike Iron Fang, Utros was not a sadistic man, and he did not en-joy causing such pain, but he realized the military ne-cessity of it. After he committed just a few horrific atrocities, the other leaders could not surrender fast enough, and thus he saved lives. When his army rolled onward and his legend grew, he easily vanquished the next city and the next with little bloodshed. Even large walled citadels threw open their gates when his army marched near.

Until he reached the most difficult target: Ildakar.

Now the hot sun shone down on the soldiers as they rode back to their lost capital. Many of these men were conscripts recruited from conquered towns, and they had never seen Orogang, while others were hardened members from the imperial army, originally trained in the great capital city. They had families, sisters, wives, and mistresses back home—all long dead now, just as the soldiers themselves should have died in the natural order of things. Those men remembered Orogang, and Utros could sense their excitement as they rode toward the familiar gray mountains, knowing they were getting closer, mile after mile.

He thought of Kurgan's enormous palace, with its towers and banners, its crystal windows, its plazas and statues, and the sunken amphitheater from which the emperor would address throngs of his citizens. Great bronze bells would ring fanfares to celebrate Kurgan's every announcement. Conquered cities and kingdoms would send tributes, and such new wealth would pay for all of his extravagance.

The twin sorceresses couldn't wait to see the city with their own eyes. "My sister and I only knew our small village," Ruva said.

"Is Orogang grander than Ildakar?" Ava asked.

"Orogang is Orogang, the capital of my empire." Utros straightened. "Of course it is grander."

Fixing his gaze on the line of mountains still many days' ride away, Utros said, "I have often imagined what would happen when I returned to Orogang with the report of my triumphs. I was sure Emperor Kurgan would praise me for the victory." His heart felt heavy, and he couldn't speak the words. Regretful thoughts surrounded him. "I did it for him. Loyalty is greater than love."

"You also did it for Majel," Ava added. "Do not fool yourself, beloved Utros. We know you, and we know your heart."

Utros stared ahead as his black stallion toiled onward. "Yes, for her," he whispered. "Keeper and spirits . . ."

Though he knew their passion was forbidden, even on the bloodiest battlefield he thought of *her,* the soft skin, her long black tresses, her brown almond-shaped eyes. Iron Fang had been his emperor, but Majel had been his love.

He lifted his chin and spoke with a raw edge. "I also did it for him. I swore my loyalty, and I served my emperor."

Honor had been his armor, a shield that protected him from indecision, but his honor had also blinded him to Iron Fang's incompetence and petulant evil. No wonder the man's own wife had sought solace in the arms of another man. Majel had truly loved him, but centuries in the underworld had changed her. Through the blood lens his sorceresses had created, he had seen Majel stripped of her skin, her face peeled off to expose her teeth and staring bloodshot eyes. Speaking to him through the veil, Majel's spirit had spurned Utros and reaffirmed her devotion for the very man who had done those horrors to her. Utros knew that his dear Majel was not just dead, but dead to *him*.

Now he couldn't shake away the thoughts. After the last battle at Ildakar, when his army had suffered such devastating losses, the sour spirit of Emperor Kurgan had taunted him from the underworld, and Utros had smashed the blood lens, forever breaking contact with Iron Fang and with Majel. Now he was on his own, and his determination had not faded, merely shifted. He still intended to conquer the land, but it would no longer be for Emperor Kurgan.

"I don't know what we will find in Orogang," Utros said as they rode into the hills. "I'm a soldier of the empire, whatever remains of it. Iron Fang was a terrible leader, but if the current emperor is worthy, then I will swear my loyalty to him. If he is not worthy . . ." Utros looked at the two women, who gazed at him with yearning expressions. "If he is not, then I will claim the throne for myself, as I should have done all those years ago."

* * *

That night, when the army camped in a sparse birch forest, Utros tried to sleep in his command tent. As he closed his eyes, he pondered Orogang. The capital city had surely grown over the centuries, but he would recognize the towers, the looming buildings. Would anyone even remember General Utros from so many centuries past? The wizard Nathan had said that his name was legend, but what else had transpired in the empire after all that time?

Ava and Ruva remained outside by the fire, adding powders to the smoke, shaping and sending wisps among the sleeping soldiers to reinforce the preservation spell. Foraging hunters had killed deer, goats, rabbits, and squirrels, anything to feed the ravenous troops. Some of the more intensely desperate soldiers stripped leaves from trees, ate the fleshy stalks of plants, even tall grasses. Once this escort army reached Orogang, they could feast and resupply. That was what Utros held on to.

Orogang . . . In his mind the capital was breathtakingly beautiful, home to the lavish palace, the throne, banquet halls, meeting chambers, and high balconies from which Iron Fang had commanded his subjects. He also remembered the hidden rooms where he and sweet Majel had spent hours reveling in each other, touching, kissing, without fear of discovery. . . .

Now, as Utros lay on his sleeping pallet, he touched the hard scar that was the left side of his face. His gold mask rested on a nearby wooden table. His hideous face made him think of the mangled horror Majel had become, but in his memories, she was as beautiful as ever, and he was just as handsome.

He slept, but woke in the dead of night after the moon had set and the camp quieted. Outside his tent, he heard only the low rustle of sleeping soldiers and stirring horses. When he opened his eyes, he was startled to find a woman standing before him. He could see her silhouette in the dim light of low campfires that penetrated the fabric of the tent. Long dark hair fell down over her shoulders. He recognized her shapely figure, the curve of her hips, the narrow waist.

He sat up instantly. "Majel?"

She placed a finger to her lips and came closer. She raised her hands to her chest and undid the laces on the front of her filmy gown. She shrugged it off, letting the garment pool around her feet. Her naked breasts were full and rounded with caramel-colored nipples. Somehow the light grew brighter so that he could see her skin, the familiar mole just under the curve of her left breast, the implanted ruby in her navel.

"Majel?" He kept his voice to an awed whisper.

"Beloved Utros." She leaned over him, kissing the smooth skin of his brow just above his scarred face.

He could smell her warm breath. "It can't be you."

"I am here if you want me to be," she said. "You should have been dead centuries ago, like me, but the rules have changed. Accept that." She pressed her hands against his shoulders, forced him to lie back on the pallet. She caressed his chest, stroked the fine hair.

"I saw you in the blood lens," he said. "Your face."

"My face is beautiful, as is yours." She kissed him on the lips, silencing further questions. Majel climbed on top of him, and he wrapped his large hands around her waist, feeling the real solidity of this beautiful woman. A flood of memories came back, all the times they had made love, but this time he experienced only joy and relief, rather than fear of being caught. Majel was some-how back from the underworld, and she was here with him.

He twisted his fingers through her hair so he could pull her face closer to his, and he kissed her again sav-agely. Majel purred into his ear, then reached down to stroke his thigh. She nudged his legs so she could settle herself on top of him. He groaned as he slid inside, and her smile was filled with delicious rapture. For a mo-ment, just a moment, Utros let himself revel in the dream, sure that it was real but unable to understand.

"This is what you need, beloved Utros," Majel said as she began rocking back and forth. He ran his hands along her back, coaxing her.

Beloved Utros . . .

Majel had never called him that. Her pet name for Utros had been "my commander." When they engaged in rough play, she would instruct him to command her. Her actions now struck him as different, her movements not the familiar interchange of bodies they had devel-oped after pleasuring each other so many times.

Beloved Utros.

He grabbed her shoulders and looked intensely at her. "You are not Majel."

"I can be," she said.

He pushed her aside. "You're not Majel!"

The woman slid off of him and retreated. When she raised her hands, her body shifted to become a form that was still slender and shapely, but pale and covered with splashes of color. The long hair vanished.

Ava stood naked before him, tracing one of the painted spell patterns along her flat stomach. "I knew what you wanted, beloved Utros. Through me or my sister, you can have Majel again any time you like."

"I can never have her again! I do not want an imitation. My Majel was murdered by her own husband. Her spirit is locked in the underworld, and she renounced her love for me to stand by him."

"I was just trying to give you love, love that you seem to need." She reached out to console him, but he pushed her hand away.

"I do not need love," Utros vowed. "I need to conquer, and I intend to do so." He felt deep anger and disappointment, but he knew what Ava had done and why. He couldn't hate her for it. "I need you and Ruva. You both are indispensable to me, but I don't need . . . this." He gestured to her beautiful body.

"As you wish." Ava retreated to the tent opening and stood there in the faint light, naked and achingly beautiful. "Just remember that my sister and I will give you whatever you need."

CHAPTER 24

As the main body of the ancient army pushed into the rising mountains, Nathan and the group of defenders made their plans for the field of deathrise flowers. General Zimmer's scouts rode out to reconnoiter the enemy force, reporting on their progress climbing toward the meadow. Thorn and Lyesse indulged themselves by killing stragglers from the giant army, which also provoked the vanguard to surge after them.

While waiting to spring their trap, Nathan scouted the sea of poisonous blossoms and the trees beyond. The flowers were beautiful, their colors as intense as the silence, which was like death. On the other side of the meadow, an expansive forest stretched into steeper terrain.

He remembered when naive Bannon had come upon the deceptively pretty flowers and offered a meager bouquet to Nicci, hoping to earn her favor. Recognizing the poison, Nicci had calmly lectured the young man on the lethal leaves, stems, and blossoms, how even a drop of sap or a crushed blossom would kill him. Terrified, Bannon had dropped the flowers, relieved that he hadn't accidentally touched any of the juice. He had picked only a few of them, and this meadow contained thousands.

"This will kill a lot of the enemy," he said to Prelate Verna, "if we can trick them into running across the meadow."

"I understand it's a horrible death," she said.

"The most horrible imaginable," Nathan mused, stroking his chin. "And I can imagine many horrible deaths."

"It's what they deserve," Renn growled. Sadness still hung heavy in his eyes. "I want to march them all through this meadow so that they die screaming. I hope General Utros is with them, along with his sorceresses. They killed Lani."

Zimmer stepped up to them, frowning. "General Utros and both sorceresses have gone elsewhere. According to my scouts, First Commander Enoch is in charge of the army right now." He flashed a dark grin. "We know this because our two morazeth friends enjoy asking harsh questions of any scouts they capture."

Nathan and Verna stood at the edge of the deathrise field. "The army will stream through this hanging valley. We can provoke the vanguard, try to get them to chase us, and lead them right through this meadow. They'll be exposed to the poison, cover themselves in the deadly juices."

"As will we," said the freed slave Rendell with a deeply worried look on his seamed face. "How will we avoid dying?" Though ungifted, the old man had done everything he could to assist them in their flight. Rendell was remarkably skilled in finding edible roots and berries, even shelf mushrooms that grew on trees. Each night he managed to make a palatable meal with whatever he had scavenged.

Oron joined them. "If we can get through to the forest on the other side, a deep swift stream runs out of the mountains. We could wash off the poison—if we can get there in time."

"The poison would penetrate," Nathan said. "We wouldn't last that long."

"Then we will have to wear protection on our exposed skin," said Olgya. "With wrappings of the special silk I brought with me from Ildakar, we can cover our hands, faces, and any exposed part of our legs or arms. It is wispy thin and impenetrable."

Perri looked doubtful, her face creased with a worried expression that marred her otherwise pretty features. "Why not just go around the field without risking ourselves? We know the army is coming this way, and they are sure to stumble across the meadow. Some of them will die anyway as they cross it."

"They might even eat the flowers," said the wizard Leo. "The scouts say that the army is stripping the grasses and leaves as they march, as if they were yaxen." He rubbed his flat stomach beneath his robe. "How I miss fresh yaxen meat. When I worked the slaughterhouses, I could have a fine bloody steak whenever I liked."

The soldiers nearby mumbled wistfully with their own hunger.

Verna shook her head. "Those ancient soldiers may be familiar with deathrise flowers. We can't give them a chance to think. If they're chasing us, they'll fall into the trap."

"They want us," Nathan said. "We have given them more than enough reason to want revenge for all we have done. We need to let them see us and then run, leading them directly through the flowers. We are protected, and they are not. I believe the rest will take care of itself." Riled up by the constant hit-and-run tactics, he was certain that once the ancient army spotted their harassers, they would charge recklessly ahead into the field of poisonous flowers.

As the great army marched ever closer, the two morazeth would taunt the soldiers into pursuing them at full speed, but with so much exposed skin, Thorn and Lyesse could not be allowed near the meadow. Rather, they would vanish into the surrounding forest as soon as the enemy warriors spotted Nathan and his handful of gifted defenders waiting at the meadow. Zimmer's soldiers could not help with the trap; they retreated around the meadow and into the forest beyond, where they would wait for the group at the fast stream, and they would help dispatch any of the enemy who happened to make it through.

In preparation, Nathan put on his high boots, ruffled shirt, and black pants, with his ornate sword strapped to his side. Over those garments, he donned his wizard's robe, which protected more of his skin. After that, he wrapped Olgya's silks around both hands up to his elbows and made a scarf for his neck and face, leaving only a slit for his nose and eyes. He bound his long hair in a ponytail. Verna, Renn, Oron, Olgya, and six of the gifted scholars wrapped themselves in the same fashion, using all of her remaining silk fabric.

With the vanguard of the ancient army fast approaching, Thorn and Lyesse trotted off, eager to provoke the enemy. Everyone was ready. Nathan regarded the silk-covered defenders. "We look like corpses wound in linen strips and ready to be interred in catacombs."

"We will be nightmares to them, by the Keeper's

beard," Renn said. He plucked at his silks, adjusting them over his tattered and stained maroon robe.

That afternoon, after hours of unbearable waiting, the shouts finally came, the clash of swords, the rhythmic pounding of marching feet. Running hard, Thorn and Lyesse burst out of the trees to the edge of the meadow. Both women had joy on their faces as they bounded along like fleet deer. When they saw Nathan and his silk-wrapped companions standing ready in front of the deathrise field, the morazeth flashed glances at each other. "We will compare scores later," Thorn said to her partner. They bounded off to safety, racing around the edge of the meadow and into the trees.

Nathan said, "It's our turn now."

He called upon his gift and summoned a great wind that thrashed the branches. Beside him, Verna sent dazzling flashes of light into the trees to blind the first line of warriors just as they surged into the clearing. Oron, Leo, Perri, and Olgya joined forces to call a storm, drawing bullwhip lightning bolts that killed the first twenty soldiers who thought they were chasing only two women.

Oron said, "They have to believe we're cornered and making a last stand."

"A cornered animal is the most dangerous," Renn said.

As hundreds more of the yelling enemy rushed out of the trees, Nathan created a ball of wizard's fire and splashed it sideways. More of the enemy fell dead, screaming in agony from the incinerating flames.

Nevertheless, the front ranks of the marching army raced ahead like wolves smelling blood. When they saw the vulnerable defenders standing in front of the field of flowers, they howled with excitement.

Beneath the silk wrappings, Nathan smiled and spoke quietly through gritted teeth. "Come and get us."

For days the ragtag band had preyed upon the army, murdering stragglers, wiping out scouting parties. Even if the death toll was insignificant against the enormous numbers, fear and anger had worked itself into the minds of Utros's soldiers. At last facing their tormentors, the front ranks rushed forward, suspecting nothing.

Renn's voice was muffled through the silk as he summoned a blazing ball in his hand. "Wizard's fire seems too clean and swift for them, but I'll see them dead any way I can." He splayed his fingers as he threw the crackling ball, which shattered into separate pieces, each fragment striking the face of a helmeted warrior, exploding their skulls. Renn laughed wildly. His grief over Lani had become a vindictive weapon.

The Cliffwall scholars summoned spells that made the ground tremble or hurled hard winds into the faces of the charging soldiers. The first ranks fell dead, but the second and third lines simply trampled over the fallen corpses as they closed in on the silk-wrapped defenders.

Nathan saw they would swiftly be overwhelmed. "Run! It's time." He adjusted the coverings on his hands, then turned about to charge into the sea of poisonous flowers.

The ancient soldiers flooded out of the forest, and the line of rebels retreated across the meadow, the beautiful blossoms all around them. The moment seemed surreal as Nathan ran for his life, his boots trampling the leaves, the stems, the colorful petals. Verna crashed beside him, her skirts flowing behind her. Leo, Perri,

Oron, and Olgya threw a last wave of storm winds and lightning, just one more provocation, and then they also bounded through the colorful field, giddy and terrified.

A defiant Renn was the last, killing them with whatever spells he could summon, and then he fled just before the enemy soldiers caught up with him.

The meadow seemed to go on forever, and the flowers were an endless wave of fresh color and lingering death. Verna stumbled and nearly fell face-first into the blossoms, but Nathan snatched her collar and held her up, giving her a moment to regain her feet. The enemy soldiers roared in pursuit, convinced they had their victims in full retreat. The first wave charged at a full run, swinging their swords as they closed in on their prey. Oddly, some of the ravenous soldiers paused to scoop up the poisonous flowers and devour them like starving animals.

Nathan put on a burst of speed toward the sheltering forest. He could hear the crushing foliage, saw the people trampling countless flowers. His boots, the hem of his wizard's robe, even the silks covering his hands must be tainted with poison. He would have to scrub every bit of it off in the fast stream, if he made it that far.

He and Verna finally reached the other side of the meadow. They rushed into the trees, scrambled over rocks, and topped a rise before they worked their way down into a drainage, where a rushing stream tumbled over mossy rocks. Before he scrambled down the steep slope, Nathan glanced back to see the enemy soldiers pouring across the meadow after them. The first ones were starting to stagger and drop among the deadly blossoms. Many did not make it halfway through the meadow, while others kept on, slowing, lurching, until they collapsed into the deceptively colorful vegetation.

As countless men died inexplicably, the rest of the army hesitated, piling up in a wary crowd at the outer edge of the meadow. A few made it all the way across the field of flowers and reeled into the rocky forest, where they dropped among the trees, writhing and vomiting, clawing at their eyes.

Nathan felt a grim pleasure as he watched them die. "Those flowers will make a fine bouquet for your funeral."

Verna's shout startled him out of his reverie. "Nathan, don't just stare! We have to get to the stream and wash!"

Without wasting breath on further words, they ran down the steep slope to the fast-flowing water, where General Zimmer and his soldiers waited beside all the horses, weapons drawn and ready to fight any enemy who made it through. Nathan and his companions careened down the slope, slipping and stumbling on dry leaves and pine needles until they plunged into the rushing, cold stream. The current was frigid with snowmelt, but Nathan dove into the water, peeling the silks from his hands before the poison could soak through the special silk. He unwound the fabric from his face, then dunked his head into the stream and let his long white hair flow loose. Next, he stripped off his white robe and let it drift down the stream. He would never wear the contaminated garment again.

Verna, Oron, and Olgya scrubbed their hands in the silty stream bottom, washed their faces, wrung out their clothes. Gasping, spraying water from his mouth, Nathan looked up to see Renn stumble to the stream's edge. The other wizard moved slowly, his face aghast.

"Into the water, Renn!" Nathan called. "Wash yourself! Get the poison off."

But Renn stared at his left hand, where the silken wrappings had slipped off while he charged through the flowers, and now the fabric hung loose on his wrist. He looked at his palm, his fingers, the back of his hand, where the skin was already covered with gray blisters. His wrists were swollen and red, his knuckles puffy.

"Oh no," Renn said.

The sad defenders carried Renn's body with them, not willing to give the fallen wizard an unmarked grave in an empty forest. They moved swiftly away from the deathrise field, griefstruck.

Behind them, hundreds, maybe even thousands, of the enemy soldiers had fallen dead from the horrible poison in the meadow. The ancient army ground to a halt in shock as First Commander Enoch sent cautious scouts to find a safe route that avoided the meadow. Eventually, the great force pushed on toward the rocky peaks that led to the pass of Kol Adair.

When Nathan and his companions had gone a safe distance from the enemy army, they found a sheltered hollow in the high forest, where they took the time to build a funeral pyre for Renn.

Thorn and Lyesse patrolled, watching out for surprise attacks, while the rest of the group paid their respects to the fallen wizard. Captain Trevor and his Ildakaran guards were especially shaken, having escorted Renn to Cliffwall and back. Together, they watched the blaze burn, purifying his mortal remains.

Nathan touched the scar on his chest and felt a twinge of Ivan's anger, but he drove it back and concentrated only on his respect for Renn.

CHAPTER 25

The three serpent ships cruised down the Kill-raven River past sluggish side channels and wide marshes. When a heavy breeze stretched the blue sails, the Norukai shipped the oars and let their captives sprawl on deck, tied in place.

After being confined for so long in the hot and stinking hold, Bannon relished the small joy of open air. His skin was caked with sweat, dried fish slime, and blood. His pale skin burned easily under the sun, and his body was mottled with bruises.

King Grieve strode along the deck to remind the slaves of his intimidating presence. Bannon hated everything about the man—the chain around his waist, the iron plates on his knuckles, the implanted spines in his shoulders, the awful gash that sliced his mouth to the back of his head.

Chalk followed the king like a loyal dog, jabbering, grinning. "My Grieve, King Grieve, you'll all grieve!" The king seemed comforted by the shaman's presence, as if he were a pet.

The big captive Erik sat beside Bannon, his knees drawn up to his broad shoulders, his head hung. Though Bannon had tried to keep him strong, the large man remained in a daze of grief, walling himself off, as if to commune with the spirits of his slaughtered family. Bannon tried talking with the sullen captive, but rarely earned a response.

Several Norukai ran excitedly to the stern of the ship, looking down into the muddy river. "Get us hooks," one man cried. "Spears with ropes!"

Trying to see what they were doing, Bannon tugged against his bindings, but each movement made him wince. More Norukai rushed to the rail with boat hooks, harpoons, weighted nets. Leaning over the side, they took turns hurling weapons into the water, as if it were some kind of sports contest.

Drawn to the frenetic activity, Chalk pressed among the larger warriors, elbowing through so he could peer down. "Ah, fish! Big fish, monster fish! Fish monsters."

"Get a hook in their gills," Gara called down.

Another Norukai groaned, "That one's dead now, but we're drifting too fast down the channel. The damned thing is slipping away!"

"Drop anchor," King Grieve shouted. "It's worth the stop. That'll be enough food to get us back home."

Chains rattled through slots as heavy anchor stones dropped into the river, sinking to the mud. Two other raiders climbed the mast and rolled up the sails, tying them to the yardarm. The other two serpent ships dropped anchor as well.

"Channel catfish," said oar master Bosko as he let out a loud burst of smelly gas. "We'll have a feast, by the serpent god!"

They jabbed hooks and spears into the water, then hauled on the ropes. It took three straining Norukai to pull up the first flopping body.

Though Bannon had lived on Chiriya Island, where

fishermen brought back their daily catches, he had never seen such a huge fish before. Groaning and laughing, the Norukai heaved the beast over the rail and dropped it onto the deck with a loud thud. The catfish's body was as long as a canoe, its crescent-moon mouth gaping, the wide-set eyes small, dark, and stupid. Long whiskers were like barbed tentacles. Watery brown blood oozed from the wounds made by barbed hooks and serrated harpoons.

Chalk could barely contain his excitement as he squatted in front of the creature. He touched the slime that covered the catfish's body and danced back, holding up his finger and licking it. The dying catfish twitched and thrashed, and the albino shaman skittered away from the sharp spines on its fins.

"Fish bite, fish nibble," he said, poking the countless small scars that covered his body. He grinned at Bannon as if the two were having a private conversation. "Stay away from the fish."

The Norukai threw more harpoons into the river and pulled up a second enormous fish. Before long, the mood on the ship brightened as the Norukai hauled a third monster fish onto the deck, and they fell upon the creatures with their knives, sawing through the scaly hides to pull out the entrails. The catfish oozed puddles of slime on the deck. One Norukai man received a deep cut from a thrashing spine, and he retaliated by using his battle hammer to batter the fish's head into pulp.

Bannon felt queasy with the stench of the slime and blood, but Grieve regarded the mess with pride. He raised his heavy war axe and with a single stoke cut halfway through the catfish's neck. The whiplike whiskers continued to twitch.

Grieve hacked twice more until the head rolled loose,

and Chalk clucked his tongue in disappointment. "The axe cleaves the wood, the sword cleaves the bone! And King Grieve cuts the fish, monster fish. Fish monsters."

"Did you predict we would have a feast, Chalk?" Grieve asked.

The albino dropped to his knees and thrust his hands into the open cavity from which the guts had already been removed. "I predict . . . dinner!"

The Norukai made swift work, peeling off the tough skin, cutting up the pinkish meat. They were happy to eat the fish raw, and Grieve took a hunk for himself, chewing with his wide-hinged jaws. Before long, the three enormous carcasses were stripped down to the bones, and men heaved the skeletons overboard into the river.

Once he had stuffed himself, Grieve became magnanimous. "Let the slaves feast, too, so they have more energy to work."

The Norukai threw piles of the slick red intestines and frilled gill membranes onto the tied captives. The stinking slime crawled down Bannon's chest, but his stomach growled. The raiders hadn't fed him all day.

A flare of anger ran through him. In the past, he sometimes lost control and flew into a fighting frenzy, a reckless wild man with no thought for his own safety. He controlled himself now, knowing that foolish resistance would only get him killed. He would rather kill them.

He strained at the ropes around his wrists and grabbed a fleshy blob of organ meat. He chewed, tasting the muddy burst in his mouth, but he grimaced and swallowed.

Chalk squatted next to Bannon, munching handfuls

of raw meat. "Revenge on the fish! Fish tried to eat me, and now I eat the fish."

Bannon again noted the pockmarks on his skin. "What really happened to you? Why do you have all those scars?"

"Fish nibbled me," Chalk said. "Wish the fish! Wish the fish! King Stern didn't like me. He threw me in a pool of razorfish, and they almost ate me, but Grieve pulled me out. He saved me, took me to a healer. My Grieve, King Grieve, you'll all grieve!"

Bannon tried to piece together the shaman's ordeal from his patchwork words. Chalk had been sacrificed to a pool of carnivorous fish—because he was an albino? because he was odd?—and the fish had torn his skin to shreds before he was rescued? No wonder he was so loyal to Grieve.

The thought of what had happened twisted Bannon's stomach, even eliciting an odd sympathy for the scarred and mentally disturbed man. Considering all the Norukai had done to him, Bannon chastised himself for feeling sorry for Chalk, but the pale man had an odd longing in his eyes.

The shaman glanced over his shoulder to the bow, where the king stood. "Nibble, nibble, nibble! Fish will nibble me still. Eat my flesh and bones when I die." Chalk jammed more raw flesh into his mouth. "Now I eat the fish. Which ones will eat me, I wonder. . . ."

Bannon ate as much of the catfish entrails as he could stand. Next to him, Erik sluggishly chewed a mouthful, but he looked sick. Trying to encourage his friend, he forced himself to set a good example and eat a little more. Erik didn't seem to notice.

Impatient, the king bellowed out, "Enough wasted

time. Set the sails and raise anchor. Soon, we'll reach the estuary and the open sea. We have a war to fight."

As the serpent ships got underway again, Grieve grimaced at the slime and blood pooled across the deck. "Have the slaves clean this up. They need to earn the feast we just gave them."

"Scrub!" The shipwright Gara handed Bannon a bucket and bristle brush. She raised a threatening fist. "Scrub to make you strong enough for fighting."

Bannon knew he would be strong enough to kill any Norukai who gave him the chance. As the serpent ships sailed on, he and the other slaves got to work.

CHAPTER 26

After watching the sacrifice of the man named Cal, Nicci now fully understood the explosive threat of the zhiss. She could not just abandon these people to seek another war, hoping they would manage to keep containing the bloodthirsty black cloud. She had to find a way to stop the destructive force before it broke loose and swarmed across the landscape. Nicci was not one to walk away and leave a problem unsolved.

And the Sorceress must save the world.

While sheltered inside during the day, Nicci called some of the Hidden People into Kurgan's cavernous throne room. Restless, Mrra brushed against Nicci's leg. Her black travel dress was swallowed up in the stark shadows of the torchlit chamber.

She announced to the group without preamble, "I will help you find a way to stop or destroy the zhiss." The big cat let out a growl, as if to agree with her sister panther's new mission.

The Hidden People sounded relieved and excited. Young Asha grinned. "I knew you would!"

With a satisfied expression, Cora nodded. "The legends said a hero would come back and save us."

"It should be General Utros," said Cyrus. "That was the prophecy."

"Would you prefer to wait for him?" Nicci snapped. "Or shall I try?"

Cyrus frowned. "You may try."

"I tend to succeed." Nicci did not boast of her past victories. She had killed Jagang, she had helped Richard defeat Emperor Sulachan and his hordes. She had destroyed the Lifedrinker as well as the violently uncontrolled Victoria. She had fought the twisted society of Ildakar, and she had clashed with General Utros. The zhiss swarm was an entirely different danger.

Nicci stepped onto the cold stone dais that had once held Iron Fang's imposing throne. "I am a sorceress, and I was once a Sister of the Dark. I can use both the Additive and Subtractive sides of my gift. I don't know what the zhiss are or where they came from, but I will find a way to stop them."

The shadowy people looked at her with hopeful expressions. They pulled back their gray hoods to reveal faces white from living in darkness, but their expressions now showed a spark of hope that she had not seen earlier. Mrra thrashed her tail, and a low rumble vibrated from her throat.

Cora came forward to help. "We can tell you everything we know about them. Maybe it will give you what you need to find a solution."

The Hidden People had studied the black swarm for generations, documenting their observations, their extrapolations, and several failed attempts to eradicate the zhiss. For more than five hundred years, they had poisoned their bodies with the toxic fungus, but they had tried little else, simply clinging to the status quo and keeping the threat at least marginally under control.

Cora brought her scrolls and bound journals, ledgers where witnesses had recorded their thoughts from generations earlier. Nicci pored over the words, dismissing anything that was not relevant. She had studied for many years in the Palace of the Prophets and also learned techniques that were forbidden.

While the pale old woman made suggestions and pointed out important summaries, Nicci tried to devise a tactic that might work. She skimmed another account and mulled over what she knew. "They only come out during the day. They thrive under the light and hide or go dormant in darkness." She looked at Cora. "Do you know where they go? How I can find their lair?"

The old woman shook her head. A gray-brown strand of hair dangled down the side of her wrinkled face.

Nicci tried another idea. "Can we attract them at night? Could we call them here, under our terms?"

Cora reacted with horror. "Why would you do that? It is our only time of safety."

An idea began to form in Nicci's mind. "Because in daylight they can go anywhere, but what if we found a way to attract them to a dark place and trap them there?" Her lips curved in a hard smile. "That might be what we need."

The old woman looked disturbed. "How would you hold them? What could possibly contain the zhiss?"

Nicci raised her hand to indicate the stone walls. "Your artisans bricked up the arches and windows, sealed these buildings, and the zhiss can't penetrate the walls. A properly constructed stone structure could hold them in just as easily as blocking them out. We could imprison them permanently, maybe starve them."

As she developed her plan, Nicci had to convince the Hidden People, for she would need their help. Since she was a gifted sorceress, the primary work of trapping and holding the zhiss would fall on her shoulders, but the Hidden People were a skilled workforce and she would need them all to pull together to craft a permanent prison. Or an execution chamber. It would be a swift and ambitious job, if she could contain the cloud long enough.

When Nicci explained her idea, Cora said, "Many of us may die."

"You sacrifice one of your number every month just to keep them contained. Your people have been dying here for centuries, to no good effect. My idea may put an end to the threat forever. Isn't that what you want?"

"It's a risk we have to take," the old woman admitted, "and I pray you succeed."

"So do I," Nicci said under her breath. "You have never seen someone like me."

Over the course of planning, Nicci scouted the city every night, deciding on the right place to set her trap. She and Mrra prowled outside as soon as twilight fell. She required a large space to confine the swarming cloud, and the round sunken amphitheater seemed perfect for her purposes.

During their days inside the sealed buildings, the Hidden People scoured the imperial halls and chambers to find old mirrors that could be polished to bright reflectiveness, smooth sheets of gold and brass that gleamed in the torchlight. After all the preparations were made, Nicci began building what she called her "cauldron trap."

As soon as the sun went down, the Hidden People bustled around the stage at the bottom of the crater amphitheater, installing the mirrors, the reflective metal sheets, and angled crystals, all of which sent out rainbow shards of torchlight. The work crews took advantage of every hour of darkness. They filled the center stage where Iron Fang had once shouted his speeches to a cowed populace. They piled a mound of dry wood, split logs, and thin branches, enough to make a blazing bonfire. All of the reflective surfaces would increase the brilliance a hundredfold.

Even so, Nicci suspected the blaze wouldn't be sufficient. With her gift, she would add much more to create a dazzling, irresistible beacon. It would be as bright as the sun, bright enough to call the zhiss.

When the preparations for the beacon were complete, Nicci ordered all of the master artisans, masons, and stonecutters to prepare for a furious, desperate night of work, stacking up all the supplies so they were ready at hand. Once Nicci did her part—if it worked—they would have only one chance and very little time.

By living inside the abandoned buildings every day, the Hidden People knew the architecture from the inside out. They understood how stones fit together, and they knew how to build arches and vaulted ceilings. They could cut stone with great precision, and they knew the mixtures for fast-drying, permanent mortar and plaster that would endure for ages.

After measuring the sunken amphitheater, their architects designed support struts and mapped out the blocks that would be needed. Though they rushed back inside each sunrise when the zhiss returned, the shadowy people worked with tremendous energy and increasing hope.

Each night Mrra ran free, reuniting with the other sand panthers that lurked in the mountains. The big cat made fresh kills and feasted with her new pride, but she always returned to spend the day in the shadows with Nicci. Mrra could sense her sister panther's restlessness, wanting to attack the formless black cloud, but Nicci couldn't allow her to be in danger.

When the preparations were at last complete, a tension built among the Hidden People. They watched the daylight wane through chinks in the barricaded windows. Nicci scratched the big cat behind the ears and led her into her own bedchamber, blocking her thoughts. She had a heavy heart, knowing that Mrra would see her actions as a betrayal.

"I have to keep you safe," Nicci whispered. "This is my fight. I need to make sure you stay here." Mrra growled and tried to push past her to escape the chamber, but Nicci blocked her way. "I will come back for you." She pulled the thick door shut, locking Mrra inside.

Angry at her confinement, the panther thumped against the door. Loud scratches came from the other side, along with a frustrated yowl. Nicci suspected that by the time she returned—if she returned—the door would be torn to splinters. She had to move quickly.

Nicci hurried through the corridors to where Hidden People had gathered. Cora waited with dozens of eager and nervous people at the towering palace doors, while other Hidden People lurked inside many secondary buildings. They were ready.

"We have to wait until the darkest hour of the night," Nicci said.

Cyrus adjusted his gray cowl, frowning. "We've waited long enough."

"And tonight, if we are successful, your waiting will end."

CHAPTER 27

At midnight, before the waning moon rose over the mountains, Nicci led the Hidden People out for their attack against the zhiss. Her beacon in the darkness would be an irresistible summons to the horrible black cloud.

She would eradicate the deadly swarm that had terrorized this city since the fall of Iron Fang's empire. Once freed, the Hidden People could rebuild the capital and turn Orogang into a trading hub again. They could name their own leader to become part of the D'Haran Empire. Once she knew the zhiss were no longer a threat, she would set off overland to find the army of General Utros.

But only if her plan worked against the zhiss.

Five of the gray people carried torches down the steps of the sunken amphitheater and ignited the piled wood on the central stage. The flames caught in the kindling and flared up, sending sparks that swirled like night wisps. The bonfire snapped as it consumed the dry branches then fed upon the split logs. The flames danced and reflected on the array of mirrors and polished metal surfaces placed in the concentric rings of seats around the sunken stage. Smoke writhed in the air and the fire stretched higher.

Nicci stood on the topmost tier, watching the blaze grow. She had wrapped her blond hair and her face with scarves and veils, which she hoped would keep the zhiss away from her bare skin. She wore gloves on her hands, fabric windings down her legs. After lighting the bonfire, the Hidden People tossed their torches and backed up the steep ramps to street level. At the bottom of the crater, the fire was definitely the brightest light in Orogang, but she would make it even brighter. Irresistible.

"Go," she called to Cora and the others. "When the swarm comes, I want you all safe." She hoped the cloth wrapping her body would be enough protection, would give her enough time.

"But we need to help you, Nicci," Asha said. "We can lure the zhiss into the pit. This is our battle, too."

"Leave that to me. The flames will be bright enough." Nicci looked at the determined young woman. "You have made enough sacrifices." She urged them to retreat, and the group backed away but did not lock themselves inside the buildings.

She descended to the bottom of the sunken amphitheater and approached the low stage, which held the blaze. In order to draw the zhiss out of their lair, Nicci needed to make the bonfire many times brighter, a beacon to rival the sun, and so she drew upon her gift. She could summon wizard's fire, one of the most dramatic and deadly spells, but she didn't need such destructive heat now, only the brilliant light. So she altered her spell, removed the energy of heat, and focused on creating wizard's *light* instead of wizard's *fire*.

The bonfire flared as if a sun had suddenly appeared

at the bottom of the amphitheater, a blinding silent explosion that made Nicci shield her blue eyes. From above, she heard a collective gasp, and the Hidden People backed farther away from the rim, unable to tolerate such an outpouring of artificial light. Shielding her eyes with her palm, Nicci managed to look at the blazing orb she had created. It engulfed the speaking stage and surged like a scream of brilliance enhanced a thousandfold by the mirrors, crystals, and polished precious metals. Even from their lair, the zhiss had to see it and be drawn across the night like moths to a flame.

Continuing to release her gift, she kept the beacon shining bright and listened for the deadly buzz, but heard no sounds except the crackle of the central fire. The wizard's light pulsed with a hypnotic thrum, and the city held its breath.

As more minutes passed with no sign of the throbbing cloud, Nicci waited, tense, feeling a shred of doubt. What if the zhiss really did go dormant at night? What if they retreated to sealed lairs, like bats hanging in caves, where they couldn't see her beacon? What could flush them out?

Using both the Additive and Subtractive sides of her gift, just as when she had tried to summon the sliph, she sent out her thoughts to draw the zhiss. *Light! Come feed on the light! Come feed on the blood!*

Finally, a different sort of hum penetrated the air, a thrumming that increased to a grating buzz. She looked up, away from the dazzling beacon, and saw a featureless black swirl blotting out the starlight. The zhiss swarm broke apart and spread over Orogang, called by the irresistible glare. She raised her cloth-wrapped arms to beckon them. She pulled the cloth away from her face so they could smell her blood.

The Hidden People fled back to their sheltered doorways, but the movement attracted the zhiss. One arm of the dark cloud extended toward the gray-cloaked people.

With her wizard's light still flaring, Nicci moved up the arena steps to street level, intent on distracting the swarm. The mindless, bloodthirsty flecks had already swooped down upon two lagging people, who collapsed, covered with feeding zhiss. Nicci couldn't reach them in time to save them, but their unwitting sacrifice would kill many of the swarming creatures. As the zhiss gorged themselves on the tainted blood, clouds of swollen globules lumbered away, sated with poisoned blood. As before, the fat spheres turned a sickly purple and burst to spatter across the flagstones.

The rest of the zhiss cloud, though, hurtled toward the bright light like a swarm of ten thousand bees. Nicci stood on the rim of the amphitheater. "Here! Over here." She waved her hands, hoping that her unpoisoned and *gifted* blood would be more desirable than the blood of other victims. "Over here, by the light!" She tore the scarves away from her face and head, shook her hair free. "Here! To me!"

The black cloud swirled like a pall of greasy smoke, while the nexus of light continued to crackle and shine at the bottom of the amphitheater. The zhiss were hungry, looking for prey, and she needed to lure them to the cauldron trap. The ravenous black swarm probed doorways and windows, trying to find cracks in the masterfully laid stones.

When the zhiss sensed her, Nicci felt her skin tingle. At last the smell of her untainted blood drew them, and the black cloud surged all around her, swooping in even faster than she had expected. As if she were engulfed in thick smoke, the zhiss blanketed her body. It was like a surprising hailstorm of black ice, shapeless nuggets that moved and pulsed and *bit,* each one no larger than the nail on her little finger. They tried to penetrate the fabric, and they found folds, created small rips, worked their way to her skin. Each small *thing* was covered with pointed needlelike legs that jabbed into her skin, one zhiss on top of another, blanketing her arms, her face, her neck, nesting in her hair, covering her eyelids.

Suffocating, Nicci used her gift to summon a pulse of wind that blasted them away, but it was like coughing out a breath against pollen in the air. The zhiss came back with a vengeance. She staggered to the steep steps, trying to draw them down into the sunken amphitheater, the tantalizing fire. After feeding, hundreds of them rose from her body, swollen globules filled with dark red fluid—her blood, gifted blood. She knew that once they had drained her, the swarm would reproduce explosively. She had to stop them!

Determination gave her strength, and she pushed harder with her magic. This was her blood, *her blood!* She called on a thread of Subtractive Magic to burst every one of the rising globules, destroying dozens at a time.

But her body was encrusted with the black things, and they kept drinking her blood. Using her deadly magic, Nicci tried to stop their hearts, but the zhiss had no hearts. They were just tiny ravenous membranes.

Weakened from sudden loss of blood, she dropped to her knees on the amphitheater steps and fought to hold on to her strength. If nothing else, she would crawl down into the crater to contain them, even if she trapped herself as well. She needed to retain enough of her gift to form the shield, or the zhiss would escape. And for that, she had to be alive!

Outside, a woman's voice was loud enough to penetrate the buzzing clamor. "Here, take me! Feed on me, and follow me to the light!"

It was Cora! The old woman ran from the palace archway, throwing aside her gray cloak to expose leathery wrinkled skin.

Seeing another victim, the zhiss did not need to be encouraged. Part of the swarm around Nicci shifted course, and countless thousands of the black specks rushed in to engulf Cora. The old woman kept running even as the black things covered her skin, plastered her face. She slowed, then staggered until she barely plodded forward, each step taking her closer to the sunken amphitheater. Countless zhiss drifted up after sucking her tainted blood and burst in the air, but thousands more swarmed around the old woman.

With her last energy, Cora reached the edge of the amphitheater and collapsed on the sloping ramp. Her body rolled down the tiers of seats as the zhiss closed in, dead before she slid to a stop at the third tier. Zhiss blanketed her motionless body, but now they were also drawn to the blazing beacon at the central stage.

Nicci pawed at her face to tear away the feeding creatures, felt the countless stinging bite marks on her skin, the loss of blood. Knowing this was her last chance, she called up a powerful wave of her gift. She heated her skin, hardened it, sent rippling bursts of force that scraped the bloodsucking specks away, and then with a heavy wind she herded the entire cloud toward the shining wizard's fire, the waves of reflected light from hundreds of polished surfaces. The glow was irresistible.

She withdrew her magic from the blazing beacon, which made the light retract, like a setting sun. In the dark and empty city, the zhiss were drawn toward the light, following it like moths spiraling into their doom around a single flame.

Though drained from expending her gift and weak from blood loss, Nicci rose to her feet again and climbed down to the bottom of the crater and the blazing stage. The zhiss cloud closed in, nearly eclipsing the shrinking globe of wizard's light. When the complete swarm was within the bowl of the amphitheater, she called up another wave of magic to establish a shield, a curved shimmering barrier like a bubble over the stage.

The zhiss were bottled up, but only for as long as she could hold the shield in place.

"Hurry!" Her voice was just a croak. She hoped the Hidden People could hear her. "I need you. Builders—now! You are ready for this." A flood of gray-robed people rushed out from the sealed buildings.

Though her thoughts were dizzy, she shrank the shield, retracted the bubble to push the bottled zhiss farther and farther down toward the central fire, to contain them in a controllable space. The rim of the hemispherical shield dropped to the middle levels of seats, then kept shrinking, pushing the black swarm into a smaller and smaller confinement.

Inside the palace, Mrra finally smashed through the last shreds of the wooden door and escaped, bounding out of the building and into the streets to help her blood-spattered sister panther. Nicci fell to her knees and felt the blood-soaked fabric of her black dress. Mrra pressed against her, offering strength and protection, but Nicci could not let her concentration falter.

The bubble was now small enough that it was only a

dome over the stage at the bottom of the amphitheater, a sealed prison with the waning bonfire and the buzzing zhiss. To maintain her strength, Nicci withdrew her energy that kept the wizard's light glowing, and the fire died out, leaving the sealed bubble in darkness and all the frustrated zhiss trapped with no light and no blood. They battered against the invisible curved wall like thousands of vengeful hornets.

"Now!" she gasped. "Contain them!"

Architects, carpenters, stonemasons raced out, along with all the labor force they could need. They had drawn their plans, laid down their supplies, gathered their tools, and they were prepared. Working like agitated bees, the builders of Orogang threw long crossbars over the lower part of the amphitheater. They had already sealed the floor of the stage, caulked and bricked even the tiniest of openings. Next, they crisscrossed the beams and added a structural layer of wooden slats, which they covered with opaque tarpaulins, sealing the dome. More teams slathered the thick fabric with fast-hardening plaster. On top of that, they laid layers of bricks, building up an impenetrable cap to cover the imprisoned zhiss.

All the while, Nicci focused her effort into maintaining the shield that trapped the black cloud, holding them until the permanent containment could be finished.

The Hidden People moved in a coordinated flurry. They reinforced their solid barrier, covering any open gaps, then slathered the bricks with more thick plaster and mortar, layer upon layer, to a thickness of many feet and impenetrably black.

Before dawn, hundreds of workers had entirely sealed the zhiss in a prison that would hold them forever. No light, no blood, no freedom. They would wither away and die.

Nicci groggily realized that Asha was shaking her shoulders. "It is finished. You can rest now."

The sorceress couldn't even lift her head, but she slumped against the big panther who purred beside her. With a sigh of relief, Nicci released her hold on the gift, letting the inner shield fade. The zhiss were forever sealed within the impossibly thick and opaque walls of their enclosure. The solid barrier held, but the Hidden People would keep reinforcing it, thickening it for days.

Nicci didn't know how long it would take for the zhiss to starve, to dwindle away to nothing, but she was certain they would never get out.

She didn't have the strength to struggle as the Hidden People picked her up and carried her back into the shelter. She could rest with confidence now. As her eyes closed, she felt the weakness of blood loss and the utter weariness from expending so much of her gift. But she would recover.

She had done what she'd promised. Now all she had to worry about was preventing General Utros from conquering the world.

CHAPTER 28

The smoke from moss-covered firewood had a sour smell, but the odor of decaying flesh bothered Lila more. She cautiously hunkered down across from Adessa. The older morazeth had an unsettling gleam in her eyes as she sat by her campfire.

Lila explained, "I am pursuing the Norukai serpent ships down the river, looking for my chance. I need your help."

Adessa was puzzled. Her voice sounded distant and strange. "Why do you care about Norukai?"

"Much has changed since you left on the night of the revolt." Lila frowned. "Nothing is left of Ildakar. The army of General Utros awakened and laid siege to the city, and then a Norukai fleet attacked us from the river. Ildakar vanished under the shroud of eternity again, and I was trapped outside. We can't go back. No one can."

Adessa turned her gaze to look at the severed head resting on the matted grasses. She glowered at it. "That's what he just told me."

Black bugs scuttled over the pus-filled flesh. The head was hideously decayed, the eyes swollen shut, the mouth sagging. It took Lila a moment to recognize the dark hair, the goatee, the distorted features. "That is Wizard Commander Maxim."

"Sovrena Thora commanded me to bring back his head, and I am doing so." Adessa unconsciously swatted away a biting insect. "He was Mirrormask and he wanted to bring down Ildakar. He has paid for his crimes, but not enough." Her expression darkened, and she suddenly yelled at the decomposing horror. "You hear me, Maxim? Not enough! I will place your head on a spike before the gates of Ildakar, where the entire population can know what you did."

Lila found her comments and mannerisms tinged with madness. In a calm, even voice, she explained again. "Ildakar is gone, Adessa. We can't go back."

The other morazeth cocked her head and seemed to hear a response from the rotting lump. Adessa sat up straight as if preparing to fight. Though her hard years were showing, she had once been beautiful in a feral way, her close-cropped dark hair shot with lines of silver. Her face was lean, her body muscular, but now Adessa's dark eyes held a haunted shadow. Her gaze flicked back and forth, as if she was watching things unseen. "No, no. He was lying! Ildakar can't be gone. I still have to bring Maxim's head back to the sovrena."

Sitting near the fire, Lila laced her fingers together around one bare knee. "I am your morazeth sister. You know I would not lie to you."

Adessa sagged, then glared at the severed head. "Yes, Lila, I know you speak the truth." She grabbed the clumps of dark hair, then carried the head to the campfire. "Shall I roast you here? If the sovrena is gone, then I don't need to deliver the trophy anymore. I'd like to hear you scream as the fire cooks the remaining skin off your face."

Decaying drops of fluid oozed down the chin to drip in sizzling bursts in the coals. Lila kept her voice low and guarded. "What are you doing, Adessa?"

"Making him stop his taunts!"

The wizard commander's sunken eyes were pools of gray jelly, like rotten egg whites. With a wet sound, part of his scalp ripped from the skull, and the loose head dropped toward the fire, but Adessa rescued it by grabbing the soft neck stump. "Not yet. Not so easy for you."

Adessa returned the wizard commander's head to the stained sack. "Be silent!" Then she turned back to Lila. "If what you say is true, if the sovrena is defeated and Ildakar is gone, then my quest is ended." The disappointment on her face struck Lila's heart. The quest, the woman's reason for suffering so many hardships, was all that had kept her going. "Now where do I go? What do I do?"

"I have a mission of my own," Lila said, "and it is a morazeth mission. You could help me. There are many Norukai to fight and kill, and it will give you a chance to spill more blood. That would give us both a purpose."

"Tell me about your mission."

Lila delivered a formal report to her commander, hoping to get through to Adessa. She talked at length about Bannon, the young swordsman she had trained in the combat pits.

Adessa raised her eyebrows. "Yes, Bannon was your special pet. He corrupted my champion Ian and forced me to kill him. If you are hunting Bannon now, I will help you. He should die for the damage he did to our society. For making me waste a good champion like Ian."

Lila considered how to answer that question. "Yes, I am hunting him, but not to harm him. Bannon and I fought alongside each other to defend Ildakar, and we even battled King Grieve himself." Her voice dropped. "He was taken captive along with many Ildakarans. With the city gone and me trapped outside, I took on my own mission. I have to rescue Bannon."

"Why?"

Lila felt a flare of defensive anger. "Because I choose to do so! I consider the mission worthwhile, and if you are my morazeth sister, then you will accept that reasoning."

Adessa pondered. The mossy fire was burning low, and Lila added some green twigs to it. The darkness around them remained deep, but a low mist had risen from the marshes. Adessa nodded distantly. "Sovrena Thora disliked the Norukai, called them brutes. She would have wanted me to kill them because they attacked the city, but why would I do it to save a skinny arena slave? Bannon caused a great deal of trouble. Is he that remarkable a lover?"

Lila had already thought of the answer. "Now that the shroud of eternity is back, Bannon Farmer is the only warrior who remains. In a sense, he is the champion of Ildakar, and he could be useful."

Adessa considered that. "One should not discard useful tools or fighters."

"Then let us plan a trap together. We will fight the Norukai, and I can free Bannon, as I vowed to do." The intensity of her gaze caught Adessa's attention. "Will you help me, morazeth to morazeth?"

Adessa snapped at the unseen head inside the sack. "I don't care what you wish, Maxim! I make my own decision." The flecks of madness in her eyes grew brighter. "Stop laughing, or I'll submerge your head again and let the fish eat more of your face."

Composing herself, Adessa faced Lila across the

campfire. "If you and I are the only two morazeth that remain outside the shroud of eternity, then your mission is mine. I will battle the Norukai with you, but you can save the scrawny swordsman on your own."

CHAPTER 29

A thousand soldiers carrying flame-symbol banners pressed toward Orogang. As they gained altitude and the terrain grew more rugged, General Utros recognized the dark crags with patches of snow on their summits. He inhaled the thin, chill air, a refreshing change from the dust of the road, the thick odor of horses, and countless sweating men.

"Will we see the capital today, beloved Utros?" asked Ruva, riding beside him.

He lifted his head high, a victorious military commander coming back to report on the lands he had conquered. They were close to the city; he could taste it. "Yes, it will be today."

That dawn, while his soldiers broke camp and prepared for another long march, Utros had polished his gold half mask. He studied the burnished metal, the idealized sculpture of his features. When he entered the imperial palace, he wondered if anyone would remember the face of Utros after all these centuries. History recorded large-scale events and political consequences, but rarely preserved the details of a man's physical appearance. Would anyone know him at all?

"They will remember your legend," Ruva said.

"History is filled with stories of General Utros. That is what the wizard Nathan said."

He gazed along the widening road shadowed by tall mountains. "We shall see for ourselves. I'll face the man who now sits on the throne in Orogang, and I will determine if he is worthy."

He dispatched a pair of scouts to ride ahead to announce their arrival. He selected two men who were originally from Orogang, fighters who had left their homes and loved ones to follow General Utros, long ago. The two scouts proudly shouldered their responsibility.

"We will bring you news, sir," said a man with an unfortunately large nose. "And we'll make sure the people of Orogang prepare a welcome celebration for your returning army."

"We're going home!" the other scout cried with such enthusiasm that his voice cracked like the voice of a boy struggling with puberty. They galloped off.

Utros kept silent as he rode forward, leading his escort army. The twin sorceresses looked eagerly ahead, their bright eyes searching for the grandeur that Utros had promised them ages ago. He was perplexed and disappointed by the sad state of the main roads. This close to the great city, he expected to see overburdened caravans, farmers with wagons, travelers, military patrols. With Orogang's population of nearly a million people, even the outlying areas should have seen much activity.

Dark pines rose all around, and he knew the forests should have been cut for firewood and construction material. The rocky slopes should have shown the stair-stepped gashes of stone quarries. Why were there no fields of grain, no orchards, no grazing sheep or cattle? Where were the people?

They passed only the foundation stones and crumbling walls of long-collapsed cottages. The twins picked up on his uneasy mood. Ava and Ruva kept glancing at him, wondering how they could help. The mounted army began to display an odd mixture of impatience, joy, and concern.

By noon the pair of scouts galloped back to the general, and he could already read the grim news on their faces. The large-nosed man had tear tracks through the dust on his cheeks. Both scouts lowered their voices. "We found Orogang, sir. The city . . ."

"The whole city is empty and abandoned!" blurted the other scout. "The population is gone, the streets are empty."

"Was the city ransacked?" Utros demanded, trying to keep his dismay in check. "Conquered?"

"I don't know." The scout with the big nose had lost his sincere smile. "The buildings don't look burned or destroyed, just abandoned. The structures are intact, but they're sealed up."

"I will see this myself." Utros urged his horse forward.

The scouts turned their mounts about and led the way. "It's less than half an hour's ride, sir. Follow us."

Utros grasped the reins and kicked the stallion into a gallop. Ava and Ruva raced alongside their general. Behind them, the army let out a cheer and urged their horses faster, rushing toward Orogang like a battlefield charge.

When they reached the outskirts of the city, Utros suddenly had trouble breathing. Silence loomed like a pestilence in the air. The towering structures were washed by the sun like bleached bones in a desert. Silent and dead.

Utros trembled as he guided his stallion between imposing monoliths, stone piles that had once formed an awe-inspiring gate. The streets that should have celebrated the glory of the empire were overgrown, the flagstones buckled. Twisted trees reached up from wherever seeds had found cracks or crannies.

His army crowded behind their general as Utros halted to stare at the vacant gate. Ava and Ruva were silent, dismayed for the general's sake. "It's gone," he said. "My empire is gone. Who leads it now?"

"He would only be an emperor of dust," said Ruva.

Ava said, "The slate has been wiped clean, beloved Utros. This is Orogang. It could be your own capital, and you will rebuild the empire."

Ruva agreed, "*Your* empire."

He could not let the men see his crippling disappointment. Still picturing himself as a conquering hero, he proudly rode his stallion through the remains of the grand arch. Behind him, his army flowed into the empty capital.

As he looked around, he remembered the palace, the observatory pyramid, the tall lookout towers. Utros recognized the ministry building with its line of fluted columns and multiple entrances, all of which were now barricaded shut. The palace had sported myriad multicolored windows, but now he saw only a wall of mortared bricks.

"Someone turned my city into a tomb." He had expected bustling streets, crowded bazaars, craftsmen districts, moneylenders, temples, stonecutters. Now there were only ominous silence and shadows, even in the bright afternoon.

As his army moved through the streets, other scouts

came back with good news. "We found storehouses, General! Many sacks of grain, barrels of apples, potatoes, even kegs of wine and ale. Those supplies will help our people."

"Seize everything," Utros said, pleased. Ava and Ruva had worked their spell so the soldiers could not feel the gnawing hunger, but now, thankfully, they had real supplies, enough for a well-deserved feast.

The clatter of iron-shod horse hooves echoed against the stone walls, but the sound was no substitute for massed crowds and loud cheers. In the central plaza, Utros pulled his stallion to a halt and dismounted. He stood before a colossal statue that had toppled from its base. The massive stone arms were broken, the booted feet still secured to the marble pedestal. The figure sprawled on the ground in several pieces, weathered with age. He looked down at the carved head and recognized the sneering self-important expression as well as the distinctive iron fang. Kurgan's statue had been brought down when his own people overthrew him.

"General!" one of the scouts shouted from the other side of the square. "You must see this."

The sorceresses slid from their saddles and stood next to him on the ground, ready to fight. He could sense a crackle in the air as they summoned their gift to defend him. The ominous tension around the city put them all on edge.

With a brisk stride, Utros went to an adjacent plaza, where he saw a second great statue, this one even taller than Kurgan's and well maintained, the stone polished. Fresh flowers were strewn around the base. His gaze was drawn upward to look at the stone face, the full beard, the strong jaw, the features that so closely matched the shape of his gold half mask. The base of the statue marked out his name in chiseled letters. UTROS.

More soldiers filled the open areas, a full army conquering an empty city. Questions rustled among them like breezes in a brewing storm. Utros had no answers for them, but they could draw their own conclusions. The weight of mysteries was oppressive.

The gigantic statue proved that Utros was indeed remembered, that his legend had survived, but he also sensed that the city wasn't as empty as he had first thought. Silent threats lurked there. Hidden eyes watched them from shadowed recesses in buildings, no doubt plotting something. All the men were tense, their guard raised.

Ava and Ruva also looked uneasy. His soldiers drew their weapons, waiting for something to happen. The tableau seemed ready to explode.

General Utros had returned! Cyrus knew it the moment he saw the military leader astride his black horse, wearing armor much as was depicted in the towering statue.

Nicci had told the Hidden People that Utros still lived, and although Cyrus and his followers had prayed for that all their lives, he had merely hoped to find a worthy successor to Utros, not the legendary general himself, in the flesh. But that was what the prophecy had said. It was true! Now the great commander rode into the city with a thousand well-disciplined soldiers, returning to Orogang just as Cyrus had hoped.

The general wore an imposing helmet adorned with the curved horns of some massive beast, and half his face was covered with a burnished gold mask that made him look less human, but more terrifying. Two beautiful hairless women rode on either side of him, and Cyrus remembered legends of the fearsome twin sorceresses that accompanied General Utros.

Huddled in their shadows, the Hidden People were exhausted and battered after helping Nicci contain the zhiss the night before. Many of them were weak from loss of blood, but they had survived the ordeal. Nicci was unconscious, recovering deep inside the palace.

Because of her efforts to save the Hidden People, Cyrus had begun to forgive her. She had indeed imprisoned the bloodthirsty black cloud, freeing them from their oppressive obligations. But she had also declared that the legendary Utros was an untrustworthy tyrant who meant only to conquer the Old World. Cyrus didn't believe Nicci. She lied, and her lies uprooted all the beliefs that he and his followers held so dear.

And now Utros had returned!

Cyrus looked through the open windows—open windows, even in the daylight! He watched the armored soldiers ride into the great plaza, saw the magnificent uniforms, banners with the flame symbol of the once-great empire. Oh, this was a glorious day in many ways!

"Hurry!" Cyrus called his followers. "Take your swords and whatever armor we still have. To arms! We must show General Utros that we still remember, that we are worthy of him. Hurry!"

Twenty of his followers seized weapons from the stockpiles, battered helmets, ragtag breastplates and capes, anything that would make them look impressive. They were pale from living in the shadows, and many had scabs and blood blisters from the attack of the zhiss. Cyrus knew they must look horrific, but they could not wait. Utros was here! There would never be a better chance. He had lived all his days for this moment.

Cyrus rallied his people. "Our general has returned at last. Run out to meet him!" He grabbed his own sword, raised it, and ran out at the forefront.

With a triumphant roar, unable to contain their exuberance at seeing the legend proved true at last, Cyrus and his followers surged out into the square.

A door creaked open in a council building and pale figures appeared. They wore sinister, hooded gray robes, and all of them carried gleaming swords, scraps of armor obviously scavenged from elsewhere. "It is Utros!" one of the strangers called.

Figures rushed out of the building with furtive spiderlike movements like a small, shouting army. They scuttled quickly, swirling their cloaks around them. Nearly a hundred of them ran forward, raising their swords. "General Utros!"

As soon as the first man charged into the dazzling sunlight, though, he staggered and shielded his eyes, swinging his blade in the air. The bright sun blinded them. The threatening army behind the first man also covered their faces with their hands and cringed from the light, but they blundered forward, all of them armed.

Ava and Ruva reacted without waiting for orders from Utros. Seeing the danger to the general, they launched a burst of fire that engulfed the leading group of pale, threatening figures. Even as the flames incinerated the front ranks, the twin sorceresses followed with a bolt of lightning that blasted more of the intimidating figures.

Ava sounded satisfied as the ominous people col-lapsed. "We will protect you, beloved Utros."

Utros frowned at the blackened skeletons. "I wanted to know who they were. Why did they attack me?"

From inside the ominous buildings, they heard more threatening movement, multiple doors opening. Faces pressed against hidden peepholes, and muttering voices rose with an undertone of anger.

CHAPTER 30

W hen Nathan's party reached the high pass of Kol Adair, he felt a sense of purpose, if not triumph. With Nicci and Bannon, he had originally climbed the rugged mountains above the lands of the Scar, intent on reaching this singular pass.

Prelate Verna had ridden beside him up the last rocky switchbacks until the glorious top of the pass unfolded before them. Nathan breathed hard in the thin air, but he couldn't seem to fill his lungs.

General Zimmer and his soldiers gathered on the open tundra. A large rock cairn marked the high point of the pass like a monument to fallen kings. By now, they were quite far ahead of the enormous marching army. Zimmer called out, "We rest here for an hour. Eat your food, drink your water. There will be plenty of streams on the other side. We need to keep moving toward Cliffwall."

Amber and Peretta mingled with the Sisters of the Light, while Oliver shaded his eyes and squinted into the distance, as if amazed at how far he had come. Rendell hunched his head, the expansive panorama seemingly too much for him to endure.

Captain Trevor said sadly, "The first time we reached

this point, Renn dropped to his knees and kissed the stones, but on our way back I don't think he paused to admire the view, he was so anxious to get home to Ildakar." Trevor heaved a sigh. "Now he will never go home."

The two morazeth showed no discomfort from the brisk wind. They studied the steep route down the other side of the pass. "It looks like a rugged journey ahead," Lyesse said.

Nathan looked down the western slope to where he could see broken glaciers that had tumbled down in a recent avalanche. "It will be a far more difficult route for that giant army. In many places, the soldiers will have to move single file. We'll pull even farther ahead."

He claimed a boulder for his seat and removed the life book from its pouch. With numb fingertips, he traced the leather cover. The book contained a chronicle of history and adventure, everything he had done since leaving the Dark Lands far to the north. He had filled many of the pages, and he could hardly believe all he had done and faced.

Verna sat next to him on the large rock. "You've been here before, Nathan. What drew you to Kol Adair in the first place? Did you know what was on the other side? Were you looking for Ildakar?"

"Kol Adair was where I hoped to regain my gift," he said. "But it was just a step in a longer journey." Now that he had discarded his stained wizard's robe in favor of more familiar black pants and ruffled shirt, he rested his hand on the ornate hilt of the sword. Nathan stroked his smooth chin. "It was a prophecy, of sorts."

"A prophecy?" Verna was surprised. "You of all people know how misleading any prophecy can be, even back when prophecy still worked. All the forked paths, true ones and false ones."

"Indeed, my dear prelate. That is why the Sisters of the Light locked me up for a thousand years." He raised his eyebrows. "And look what good that did you! It only led to the ruin of the Palace of the Prophets and caused great dismay to your entire order." He sniffed. "Serves you right. You should know what happens to anyone who attempts to thwart prophecy."

"Yet you came here yourself following a prophecy. Weren't you aware of the danger?"

"A desperate man will grasp at any hope, and a desperate wizard has ways to believe what he wishes to believe. Besides, my dear, I wasn't attempting to *thwart* prophecy, but to follow it."

He opened the life book, flipped back through the pages, ignoring his neat handwriting. On the very first page he read lines in a different hand. "This is what the witch woman wrote. We didn't know what it meant at the time." He ran his fingers along the words as he read them aloud. "'Future and Fate depend on both the journey and the destination. Kol Adair lies far to the south in the Old World. From there, the Wizard will behold what he needs to make himself whole again. And the Sorceress must save the world.'"

He paused. "My gift had abandoned me aboard the *Wavewalker,* you see. I couldn't perform even the simplest magic, not so much as a spark of flame in the palm of my hand. Red had written those lines while my gift was at full strength, yet she knew somehow I would lose it."

"*If* you're interpreting the words correctly," Verna said. "You, Prophet, know that a reader reads the details of a premonition according to his own wishes."

"I did know that, but I didn't remember it. I was convinced that once I reached Kol Adair, my gift would suddenly return, that I would achieve the end of my quest. But no, the words say only that I would *behold* what I needed." He looked eastward beyond the pass. "And from here, through a trick of a mirage, we saw Ildakar, far away, shimmering as the shroud of eternity flickered. That is why we headed there, and eventually I did indeed get what I needed, the heart of a wizard."

Nathan suddenly winced as pain shot through his chest. Ivan's heart beat harder, pounding as if trying to break free of his rib cage, fighting back against its new owner.

Verna saw his grimace. "What is wrong? I've seen you rub your chest before. Does your heart still bother you?"

"The heart is not entirely mine." He gave her a wan grin. "At least that is what Chief Handler Ivan seems to think."

Loosening the laces among the ruffles of his shirt, he tugged open the front to reveal the long white scar on his breastbone. "This was where Fleshmancer Andre tore out my heart and replaced it with Ivan's to give me my gift back. Andre wasn't sure the scheme would work, and I'm quite certain that *Ivan* had no wish to participate." He tugged the laces tight against the chill breezes on the pass. "It wasn't my choice either, but I had tried everything else. A prophet without prophecy and a wizard without the gift—I felt quite useless, Verna." He wondered whether he had ever used her first name before. "At the time, I accepted what I had to do, and now there is no reason to second-guess it. I do have my gift back, and I will fight against the enemies of the land. That is all I can do."

Verna placed a comforting hand on his knee. "And

what does the rest of the prophecy mean? 'And the Sorceress must save the world.'"

"That part is for Nicci, I believe, but she's been doing that all along."

After a brief rest, the company moved on down the western slope. The lead horses picked their way in single file along the rougher and more jumbled terrain. In many places the road had been damaged, strewn with fallen boulders or swept away by sheets of ice and snow.

Holding on to the saddle horn, Zimmer rocked back and forth as his horse traversed the uneven ground. He glanced back over his shoulder. "Our avalanche certainly caused a lot of damage, Prelate."

Nathan raised his eyebrows. "Your avalanche?"

"You'll see soon enough," Verna said as the first line of horses picked their way across an angled white field.

Dislodged pebbles and ice chunks still pattered down the slopes. Though Nathan felt uneasy about the unstable terrain, he could only imagine how difficult this passage would be for many thousands of marching men in full armor. By the time they reached Cliffwall, their small group should be a week or more ahead of the main army.

As the party veered around the broad fan of a fresh jumbled snowfield, Nathan realized the white blocks were studded with dark forms, a glint of polished armor, the sharp edge of a shield. A gauntleted hand reached out of the frozen mass. As the company approached, cawing ravens took wing from their feast of frozen meat.

"Those are bodies!" Nathan realized just how many corpses there were; not just hundreds, but thousands. "Dear spirits!"

"One of General Utros's expeditionary armies,"

Verna said. "We found them camped just below Kol Adair, beneath the heavy glaciers."

Zimmer pulled up to a halt beside them. "We estimated they were ten thousand men marching in the general direction of Cliffwall. We stopped them."

Amber, Peretta, and Oliver called out as they stopped by the edge of the avalanche field. "Some of the ice melted, but the bodies are still frozen!"

"Not so frozen that the crows can't eat them," Peretta said. "By summer, all these bones will be picked clean."

Nathan tried to grasp what he was seeing. "What did you do? How did you cause this?"

Verna seemed quite pleased with herself. "Renn was the only wizard among us, but there were Sisters of the Light and many gifted Cliffwall scholars. Together, we used magic to melt the ice in strategic places, which lubricated the glacier sheets. Gravity did the rest." She shrugged as if it had been a simple exercise.

At the edge of the ice field, Nathan stared at the innumerable buried bodies, the armor, helmets, and the exposed faces with pecked skin.

The morazeth nodded with admiration. "Ten thousand?" Thorn asked.

"An impressive score," Lyesse added.

Nathan turned to the prim prelate, seeing Verna in an entirely different light. "I had no idea you were so bloodthirsty, my dear."

"I can be, when it's necessary."

"Yes, I suppose you can. I have seen you do many hard things over the years."

Nathan and the prelate had an often contentious relationship. She considered him dangerous due to his gift of prophecy, and after he'd escaped from the Palace of the Prophets, she had tried to hunt him down. Nathan had only wanted his freedom, living his life for the first time, even though he was already a thousand years old. He had indeed found adventure and love, more than once.

He sighed. "After Clarissa was killed, I was so angry at you that I broke your jaw."

Verna hung her head. "I am sorry about that."

"You're sorry? I'm the one who smashed you in the face."

"Many things were different then. It healed."

Nathan thought of beautiful, innocent Clarissa, and then Prelate Ann, whom he had also loved . . . and much more recently there was Elsa, who had sacrificed herself in a blaze of glory with her transference magic. "Not everything heals completely."

He kicked at the armored glove of a body that was buried in ice and snow. Without gloating further over the massacre, he and his companions moved on toward Cliffwall.

CHAPTER 31

Yes, she would take the head of the Norukai king. That would be her new trophy, her new quest, and Adessa considered it a worthy one.

She felt alive again with a purpose, a true morazeth purpose. The sack with the wizard commander's head bumped against her hip as she sprinted along the river with Lila beside her.

The severed head had fallen silent, and Adessa was glad not to listen to his taunts, not to look at his rotting face. Maybe the Keeper had silenced him for good. What worried Adessa, though, was that Lila didn't seem to hear the wizard commander at all.

When the young woman explained what had happened to Ildakar, Adessa felt the solid ground of her life drop out beneath her. She had asked herself repeatedly whether killing Maxim was enough of a purpose, in and of itself. And now that he was dead, what did she have left, other than carrying the head back to Ildakar? A city that no longer existed.

Even that had been taken from her. The emptiness was a void filled only with Maxim's mocking laughter, but now Lila had given her a new mission. Bannon meant nothing to her, but Adessa did care for her morazeth sister. Therefore, Lila's quest was her own quest. Besides, she liked the idea of killing King Grieve.

The two women could run for hours with only brief rests. Lila had insisted on the need for speed, because although the Norukai would stop to anchor at intermittent times, the serpent ships moved swiftly along the Killraven. In order for their plan to succeed, they had to get ahead of the three vessels so they could lay their trap.

The game trail turned into a footpath, then an actual road as they reached the outskirts of a tiny fishing town. The two women gave it a wide berth, because encountering people would only delay them. But when they stumbled upon a hunter trudging back to his home with a small gutted deer over his shoulders, the man was so startled to see the morazeth running toward him that he dropped his kill and grabbed his bow. The two barely paused as they raced past him.

Lila called over her shoulder, "Warn your village! Norukai ships are coming, and they will kill your people, burn your homes. Get everyone to safety."

The man gaped at them, but they had already vanished into the forest. Adessa pointed out, "This means we must be ahead of the raiders. Otherwise that village would have been destroyed already."

Lila pushed on with greater speed. "We have a chance to set up an ambush, if we find the right place to do it."

By late afternoon they came upon an elbow of dry land that jutted into the river. Lila paused and looked around with a critical eye. She smiled. "We can build a bonfire here where the Norukai ships are sure to see it. We will taunt them and bring them closer."

"I will challenge them." Adessa responded with a predatory grin. "If he is not a coward, King Grieve will face me."

As sunset approached, knowing the raider ships were coming, though they would anchor when night set in, the two morazeth moved through the underbrush breaking off dead branches and hauling dry marsh grasses, which they piled out on the spit of land to prepare a big fire.

Adessa found a fallen tree with a hollow interior that would make an adequate drum. Together, they dragged the hollow log to the edge of the water, where Adessa could sit in front of the bonfire and make loud, rhythmic pounding. One way or another, she would command the attention of the Norukai.

The two women waited as darkness fell and the river sounds grew louder, more sinister. Adessa stared out at the empty river, penetrating the gloom with her eyes, listening intently. She smiled at her companion. "Can you hear it?"

Gruff voices carried on the water, along with the creak of wood.

Lila tucked her dagger into its sheath, checked the small agile knife at her side and Sturdy strapped to her back. "I will get ready. Give me the diversion I need, and I'll save Bannon. That is our mission."

Adessa responded with a wolfish grin, then a glance at the sack. "We will keep their attention, don't worry."

Lila sprinted off along the riverbank to take her position in the bushes, while Adessa ignited the bonfire. The flames quickly caught the reeds and grasses, burning fast and hot. The signal blaze rose high, demanding the attention of the serpent ships.

As she moved to the hollow log, a muffled voice came from the sack at her side. "The Keeper wants you."

"The Keeper will have all of us in our time. I wish he would take you now."

"Poor Adessa . . ." Maxim said in an oily mocking voice.

"Silence!" Adessa's shout echoed across the river, and she heard surprised responses from the Norukai vessels.

She sat cross-legged next to the hollow log and hammered on the trunk with a wooden branch, pounding out a loud drumbeat. When Maxim's head continued to mock her, she just beat the stick louder, drowning him out.

When the fearsome serpent ships came closer, attracted by the blazing fire and the pounding beat, Adessa stood and went to the river's edge. Her silhouette would stand out clearly against the bright flames. From the ships she heard taunting jeers, burly raiders pointing at her as if she were a fool.

She shouted loudly enough to be heard over their catcalls. "I am a morazeth from Ildakar, and I challenge King Grieve to a fight. I mean to kill someone tonight."

Cloaked in the last light of dusk, the serpent ships approached closer in the main river channel. Raucous shouts came back over the water in response to her challenge.

Adessa stood her ground, calling back to them. "Is Grieve a coward to face me himself? Very well, let him send a lesser Norukai, or two, if you think that is what you need to fight a morazeth."

A smaller boat dropped into the water from the lead ship. Two barrel-chested Norukai, their faces slashed into permanent hideous grimaces, rowed to where she waited on the spit of land by the bonfire. Each man carried ominous weapons, which Adessa ignored. She had her short sword, her dagger, and her agile knife, which was little more than a rune-marked handle that no Norukai would recognize. She also carried the blood-stained sack with the head, refusing to relinquish her trophy. Maxim would come with her.

She waded into the shallow river to meet the landing boat. Adessa glowered at the Norukai greeting party as if their presence were an insult. "A disappointingly small escort. The Norukai don't fear me enough yet."

The raiders growled, as if incapable of normal human speech. She climbed into the boat even before it came to shore, then sat imperiously at the bow while the Norukai rowed toward the serpent ship. She turned her back to the men and cradled the stained sack on her lap.

Norukai crowded the rail on the upper deck, watching her with strange curiosity. From the waterline, Adessa scanned their faces, trying to determine which one was Grieve.

She saw a scarred, white-skinned man poking his head up and down, scuttling sideways to get a better view. "My Grieve!" The albino cocked his head at the burly man beside him, who wore a thick chain around his waist and had bone spines implanted in his shoulders. "My Grieve, King Grieve! Make her grieve."

With the sack secured to her waist, Adessa left the landing boat and climbed a ladder up the side of the serpent ship's hull. She showed no fear as she stood among the raiders.

"Death is in the air," Maxim whispered from the sack. "Someone will die. Who will you fight? Who will you kill, or who will kill *you*? Best prepare yourself, Adessa."

"Be quiet." She climbed onto the deck and planted her feet firmly on the scrubbed wood. As the Norukai crowded around her, she drew her sword, standing defiant. "Is King Grieve brave enough to face me? I want his blood."

The raiders guffawed. Grieve stepped forward, a truly hideous man. "Why would I waste my time fighting you? If I need practice, the Norukai are more worthy sparring partners."

"You'll fight me because I want to kill you," Adessa said.

The Norukai laughed at her audacity, and even Grieve chuckled. "A woman doesn't always get what she wants. I have disappointed many who lusted after me."

The scarred sailors snickered. Adessa stared at him without answering. Grieve looked at the bloodstained sack at her side. "What is that? A gift for me?"

She set the sack on top of a barrel and pulled down the cloth to reveal the rotting head.

The albino shaman capered in delight. "The axe cleaves the wood. The sword cleaves the bone!"

"Quiet, Chalk." As Grieve leaned closer, his scarred mouth drew down in a frown. "Who is this? Why would I want such a gift?"

"It is not a gift for you. This is Wizard Commander Maxim from Ildakar. I was ordered to take his head." She remained stony. Now that her hands were free, she touched her short sword. "I intend to take your head as a second trophy."

The Norukai crowded closer, amused by the impending fight. As the darkness thickened, they brought lanterns to illuminate the open deck, clearing an area for combat. Grieve held his wicked war axe in his right hand.

"All right, let's play," he said.

The two faced off.

CHAPTER 32

Disheartened and angry after so many soldiers had died in the meadow of deadly flowers, General Utros's army marched into the mountains. As their provisional leader, First Commander Enoch rode his warhorse, donning a crimson cape to indicate his rank. His brass helmet gleamed in the sun, but his entire body felt like iron, heavy and harder than the stone he and all the soldiers had been for centuries.

With the general himself on his way to Orogang, Enoch needed to lead more than a hundred thousand fighters, but he had never been an inspirational commander like Utros. So many soldiers had already died since awakening from the petrification spell, and they had all lost their families many centuries ago when they had left home for the last time under the banner of General Utros.

Utros was the one who inspired that undying loyalty, and although Enoch tried to hold the army together, he could tell that cracks were showing in their ranks. A handful of stragglers from Ildakar had picked them off, one by one, and then hundreds more died in the field of poison flowers, a trap. That had been a great blow to their confidence in him.

Enoch had not been at the forefront that day, but riding among the ranks to encourage the marching companies. His vanguard had been so easily provoked by a few gadflies, so heinously tricked. By the time Enoch had arrived to join the charge, the broad meadow was already strewn with writhing bodies.

Now, riding endlessly through the mountains, Enoch squeezed his fists, feeling the stretch of his leather gauntlets. He wanted to bash each one of the rebels against a rock. Even a thousand casualties had no significant effect on the gigantic force, but it was like a sword thrust through the heart of their morale.

And he was in command.

The soldiers were without supplies and starving, and they knew it, though kept alive thanks to the unsettling spell that altered their digestion and metabolism. Their instinct forced them to strip the greenery off trees, grasses, and bushes, like locusts. They devoured any animal they caught. Enoch had a sick suspicion that if the bodies of those fallen soldiers had not been impregnated with the deathrise poison, some of his most desperate troops might even have eaten the human flesh. But he had rushed the thundering force up to the next ridge, away from the poisonous flowers and all that tempting meat. . . .

Enoch drove the army harder as they climbed into the more rugged mountains. He wished General Utros would come back and join them again. The army needed their general, though Enoch dreaded explaining such a failure to Utros once he returned. . . .

The marching force stretched out for half a mile, heading into the mountains, up above the tree line and toward the highest pass ahead. Raising a gloved fist, he shouted loudly enough for the front ranks to hear his words, which would then be passed along down the line of soldiers. "Scouts have found a large mountain lake ahead! We will camp there for the night. Just another hour, and we'll be there."

Finally, they reached a cliff-ringed bowl below the last line of high peaks, where a clear mountain lake welcomed them. This would be their final camp before a vigorous push up and over the pass of Kol Adair. The first ranks set up camp around the lake, finding patches of dry ground to sleep on.

The pristine hanging valley looked peaceful and spectacular, and Enoch inhaled deeply of the crisp, cold air. Though stark and forbidding, the crags were beautiful in a wild way. Filled with snowmelt and stream runoff, the lake reflected the veils of late-afternoon clouds like a broad mirror.

The sound of his soldiers setting up a camp, scrounging whatever scrub wood they could find for campfires, created a comforting drone. Normally he would have heard more chatter, boisterous challenges, gambling games, but the troops were sullen and exhausted.

Enoch had devoted his life to serving in the army. He had marched proudly alongside General Utros, but he had given up hope of a normal family, of the contentment a retired veteran might expect with a small farm and an orchard outside of Orogang. The general had handed him this responsibility now, and Enoch took satisfaction from leading this great army, although he was aware that if Utros did not come back soon, some of these soldiers would desert the army and go somewhere to live out their lives however they wished.

As endless troops continued to march into the basin, supply sergeants filled barrels of drinking water from the lake, and the cooks prepared scant meals with whatever rations they had left. The rest of the fighters stripped out of their armor and rushed to the cold water to wash themselves. They splashed their faces, rinsed dirt-encrusted hair. Though the water was frigid, some swam out to rocks protruding from the lake. At last, their tension began to ease, washed away like the dust of the long march. Some soldiers even made makeshift fishing poles from willow branches and went in search of trout.

Suddenly an odd hush fell over the men on the shore, and Enoch felt something change in the air. A few swimmers cried out in shock, then sank beneath the surface, never to emerge. Others stood at the lake's edge, wary, searching for an enemy.

Far from the shore, Enoch cried, "Beware of the water!" He pushed his way through the troops, trying to get to the lake.

The soldiers already crowding the shore peered transfixed into the deep water and gasped. Several voluntarily dove in, still wearing armor, as if tempted by an irresistible force; they swam deep and did not resurface.

More soldiers came running. One subcommander yelled at his company, grabbed the shoulder of a struggling man, and tried to drag him away from the shore, but then he, too, stared in fascination, as if caught in a spell. He dropped to his knees and plunged into the water, still wearing full chain mail. He drowned before he got far.

Rather than being terrified, the soldiers at the lakeshore began calling out names, full of yearning and wonder. "Alice! Alice, how are you here? I've missed you so—!"

"Jane! Oh, and our dear daughters! I'll save you. I'll join you!"

"Ma! I can hear you. I can see you. Ma! Wait for me."

As if caught in their own bubble of obsessive focus, the soldiers didn't hear their own comrades right beside them. They could only see whatever had hold of their eyes and minds. In desperation and with no sense of self-preservation, they jumped into the water and swam away from shore. More warriors charged forward, trying to stop their fellows, but the transfixed men fought back, refusing any rescue. In moments, the would-be saviors were also captivated by some illusion and plunged to their own doom as well.

They stretched out their arms, several of them sobbing. "I thought you were dead. How can you be here?"

"I am coming for you."

Enoch had to save his men. "Retreat! Stay away from the lake." He stormed forward, knocking soldiers aside, shoving their shoulders, pushing them to the ground. "Are you fools? The water is dangerous. Get back!"

He bowled men over and called for more troops to rescue their comrades, to drag them away from the shore no matter what it took. "Don't look in the water!" He kicked others, heaved them aside, forced his way to the edge. It was madness, complete madness! He could not see what was attacking his troops.

When Enoch looked at the lake, even though it was churned by struggling bodies, he caught sight of a patch of smooth water, and just beneath the surface he saw submerged faces, heard voices that tugged at his heart. Gritting his teeth, he tried to force himself to turn away . . . but the woman's eyes caught him like a rabbit in a snare. He recognized her face, the familiar smile with its endearing chipped front tooth, her wavy brown hair, her arched eyebrows that had drawn him in when she first smiled at him, so long ago.

"Camille?" he whispered, and suddenly he could hear none of the commotion around him. He was interested in nothing else. This was not possible!

The very mention of her name strengthened the apparition. She reached up with delicate fingers, straining toward the surface of the water from below. "Enoch, my love. I've waited for you, waited forever."

He felt as if his entire body had turned to stone all over again. "Camille?"

"Enoch, why didn't you join me? You left me behind. It was so long ago!"

She was the closest thing to love he had ever allowed himself. Camille was a barmaid in a tavern in Orogang, and he saw her every time he returned to the capital city. She always had a warm bed for him, but he refused to marry her, because he was a dedicated soldier. He knew he would be gone for months or years at a time and would likely die on a distant battlefield; he was too fond of Camille to bind her like that.

Still, she swore herself to him, said that she adored him. They had two young sons, boys that Enoch barely knew, Aaron and Alex. As soon as he thought of them, the boys appeared beside Camille under the water. They had bright eyes, freckled faces, and curved noses, features that bore a hint of his own.

"Father, come to us," the boys cried in unison.

Enoch gasped. He couldn't stop himself from reaching forward. His heart ached. "Yes, I left you so many years ago. I didn't mean to." Although thousands of soldiers crowded in the basin around him, he heard nothing else, saw nothing but his loved ones shimmering beneath the mountain tarn.

"Come to us," Camille pleaded. "The Keeper wants you. You are long overdue."

The grizzled face of his father appeared beside Enoch's beloved woman and their two sons. The old man had shown him much, taught him many hard lessons in life. His father had always retained a sense of humor along with a sense of wisdom.

Enoch's world spun, and the deep water seemed to call to him.

The old man said, "You belong here in the underworld. With us."

Remembering his duty, Enoch dredged up a firm tone of command. He tried to keep his thoughts straight. "Who are you, truly? My father and family are long dead."

"Yes we are, and so should you be," young Alex said in an eerily mature voice.

"Come to us," Camille said again.

"Now that you and all your soldiers awakened, the Keeper has tasted your souls. He knows what he has been missing," Enoch's father said. "He knows what has been stolen from him for all these years. You belong in the underworld. All of you. With us."

Knowing his father's stern voice, Enoch flinched at the scolding.

Aaron said, "You should have been here with us centuries ago. Now the Keeper wants you."

All of them said in unison, "He wants you all."

With a remarkable effort, Enoch broke his connection to them. He squeezed his eyes shut and shook his head. He forced himself to lurch away and stumble back onto the shore, where he collapsed. The clamor around him returned with a rush of uncontrolled sound.

Staring up at the sky, he suddenly heard all the moans, the longing outcries from his soldiers. They were dying by the hundreds, sacrificing themselves to the lake, giving themselves to the Keeper.

"No!" Enoch dragged himself to his feet. His army was perishing before his eyes, countless ranks rushing into the lake. This was far worse than the meadow of poison flowers.

The rear divisions still arriving at the lake saw that something terrible was happening, but they didn't understand. Enoch pushed into the main encampment, bellowing commands in the voice that General Utros had taught him. "Do not listen! Do not look into the water. *Stay back!*"

He knew the ranks at the shore were lost, so many bodies already bobbing facedown in the water. He wept as he turned his back on the desperate pleas of his beloved family, but he refused to take the easy way out. He yelled at the nearest lieutenant. "Rescue the ones you can, but do not approach the water!"

The frightened soldiers passed his instructions along, spreading the warning like wildfire. Enoch grappled with his own men, pulling as many as he could away from the shore. Those who came too close looked in horror at the countless floating corpses, yet they did not comprehend the danger.

Tears poured down Enoch's battle-scarred face as he forced his army to skirt the lake and head directly toward the mountain pass. "Abandon camp! Keep riding! We cannot stop here."

He mounted his horse and led them away from the trap at a full gallop. Tens of thousands of soldiers followed him in confusion and terror, pushing on into the cold mountains. Enoch felt his heart turn to stone again as he rode higher toward the pass, wondering whether his entire army was truly alive, or if all these soldiers had actually died long ago and just didn't realize it yet.

CHAPTER 33

Weak from blood loss and utter exhaustion, Nicci fell into a sleep as deep as a coma. Mrra remained in the cool bedchamber, protecting her sister panther from danger. The big cat curled up beside her, and Nicci took comfort in the dense, soft fur, the powerful feline body.

The bloodthirsty zhiss were bottled up, dwindling and starving, and the Hidden People could at last reclaim their city and emerge into the sunlight again.

In the depths of her sleep, though, loud sounds reached her. Nicci awoke to turmoil inside the stone buildings. She sat bolt upright despite her lingering weariness. Mrra sprang to her feet and faced the splintered remnants of the door she had shredded with her claws in order to break free the night before. Nicci slid off the bed, her head throbbing with pain, her knees shaky. Thanks to hundreds of the biting zhiss, her pale skin was mottled with maroon blood blisters. She tried to shake off the fuzziness. "Come, Mrra. Let's go see."

With the cat loping along beside her, Nicci ran down the torchlit corridors toward the main entrance. The Hidden People were crowded at the high doorway, staring out into the daylight as if still fearful of the sun.

Crouching in the shadows, young Asha turned to her with an expression full of hope and desperation. "Nicci, we need your help!" When the girl clutched her arm, Nicci winced, feeling the bruises and bite wounds across her skin.

She felt intensely weary. "I already saved you. Have the zhiss escaped?"

A man nearby shook his head. "No, not the zhiss—an army! He's come back!"

She was surprised and confused by the statement. "What army?"

"A thousand soldiers bearing the emblem of Emperor Kurgan! Cyrus said it was General Utros." Asha hung her head. "He's dead now."

That made no sense. "General Utros is far away. Why would he come here?"

"This is his capital," said another man, hiding in his gray robes. "He has two sorceresses with him. Cyrus and a dozen followers went out to greet him, but the sorceresses blasted them to bones and ashes."

At this news, Nicci felt her strength return in a surge, though her ears still rang and her head throbbed. She worked her way past the drab people and stood in the towering doorway. "Two sorceresses?"

Out in the sunlight, she saw the glare reflected from countless shields, swords, chain mail, and armor plate. Hundreds of mounted troops filled the main plaza. Riding a black stallion, General Utros wore his distinctive horned helmet and golden mask. Beside him, dismounted, stood two bald women with designs painted on their skin.

Without hesitating, Nicci strode out into the bright sunlight to challenge them.

* * *

The stench of roasting flesh wafted into the air. Utros held the reins as he looked down at the gray-clad bodies his sorceresses had blasted. Now he needed new captives he could interrogate.

Ava looked downcast that she had disappointed her general. "Surely, they meant to attack."

Ruva said, "Look in the shadows. Many more are lurking here. They infest your city, what is left of it. We must eradicate them."

Fine swords were clutched in the blackened skeletal hands of the strange victims. Utros wondered if the furtive, gray-clad men were the remnants of some lost army left behind in the ruins. Wary now, he looked around at the great towers, the carved monoliths that depicted the exaggerated glories of Iron Fang. The city seemed more ominous now that the sorceresses had destroyed the first attackers—or were they merely emissaries? Curiosity seekers? They shouldn't have been killed so quickly.

He shouted out to the shadows. "I am General Utros, and I have returned to Orogang. If your emperor is not worthy, then I will be your new ruler."

His words were loud enough to startle pigeons from the high eaves. His soldiers flooded into the plaza, lining up their horses in ranks. He heard the jingle of tack, the rustle of leather armor, the sliding musical note of swords being drawn from scabbards as they waited in the ominous silence.

"Show yourselves!" Ava cried. "Bow down before General Utros."

Ruva muttered, "Like beetles hiding inside a rotted

log." In disgust, she looked at the blackened corpses on the flagstones in front of them. "We will eradicate them all so we can take back your city."

Since the pale figures seemed frightened of simple daylight, Utros decided they must be mere scavengers, human leftovers who did not belong in this glorious capital. Utros turned to his troops. "Break into companies and move through the major buildings. Sweep them clean. Round up those people. We will interrogate them."

He faced the still-imposing palace that had been Iron Fang's seat of power. He remembered the towers that stretched toward the heavens, the supporting buttresses, the arched windows that were now all bricked up.

The main palace entrance was open, though, and figures huddled inside. They must have seen Ava and Ruva blast the first group of emissaries, and he planned to strike greater fear in their hearts. He would ride his black stallion through the gates and directly into the grand throne room like a conquering hero.

Then one person strode boldly into the daylight, carrying herself with pride. Unlike the tattered gray rags that covered the others, this woman wore a black dress that clung to her shapely form. Her blond hair was raggedly cropped, and her piercing blue eyes stared at him as if his soldiers and sorceresses simply weren't there. She had eyes for him, and him alone.

"I was ready to defeat you at Ildakar, General Utros," Nicci said. "Now I will drive you from Orogang as well."

* * *

With the bright sunlight on her blood-mottled skin, Nicci dredged up all her strength. She didn't dare let Utros or his sorceresses see how drained she remained from the previous night's battle.

Ava and Ruva skewered her with their glare, and then the two raised their hands in unison, ready to attack. Nicci could sense the waves as they summoned their gift, and she readied her shields. She had every intention of destroying the twins, but her real enemy was the ancient general.

Nicci called back to all the downtrodden Hidden People watching from shadowed doors and windows. "Behold the man whose statue you revered, whose legends you told. General Utros." She glared at the blackened skeletons sprawled on the flagstones in front of his black horse. "Cyrus and his followers worshiped him, came to offer their swords to him—and he wiped them out. What will he do to the rest of you? General Utros is not your hero. He wants to subdue the Old World for his own gain."

"We thought you had vanished along with Ildakar," Utros growled at her. "Who are these people huddled in the shadows of Orogang? Why do they infest my capital city?"

"They are the descendants of those who overthrew Emperor Kurgan and claimed the city as their own." Nicci took another step closer. "You are not welcome here."

Ava and Ruva called on their gift, and an angry knot of clouds appeared over their heads. The wind whipped up, startling the horses of the ancient army.

Nicci called up an invisible shield to deflect their initial forays, though it cost her an alarming effort.

Showing no weakness, though, she didn't tear her gaze
from Utros. "If the great commander needs lackeys for
protection, then the legend of General Utros has dwindled indeed."

The twins snarled, curling their fingers to build another attack.

Utros halted them with a gesture. "I don't need them
to protect me, but I can let Ava and Ruva play." He released them.

On foot, the twin women glided toward Nicci like
reptiles on a hot rock. She met them with a smile that
was sharper than any sword edge. "You tried to kill me
and my friends, attacked me with my own hair." She
touched her ragged blond locks. "It's time I repaid you
for that."

With a thought and a push, she created wizard's fire,
a shimmering and searing globe in her hand, which she
hurled into the crowded soldiers in the plaza. The molten flash incinerated five of the warriors and threw the
remaining ranks into disarray.

Unexpectedly, the heavy doors of the stone buildings
swung open behind her, and crowds of Hidden People
emerged, angry at what they had seen and inspired by
Nicci's words. Shouting, they rushed out in a surpris-
ingly coordinated assault, carrying weapons from the
armory that Cyrus and his followers had maintained for
centuries.

The general's army swung their horses around in the
plaza, and their once-coordinated ranks faltered as they
faced ghostly attackers who swarmed toward them
from every building in surprising numbers.

Utros lifted his gold-masked face and shouted orders.
"Eradicate them! You outnumber the enemy ten to
one."

In a great clash across the plaza, the ancient soldiers fought the cloaked opponents, hacking them down. But more and more Hidden People emerged from the buildings, the force growing every minute.

Ava launched a wave of dazzling light at Nicci, whose shield deflected the blast. The effort made her stagger backward, though, and she shored up her defenses, trying to find more strength in her core as she pushed herself toward the twin sorceresses.

Ruva made a whiplike gesture with her arm, and the black thunderhead overhead swirled into an ominous storm. Nicci retaliated with a curtain of air that slammed the woman into her sister. The general fought to keep his stallion under control as it reared.

Facing the reckless charge of the Hidden People, the ancient soldiers broke ranks and fought in individual battles. Many wheeled their mounts and used the sharp hooves to strike down their pale attackers, while others hacked down with their swords.

The surging Hidden People stabbed the warhorses, chopped at the soldiers' legs, and pulled them from their saddles. The air rang with screams and the clang of weapons.

Amid the clamor, Nicci heard a primal snarl, and Mrra leaped into the fray. The big panther pounced on the ancient soldiers and tore out throats and ripped open chests.

Pushing forward, Nicci swept her hands apart and sent waves of wind that buffeted the mounted soldiers as if they were game pieces on a har'kur board. The Hidden People darted into the disarray with their sharp blades, while Mrra lunged in with fangs and claws.

Utros kicked his horse into a gallop as he charged to

the other side of the plaza. The twin sorceresses each sent searing lightning at Nicci, which she deflected. The ricocheting bolts shattered the flagstones. With her eyes on her real enemy, she focused on Utros.

Carefully manipulating her gift, Nicci found the stone resonance in a granite monolith that loomed thirty feet high above the general. The segmented column shuddered and wobbled as she moved the foundation stones. When she weakened the underpinnings of the column's base, cracks raced up through the bottom block and crumbled it into powder. The great pillar began to topple toward Utros.

He leaped off his horse and scrambled out of the way while the terrified stallion galloped off. With a tremendous crash, the monolith smashed into dozens of fragments, spraying rock splinters in all directions.

"You are mine, Utros," Nicci said, stalking after him. "Why bother to run?"

The general turned his golden half mask toward her and drew the long sword at his side. "Run? I will squash you."

As she focused on him, Nicci was caught unawares from behind when Ava and Ruva threw a combined blow of magic. The fabric of her black dress smoldered and burned her skin, but she extinguished it with a thought. Even though her legs shook with the exertion, she pressed forward. The air burned in her throat and nostrils.

As the increasing battle swirled across the central complex of Orogang, Nicci mentally sneered at the fallen statue of Emperor Kurgan, his arms and head broken off, the features scoured away by time. Not far away, the mysterious sliph well sat empty and silent among the other monuments, and she thought it might be fitting to throw General Utros down the bottomless pit.

Unified against her counterattack, the twins hurled more lightning at Nicci, but she strengthened her shields and turned to face them. Utros was just a man, no matter how powerful or legendary he might be. The two sorceresses, however, were genuine distractions.

Ava sprang onto the body of the Kurgan statue and called another flash of light that dazzled Nicci. Below her, Ruva stomped hard, pounding her heel to send a shock wave through the flagstones, which rippled across the plaza.

At just the right moment, Nicci leaped into the air and landed on the unstable flagstones after the wave had passed. She retaliated with a bolt of lightning, pure energy called from the sky. The twin sorceresses cast desperate shields that crackled and sparked against the barrage.

"I am stronger than you," Nicci said.

The twins retreated into the next plaza, and Nicci followed, vowing to eradicate them. Without his horse now, the general charged toward them, his sword drawn and ready to fight alongside his sorceresses. They gathered beneath the titanic Utros statue that loomed over the high square.

Ava and Ruva faced her, building their magic to defend their commander. Nicci concentrated the air into a single force, forged an invisible knife, and slashed sideways with a razor of air. Ruva thrust up her shield and blocked the brunt of the attack, though Nicci's unseen blade sliced a long furrow down her right arm. Ruva cried out in pain, and her sister responded by hurling a shock wave woven with a wall of fire.

Nicci dodged, and the magical hammer blow swept

past her and smashed the base of the Utros statue, cracking its pillar legs.

Ruva wailed to see fractures spread through the muscular stone legs. Both women screamed as the enormous statue toppled toward them. Utros and Ruva scrambled away from the impact area, but Ava darted in the other direction. She staggered two steps away as the stone figure thundered to the ground. Waves of dust and rock chips flew in all directions.

Ava stared, horrified, her mouth agape. "Utros!"

Nicci used that moment of vulnerability to call down another bolt of lightning, braided and twisted with both the Additive and Subtractive sides of magic. The fierce energy slammed into Ava like a bright and dark spear, piercing her chest, shattering her spine, and blowing out her back.

Ruva screamed. The agony and dismay in her voice nearly tore her throat open.

Nicci could barely hold herself up after expending so much energy. Her knees buckled.

Ruva bounded over the broken statue and grabbed her fallen sister. Wailing, she dropped to her knees and clutched Ava's body, holding her sister against her chest.

Next to the sorceresses, Utros raised his long sword, ready to kill Nicci.

In her last moment of life, Ava clasped her sister weakly with one hand, but her chest was burned open, and she sagged into death.

Nicci climbed back to her feet and summoned her gift again, created a ball of wizard's fire in each hand, and prepared to throw the pair of boiling suns at Utros.

Ruva was absolutely destroyed, emotionally wrecked. "No! You can't have him!" Wrapping her arm around her dead sister, she grasped Utros and squeezed her eyes shut, invoking some spell that Nicci didn't recognize.

With her last effort, Nicci hurled both spheres of wizard's fire, an insatiable blaze that could burn through any substance. Ruva and Utros didn't have a chance.

But before the fires struck, Ruva, Ava, and General Utros simply vanished, as if they had winked out of existence. The fireballs smashed into the broken plaza, but they burned only emptiness.

Chapter 34

As the three serpent ships prepared to drop anchor for the night, Bannon continued scrubbing the boards with a stiff-bristled brush, though he had long since removed any visible remnants of catfish blood and slime. With his ankle shackled to a pin in the deck, he had been on his knees for hours, and his hands were raw and bleeding. Several other slaves, including morose Erik, were tied on deck nearby, forced to watch him.

Bannon knew that if he could get free for only a moment, he would fling himself over the side of the ship. He could stroke across the river and hide in the thickets—if he made it to the bank. The Norukai were skilled with their bone-tipped spears, and one of the jagged weapons might skewer him before he made it halfway to the shore.

Then he wouldn't be able to help Erik and the other captives either. He had to find a better way.

In the thickening dusk, he saw a bright bonfire ahead. He heard a pounding drumbeat and loud voice as someone stood out on a spit of land, challenging the serpent ships. A lone woman stood silhouetted by the flames, lean and clad in black leather wraps. A morazeth!

At first he thought, he hoped, it was Lila, but he recognized the voice of Adessa, the cruel morazeth leader from the combat pits of Ildakar. Adessa had taken his best friend Ian as her lover and then killed him in front of Bannon. He would never forgive her for that.

But here she was, calling out a challenge to King Grieve. He hated Adessa, but she was certainly no worse than the Norukai.

Her challenge amused the scarred raiders, but Bannon knew they were fools to underestimate her. When the two raiders rowed a landing boat out to fetch her from the shore, others checked the bindings of the slaves on deck. Shipwright Gara grabbed Bannon by the hair and dragged him to the side rail. "Enough scrubbing for now. You can spend tomorrow scouring the deck. Again." Gara lashed Bannon's wrists together and checked the chain around his ankle, but she kept looking toward the serpent ship's bow, where King Grieve waited for his morazeth challenger to climb aboard.

Chalk pranced back down the deck, squatting next to Bannon. "She challenges King Grieve! She will grieve." He whispered close to Bannon's ear, "Blood on the deck, scrub, scrub! You'll see." Then he scuttled back to the bow, where Adessa faced the Norukai king.

She revealed the rotting head and set the hideous trophy on a barrel. Although decay had distorted the features, Bannon recognized Wizard Commander Maxim. "Sweet Sea Mother."

Ugly raiders crowded at the rails to watch the duel as Adessa and Grieve faced off in the flickering lamplight. The king let out an explosive laugh and lifted his heavy war axe while Adessa drew her short sword.

With their backs to him, the crowded raiders blocked Bannon's view, so he could see only glimpses of the

combat. All the Norukai were focused on the unexpected amusement of the battle. Meanwhile, the slaves
remained silent, huddled and trying to stay unnoticed
at the stern.

Against the jeering, laughter, and catcalls from the
rowdy Norukai, Bannon heard a stirring from the river,
a furtive splash along the hull. He heard a soft thump,
and realized that someone was climbing up onto the
ship!

He turned away to see a lithe figure clamber over the
rail and quietly roll onto the deck—another morazeth,
her skin covered with branded runes, her short brown
hair plastered to her head. Lila! A surge of hope set his
pulse racing. He nearly leaped to his feet, despite the
chain, but her gaze swung over him like the lash of a
whip. She held up a hand to silence him.

At the front of the ship, the Norukai let out a loud
cheer, and the clash of blades rang out.

"What are you doing here?" Bannon whispered. Optimism flared inside him.

"Don't be a fool, boy. I'm here to save you."

Adessa confronted the Norukai king, who looked
even uglier than many of the combat beasts she
had fought in the Ildakar arena. Maybe Grieve thought
his slashed cheeks and implanted bone spurs made him
more fearsome. Adessa just found them all the more
reason to kill him, which was what she had promised
to do. It would give Lila a diversion to free the young
swordsman, and Adessa enjoyed the task. Throwing
herself upon the Norukai king, she swung her sword,
letting out an explosive breath with the effort.

King Grieve was an ox of a man with a broad chest,

swollen muscles, and a sharkskin vest. He had the strength to wield his heavy war axe as if it were no more than a dagger. Despite his size, he showed surprising agility as he arched himself backward to avoid the point of Adessa's sword. The Norukai spectators whooped at the near miss.

Adessa put so much effort into her swing that she overbalanced herself when the weapon struck only air. As she caught her balance, the king smashed the side of her head with his iron-augmented fist. Her skull rang, but she managed to dance out of the way while he swung his axe at her.

Judging by their howls and laughter, the Norukai were convinced she would lose.

On top of the barrel, Maxim regarded her with jellied eyes. She could hear his malicious taunting in her mind, but the rotting head did not speak aloud so that others could hear. He was too devious for that, but she heard him laughing inside her head, louder than the rowdy Norukai. She shook her head fiercely, as if to drive away annoying gnats.

She blocked Grieve's axe with her sword, and even though her blade was much smaller, the blow deflected the king's weapon. After his big axe swept past, Adessa lunged with her right foot and kicked him in the abdomen hard enough to knock the wind out of him.

Enraged, Grieve swung his axe like a bludgeon, without finesse, but with enough strength that she barely avoided it.

Hooting and whistling, the Norukai taunted her by throwing slimy objects that splattered her skin. Fish guts. It was a common trick from desperate fighters in the combat arena, and she refused to let herself be distracted. She had faced altered bears, spiny wolves, and sand panthers without flinching, and Grieve was a monster just like the others.

She and the king smashed together again, attacking, neither managing to land a mortal wound.

The albino shaman darted in among the spectators, then flitted out of view again. The simpering man made her skin crawl, but she concentrated on Grieve while keeping her peripheral vision alert for treachery. She did not trust the Norukai to fight by honorable rules.

The king grunted again, straining with the weight of his heavy axe. His studded boot stepped on a pile of slippery fish guts, and he stumbled. The disorientation lasted no more than a heartbeat, but Adessa seized her chance. She raised the sword in her right hand, forcing him to defend himself, and with her left hand she snatched the small engraved wooden handle from her hip. The agile knife—the specific morazeth weapon used to cause intense pain in their victims.

Grieve regained his balance as she plunged in. He twisted his axe to block her short sword, exactly as Adessa had expected him to do. He wasn't watching the insignificant object she held in her other hand.

Adessa struck with the agile knife like a stinging bee and pierced him. The tiny blade was needle-thin, no longer than a knucklebone, but that was not where its power lay. She doubted he even felt the puncture through his sharkskin vest. Until she slid her thumb over the rune and activated the magic.

An overwhelming thunderclap of pain rocked through the Norukai king. Grieve snapped back, all of his muscles contracting with seemingly enough force to crack his spine. His scarred jaw dropped open in a yawning scream that was horrifying enough to shock the Norukai observers. They gasped in disbelief.

Adessa twisted the agile knife and continued to release the litany of pain. With this tiny weapon, she had made her bravest, strongest warrior trainees fall to their knees and sob for release. She pressed harder.

Then Maxim's head began to laugh. With the soft neck stump squished on the barrelhead, the hideous jaws stretched and the hollow, mocking voice slithered out. "You won't beat him. Come, join me in death, dear Adessa! That is where you belong!"

The voice was shocking, jarring. The Norukai were shouting, howling, demanding blood. Their king writhed under the pulse of the agile knife, and Adessa drove it in harder.

"You are weak, Adessa!" Maxim taunted. "You know it!"

She flinched, flung a poisonous glare at him. "Be quiet!"

In the instant she was distracted, somehow, even with the needle of the agile knife still inside him, Grieve grabbed her left hand. He squeezed her wrist with unbelievable strength, a vise enhanced by the desperation of pain, and crushed the bones, turning Adessa's hand and forearm to pulp.

A black thunder of unbelievable pain swirled behind her vision.

Somewhere in the background clamor, Maxim was laughing again.

Grieve grabbed her broken hand, snatched the agile knife from her mangled wrist, and shoved her backward.

Adessa tried to lift her short sword, but the big man knocked her flat to the deck. Her head struck the wooden boards, and more pain rang through her skull. She raised her knee to push him away, but Grieve had the agile knife now. He could not unleash the pain spell, and as a weapon it was no more than a cobbler's awl, but he stabbed her throat, then stabbed again, puncturing her jugular. He viciously dragged the small blade across her neck.

Adessa felt warm blood splashing out. In a distant part of her mind, she realized that her struggles were growing weaker.

He hammered the tiny blade down, pounding and pounding like a butcher tenderizing meat. With a constant wordless roar, Grieve stabbed her countless times in a fury. Hundreds of puncture wounds mangled her face, throat, and chest into a horror of ripped flesh. He kept stabbing long after she was dead.

The Norukai howled with victory.

As soon as Lila dropped onto the deck, Bannon realized that he had always expected her to come. Optimism hadn't failed him. While Adessa and Grieve fought at the front of the ship, Lila darted over to him. Then Bannon saw that she had a familiar sword strapped to her back—Sturdy! For the first time in many days, genuine joy filled him.

Lila used her knife to slash the rope around his wrists. He twisted until the cord snapped, and she set to work on the manacle around his ankle. Bannon whispered to her, "You have to free the others too. They are my friends."

The slaves groaned. Some were panicked, others distraught. Erik pulled against his chains.

Lila turned her hard gaze up to Bannon. Sweat ran down the side of her face, mixed with the drying river water. "I don't have time, boy. I did not swear to protect these others. I came to rescue you."

Inspecting the cuff around his ankle, Lila followed the chain to the pin screwed into the deck boards. With Sturdy still strapped to her back, she dug into the wood with the point of her dagger, trying to uproot the pin.

At the bow, the Norukai roared louder than before, and Bannon saw Adessa fall. King Grieve was upon her, stabbing and stabbing. Blood flew everywhere, spraying high.

Bannon groaned. "Sweet Sea Mother, he just killed her!"

A flicker of shock and disbelief crossed Lila's expression. She hesitated only a moment, then she worked harder at the chain. "I thought I would have more time." She did not look up as Grieve continued mutilating the fallen morazeth. She was breathing harder.

Bannon reached out. "Give me Sturdy! Please, I can help."

The raucous Norukai were still celebrating Grieve's victory, but a pale figure scampered down the deck toward them. Bannon looked up as Chalk saw him, then spotted Lila as well. The shaman suddenly jumped up and waved his arms, shouting, "Another fish! We caught another fish."

Even with their shouts of victory, some of the Norukai heard Chalk's shrill outcry and turned to see what had excited him.

Lila yanked at Bannon's chain, tugging as she tried to rip the anchor bolt loose. Giving up all attempt to remain quiet, she hacked at the deck board. Trying to help, Bannon strained against the manacle, gritting his teeth.

Chalk capered up to them, shouting for the Norukai to come. "Here! Here! Another fish! Come quick!"

Lunging up, Lila punched the shaman hard in the face, doing anything to silence him. Her blow knocked him backward as if he'd been thrown from a catapult. Chalk crashed to the deck, squealing in pain and disbelief, pressing a palm to his split lip. He curled up into a ball and wailed. Bannon felt an unexpected guilt at seeing the albino hurt, but he pushed it away. They had no time!

At the front of the ship, under the lantern light, the rotting head of Wizard Commander Maxim began to shine with a sickly greenish glow. Its jaws moved and the gelatinous eyes gleamed, as if rejoicing in the death of Adessa. The dead man let out a chilling nauseating laugh, mocking them all and horrifying them.

Even Bannon heard it, and the sound made his skin crawl. The Norukai backed away, breathless and uncertain. They stared at the head. When Maxim finished laughing, his remaining skin liquefied and slid down the skull, oozing into a puddle on the barrelhead. Then even the bones crumbled into fragments.

But while Chalk kept screaming, the Norukai ran down the deck, saw Lila, and roared in alarm. Many scarred raiders thundered toward them, their weapons raised.

Lila drew Sturdy from its lashings on her back and held the blade in front of her. She crouched as if facing arena monsters, ready to defend him with her life. Bannon kept straining on the chain, planting his feet, but he couldn't rip the bolt free.

Erik and the other slaves also pulled against their bonds, shouting, desperate to get away. Bannon thought that if they all fought back at once, some of them might even break free. But his hope dwindled as the howling Norukai closed in.

King Grieve stormed forward, his boots crashing on the deck, his skin and sharkskin vest splashed with Adessa's blood. When he saw Chalk sprawled on the deck, nursing his bruised face and whimpering, he let out a roar of rage.

For an instant Lila was ready to face all the Norukai, refusing to admit failure, but Bannon groaned. "You'll die, Lila. You can't save me." He knew it was the right thing to do.

Lila struggled with the impossibility, but when her expression changed, Bannon realized that she knew he was right. She growled, "Not this time." As the Norukai charged in to kill her, she vowed, "I will be back for you, boy." She flipped herself over the side of the ship, and Bannon heard the splash as she plunged into the river.

Ignoring the bound slaves, the Norukai snatched up spears and raced to the rail, looking for the ripples as she swam away. Some hurled their weapons into the water as if Lila were a channel catfish. They missed.

Seething, Bannon knew they wouldn't kill her. Lila would get away, and she would return for him.

Miserable and shaken, King Grieve bent next to a whimpering Chalk, rocking his gangly friend back and forth. The shaman poked at where blood dripped from his split lip and swollen cheek. Though covered with gore, the king tenderly touched the albino's smashed face. "So sorry, Chalk. I should have protected you. I should have known Adessa was part of a plan. They tried to trick us."

Grieve rose ominously to his feet and glared at Bannon, whose hands were free though the chain still pinned him to the deck. The king stalked forward. "That woman hurt my Chalk. Now I repay the favor."

Grieve swung his iron-plated fist like a boulder into Bannon's face, nearly dislocating his jaw. Stars erupted through his mind as he crashed against the side of the ship and slumped to the deck, stunned.

"You deserve to die," the king growled. "But I will give you pain instead."

CHAPTER 35

The general's army clashed with the Hidden People in the streets of Orogang. The regimental commanders rallied their troops to face the ragtag inhabitants, who put up a surprising resistance, but Utros's well-trained soldiers needed no further orders to slaughter the enemy.

More and more pale, gray-clad fighters rushed out of the dark buildings. While the disciplined army used well-practiced battle maneuvers, the Hidden People fought with a frenzy that disrupted the rigid plans. It was like two thunderheads colliding with a sound of thunder.

Nicci struggled to recover after Ruva and General Utros vanished along with the body of the dead sorceress. The clamor was deafening, and she heaved hard breaths, looking at the shattered marble face of the toppled Utros statue. She had expended so much of her gift that she could barely stand. Nicci brushed stone dust from her black dress as she dredged up energy within herself. She had to help the Hidden People in their fight before they were slaughtered. Though her gift was weak, she touched the daggers at her waist, knowing she could always fight with knives.

As the battle raged in the main plaza, the ancient soldiers did not at first realize that their commander had disappeared. They simply kept massacring the poorly trained refugees who threw themselves recklessly upon them. Bodies lay strewn across the plaza, but Nicci realized the Hidden People were inflicting numerous casualties themselves. They were hardened to sacrifices, and they were determined to win this fight.

But they stood against a thousand well-trained warriors in full armor.

Sword fights swirled through the streets, between buildings, under the imposing archways. In hand-to-hand combat, the fighters dodged the rubble of toppled monoliths and shattered statues.

An ancient soldier lurched in front of Nicci, raising his bloody sword and leering at her, as if he assumed she would be an easy kill. He slashed, intending to gut her, but she deftly avoided the strike, slipped in under his backstroke, and jammed one dagger between the man's legs. She drove upward into the soft but crippling target, and the soldier collapsed with a squeaking wail. She could have taken the time to kill him, but decided to let him lie there screaming as she ran onward. She had to turn this battle and save the Hidden People.

Mrra let out a roar that shattered even the din around them. Thanks to their spell bond, Nicci felt the big cat's joy, the hot iron taste of fresh blood in her mouth. The sand panther drove a soldier to the ground and tore open his leather armor. With blood dripping down her muzzle, Mrra let out an even louder roar, a summoning.

Sleek, powerful feline forms bounded in, more than a dozen sand panthers in a new bestial army that struck primal fear into the enemy. The ancient warriors screamed as the huge cats bore them to the ground and ripped them open. The panthers somehow knew to avoid the gray-cloaked Hidden People and attacked only the soldiers of General Utros.

Nicci strode in among the enemy, wielding a bloody dagger in each hand. Desperate men cried out for the general, and subcommanders demanded orders, but their leader could not respond. The mood changed like a shifting storm wind as rumors started to spread that Utros had left them. The mounted army started to fight with an increased intensity that bordered on violent desperation.

The poor Hidden People had just been released from their heavy burden with the zhiss, and now it looked as if they would all die before they could reap the benefits of their well-deserved freedom. Nicci felt a flare of anger and sadness as she fought her way back toward the towering palace. Somehow, she would rally the poor people and help them fight such an overwhelming enemy. Nicci did not accept an impossible situation.

She paused to assess what remained of her gift. When she felt the magic resonating within her, she knew that even diminished she was still a powerful sorceress. She could help the Hidden People and save as many as possible.

As she passed the empty sliph well, Nicci called on a few threads of her gift and created a small sphere of wizard's fire in her palm. She paused there and faced the fighting, ready to make a difference, to help the Hidden People win. Pulling on her magic, she tossed the ravenous fire. The looping, twisting flames flared, then swelled into a greater flash as the fireball engulfed three enemy soldiers before fading. She had hoped for more.

She struggled to find enough of her gift to create more

fire. From behind her, she heard an unexpected rushing sound of gurgling liquid that pushed upward.

She whirled to face the low sliph well in the plaza, where a roiling pool of quicksilver rose above the mouth, shaping itself into an icily beautiful human figure. Nicci was taken aback. "Sliph!"

Looming above the well, oblivious to the clamor of battle, the silver woman glowered at Nicci.

Why had the sliph come *now*? "I called you many times," Nicci said.

"I heard, but I am not required to heed you." The sliph's face pinched into an angry expression. "I accept your terms. I will know about my Emperor Sulachan. Tell me everything."

"Not now, sliph! I will summon you later."

"Now," the sliph said. "I will take you back to Serrimundi as you demand, and you must tell me about Sulachan. That is the bargain."

Nicci raised a shield, trying to repel the sliph, but it wasn't enough. "No, sliph! Not now."

"Breathe!" The quicksilver wave plunged down to engulf Nicci and dragged her down into the well.

CHAPTER 36

O nce the group descended out of the rugged mountains beyond Kol Adair, Nathan felt heartened. General Zimmer led the horses at a faster pace across the now-fertile valley. "On this terrain, we can get even farther ahead of the enemy army."

Nathan rocked in his saddle as the horse moved alongside the prelate. "The sooner we get to Cliffwall, the more defenses we will be able to create."

Verna mused, "The scholars have been cataloging the materials for years, and the memmers are sorting the vital missing pieces. By now they must have found many books containing deadly spells."

Nathan looked across the bowl-shaped valley, remembering what it had been not long ago. Those lakes and streams, the green expanses, the lush trees, had been devastation for as far as he could see: cracked dry terrain, volcanic glass, broken fissures, all caused by the Lifedrinker, a hapless gifted student who had triggered more magic than he could handle. "It's not *finding* the deadly spells I'm worried about, my dear prelate. It is *controlling* the awful magic that can be released."

Verna looked doubtfully at the verdant landscape in front of her. "I know the stories about the Lifedrinker,

but Victoria restored all the vegetation with a rejuve-
nation spell she found in the archives. Wasn't the world
saved because of her?"

Nathan clucked his tongue. "Dear spirits, who told
you such nonsense? Victoria was as dangerous as the
Lifedrinker, but in a different way! She also triggered a
spell she didn't understand, and her explosive vegetation would have engulfed the world. We stopped her
only at a terrible, terrible cost." His heart suddenly beat
harder, as if Ivan's dark remnants relished the painful
memory. "The poor girl Thistle sacrificed her heart's
blood to give Nicci the weapon she needed."

His long white hair blew about his shoulders as he
stared toward the desert highlands where they would
find Cliffwall. "Even if we do find powerful spells, will
we be strong enough and wise enough to use them
properly? That is what worries me the most."

The maze of canyons had hidden Cliffwall for millennia. The young scholars Oliver and Peretta now
led the way, eager to get back home. The horses clattered along the stony floor of the wide entry canyon.
Ahead, the towering tan walls closed together into what
looked like a dead end, but it was merely an optical illusion, with a hidden gap wide enough for two horses
to travel side by side.

The party worked their way through the gap, turned
left then sharply right, and emerged into a wide sheltered canyon that looked like a paradise.

Captain Trevor, the leader of the remaining Ildakaran
escort guards, let out a dry chuckle. "I don't know how
we ever found this in the first place. Our party was stag-

gering, weak, starving. We thought that Renn had led us astray."

Oron looked around him in amazement. "If the knowledge here is as extensive as you suggest, then we will find some way to defeat General Utros."

"In that case," Leo said, "the final result justifies all sacrifices."

Lady Olgya's face pinched in a bitter expression. "Says a man who has made no sacrifices! You didn't even have a wife or family in Ildakar. What have you lost? My son was *killed* by those soldiers!"

Oron grumbled, "As was mine."

Nathan didn't comment, since those two young men, Jed and Brock, had been despicable people who had caused Bannon great pain. But grieving parents would remember a child however they wished.

He raised his voice as they rode into the Cliffwall canyon. "The important thing is that General Utros and his army must never find this place. Cliffwall's greatest defense is its camouflage. Those thousands of enemy soldiers are on a forced march, and no doubt starving. They should walk right past these canyons."

"Then we could spring a trap," said Perri, the youngest of the gifted defenders from Ildakar. "If we can figure out how." She had been a shaper back in the city, manipulating trees and vines into interesting topiary shapes. Her gift, though powerful, was likely too subtle to be useful in any large-scale attack against General Utros.

"The Cliffwall records may suggest dozens of new methods of attack," Verna said. "We could create a powerful gifted army of our own."

As they proceeded forward, Nathan drank in the

view. A stream ran along the canyon floor, flanked by fruit and nut orchards. Sheep grazed in open meadows, and terraced gardens lined the steep hillsides. People tending their flocks, working in their gardens, and fishing in the stream all looked up to watch the party enter the canyon.

The high, sheer walls were pocked with natural alcoves and overhangs, some of which held a personal dwelling or two. The largest overhang held a veritable city of knowledge. High up the cliff wall, a grotto contained buildings made of adobe and hardened brick, some structures so tall they reached to the curved rock ceiling. Stonemasons had added beautiful ornamentation on the façades and carved archways over the grand doors of the main archive.

Oron shaded his eyes and peered at the vertical cliff with a skeptical expression. "How do we get up there? Is that supposed to be a path?"

"There are stone steps, narrow but safe," Oliver said. "You can climb them, if you have no fear."

Peretta added, "And anyone who is afraid should not look in the books and scrolls stored there."

Oron let out a snort in response to the implied insult.

They dismounted at the base of the cliff beneath the great alcove, and General Zimmer's soldiers led the horses away to join the soldiers who had remained camped in the canyon to guard the archive.

Nathan set off up the steep zigzagging path chiseled into the sheer stone. He adjusted his sword so that it hung on the opposite hip as he climbed the precarious trail. Not only did he look forward to studying the ancient documents, but he also wanted to patch and clean his clothes, repair a crack in his boots, and replace his frayed laces with new ones.

Verna toiled up the path behind him. When they finally reached the alcove high above the canyon floor, Nathan paused to rest, breathing hard.

Several Cliffwall scholars came running out to greet the returning party. "Nathan! And Prelate Verna!"

He recognized Gloria, the matronly leader of the memmers, who had committed every word of countless written volumes to memory. She was a round-faced woman with short dark hair in an unattractive cut. Beside her walked Scholar-Archivist Franklin, a studious, serious man in charge of all the students inside Cliffwall.

The Sisters of the Light who had stayed behind also emerged from the main building. "You've returned," said Mab, one of the Sisters. "You've been to Ildakar, and now you're back. Tell us what you saw."

Another Sister, Arabella, asked, "Was Ildakar as grand as Renn claimed? Where is he? Did he stay behind?"

Nathan drew a deep breath. "We have a tale to tell indeed, but I'm afraid it is not good news. Once more, we must search the knowledge in Cliffwall in order to defend the whole world."

CHAPTER 37

Light sizzled around General Utros, a crackling web that swallowed him and tore him away from Orogang, the fighting soldiers, the wailing Ruva and her dead sister. His body went numb, completely blinded.

Buffeted, weightless, tumbling in a void. He screamed, his skull twisted like the lid of a jar, and his thoughts howled, detached. His bones elongated, tangled, flailed like limp ribbons. The air, the world—existence itself— folded around him, then refolded, and he could hear a scream outside him and within, wrapping around his thoughts.

Ruva had caused this—he knew it. The sorceress had released some extreme form of magic to save them, but it had plunged him here. The light around Utros flared brighter until it became a wall of molten pain that hung and then shattered.

The world unfolded again, and he spilled out.

Reality crystallized in front of him, a landscape of mountains and sky. He staggered forward two steps, then his legs simply could not support him anymore. Utros crumpled to his knees, sprawled forward, and caught himself with splayed hands. He couldn't breathe.

His chest had been squeezed as if under an impossible weight of rocks.

Nearby, Ruva appeared in a slash of lightning-intense glare. She clung to the corpse of her twin sister. Smoke and the stench of burned flesh wafted up from the blackened crater in the middle of Ava's chest.

Disoriented, Utros looked up. His gold half mask had slid down his face to cover one of his eyes, and he adjusted it so he could see. The horned helmet tumbled onto the ground beside him, clattering among the stones and patchy alpine tundra. In front of him he saw countless armored figures, an encamped army. Having seen the flash of light from Ruva's spell, they turned to him and suddenly recognized their commander.

"General!" one man cried. "General Utros has returned!"

He sucked in a deep breath of biting air. He glanced around, noted the mountain peaks, and realized that his huge army had already crossed the highest mountains and was marching down the western side of the range.

This didn't make sense. "But we were in Orogang. How did we get here?" He turned to the grieving sorceress, whose arms were still wrapped around the limp body of her twin. "What did you do?"

Ruva made inhuman sounds of sorrow. Her sister's pale arms dangled, her fingers curled in death. Ruva rocked her back and forth, rubbed the markings of soot and dried blood into a muddy smear of sadness. Utros shook her shoulders with both compassion and command. "Ruva, tell me what happened! How did we get here?" They had to be many hundreds of miles from Orogang.

The sorceress let Ava's corpse drape across her lap. The dead woman's eyes were merely blackened sockets. Nicci's surge of combined Additive and Subtractive lightning had raged through Ava's heart and blasted out of her eyes.

The nearby soldiers rushed closer. As word was passed, lieutenants came running, and he recognized First Commander Enoch. Utros had only a few moments to get answers from the sorceress. Utros shook her again. "What did you do to us? You left a thousand soldiers in Orogang in the middle of a battle. Speak quickly!"

A growl of vengeful fury boiled in Ruva's throat. "I couldn't leave you there to die, beloved Utros. Nicci killed my sister. I had to get us away from there, had to save you. Ava . . ."

"But how? How long have you known how to travel like this?"

"I didn't," she said. "I didn't think it would work, but I had no choice. A long time ago, Ava and I learned of a dangerous distance-eating spell that would erase all the miles between one point and another. I knew many anchors here among the soldiers, their keepsakes, even the sword and tack worn by First Commander Enoch. I pulled us here, though I thought we might die in transit." Tears smeared the paint she had marked on her face. "I did it for you. My sister was dead, and I had to save you."

He felt a pang of sympathy for Ruva. As twins, their bodies fused at birth, the two had shared an immeasurably intimate connection, their gift entangled, their thoughts practically identical. Even though they had been cut apart, Ava and Ruva were inextricable. And now one of them was dead.

"I am sorry for you." He knew the horrible pain of losing his beloved Majel, but this must be far worse.

"You have always been loyal. I never questioned your service. You and your sister were the best among us, the finest."

"I'm sorry I left the army behind," Ruva said. "Those soldiers are without a commander in an empty city."

Utros tried to console her. "They are a thousand of my best soldiers. If they can't wipe out a handful of refugees living in the shadows, then they do not deserve to be part of my army." He smiled gently with half of his face. "In effect, I now have a strong military contingent in Orogang, and once my soldiers have flushed out the vermin, they can reclaim the capital in my name. It is an accidental victory." He stroked her cheek, used the moisture from a fallen tear to smudge the paint in a straight line. "We just inadvertently placed the first occupation force to rebuild the empire."

The sorceress's expression softened. "I cannot take us back there. The distance spell was dangerous. I nearly lost us in the void, and then we would never have returned. I even used some of Ava's gift as her spirit dwindled."

Utros lifted Ruva to her feet. Her dead twin lay on the tundra grasses. "I don't wish to go back to Orogang. I am here where I belong, with my army. I have to lead them across the Old World."

First Commander Enoch rushed up to them, his expression a mixture of relief and unanswered questions. He dropped to his knee, pressed a fist to his heart, and bowed before his general. "You are here! How is it possible?" He looked in horror at Ava's corpse. "What happened, sir?"

"I am back. That's what matters," Utros said.

Other subcommanders and curious soldiers rushed up, eager to hear the story. They dropped to their knees.

Utros raised Enoch to his feet. "Report, First Commander. Tell me what happened while I was away."

Enoch briefly looked aside, nervous and distressed, then steeled himself to report. "Your army has crossed the mountain pass of Kol Adair, sir, and we are descending to the foothills. The soldiers keep marching, but they are very hungry. Even with the spell."

"They will survive." Utros looked at Ruva, and the sorceress gave a brusque nod.

"But we have suffered many losses while you were gone, General." Enoch hesitated, then explained about the field of poison flowers and then the high mountain lake where so many troops had been lured into the water by their dead loved ones.

"Keeper and spirits," Utros whispered.

"I do not blame them, sir," Enoch said. "I felt it too. I saw my Camille, our two sons, even my father. I barely broke away myself. We lost more than a thousand fighters before I pulled the army away."

Utros absorbed another blow to the countless soldiers who had followed him under Iron Fang's banner.

Enoch continued. "The Keeper wants us, sir. He knows we've avoided him for fifteen centuries, and now we are marked, more than a hundred thousand souls. We all should have gone to the underworld long ago. They are effectively dead, but still marching."

Utros felt a flare of anger. "The Keeper can't have us yet. I need my army, and we still have a war to win."

W restling with grief while also stoking the fires of revenge, Ruva washed the body of her sister and used a razor-sharp knife to shave any hint of hair from her cold body, not a strand left behind.

Ruva applied herself with reverence to this last task for her sister. She placed small round stones in Ava's burned eye sockets, and wrapped boiled white cloth around her sister's breasts to cover the black hole where her heart had been. When Ava was clean and pure again, Ruva made fresh pots of paint, blood red and pitch black, and painted new designs across the pale flesh, then reproduced the symbols across her own body.

When Ruva proclaimed that she and her sister were ready, General Utros commanded two of his soldiers to carry the bier and place it carefully atop an unlit pile of wood that would serve as a funeral pyre. Except for the white wrapping across the burned hole in her chest, the slender woman lay naked on the kindling.

Letting his arms hang at his sides, Utros turned to Ruva. "You are my sorceress now. I trust you to be strong."

"I cannot be as strong without my sister," Ruva said. "But I would do anything for you."

"As would we all, General," said First Commander Enoch.

His soldiers raised their voices in a shout of affirmation. Utros absorbed it all, and when the cheers fell silent, he called for torches to light the pyre. The dead willows caught fire quickly, and the flames grew to an intense blaze.

"The Keeper will have to be satisfied with Ava for now," Utros shouted to his army, "for the rest of you are needed here!"

The pyre roared so bright and hot that Utros had to step back. Transfixed, Ruva stayed close to the blaze as the fires blackened her twin's flesh and destroyed the painted markings. Ava's skin cracked as the fire consumed her. Her face fell away, leaving only a skull with two pebbles inside the eye sockets. Though the intense heat reddened Ruva's own skin, she refused to retreat. Utros grasped her arm and pulled her away, pressing the slender woman's shoulders against his chest armor.

As the orange fire devoured the remnants of Ava's body, the pyre shifted and the flames swirled as if a whirlwind had caught the embers in a circle. The color changed from a bright yellow to a sickly green as Ava's bones fell apart into the core of the fire. A translucent green image rose from the flames, insubstantial and shimmering.

The soldiers gasped in superstitious terror. Ruva let out a low moan that sounded like surprise, not fear. The apparition sharpened, became more intense, and Utros recognized the dead sorceress.

"Ava, you aren't in the underworld!" Ruva cried.

"I cannot go." Ava's spectral form brightened to stand out against the bonfire, where her blackened bones crumbled into the embers.

Utros held on to Ruva with his powerful arms, although she struggled to break free and throw herself into the flames. He needed to know Ava's purpose. "Has your spirit decided to remain with us? Did the Keeper allow it?"

"My sister and I are twins," said Ava's shimmering form. "We are bound together, heart and mind and soul. We share the same Han. The Keeper marked both of us. As infants, after our bodies were cut apart, we two died briefly and traveled through the veil, but a healer brought us back to life and snatched our souls from the underworld. The Keeper knows us. He is waiting for us . . . but he needs both of us." The shimmering spirit hovered before Ruva. "My sister must pass through the veil with me. I cannot go alone."

Ruva looked longingly at her twin, but pressed her shoulders back hard against the general's chest. "No, I must remain here. You know it."

Ava laughed. "And therefore, I must remain! You are an anchor that keeps my spirit here in this world. I am trapped between life and death." The greenish spirit flitted directly through First Commander Enoch, shocking him, and then she circled the soldiers, who scattered in panic. She wafted back through the fire, entirely unharmed. "I am a spirit unfettered by physical form. I can go wherever I wish, see whatever I like."

She swooped closer to Utros. He was not afraid, but intrigued. Her spectral face was very close to his as she hovered before him. "And then I can report back here." She smiled. "Beloved Utros, I will be your perfect spy!"

CHAPTER 38

When she plunged into the river from the stern of the serpent ship, Lila swam deep. The shouting Norukai hurled their spears into the water, but she didn't head toward the shore as they expected. Rather, she stroked powerfully down the current and moved far ahead of the three anchored ships. When her lungs were about to burst, she surfaced again and forced herself to exhale with only a whisper of sound. Far behind, she could still hear the raiders raging at her escape. She suspected Bannon would pay a price for her failure, but she knew he could endure it. She had made him tough.

She wrapped her arm around a floating log, and it kept her above the surface as she drifted downstream. With the serpent ships anchored for the night, Lila realized she would be able to cover a great distance if she simply floated on the current all night long.

Then she would be far enough ahead to make another attempt to rescue Bannon.

Resting, she let her thoughts drift just like the brown water around her. Lila tried to process how she had failed, and how Adessa could have been so brutally defeated. Lila felt dismayed and empty; although she had seen many trainees and morazeth sisters die in combat, Adessa had been different, seemingly invincible. She had fought the Norukai king so Lila could rescue Bannon. And they both had failed. Adessa was dead, and the young swordsman remained a prisoner.

"I will not give up on you, boy," she muttered as river water lapped against the floating log.

Locking her arms and legs around branches, Lila dozed for an hour or two and woke when her feet brushed against a large slimy creature beneath her. Startled, she grabbed her dagger. The sword was still strapped to her back, but she couldn't get it in time. As faint dawn suffused the eastern sky, she could see large forms swimming next to her, each smooth tan body as large as a canoe. The channel catfish lumbered along, not predatory, only dangerous because of their size. Lila drew her legs against the floating log, and the catfish swam past her into the widening channel.

In the light of sunrise, Lila looked around and saw how far she had traveled during the night. The sight struck her with awe, then alarm.

The widening river sprawled into a diverse delta of numerous channels and sandbars. Beyond the land's end, she saw the estuary spill into the ocean, an open expanse of blue water that extended to the horizon. Lila had never seen such a sight in her life. The Killraven River ended here.

She released the log and drifted in the water, swimming to a low sandbar covered with tufts of grasses. Lila had gotten a substantial head start on the serpent ships, but they would come soon, on their way to the sea. Once the big ships passed the estuary and reached the open ocean, Lila knew she would never be able to catch them. This was her last chance to free Bannon.

She had to stop them.

For half an hour after Lila escaped, King Grieve coddled Chalk, touching the shaman's battered face, wrapping a big arm around his scrawny shoulder. Consoling his albino friend seemed to make him even angrier. "I'll make them all grieve."

Chained to the deck while the ships remained anchored during the night, Bannon could not escape King Grieve's fury. The big man strode up to him, his heavy boots ringing loud on the boards. His war axe was still stained with Adessa's blood spray.

The bolt holding Bannon's chain remained set in place, and when the young man tugged on it, he felt the sharp scabs and bruises of the manacle around his ankle. Big Erik sat nearby in the darkness, knees drawn up to his chest, shoulders hunched with contained sobs.

Bannon steeled himself, sure that Grieve meant to lop his head off, but Chalk scuttled over to them. The shaman was miserable from his smashed face, but he touched the king's arm to stop him. Grieve shook him off and stood over Bannon, raised the weapon. The young man glared at him, knowing he couldn't escape, and the Norukai king brought down the heavy weapon with a hard thunk into the wood of the deck, smashing the plank so he could uproot the anchor bolt.

Chalk bobbed his head and clapped his hands in delight. "The axe cleaves the wood! The sword cleaves the bone!"

Grieve uprooted the chain and dragged Bannon by

the legs toward a pool of light from one of the lanterns. "Scrub the blood from the deck and get rid of the dead woman. Feed her to the catfish."

Grieve kicked at Erik. "You! Help him!" The big man shuddered and moaned, paralyzed.

"I'll do it myself," Bannon said, climbing to his feet and grabbing the brush. "Leave my friend alone." He realized it was the wrong thing to say as soon as the words passed his lips.

"You have no friends," the king said.

Dropping the axe, he wrapped his big hands around Erik's head and pressed hard against his temples and cheeks. The captive's eyes went wide, and his mouth dropped open in a wail. Grieve's muscles bulged with the effort as he snapped the other man's head sideways in an abrupt vicious turn. The bone cracked, and Erik's feet jittered on the deck, clanking the ankle chain.

Bannon felt sick, his knees weak as he forced himself to remain standing. Other Norukai crowded close, making sure he did not try to dive over the side, but Bannon was paralyzed by the sight of his dead friend.

King Grieve wasn't finished, though. With an additional grunt he twisted the head around even more, snapping and grinding the neck bones, stretching the skin and tendons. Erik's head faced entirely the wrong direction. With another severe jerk, Grieve twisted again until the neck popped and tore, and then he wrenched Erik's head off his shoulders, uprooting the spine with the ragged cord still dangling down.

Grieve shoved the limp body onto the deck boards. "Now you have another mess to clean up."

The remaining slaves whimpered, but Bannon refused to reward the king with any reaction. He clenched and unclenched his fists, feeling murderous rage toward

Grieve and all Norukai, as well as dismay that he had let his friend down. If only he had a chance . . .

With an offhand gesture the king tossed Erik's head overboard, and Bannon heard it splash into the dark river where Lila had vanished more than an hour ago. If she came back, the young man imagined he and the morazeth together could kill a dozen of the ugly raiders . . . but it wouldn't be enough.

"Clean up the woman's body," Grieve sneered. "I'll dispose of this garbage." Seeming to take pleasure in the labor, he raised his axe again and brought it down in an abrupt stroke that struck off Erik's foot just above the iron shackle so he could drag the body from the chain.

Chalk let out a high-pitched laugh. "The axe does cleave the bone!"

Bannon knew that the albino had saved him, staying King Grieve, but he could have saved Erik, too. Chalk's eyes were bright as he capered around, distracted.

Grieve heaved the headless body over the side of the serpent ship. Eager to help, Chalk ran up, grabbed Erik's severed foot, and flung it into the river, following the larger body with a smaller splash.

"Feed the fish!" Chalk cried. "Make them grow big."

Bannon hardened his heart with the certainty that someday he would be free and someday he would kill King Grieve.

Moving stiffly with pain, he went to the bow, where Adessa's disfigured body lay on the deck. Her face, throat, and chest were like pounded meat. The king thought he was punishing Bannon by forcing him to see the bloody morazeth leader, but Bannon had hated Adessa, too, although he felt no elation at seeing the woman dead. He couldn't understand why Adessa would have been any part of Lila's plan to help free him, but she had provided a distraction that gave Lila a chance, though not enough.

Bannon slung the morazeth leader's mangled body over his shoulder and grimaced when he felt the wet pulp of her skin, the oozing blood and tissue. She felt light, empty, for such a fearsome warrior. The Norukai sailors watched, amused, as he rolled her overboard into the darkness.

"Feed the fish!" Chalk cried. "Big fish."

With a queasy stomach, Bannon turned to Maxim's collapsed skull and sloughed, rotten flesh. He shuddered as he remembered the unmistakable maniacal laugh, the taunting voice of the dead. He feared the slain wizard commander's spirit might return.

Bannon upended the barrel and dumped the mess overboard, where it joined Adessa's body in the river.

Many of the Norukai lounged back and snored for the remaining hours of the night, though edgy guards stayed close to Bannon. He concentrated on scrubbing the blood and washing the deck clean with buckets of river water. The work wasn't much different from cleaning fish guts and slime, but this was the smeared remnants of human beings.

As if keeping him company, Chalk pestered him for hours, even if his words were slurred due to his split and swollen lip. Bannon did his best to ignore the bothersome shaman, though each time he saw the scars from the myriad bite marks on the pale skin, he shuddered from the ordeal the outcast had endured.

After sunrise, when the deck was scoured clean five times over, the Norukai tied Bannon next to the other slaves again, and Chalk found a spot beside a wooden crate, where he curled up and went to sleep.

When the morning brightened enough for them to see

the channel ahead, the Norukai raised their anchors and stretched the dark sails to drift down the river again. The slaves sat quietly under the hot sun, searching for remnants of hope. If they tried to speak to one another, the Norukai would beat them.

Near noon, the crew grew visibly excited when they could see the estuary ahead, the widening mouth where the river spilled into the vast open water.

"I can't wait to be out on the ocean again," Gara said, then let out a mournful whistle. "My ships were made for the open sea."

With longing in his heart, Bannon remembered spending time on sailing ships, even the doomed *Wavewalker*. As a boy on Chiriya Island, he had watched the graceful vessels sail off to places he could only dream of. He had always wanted to sail the seas, and now he was a captive of the hideous raiders. He had no hope of escape, unless Chalk could help him. . . .

As the raider vessels cruised into the delta, shouts of surprise came from the bow. Norukai hurried to the front of the ship. Some of the raiders guffawed and joked, pointing over the side. Bannon strained against his bindings to see what had drawn their attention, but too many burly bodies blocked his view.

King Grieve stood by the carved serpent figurehead, and he let out an angry snort. "I can kill her just as easily as I killed the last one. Go get her."

Out in the widening estuary where sandbars and hummocks confused the direct route to the ocean, a woman stood alone on a sandbar in the middle of the river, waiting for the serpent ships to arrive.

Lila.

* * *

When Bannon watched the Norukai bring the new prisoner on board, she was trussed like an animal killed in a hunt. Her wrists and ankles were bound, as if the raiders feared her, and with good reason. They dropped Lila heavily onto the deck, and she smothered her grunt as her head struck the wood. She glared at them in defiance.

When she saw Bannon, her stony expression softened and her eyes lit up. Chalk cringed and scuttled away from the woman who had struck him.

Grieve bent down to relieve Lila of her dagger, then—gingerly—her agile knife. "You won't be using these again." He threw both weapons over the side.

Next, he pulled the sword that was bound to her back, holding up Sturdy. Bannon's heart surged at seeing his trusty weapon. He had bought the discolored blade from a swordsmith in Tanimura. Nathan had trained him in its use aboard the *Wavewalker,* and Bannon had killed many enemies with it, including countless Norukai. He strained against his bonds. If only he could get the weapon, his familiar blade—

"Ugly sword," Grieve said. He unceremoniously threw it overboard into the river.

Bannon bit back an outcry. Sturdy! The sword tumbled and spun in the air before it splashed into the deepening water. The serpent ships sailed on, past the estuary toward the open sea.

Bannon slumped back. Sturdy was gone, sunk to the bottom of the river's mouth.

Lila managed to sit upright, and Chalk pranced over to her, reluctant to approach the morazeth. His cheek and mouth were swollen, puffy with blossoming bruises, and blood from the split lip caked his pale mouth.

Glancing at the shaman's damaged face, Grieve

glared down at Lila. "This is for what you did to my Chalk." He slugged her face hard, knocking her to the deck with blood pouring from her smashed nose and split lip. Though Lila didn't make a sound, Bannon groaned in anticipation of what he knew was to come.

The serpent ships left the coast and headed out to sea.

CHAPTER 39

After their reunion at Cliffwall, Nathan and his companions prepared to defend the world. They didn't have much time.

Even the staunchest fighters could not hope to drive off the gigantic army, should Utros find the isolated archive, so their best defense lay in remaining hidden in the maze of canyons. On a forced march to the coast, General Utros would have no reason to explore these side canyons, so the scholars should be safe while they planned.

As he stood outside in the open alcove in front of the main building, Nathan regarded the prophecy building that now lay slumped and melted against the far wall, its windows scarred over like wet clay. It had been destroyed by a foolish student who accidentally released a "Weeping Stone" spell without understanding how to control it. Nathan sighed at yet another reminder of the dangerous knowledge in the archive.

A knot of dread formed in his stomach as he considered so many naive and untrained scholars ransacking the archive for equally powerful magic. What if another eager but foolish scholar unleashed a dangerous spell that got out of hand? He, Prelate Verna, and the Sisters of the Light would have to serve as a check before anyone used such destructive magic.

He stroked his chin as he gazed out to the green canyon, the orchards, the flocks of sheep. These isolated people had vanished from the world thousands of years ago, during the great war. When Sulachan declared that all magical lore be rounded up and destroyed, many valiant wizards had secretly stockpiled old books and scrolls, preserving the information here in the wilderness. Now, perhaps that knowledge could be used to defend against General Utros.

Nathan sighed. Every time one terrible enemy was vanquished, another appeared—a discouraging thought. But maybe he should look at it the other way around. For every enemy that threatened the world, there would always be defenders like himself, Nicci, Richard, and Kahlan to stand against tyranny, proving to be stronger than evil, again and again.

This time would be no different.

Inhaling another breath of fresh air and solitude, Nathan turned back to the main archive building, which contained far too many books to read. Somewhere, there would be at least one good solution.

Inside the vaulted library chamber, glowing lights hovered above study tables, illuminated by simple spells that the young novices used for practice. Scholars sat at individual desks or at long tables piled with books. They all searched for new ideas, some unorthodox spell that could help stop the ancient army. Gloria distributed volumes for her avid memmers to peruse. Traditional scholars searched volume after volume, categorizing the books so that the Sisters of the Light could locate relevant subjects for more careful study.

Nathan was impressed by how engrossed they were in their search. The men and women bent over faded words, compared notes, and deciphered near-forgotten languages. The air in the chamber seemed to throb with the intensity of their thoughts.

Verna looked up from a long scroll spread out on the main table. Novice Amber and Sisters Mab, Sharon, and Arabella sat close to the prelate, sharing books and indicating passages they found of interest. Seeing him in the doorway, Verna raised her voice. "Can you read the documents by standing all the way over there, Nathan? Your eyesight must be extraordinary."

"I was pondering, my dear prelate." He came in and seated himself on the bench beside Amber, and the prelate handed him a stack of books as if she were a schoolmistress. "We haven't reviewed these yet. Of the five hundred tomes we studied today, we set aside fifteen that are worth a second look. It is hard work."

"Well, well, fifteen are better than none." He opened the cover of the first book, which was filled with nautical charts. He wondered how such a book had ever found its way so far inland, but he doubted it would contain anything they could use against the marching army. He set the tome aside.

For the next several hours, Nathan fell into a routine, studying spines and titles, occasionally recognizing an author. Some books were written in the alphabet of Ildakar, which he had learned from Elsa during their stay in the city. Some languages were incomprehensible to him, so he returned those books to the stack in hopes that someone else might recognize the writing. Several books were written in High D'Haran, and one volume sent a tingle through his skin. He leaned closer. "This is in the language of Creation."

"That bodes well. It must be extraordinarily powerful," Verna said. "If you can read it?"

Nathan took that as a challenge. "I am somewhat versed in the language of Creation, but it requires a great deal of interpretation."

He spent an hour on that book alone, while the scholars and the Sisters cataloged, studied, and discarded dozens of volumes. Finally, he admitted defeat. "Too much of a challenge, even for me." He clucked his tongue against his teeth. "I was adept at constructed spells, but these words have an unknown foundation. If only Richard were here! That boy was quite skilled in working constructed spells, far beyond my talents."

"Yes, Richard was the best student ever, the only war wizard born in thousands of years." Verna closed a green leather-bound book, which sported a prominent dried bloodstain. "But we don't have him now. We have only ourselves. And we have all this." She gestured to the crowded shelves that lined the walls of the library, as well as the countless tunnels and archive vaults, the satellite buildings, even the innumerable sealed chests preserved by spells long ago. "That should be enough."

"We just need to find out how, my dear," he said.

Alone in the small austere chamber they had assigned him, Nathan fell into a deep sleep, still exhausted from the long and arduous trek. His mind and heart felt bruised from the loss of dear Elsa. Ildakar was gone, and he didn't know whether Bannon and Nicci were alive or dead.

He tossed and turned on his narrow pallet. In his dreams he went back to Ildakar, but he felt a darkness around his memories. His heart pounded like a drum inside his chest, and he sank deeper into the dream. Sub-consciously, he realized that he wasn't looking through his own eyes.

Nathan saw himself in the combat arena, but his body felt different, solid and muscular. He brushed the front of his vest, finding not his usual ruffled white shirt, but the pelt of a sand panther . . . a sand panther he himself had skinned after killing it. After *Ivan* had killed it!

The chief handler's heart thundered in his chest. Ivan had been a cruel man who enjoyed torturing the beasts he created. He would beat them into submission, but he valued them, if only because they served as his killing machines.

Still sleeping, captured by the unwelcome dream, Na-than felt a rush of exhilaration as he remembered ha-rassing a huge, caged combat bear. Fleshmancers had created the beasts for the arena, and Ivan's gift could control the creatures' rudimentary brains. He remem-bered jabbing the bear with a sharp stick, making the monster crash into the iron bars of his cage. It had claws that could rip a horse apart.

Deeply asleep, Nathan stirred, tried to fight off the nightmare. Ivan was dead, mauled to death by his own animals. The man's heart had restored Nathan as a wiz-ard, but it was *Nathan's* gift, and *Nathan's* heart now! Not Ivan's.

Some lingering part of the chief handler's spirit brought back memories of tormenting monstrous bulls with branched horns, spiny boars with razor tusks. Ivan had wrestled each beast himself before turning them loose in the arena against their victims.

As Nathan dreamed, his hands flexed, and he smelled blood and dust in the air. He poked and prodded three sand panthers until they lashed out at him with fangs and claws, but Ivan just laughed and drove them away. In the dream, Nathan saw the sand panthers turn on him, snarling. They bounded closer, ready to tear him apart—

He woke up, sweating. He clenched his hands, appalled at what his heart remembered, and he realized that a part of him had enjoyed the torture. It was not a real part of him, though, just some leftover contamination from the chief handler's heart.

"Stay away from me. Get out of my head!" With an effort, he drove Ivan's presence away, and the dead man faded to whispers in his mind and in his heart.

Shaking, knowing he would never go back to sleep, Nathan went to the small desk and took out his life book. He opened it to the last few blank pages, where he would write down his real thoughts, his real adventures. That was what he wanted to remember.

CHAPTER 40

T he silver whirlwind of the sliph swept Nicci away from Orogang. She had been so desperate to leave, had tried repeatedly to summon the sliph, to no avail. But now she couldn't leave the city, not in the middle of the battle! If Nicci wasn't there to help the outnumbered Hidden People, Utros's army would conquer the ancient capital. All of the people would be slaughtered.

Yet the sliph had her, filled her, carried her along. Nicci struggled to stay where she was, but she couldn't break free. The molten silver rushed into her mouth and nostrils, plunged into her lungs, abducted her. She didn't want to go! She felt as ineffective as a small child battering at an adult in frustration.

Nicci lost track of time and distance. She was helpless, and not in gentle hands. This rebellious sliph was malicious. In transit, Nicci experienced the primal fear of suffocating, drowning. She tumbled along, disembodied.

Finally, after an infinite yet unknown amount of time, she hurtled back to the real world, and there was nothing calm about their arrival. The sliph burst out of her well at the temple in Serrimundi, and the metal froth boiled up over the lip, dumping Nicci onto the ground.

She sprawled onto the flagstones, retching to purge the substance from her lungs, mouth, and nose. She scrambled to her knees, glaring back at the well, and shouted, "Why did you take me? I did not wish to travel now!"

Orogang was on the other side of the land. Even without General Utros to lead them, those thousand regimented soldiers would make short work of the gray-clad refugees. She thought of Mrra and her sand panthers against the ancient warriors, and all those poorly trained Hidden People who fought for their lives, defending the ruins of the city that had been their home.

Nicci glared up at the shifting metallic sliph that loomed up from the well. "I called you repeatedly, but you were silent. Why now? Why did you take me when I was needed in Orogang?"

The creature's expression was like a thunderstorm as it grimaced in anger, and her hair flowed and squirmed like silver lava. With high cheekbones and thin lips, she had been a beauty in life, but now she looked blank and inhuman. "Because I wished to." The sliph sounded petulant. "I never wanted to taste you again, nor serve you. You are a traitor. You tricked me."

Nicci rose to her feet and faced the sliph without fear. "I served my own cause, and your cause was long gone, a failure from thousands of years ago."

"So long as I exist, the cause is not dead." The sliph's sculpted metal garment flickered and shifted. The molded silver of her cheeks hardened, and her mouth twisted in a sneer. "Now you will tell me what I need to know. I fulfilled your demand. I brought you to Ser-rimundi. Tell me about Sulachan!"

The sliph grew more powerful, more terrifying as she drew silvery material from the depths of the well to swell her form. Her metallic locks of hair thrashed like twisted whips.

Seeing her, Nicci remembered the huge carving at the entrance to Serrimundi Harbor, the Sea Mother, protec-tor of the Old World, a hard yet benevolent goddess that many people along the coast revered. The Sea Mother looked exactly like the sliph. No doubt in some forgotten past a superstitious city dweller had seen the sliph, imagined some kind of deity, and created a whole religion around that misconception. But Nicci knew the sliph was just a being that had been altered by ancient wizards, not a goddess.

Nicci kept her gaze locked on the gleaming woman. "I will tell you about Sulachan. I fought him myself, and I helped bring about his downfall, but it was Lord Rich-ard Rahl who finally destroyed him."

Distraught, the sliph loomed and listened as Nicci told the known history of Sulachan, how he had forged the People's Alliance and commanded his wizards to create an army of subhumans to fight the New World, and how he was eventually defeated, bottled up behind the great barrier.

As she listened, the silver woman's expression roiled and her shoulders slumped, but then she straightened with a bitter anger. "If Sulachan was dead three thou-sand years ago, then how did he return? Why was he not victorious?"

"He was resurrected with some of Richard Rahl's blood, thanks to a traitor named Hannis Arc. Sulachan returned with an army of soulless half people, but they were all wiped out. Defeated completely." Obligated to fulfill her promise, Nicci described the last war in the Dark Lands, how the armies of D'Hara had fought against the undead hordes, and how Richard Rahl had finally destroyed Sulachan beneath the Garden of Life in the People's Palace.

Her voice had an edge of hard satisfaction as she wrapped up the tale. "Sulachan was vanquished, hurled back into the underworld. Lord Rahl was a war wizard. He changed the underpinnings of the world using the language of Creation, and Sulachan was too weak to beat him. He failed completely." Her voice rose as she found more energy, more anger and satisfaction. Nicci crossed her arms over her chest. "Sulachan is dead, never to return. Your cause, the People's Alliance, is no more."

The devastating news was the only weapon Nicci could use to punish the sliph for what she had done. "Your cause is not only ended but it is useless. It was always useless. Sulachan's plan was doomed to fail from the beginning. You are the only thing that remains of it."

The sliph cringed at the information, as if the words whipped her with barbed lashes. The quicksilver face stretched, melted, twisted, and then her mouth widened in a distorted and horrific snarl. "You are lying!"

Nicci stood before the well, adamant. "You know I'm not. You hear the truth in my words. You gave up your life for nothing all those years ago."

The metallic fluid brightened as if it had become white-hot, and the amorphous molten shape changed as the beautiful woman transformed into a ferocious demon. Her body enlarged and her two arms elongated, stretching into tentacles that struck down with hooked

claws. Nicci dove to the flagstones and rolled, dodging
the blow, but the sliph shifted her entire form, forsak-
ing her human figure. Four more quicksilver tentacles
boiled out of her torso.

"Yes, come travel with me and never return!" The
hooked tentacles lashed at Nicci. "I will drag you down
and keep you within me forever. I'll drown you and
crush your lungs so that you will be as dead as my master Sulachan."

A silvery arm wrapped around Nicci like a twisted
iron bar, but she summoned her gift to flood the silver
form with heat until it ran like hot liquid. She broke free
of the appendage and ducked under it, pulling herself
away. Her black dress was smoking, and the skin on her
arms reddened with burns.

Nicci backed away, giving herself just enough time to
create wizard's fire. She threw the blazing sphere at the
sliph, but curtains of silver folded around the fire and
swallowed the destructive flame. The metal body bubbled and twisted, but somehow absorbed the energy.

Nicci retreated from the sliph well until she reached
the wall of the empty temple. The silver tentacles
stretched toward her, as flexible as hot wax and as hard
as steel. The tentacles slammed down, trying to crush
Nicci, but she dodged again. The blow shattered the
stones on the temple floor, and the backlash from another appendage struck a figurine of the Sea Mother inside the temple, smashing it into splinters of stone.

The tentacles grew spines as they whipped past Nicci.
She called sharp bolts of lightning and blasted the sliph,
searing jagged holes through the quicksilver, which
shifted and sealed again. A tentacle wrapped around
Nicci's arm and squeezed tighter than a manacle, while
another surrounded her waist, winding so tight that she

couldn't breathe. The mass of appendages pulled her back toward the well. "I will drag you down, and you will never breathe again!"

As Nicci fought, the malleable sliph could reshape herself and recover from any damage. She had already used so much of her gift battling Ava and Ruva, and before that the zhiss cloud had weakened her. Nicci was spent, but she had to find strength or she would die. She realized she had only enough power left for a single strike, but she didn't dare waste her last chance on another failure.

As the tentacles dragged her closer to the well opening, Nicci found a different target and decided to gamble, hoping it would be her best chance to free herself from this monster. She used the destructive energy to make the ground shake and shift, then unleashed a final heavy blast of lightning—but not at the sliph. Instead, she struck the circular stone wall around the well, blocking off the deep hole. The explosion came from several different directions, and the stone blocks tumbled in. The barrier collapsed, and the well opening fell in on itself.

The sliph shrieked as the walls crashed down like an avalanche. The fallen blocks severed the quicksilver tentacles, lopping off three of them, and the metal appendages dropped loose onto the cracked temple floor. Wailing, the main body of the sliph retreated by plunging down into the endless tunnels. More blocks fell in and closed over the top of the well. Breathing heavily, Nicci crawled forward and fused the edges to hold the stones in place.

She dropped to her knees, but she wasn't done yet. She raised her hand and used her gift to reshape the unstable stone blocks, softening and smoothing them so they formed an impenetrable lid to seal the sliph well forever.

She slumped in utter exhaustion while her thoughts swam.

Something cold and metallic seized her leg like the grasping hand of a dying man. She kicked out to break free. The three severed tentacles flopped about like headless snakes. They were discolored now, no longer bright silver, but tarnished. The twitching slowed, and the writhing tentacles finally fell motionless, no longer metal, but an oily black mucus that oozed between the cracks in the flagstones.

Nicci climbed to her feet again and heaved deep breaths. The pale yellow light of daybreak filtered through the temple of the Sea Mother. She had gotten back to Serrimundi, as she wanted, although she had left Mrra and the Hidden People behind. And now she couldn't ever get back to Orogang in time to help them. The sliph well was completely sealed, and she knew she would never travel in that manner again. She could not say whether the sliph herself was dead.

Nicci was stranded in Serrimundi. But there was another war to prepare for.

She heard quiet weeping and gasps of misery behind her, and she turned, ready for another battle. Her black travel dress was tattered, her blond hair a tangled, sweaty mess, but she was *Nicci*, Death's Mistress, and she could defeat anyone else who threatened her.

Five terrified supplicants stood just outside the temple. They had come at dawn carrying baskets of fruit and fish as offerings, which they had dropped as they watched Nicci battle the frightening silver apparition. Now the supplicants stared at the shattered statue, the collapsed well.

"The Sea Mother," one of them sobbed. "You killed the Sea Mother!"

"Your Sea Mother was not what you believed her to be." Nicci hardened her voice and strode to the entryway. "Now, take me to the harborlord."

CHAPTER 41

The Cliffwall scholars worked all day, every day, poring over the wealth of documents. The kitchens served the scholars their meals at the library tables so as not to interrupt their frantic searches. With the army of General Utros marching relentlessly over the mountains, they had little time.

Cliffwall banked everything on the hope that the archive would remain hidden, since no one in the ancient military force knew it was there. But with a threat to the entire Old World, Nathan didn't just want to hide. Somewhere in this vast treasure trove of magical lore they would find something to stop General Utros from conquering the cities and lands of the Old World.

Nathan and Verna moved through the corridors that honeycombed the mesa to a cavernous document storeroom. The rock-walled chamber had high shelves filled with books, some piled haphazardly, others neatly arranged. He smelled the dust, the paper, the leather. Inside the chamber, he could hear workers sorting, shelving, discussing what they found.

Stepping inside the door, he ran his fingers along the spines on the first shelf. His nails made a clicking sound from cover to cover to cover. "The sheer number of volumes is exhilarating, my dear prelate." He gave her a wry smile. "Perhaps if I were imprisoned here for a thousand years, I might be able to grasp it all."

"One man for a thousand years," Verna said, "or thousands of scholars working together. We can put in the same number of hours in far less time. But if each person's knowledge is separate and incomplete, how will we know which pieces to put together?"

He stroked his chin. "Dear spirits, so much to organize. We know how powerful the right spell could be—and how dangerous."

"We don't have the luxury of being cautious," Verna said. "If we find something that might work, we have to hope we can control it. I'm confident in my abilities, and you never had any doubts either." She looked intently at Nathan. "In fact, the Sisters of the Light were terrified of you."

"Terrified? Prelate Ann was never fooled. She would come and keep me company even when I raged with my visions of prophecy. Ah, I miss her."

Just inside the doorway of the document-storage chamber, a heavyset man with a fringe of hair hunched over an open volume on a tiny table. As the scholars came to him with books, he transcribed the titles in his ledger. His quill swirled like a bumblebee as he scribbled the letters, dipping like a stinger into the inkpot and writing another line without ever mistakenly letting a drip of black fall onto the page.

Young men and women scurried from shelf to shelf, arms laden with volumes, moving with a hush that seemed natural inside such a sacred library. The room was lit only by an illumination spell, since candles or torches might ignite all the paper tomes and scrolls.

One spindly man carried a load of books stacked up

to his nose, while his fellow scholars removed volumes from his pile and arranged them on shelves. A flustered, mousy woman pushed a cart past them with volumes that belonged in a different storeroom.

Scholar-Archivist Franklin guided a team of novices along with Sisters Rhoda and Arabella. Franklin's robes were rumpled, and his eyes were bloodshot and shadowed. When he saw Nathan and Verna, he flashed a relieved smile. "I'm glad to report significant progress. We have brought the books containing powerful spells here to this chamber." He sighed and gestured to the creaking shelves. "This is where you start, your best bet. Once you've finished reading all of these, we will bring more."

"We will get right to it," Nathan said.

"I hear you've already found the Weeping Stone spell that melted the prophecy archives," Verna said. "The one your student couldn't control."

"Elbert was a fool to attempt it," Franklin said. "Not power-mad or ambitious, but untrained and not inclined to consider consequences."

"Too foolish even to know how great a fool he was," Nathan said, clucking his tongue. "That is the most dangerous kind."

The prelate was more intrigued than frightened. "We should make note of such a powerful spell. It must be based on braided magic tied to the fundamental structure of stone. It could allow us to melt a mountainside."

"Melt a mountainside? Against General Utros?" Nathan felt uneasy. "And what if you can't stop the spell once it gets started?"

Verna pulled a faded gray book off a shelf and looked at it, but she was distracted. "It is still worth considering, if we should need it."

Franklin showed them an ornate urn of glazed blue porcelain sitting on a shelf. "We found this in Elbert's quarters after he accidentally melted the prophecy archive. I decided to keep it next to the documentation of the Weeping Stone spell." He removed the lid of the urn, and Nathan and Verna peered closer. "This was a necessary component of the spell-form."

Nathan saw fine grains at the bottom of the urn, white sand with an unusual prismatic shimmer. "Dear spirits, that's sorcerer's sand!"

Verna nodded. "I can see why that would be a key to triggering a great spell." She looked worriedly at Nathan. "If Elbert used half an urn of sand without knowing what he was doing, no wonder the walls collapsed! So much power! We're lucky he didn't destroy the whole archive."

"So this isn't just plain sand?" the scholar-archivist asked. "We were going to dump it out as we cleaned up the clutter."

Nathan gasped. "Oh no, don't do that!"

Verna relieved Franklin of his burden, protectively holding the urn. "We'll keep this ourselves. Sorcerer's sand is powerful and rare, but even a few grains can act as a catalyst for releasing enormous magic." She secured the porcelain lid in place. "This is very important."

Two scholars shelving books on the far side of the chamber cried out in surprise. Nathan heard the muffled clatter of volumes tumbling to the floor in an avalanche. A young man bolted around the end of the shelves. "A spirit! A spirit in the archives!"

Hearing more shouts, Nathan and Verna ran toward the last row of stacks, where another cascade of disturbed books thumped to the floor, pages strewn everywhere. The wooden shelves rattled. A second scholar tripped on the hem of her robe and sprawled, knocking an armful of scrolls onto the floor.

A shapely but insubstantial female figure flitted toward them in a shimmer of green glow. She was hairless and painted with symbols, but she seemed only partially there, a whisper of a human being.

Nathan's boots slid on the smooth stone floor as he skittered to a stop. "You're one of the general's sorceresses!"

Her image wavered, and her face shifted from beauty to hardened vengeance. Her flickering form became razor sharp. "Such a lovely archive. Such interesting information."

"Begone from this place!" Verna shouted, calling power into her voice. The other Sisters of the Light joined her, staring at the image.

The spectral image just laughed. "I found you! Now I know where you hide." Her voice had the hollow coldness of a winter wind.

"Which one are you?" Nathan demanded, stepping forward to face the green-tinged spirit. "Which sorceress? Ava or Ruva?"

"I am the dead one. I am Ava." She flitted to the ceiling before she swooped down, unbound by gravity or any physical form. "Nicci killed me, but I am still here. I will help destroy you all!"

As the glowing figure lunged toward them, Nathan lashed out with his gift to defend them, though part of his mind rejoiced in the knowledge that Nicci was still alive and had fought the sorceress. As the spirit came closer, he called a wind that blasted directly through the insubstantial form and succeeded only in rustling the piled books on the shelves behind her.

"I am here, but not here!" Laughing, Ava swooped through the bookcases, but made herself substantial enough to knock volumes loose and send them flying. Nathan and Verna ducked as Ava pelted them with a hailstorm of tomes. One sharp-edged book struck Franklin in the forehead, and he collided with the shelves beside him.

Ava taunted as she rose up, her green shimmer flaring brighter. "I will tell General Utros about this magical archive and guide the entire army here. My sister will help him ransack it and seize all the knowledge." She seemed amused. "You are all doomed."

Alarmed, Verna called up a shield. "Block her, Nathan! We can trap her, bottle her up." Sisters Rhoda and Arabella also called on their gift and joined the effort. "We don't dare let her escape now that she knows where Cliffwall is."

Nathan helped weave an invisible wall of magic, but Ava's spirit was too swift and insubstantial. She slipped through them, darting along the lines of shelves as more young scholars scattered in panic.

Sitting at his little table, the portly recorder lurched out of his unsteady seat as the spirit blasted past. His inkpot spilled all over his ledger, and a fountain of black liquid sprayed in the air as Ava swooped by. She careened through the archive shelves like a phantasmal battering ram, knocking the books into disarray. The wooden shelves creaked and bent, on the verge of collapse.

Ava's spirit reached the stone wall and vanished directly through the rock, leaving only the chaos of settling papers and slumping books in her wake.

Franklin groaned in dismay as he looked at the storm

of disrupted volumes. Books lay scattered with broken spines. Many pages had torn, the covers sheared off.

Nathan looked at Verna in deep concern. "We can't remain hidden anymore. General Utros knows where we are."

In camp after another day of marching through the foothills, the general stared at his campfire, trying to read messages in the flames. He felt the sadness of all he had lost, the loyalty to his emperor, the illicit love of an empress, and the fresh grief of Ava's death. Utros shouldered the responsibility for those many thousands of loyal soldiers who had died in his service. Was conquering even a continent enough?

Ruva squatted by the fire, hardened and disturbed by the loss of her twin. When Ava's spirit had manifested itself, Ruva's broken heart had twisted with an even more intense determination, and now the painted sorceress stared into the flames at the general's side, both lost in their own thoughts.

The flames flared, and Ava's insubstantial figure rose from the fire, perfectly formed as in life, identical to her sister except for the mirror-image scars on their outer legs. Ruva gasped and opened her arms in an embrace. Ava drifted close and matched Ruva's position, overlapping as if the two of them were fusing their auras into one united being.

General Utros faced the oddly doubled figure, awaiting the report of his spectral spy. Seeing the incorporeal image, First Commander Enoch also hurried over from his nearby tent.

When Ava spoke, Ruva's mouth moved in tandem.

Their words overlapped with an eerie resonance. "Beloved Utros, I have vital information. I searched the land, I followed connections, and I found the wizard Nathan Rahl and his infuriating companions."

Her expression brightened with hungry anticipation. "They have a hidden archive of powerful lore within a few days' march. The countless books are filled with incredible magic, devastating spells that Ruva could use to help you subdue the land. If you conquer Cliffwall, General, we could take all that information for ourselves." Her shimmering face smiled. "It would guarantee your victory over the land."

This was something Utros had never considered. An arsenal of forgotten magical lore? "Can you tell us where to find this archive?"

"Yes, beloved Utros," the two women said in harmony. "It is hidden in a side canyon, and they have almost no defenses. They rely on camouflage to protect themselves. We would easily take the archive."

Utros smiled. Even here at night, he kept the gold mask in place as part of who he was. He looked up at Enoch. "Cliffwall is our new target, First Commander." He stared around at all the bright campfires like winking eyes spread across the hills where his army had camped. "Once we overwhelm the archive, we will strip it clean."

CHAPTER 42

The sea was wide open around the Norukai ships as they lost sight of shore. Bannon took no joy in the expansive sight, even though it reminded him of how he and Ian had once stood on the beach at Chiriya Island, watching the ships sail by. The two had dreamed of seeing the world, though Bannon mostly just wanted to escape his father.

Now he dreaded where King Grieve was taking them, to the main Norukai islands.

Belowdecks, the oar master pounded on his drum, and the unfortunate slaves chained to the benches pulled at the oars to drive the serpent ships faster than the sluggish breeze.

After being beaten unconscious at the river mouth, Lila had been tossed to the deck near Bannon, her ankle also secured with a chain, the chain that had once imprisoned Erik. Now the morazeth lay bruised and battered, a captive just like him. Bannon couldn't understand why she had allowed herself to be captured. She had caused it! It seemed a foolish risk.

As she lay motionless under the hot sun, he studied the symbols that marked her skin. The runes protected her against magic, but they did nothing against the brutal Norukai. Her body was mottled with bruises.

Lila finally groaned, and her eyelids flickered open. She snapped awake in an instant, fully conscious and alert. She thrashed against the ankle chain, and her wince told Bannon just how much pain she must feel. When her gaze locked on to his, she visibly relaxed. "So, I succeeded then. My memory is . . . fogged."

"You certainly drew their attention." The words bubbled out of him, rising in intensity. "That was a foolish stunt! Why would you do that? We're both prisoners. Now you're in as bad a place as I am."

"I am in the same place as you are," Lila said, as if that were reason enough. "That was my intent."

"But *why*? What can you hope to achieve here?"

"More than I could achieve if these ships sailed off and I never saw you again. It was the only way I could stay with you. Now we have a chance."

Bannon hung his head, and his long hair drooped over his face. "A chance? You are maddening. I don't understand how you think."

She frowned. "It is perfectly obvious. The Norukai ships were going out to sea, and that was my last opportunity to intercept them. If they had sailed into the ocean, how else could I rescue you?"

"This isn't much of a rescue," he said.

"Obviously, I am not finished yet." She winced again as she shifted her body to inspect her bruises. She flexed her fingers, ran her tongue over the caked blood on her smashed lip. "I will heal." She strained at the bindings around her wrists until blood stained the knotted rope. "I can work myself free eventually, but the ankle chain will be problematic."

He looked across the open water, but he could no

longer see the coastline, only endless ocean. "I have no doubts about you, Lila. I know what you're capable of."

"Of course you don't have any doubts. I have never given you any reason to."

Now that she was helpless, he feared the Norukai would drag her across the deck and rape her, although most of the raiders seemed to prefer their own beefy women, and their nightly lovemaking on the open deck sounded more like a brawl. Still, he had seen Norukai men ravish three of the female Ildakaran captives, treating them so brutally that two were mad and one was dead and tossed overboard. They thought of their slaves as nothing more than "walking meat." Lila was a beautiful woman with a lean and shapely body. He dreaded what would happen to her, but he also felt a sick inevitability.

The first night at sea, a sneering young Norukai with fresh red scars on his face grabbed Lila's leg chain, unfastened it, and dragged her away. She didn't scream. Instead, she coiled, made herself ready. Bannon threw himself to the end of his own chain. "Leave her alone!"

The Norukai laughed, but Bannon was more stung when Lila turned and snapped at him, "Be quiet, boy! You only make it worse. I can handle this." She tugged on her own chain, pulling back against the raider, but the Norukai yanked the metal links, nearly dislocating her shoulder.

After the Norukai man dragged her into the shadows beside stacked crates of stolen supplies, Bannon strained to hear her voice, sure that Lila would challenge her attacker, but she spoke no words. He heard a scuffle, a grunt, then a scream—but it was not Lila's scream.

The Norukai man reeled back out of the gloom, drunk with agony, as he staggered across the deck.

Holding her own chain, Lila stalked back to return to Bannon's side. Several Norukai came running in response to their comrade's groans. He pressed his palms to his crotch and blood dribbled between his fingers. The angry Norukai stared at Lila, but she faced them defiantly, holding up a fleshy handful in her palm. "I tore off his testicles, but I stopped at that. If another man tries to take me, I will make him eat them as well."

She tossed the bloody sac with a splat onto the deck. The would-be rapist whimpered, then collapsed in a bloody mess. The Norukai prowled toward Lila, ready to tear her to pieces.

Bannon hoped his leg chain would be long enough for him to fight. Lila stood her ground and prepared to die.

King Grieve strode over and saw the writhing, moaning man on the deck, the bloody testicle sac next to him, and he guffawed. Moments later, the other Norukai joined the king in bellowing laughter. "Throw him overboard," Grieve said. "Worthless."

They tossed the moaning raider, still alive, into the sea.

Lila went back to her place beside Bannon, and the angry Norukai men glowered at her before loudly declaring that she was too scrawny for their tastes.

The next day, after several captives were worked to exhaustion belowdecks, the oar master herded them back up on deck with shouts and growls and cracking whips. Bosko released Lila and Bannon from their manacles on deck and commanded them to go down to the benches. A foul stench wafted around him, which even the sea breezes couldn't dissipate.

During the stifling heat of the afternoon, Bannon and Lila sat side by side as they pulled on the oars. Lila was a friend and sometimes lover, but she had never been much for conversation. As they pulled on the oars, Lila stared with hatred at the Norukai captors, yet with a calculating gleam in her eyes.

Chalk came down to jabber, fearful of Lila, but fascinated by her as well. In a clumsy whisper that was easily audible over the creaking oars, he muttered to Bannon as if it were a secret, "Pretty lady. Dangerous lady." His pale face was mottled purple and yellow from where she had struck him. "No love for Chalk, though. Not me. I'll never have love."

Lila growled, "Cut me loose and I'll love you until I break you into tiny pieces." Chalk scuttled away with a last look at Bannon and retreated up the wooden ladder to the deck above.

"Pull!" the oar master scolded.

The serpent ships sailed north from the estuary for days. Grieve paced the deck, and Chalk followed him like a puppy. The king placed his iron-knuckled hand on the shaman's bony shoulder. "We'll be at the Bastion soon."

"The Bastion," Chalk cried. "Home!" He ran up to Bannon, leaned close, and repeated, "Home!"

Grieve's expression darkened as he turned to his shaman. "I hoped Ildakar would be the center of my new empire. What went wrong? What didn't you foresee? We should have been victorious!"

Chalk's pale eyes gleamed with a cracked edge of madness. "There will be war, a big war! I promised a war. Many ships. My Grieve, King Grieve! They'll all grieve!"

"Soon," the king vowed.

The serpent ships sailed onward. For Bannon and
Lila, the days were an endless blur of being chained on
the open deck or sweating in the miserable hold as they
worked the oars. When the wind picked up and
stretched the sails, the oars were withdrawn, and the
slaves remained bound with nothing to do but fear their
fates.

One afternoon, the lookout called from the top of the
mast. "Selka in the water! Starboard side." Grieve strode
to the bow, where he shaded his craggy brow and stared
out on the waves.

Bannon raised himself up so he could scan the water.
"Do you see them?" he asked Lila.

"What are selka?"

Squinting across the choppy water, he felt a thrill of
terror as he spotted five swimming figures. "They look
human, but they are definitely not human."

Lila's brow furrowed. "Fish people?"

"That's as good a description as any. A race of humans long ago altered to live under the water. They can
rip sharks apart with their claws." He shivered even under the hot sun. "Nathan told me that during the great
war thousands of years ago, powerful wizards manipulated captives, gave them gills and changed their skin
in order to form an undersea army. The war is long over,
and the selka have built an entire civilization beneath
the surface. They hate humans and they still prey on
ships." He swallowed hard as the memories washed
over him.

"They attacked the *Wavewalker* when we were traveling south. The selka swarmed over our ship at night,
killed the entire crew to get revenge against the wishpearl divers that raided their reefs. Nicci, Nathan, and
I were the only ones to survive when the *Wavewalker*

wrecked on the Phantom Coast. The selka queen had some connection to me, didn't want to kill me . . . for whatever that was worth. But they were unstoppable."

"The odds are better now. This time you have me to fight beside you," Lila said. "And I am a morazeth."

With her hands bound and her ankles shackled, Bannon doubted even Lila could do much against a selka attack.

At the railings, the Norukai held their bone-tipped spears, ready to hurl them at the swimming figures, but the selka kept their distance. Grieve bellowed a challenge out on the water. "Come close enough for us to kill you!" The selka remained tauntingly out of reach.

Chalk groaned with fascination. "Selka fish! Fish people!" He nervously ran his palms over the puckered, scarred skin of his stomach. "I don't want to be gutted, King Grieve, my Grieve."

The king glowered down at him. "I won't let them gut you, Chalk."

The shaman chanted in a singsong voice, "Wrong, wrong, wrong!"

As if bored, the selka swam away, while the Norukai doubled their lookouts to keep watch on the water.

Lost in his memories, Bannon mused quietly to Lila, "I don't know why the selka queen spared me the first time." When he was much younger, he had stolen a small fishing boat and sailed away from Chiriya Island without charts or knowledge. He drifted for days until he ran out of water and food, sunburned, in despair. He'd been sure he would die at sea.

"I knew stories of the selka," he told Lila, "but I'd never seen one. I thought they were just fisherman's tales, but that night when a sea fog closed in, I huddled in my boat and fell asleep. In the darkness, something pulled my boat, brought me back to the island. When I woke, I was home, and the boat was dragged up on the rocky shore. I saw only the imprint of a webbed foot in the beach." He looked at her. "When they attacked the *Wavewalker,* the selka queen seemed to recognize me."

Lila gave him a skeptical look. "I believe you overestimate your charm and attractiveness, boy." Her voice was flat, but he thought she was teasing him. "But if the queen wishes to be your lover, I will fight her."

He shuddered at the thought. "I don't ever want to see her again."

CHAPTER 43

After Ava's spirit ransacked the archives, Cliffwall went on high alert. General Zimmer dispatched scouts out of the canyons to monitor the oncoming army that was already marching out of the mountains. Nathan called an emergency meeting so that everyone could discuss how they might possibly prepare against such an overwhelming force.

As he and Verna hurried toward the gathering chamber, the prelate said with hard skepticism, "I'm not confident we have any viable options. This archive is no longer hidden, and Utros is on his way. How can we defend Cliffwall?"

Nathan clucked his tongue. "I'm sure we'll find something, my dear, if we just think hard enough."

She walked ahead of him into the large gathering chamber. "You sound like a naive fool."

"I prefer the term 'optimist.' Remember, I've helped save the world before." But he'd had the help of Nicci, and Richard, and others. Knowing that Nicci was still alive did not help him, because she wasn't there. He had no idea where she actually was, only that she had somehow killed the sorceress Ava.

The prelate responded with only a roll of her eyes.

Franklin and Gloria sat at a speakers' table before the anxious audience. Zimmer shifted uncomfortably in his seat; his D'Haran armor was clean and professional, as if he were reporting to Lord Rahl himself. Nathan and Verna took the remaining seats at the front table before the gathered crowd. Intent scholars filled the room, sitting on the available benches while others stood shoulder-to-shoulder. The low buzz of conversation was not the casual talk usually heard at such meetings.

Thorn and Lyesse stood with weapons at their sides. Eight Sisters of the Light sat watching the prelate, confident and waiting to learn how they could help. Oliver and Peretta remained close to Amber.

Gloria nodded to her memmers as the Cliffwall inhabitants asked questions of one another. Scholar-Archivist Franklin folded his hands in front of him, waiting for the crowd to quiet down. Crowded at the entrance to the chamber, some of the ungifted workers listened in, deeply worried.

Nathan cleared his throat. "We don't have time to waste, and someone needs to call this meeting to order, although I believe meetings are often a waste of time when action is required. The enemy army knows exactly where to find us. A hundred thousand soldiers will take over this archive, unless we figure out a way to stop them."

"How can we possibly stop that many?" cried one of the memmers.

"By killing them," Thorn interjected, as if the answer were obvious.

Verna looked annoyed. "An excellent suggestion, but unhelpful. We have to prevent them from capturing all the knowledge stored here. They cannot have it!"

"At the pace of their march, they are maybe four days

away," Zimmer said. "But my scouts suggest they have picked up speed."

A wave of anxious whispers rippled through the chamber.

Lyesse said, "The soldiers are gaunt and hungry, and they are stripping the landscape clean, devouring everything in sight."

"But they continue to march nevertheless," Thorn added. "On our last reconnaissance, we killed six of them."

"Each," Lyesse added. "For good measure."

Captain Trevor spoke up, frustrated. "We cannot stop them one or two at a time."

"With the maze of narrow canyons, the sheer cliffs, the mesa rising above the valley, Cliffwall is defensible," Zimmer explained. "A small number of fighters can hold the bottleneck at the mouth of the canyon. With the proper preparations, we could ambush the enemy, slay thousands as they funnel into the canyon."

"Their piled bodies form another wall of defense," Lyesse said, relishing the thought.

"You are quite ambitious, General," Nathan said, "but with so many thousands of warriors who refuse to give up, Utros will overwhelm us no matter what his losses are. The soldiers will keep coming and keep coming. Given what his dead sorceress told him, he will want to possess the knowledge stored here, and he is not a man to give up."

"We can still try to hold them off," said the wizard Leo. "Can't we?"

"It remains an incredible risk," Franklin pointed out. "We must evacuate as many people as possible, get them to safety. I won't let all those innocent families just huddle here waiting to be slaughtered. We have to accept that Cliffwall may be captured. We could pack up some of the most important volumes and rush them in pack trains up into the highlands above the canyon."

"I concur," said Gloria. "If my memmers go with them, at least they will take the knowledge they carry in their minds, and that is the equivalent of thousands of books."

"The knowledge in the archive is too dangerous," Verna said. "We must not let that information fall into enemy hands. We cannot!"

"It took years and years to install all those works here," Franklin said. "Even if we took wagonloads of books above the canyon, we could only save a tiny fraction. It's simply not possible! We haven't even sorted them yet."

"We can't move the archive," Nathan said. "That much is obvious. Who would choose the volumes to save? Even if we merely hid the most dangerous books in caves, then what? With limitless enemy soldiers to search the surrounding areas, Utros would find the books. And the spirit of his sorceress can flit anywhere."

"We don't dare let General Utros have any of those books. The knowledge is too dangerous," Verna insisted.

"My memmers are meant to preserve information," Gloria said, "but if they were captured and tortured . . ." She looked at her gifted followers in their blue robes. "What might they be forced to reveal?"

Groans of dismay went through the audience. The scholars began to talk heatedly.

Zimmer rose to his feet, crossed his arms over his chest armor. "We have to defend Cliffwall. Evacuate all the civilians to safety, but my defenders must stop the army from breaking through into the canyon. We will stay here and use every possible defense to block the invasion."

"Ava knows exactly what the archive contains," Nathan said. "Her sister Ruva is likely still alive, too, unless Nicci killed her as well." He stroked his chin.

"She is just one sorceress," Oron said.

"And a hundred thousand soldiers," Leo pointed out.

"All the wizards of Ildakar could barely scratch that giant army," Olgya said. "We have far fewer defenses here."

Zimmer placed his fists on the table in front of him. "Let us be realistic." Black stubble shadowed his cheeks, and his forehead glistened with perspiration. "I have about fifty D'Haran soldiers as well as a few city guards from Ildakar. We have Oron and Leo, Olgya and Perri from Ildakar, along with Nathan, Prelate Verna and her Sisters of the Light, and some gifted Cliffwall scholars who can fight with magic." He drew a deep breath. "Even with the natural defenses of the canyons here, I doubt we could hold against General Utros and his army."

"But we will try," Captain Trevor said. "We will fight to the last, and make them pay a very high price!"

"Yet they will still break through," Verna interjected. "No matter how brave and desperate our defense is, if we don't hold that canyon opening, then all is lost. If this archive falls into enemy hands, then *all is lost*!" Her voice rose as her anger intensified. "General Utros could use that dangerous information to crush the Old World." She placed a hand on Nathan's sleeve as if to draw strength. "The Sisters of the Light revere knowledge, and this is a hard conclusion for me, but I believe it's the only one." She stared around the room, her gaze finally resting on Gloria and Franklin. "If that army breaks through, we have to destroy Cliffwall."

Franklin gasped. "But we haven't completed our work!"

Gloria cried, "Still so many volumes to memorize."

"Utros will ransack it. He will find the same deadly spells we are searching for, and he'll use that magic to destroy the world."

Nathan could feel the heart beating louder in his chest, and he grimaced as a twinge of dark pain shot through him again. "I remember when Richard brought down the Palace of the Prophets. Such a landmark, so much information in those vaults." He bit his lower lip. "But the world has survived fine without that knowledge. While I appreciate General Zimmer's confidence and bravado, Verna pointed out to me that misplaced optimism is only a fool's weapon."

"But think of all the sacrifices that went into creating Cliffwall!" Gloria groaned.

Peretta spoke up. "Cliffwall's magic belongs to humanity, to someone who knows how to use it."

"For good, not evil," Nathan said. "We have to face facts. This archive remained safe behind its camouflage shroud for three thousand years, and no one used any of the magic for good or ill. Our civilization bumbled along nevertheless. The world went on." He tapped his fingernails on the wooden table surface. "Very shortly after the archive was opened again, though, Roland the Lifedrinker abused a spell and made himself into an insatiable monster, as did Victoria after him. Better that the magic had never been discovered at all. We would have been safer."

Gloria looked away, embarrassed at the mention of her mentor. The other memmers also muttered.

Verna picked up the discussion in a hard voice. "And then there was the student Elbert, who melted the prophecy archive by unleashing the Weeping Stone spell, which he couldn't control. And those were merely accidents! Think how much worse it will be if Utros *intentionally* uses that lore to destroy anyone who opposes him."

Zimmer was impatient. "We should still try to defend the canyon. My men are ready. We can make plans, set traps, kill countless numbers of the enemy. We will never have a better opportunity." He swallowed. "But if we fail, if General Utros overruns the canyon, can we find a way to destroy the archive? Only then, not before?"

Olgya said, "How will we do that? Burn all the books? Seal the tunnels? How could we do it fast enough if the enemy army has already broken through?"

Verna had a distant look on her face, and Nathan frowned at her. "What are you thinking, my dear?"

"The Weeping Stone spell. Maybe we just need to use it on a larger scale."

CHAPTER 44

After leaving the damaged sliph temple, Nicci made her way to Serrimundi Harbor, where the aftermath of the Norukai raid was still apparent. At the mouth of the sheltered harbor, a high rock outcropping protected the entrance with a huge carving of the Sea Mother. Sunken ships with splintered masts rose from the water like grasping hands. Several docks were shattered, pilings uprooted and collapsed.

The harbor was an obstacle course of scuttled cargo vessels, fishing boats, and destroyed serpent ships that had held murderous Norukai. Fishermen, foreign sailors, Serrimundi seamen, and dockworkers all labored together to help the city recover.

Out in the water, some ships had burned to the waterline, and others listed to one side, taking on water. Like flesh beetles stripping the meat off a corpse and leaving only bones, harbor workers crawled over a sunken ship that blocked the main docks. They used saws, pry bars, and mallets to dismantle the wreck, stripping it down to its ribs and keel.

"Tie this rope around the lowest rib under the waterline," shouted a bare-chested man with a deeply tanned bald pate and a voluminous black beard. He stood at the end of the dock and threw a coil of rope into the water. "We'll rig a winch on the shore to drag that damned serpent ship out of the main channel."

In the water, four muscular young men took the rope and swam toward a half-sunken serpent ship just beyond the pier. Nicci recognized the swimmers as arrogant wishpearl divers, surprised to see them pitching in. The divers swam out to the wreck and plunged deep, pulling the rope along with them.

Men rowing small dinghies towed floating debris to a stony beach at the far end of the harbor, where more people pulled wreckage out of the water. They stacked salvageable planks and logs above the tide line and burned other debris in a large garbage fire.

Despite Serrimundi's ambitious recovery, Nicci was sure the Norukai would strike here again. She had originally come to warn them about General Utros's army, but instead she had faced the bloodthirsty raiders. Before she'd killed Captain Kor, he had boasted that the Norukai were also attacking Ildakar.

Yes, Nicci had plenty of enemies to fight.

She came upon a merchant dressed in unseasonably warm clothes, a dark woolen jacket and a vest buttoned across his ample belly. He worked alone in front of an open warehouse near a stack of scorched wooden crates. With a pry bar he cracked open the lids to inspect the contents.

Nicci stopped in front of him. "Tell me where to find Harborlord Otto."

The merchant sweated profusely in his stifling clothes. "I'm ruined. I've lost half of my goods."

"At least you didn't lose your life."

He blew air through his lips, grudgingly accepting her statement. "The harborlord is tallying the damaged ships." He gestured toward one of the main docks. "Look for him aboard the *Mist Maiden*."

Nicci knew the ship. That was where she had fought the Norukai and killed Kor. As she walked off, the merchant pulled green and blue silks out of a crate, frowning at the blood that had soaked into the contents. "Ruined, just ruined."

It didn't take her long to find the three-masted cargo ship. Crews continued to scrub the bloodstains from the deck of the *Mist Maiden*. One man hung on a high yardarm like a spider restringing the rigging.

She called out as she approached. "Harborlord!"

Sailors came to the rail to stare down at her. Some cheered. "It's Nicci. We're safe again!"

"You're not safe until you learn how to fight for yourselves," she replied. Without being invited, she walked up the gangplank to the deck where Harborlord Otto sat on a barrel next to the *Mist Maiden*'s Captain Ganley, who was betrothed to Otto's daughter.

The harborlord looked at Nicci from beneath a floppy hat. His caramel-colored eyes were heavy with the sight of too much death and blood. "Nicci! I thought you went back to Ildakar."

"I tried to. How long have I been gone?"

Otto scratched his beard, considering. "The Norukai attacked ten days ago." He let out a long sigh. "Without you, my sweet Shira and her children would have been killed. I would have been killed. But you made us stand strong. Serrimundi will never forget that."

Captain Ganley stepped toward her with a relieved grin as if he meant to hug her, but he hesitated when he saw the razor edge of her demeanor. "There is so much wreckage, it'll take a year before the city is back to what it was."

"If the Norukai don't attack again," Nicci said, and both men turned pale. "And there is also the army of General Utros to contend with. This is no time to be complacent."

"Will it really be that bad?" Otto asked. "Serrimundi has prospered for centuries. We kept our independence even under the Imperial Order."

"This is different," Nicci said. "Utros is intent on conquering the Old World, and the Norukai are wild animals. They want to raid and pillage, not engage in peaceful trade."

At the harbor mouth, a lookout on the high promontory of rock banged on a brass gong, and a signal fire took hold, sending pale smoke curling into the air. Otto shaded his eyes. "There's a ship coming in."

Tension thickened like a thunderstorm in the air. People gathered along the docks, looking to the mouth of the harbor and the giant Sea Mother, afraid it might be more Norukai serpent ships.

Ganley swallowed hard. "We are not ready to fight again so soon."

When the lookout banged twice more on the gong, Otto visibly relaxed. Nicci waited for a report. "What does it mean?"

"We know it's not a warship," Otto said. "That wasn't a call to arms."

A low vessel with patched gray sails slipped past the giant cliff carving. The hull was dark and dirty, but it seemed to be a swift ship, judging from how easily it sailed into the harbor.

"A kraken hunter," Ganley said with distaste.

"Not just any krakener," Otto said. "That is the *Chaser*, my brother Jared's ship."

As the dingy ship nimbly dodged the sunken wrecks

and protruding masts in the harbor, Nicci admired
the captain's skill. Captain Jared seemed to know every sail, every rigging rope, and every vagary of the
winds and currents. He steered and dodged with little room to spare. People crowded the *Chaser*'s deck,
hundreds of bedraggled men and women, even children, packed together. Loaded with so many passengers, the krakener rode precariously low in the water,
but the captain deftly guided the vessel to the nearest
open slip. At the bow stood a man with dark hair, a
gap between his front teeth, and eyes and nose similar
to Otto's.

Nicci followed the harborlord to where the *Chaser*
was tying up. Three narrow planks were thrown down
from the krakener to the dock, and the refugees began
to disembark, jostling one another in their eagerness to
get back on dry land. A crying girl clutched her mother's hand, and the mother's head had angry red scabs
from severe wounds. The people flowed off the *Chaser*
and milled around the pier, disoriented and lost. Some
dropped to their knees, praising the Sea Mother. Many
had bloodstained bandages, splints, slings, or obvious
bruises.

Nicci and Otto moved among the jabbering refugees, asking questions. The bedraggled people looked
shocked and lost. "The Norukai destroyed Effren,"
said one man with a prominent black eye. "Our city
is burned to the ground. Hundreds taken captive, our
women raped."

An old woman beside him groaned. "Ten serpent
ships came at night, led by a man named Lars."

"The Norukai never attacked Effren before. They
don't come this far north," the man said. "Some of us
hid in our root cellars. Others ran into the hills. Those

who stayed to fight—" He swallowed hard and couldn't find the words.

The old woman finished for him. "Those who fought back were all slain."

Nicci felt a flash of anger. "I killed Captain Kor, but I remember Lars too. They came to Ildakar with a load of slaves."

The refugees seemed in a hurry, though they had no place to go. Nicci and the harborlord wove their way through the milling crowd to reach the krakener. Nicci caught a foul whiff as soon as she approached. The *Chaser*'s hull and deck were impregnated with oil and long-hardened slime. She remembered kraken hunters from her time in Tanimura with the Sisters, where the ships would come in with loads of smelly kraken meat, oil, and leather.

After all the refugees had disembarked, Captain Jared hopped down from the raised bow and came toward them. "Brother, it looks like Serrimundi has had some excitement since I've been away."

"The Norukai attacked," Otto said. "We defeated them, but not without suffering great damage."

"You are better off than Effren, I guarantee you that," Jared said, and his expression darkened. "The Norukai left nothing but wreckage and bodies. When the *Chaser* arrived, I loaded as many survivors as I could and brought them here to sanctuary in Serrimundi, though some of them stayed behind to pick through the rubble."

Otto looked at all the people streaming aimlessly down the docks with no place to go. "These refugees can earn their food and keep by helping us rebuild, but with the harbor damaged and the traders skittish, we won't have many supplies coming in to feed the extra mouths."

"Nevertheless, you will make do," Nicci said, allowing no argument. "Those people are all potential fighters who could fend off another Norukai attack or stand against the army of General Utros. You need them."

Jared flashed her a bright smile, revealing the gap in his front teeth. "And who is this?" Even after the harshness he'd experienced and all the miserable refugees that had crowded aboard his ship, the captain seemed to have inordinate good cheer.

"I am the one who warned Serrimundi to build up their defenses, although a little too late." She kept her voice neutral, taking no satisfaction in being proved right. She was curious to hear accurate and recent information. "If Captain Lars attacked Effren, that means more than one Norukai raiding party is attacking the coast. More ships may well strike Serrimundi and other cities."

Jared gave a grim nod. "The Effren survivors say there's been no word from Larrikan Shores for several days, and that's farther south. I expect we'll find that city in ruins as well."

Nicci already knew that General Utros's great army was on the move, and now the Norukai threat had grown more severe. She turned to the harborlord. "I need to go north to Tanimura and the D'Haran garrison there. The Old World must unite against this common threat." When Otto looked at her blankly, not reacting as quickly as she wished, she snapped, "I need a fast horse so I can ride up the coastal road to Tanimura. I want to depart within the hour."

Jared scoffed. "Why would you want to ride a smelly horse? You'll be saddle sore and covered with dust before you get there many days from now." He gestured toward the gray, patched sails of the *Chaser* and spoke with a heartfelt pride as if he were praising a beautiful woman. "My *Chaser* is ten times faster than a horse, if we have fair winds."

Nicci realized that sailing was indeed a faster option. "With my gift, I can guarantee fair winds."

Jared laughed. "A sorceress aboard my ship. It'll be a refreshing change."

"There's very little refreshing about a krakener," Otto said with a grimace. "But that is your best choice, Nicci, if you can stand the smell."

She thought of all the miserable experiences she had endured in her life. "I can stand a bad smell."

Chapter 45

Out on the open sea, the Norukai grew restless, boisterous. They pounded on their shields and stomped on the deck, as if their raid on Ildakar had somehow been a victory instead of a defeat. As the sun set, they began chanting, "Serpent god! Serpent god needs blood."

Chalk waved his hands in the air. "Serpent god will save us, but serpent god is hungry." He ran to cling to King Grieve. "Serpent god needs blood, my king, my Grieve."

The king frowned down at him. "You're sure the serpent god will save us? You've seen it in a vision?"

"Serpent god will save some of us." Chalk cackled. "But I won't tell which ones! A secret."

King Grieve scanned the huddling slaves chained to the deck, and his eyes lit on the weakest, most exhausted captive. "Take that one. We'll whet the serpent god's appetite."

The slave wailed and struggled while the others crouched against the sideboards, as if they could become invisible. Bannon pulled on his chain, straining to break free, though he had no idea how he could help the poor man. Lila glared daggers at the king, straining against her bonds until her wrists bled.

For good measure, Grieve cuffed Bannon on the side of the head, then ignored him. The scrawny, doomed slave struggled, but to no avail. He was shirtless, and his sunburned back was blistered and peeling. Ages ago, it seemed, the man had been a minor noble from Ildakar.

The raiders went to the side of the ship and hammered on the wood with their spear shafts, their war mallets, and the hilts of their swords in a resounding call to some monster beneath the surface.

"Serpent god is deep," Chalk cried. "But serpent god is hungry! Serpent god will save us." He suddenly whimpered and cringed. "But not all of us."

The Norukai performed no ceremony. Grieve simply dragged the captive to the rail and leaned him out over the water. With a vicious slash, he drew his dagger across the man's throat, cutting deep. The victim's blood fountained out, and Grieve dangled him by the waist of his pants over the waves so the blood ran down the hull and into the sea.

The Norukai kept pounding on the deck in anticipation, while the captives groaned in terror.

"Serpent god is deep," Chalk said, "but he will eat."

When the blood had drained, Grieve heaved the body overboard into the waves. The dead man drifted behind the three ships and slowly sank, but no serpent god appeared, even though they waited in tense silence for many minutes. The Norukai grumbled with disappointment.

Bannon felt sick anger for the loss of one of his comrades, and Lila seethed in silence as she watched the sacrifice. Surreptitiously, she kept working, twisting,

scraping her hands against the ropes, but even if she
freed her wrists, the chain still anchored her to the deck.

T he serpent ships sailed on during the night while
    the Norukai navigated by the stars. Bannon lay
bound under the dim lantern light, unable to sleep. Lila
lay like a coiled spring ready to be released, and her
mere presence offered him some comfort. The dark sails
were invisible against the night sky except for where
they blocked out the stars. He listened to the stirring
waves that caressed the hull.

Chalk curled up on the deck and slept, then woke up
and scuttled to a new resting place, where he slept again.
He seemed nervous.

Bannon knew that even if he and Lila managed to
break free, they had nowhere to go. They were in the
middle of the ocean and would never survive long
enough to reach land. He lay on deck grinding his teeth.
Lila was so silent he couldn't tell whether she was asleep
or awake. His pulse ticked off the seconds of his captivity, appreciating every moment he remained alive.
Once the serpent ships reached the Norukai islands,
though, the situation would be even worse.

As he listened to the breeze, the creaking canvas and
wood, the whisper of waves and the snores of the Norukai, he heard a different sound, a wet scuffling, as of
something slithering up the hull. Next to him, Lila became instantly alert. She twisted herself upright and
strained against the ropes around her wrists.

Bannon felt an icy trickle of terror when he saw a
shadow appear at the rail, slip over, and drop to the
deck. Another silhouette followed a moment later.

Sudden shouts of alarm erupted from the two nearby

ships. From their decks he heard the ring of steel and hard blows, the clamor of fighting. Bannon lurched to his feet and tugged on his chain. Lila stood close to him like a cornered guard dog.

The Norukai roused themselves and grabbed their weapons, ready for battle. Bannon saw a third scaly figure climb over the side and land on the deck, moving as swiftly as a flash of minnows darting away in a stream. Five other creatures appeared, their bodies glistening with water and slime. They had large eyes and wide mouths full of needle-sharp teeth, and gill slits like wet wounds along their necks. Their webbed hands were tipped with powerful claws.

"Selka . . ." Bannon's stomach twisted, and then he yelled at the top of his lungs, "The selka!" The chain burned his ankle, and he wrestled with the ropes on his wrists. He snapped at the scrambling Norukai. "Free us! I don't want to die here like a gutted fish. Let me at least fight them!" He knew what the selka would do.

Lila grimaced as she twisted her wrists and more blood flowed down her forearms. "I won't let them kill you, boy, at least not without a fight."

Roused, the raiders grabbed battle-axes, war hammers, and curved swords as the selka swarmed the ship. The sea people were greenish gray, but their fins had splashes of color, some with jagged stripes, others with a tinge of blue. They flung themselves in among the Norukai, slashing with claws, ripping open broad chests.

One selka grasped a Norukai woman's forearm and bit down viciously. The fangs crunched through the skin and bone, severing the hand so that the woman's sword clattered to the deck. As if she didn't even feel the pain, the Norukai swung back her arm and punched the bloody stump into the selka's face, gouging out its slitted eye with the jagged end of bone.

Three at a time, the selka fell upon individual raiders and ripped them to pieces, slashing out throats, yanking off scarred jaws, cracking open chests to feed on red quivering hearts. But the Norukai killed many selka as well. King Grieve swung his war axe, decapitating two creatures in a single stroke. The wide mouths gaped on the rolling heads like fish drying under the sun.

Chalk darted about the deck, a pale scarecrow in the starlight. He flailed his hands. "Fish people. Fish people! I don't want to be eaten by fish!"

With a sweep of his massive arm, Grieve pushed the shaman back toward the water barrels near the bow. "Protect yourself, Chalk. Stay behind me."

The slaves ducked into shelter wherever they could find it, rattling their chains, desperate to get free. Bannon yanked his leg, and the anchor bolt wobbled in the wood, but he couldn't pull the leg iron loose.

One female selka looked more majestic than the others, with a spatter of leopard spots on her golden-green scales. She flashed her bright gaze across the Norukai as if a banquet had just been served. Bannon recognized the selka queen.

A Norukai warrior ran toward her, swinging a spiked mace, but the queen hooked a sharp claw under his chin like a fisherman snagging a carp. She lifted him bodily off the deck and flung him overboard as if she were discarding garbage.

Closer to Bannon and Lila, one brawny male selka stalked up to the captives, extending claws in his webbed hands. Seeing them bound and struggling, the selka closed in to kill them.

With a cry of effort, Lila at last freed her wrists and flung the rope away. As the male selka prowled closer, she seized the chain at her ankle and hauled with all her might. The bolt came free of the deck with a splintering crack. She uprooted the chain just as the selka charged at them, and that was all the weapon she needed. She swung the rattling links to smash the sharp bolted end into the creature's face. He clapped webbed hands against his mangled mouth, snarling and burbling. Lila whipped the chain again into the side of his head, crushing his temple. The selka fell in a pool of slime and blood at her feet.

Glancing around, she dropped to her knees next to Bannon. Lila worked at the bindings at his wrists, clawing the thick knot until her fingernails were bloody, and finally the rope came free. He flexed his arms, ready to use his fists if nothing else, but the anchor bolt still held his chain to the deck.

Three more selka approached, snarling and ready to kill Lila to avenge the selka she had just slain. Bannon jerked against the bolt, ignoring the rush of pain that raced through his ankle and up his leg. The heavy pin began to wobble loose.

With the selka closing in on her, Lila spun, holding her own chain to defend Bannon. He tugged at the loose links, rocking the bolt, feeling the wood splinter. "Almost . . . almost!"

As Lila swung the chain back and forth, the bolt whistled through the air and the selka recoiled. With a mighty heave, Bannon finally uprooted his chain, and he was so surprised that he stumbled to his knees.

Now the selka turned to him as well.

Unexpectedly, the selka queen glided closer, sleek and strangely beautiful. She let out a scolding hiss and snapped orders to her followers. "Not this one." She fixed her golden eyes on Bannon and insisted, "Not this one." She extended one clawed forefinger toward him and added, "I remember."

The three selka warriors cowered, backing away, while the queen bounded toward the Norukai. The rest of the selka left the bound slaves alone, satisfied with many other victims to kill.

King Grieve roared as he hacked at the attackers with his war axe. He continued to fight, drenched with blood and slime. Dead sea people lay all around the deck. Chalk huddled among the barrels and crates near the front of the serpent ship. "My Grieve, King Grieve! I will grieve!"

Gnashing her teeth, clacking her jaws, a Norukai woman bounded forward to intercept the queen. "I will gut you, bitch!" She strode past the slaves as if they didn't exist at all.

Bannon lashed out with his uprooted chain, caught the Norukai woman around her thick leg, and drove her to the deck. She writhed in astonishment and lunged for Bannon, but he swung the chain and caught her on the side of the head, caving in her skull. She grunted, then wilted to the deck as blood leaked from her ears and mouth.

The selka queen saw what he had done and let out a hiss that might have been appreciation. Lila also noticed. "Don't flirt with her, boy."

The selka queen chose the brawny Norukai king as her next target. She prowled forward with feral beauty, as graceful as death. When Grieve saw her, he also recognized his main opponent. With a heavy swing, he buried his axe in the chest of a nearby selka.

The curved blade dug deep, cracked bone, and Grieve pressed his boot on the creature's chest to rip his weapon free.

He faced the queen. Four selka warriors flanked her, pressing closer, and Grieve made his stand near the confined wedge of the bow. The serpent god figurehead stared out into the darkness.

All along the deck, selka and Norukai fought and killed and died, turning the scrubbed boards into a bloody quagmire. Grieve snapped his scarred jaws and glared at the selka queen. She, in turn, splayed a webbed handful of claws, and crouched, unafraid of his great axe. All of the selka prepared to spring at the same time, and they would tear the king apart. Grieve cocked back his massive arm to fight to the death.

Suddenly, a pale figure streaked between them. Chalk yelled, waving his hands. Tears streaked his white face. "No, no! You can't have my Grieve. My king!" He threw himself in front of the selka queen, unarmed, defenseless.

With a quick slash, she hooked her claws into Chalk's abdomen below the navel, then in a flash tugged brutally upward, laying him open from his groin to his breastbone like a gutted fish. Chalk's entrails and organs slithered out of the wide wound, and he dropped to his knobby knees, gurgling, "My Grieve . . ."

The Norukai king's scarred mouth dropped open in utter disbelief. "Chalk!"

Bannon felt sickened and horrified. He loathed the scarred albino, but even so . . .

With a second gesture, the selka queen ripped out Chalk's throat, and she hurled him to the deck like a bloody white rag.

"No!" The word was ripped from Grieve's throat and heart as if his entire universe had just ended. "Nooo!"

In a mindless blood rage, he lunged forward, and the surviving Norukai joined him, redoubling their efforts to fight.

CHAPTER 46

"There is no more time," Zimmer announced, and everyone in Cliffwall knew he was right. More D'Haran scouts had returned with the expected news that the marching army was already crossing the fertile valley and leaving devastation in their wake.

"No doubt about it, sir," said the dust-covered young man who ran up to issue his report. "General Utros is heading straight for these canyons." He wiped sweat from his forehead. "They intend to take Cliffwall."

"Ava told them exactly where to find us," Verna said, her nostrils flaring.

Nathan had gone without sleep since the first emergency meeting, and he suspected it would be a long time before he got a good night's rest again. He turned to Verna. "It's time to evacuate the families and scholars to safety, while some of us remain to make a last stand. With our layers of new defenses, maybe we can save Cliffwall."

Throughout the sheltered canyon, the ungifted workers had packed whatever possessions they could carry. Many complained at having to abandon everything they had worked so hard to create.

"We can't just leave it all behind," said one shepherd

trying to chase his flock to the end of the box canyon, where steep paths wound upward to the high plateau.

Nathan shook his head. "Save your family. You will have to rebuild, but you can't rebuild if you're not alive." The shepherd stubbornly kept chasing his sheep.

Nathan walked along, touching the ornate sword at his hip. From the Cliffwall stores he had found new garments, acquiring a deep blue vest that matched the azure of his eyes. He even found a fine traveling cape that he thought matched his demeanor as an adventurer.

Men and women climbed down the stone steps or wooden ladders from the cliff alcoves, moving with a sense of urgency and sadness. Parents led their children up the canyon to the winding paths by which they could reach the highlands. Thorn and Lyesse accompanied them as watchful guardians.

The D'Haran soldiers drilled constantly and developed pragmatic ways to hold the bottleneck opening to the canyon. General Zimmer and the wizards were still confident they could stop the enemy. Trenchers dug pits, erected spiked barricades, and laid down numerous hidden traps. Soldiers scaled the cliffs and set up caches of stones that they could hurl down on the ancient army from above.

Ava's spirit was seen, flitting into the canyon, spying on them, but Olgya had worked with countless gifted apprentices, teaching them distortion spells, masking spells, even raising fog banks to confuse the surveillance of the evil spirit.

Perri, the gifted shaper, followed some of the agile soldiers up the cliff above the bottleneck opening, and she manipulated the stone to form perfect handholds and footholds. Ten D'Haran soldiers stationed themselves in hiding places for an ambush from high above, each man carrying a bow and a basket of arrows. They would rain down deadly projectiles as soon as the invaders approached the sheer cliffs that blocked the entrance. Oron, Olgya, and Leo discussed ways in which they could use their magic to fight back.

As she and Nathan watched the preparations, the prelate drew her mouth into a tight frown. "If your handful of defenders can keep the canyon safe, then I will be relieved." She sighed. "And completely surprised. If you should fail, Nathan, I am fully prepared to bring down the cliffs and obliterate this dangerous library. I have studied how to use the Weeping Stone spell. That will seal off the entire archive to make sure the knowledge never, ever falls into enemy hands."

He shuddered at the metal in her gaze. "Be very careful, my dear prelate. We've seen how powerful magic can burn like a wildfire out of control."

She gave him a skeptical frown. "You mean Elbert and the ruined prophecy building? We saw what happened when an untrained novice got out of his depth. I have a bit more experience than that." Verna softened her expression, reached out to touch Nathan's shoulder. "But yes, I will be careful."

They climbed the narrow stone path to the large primary archive. Inside the buildings and tunnels, scholars were frantically sorting the most important documents, while memmers opened the chosen volumes and scanned them, impressing more and more words upon their memories.

Franklin could not decide which volumes to salvage, because there were so many. "We have to leave soon, but what am I to do? We have only cataloged a fraction of the books. How do we even know which are the best ones?" He ran both hands through his brown hair. "When Simon was killed, I became the scholar-archivist, but I never knew I would face a decision like this. Historical chronicles will record my name as the man who let Cliffwall be destroyed. What was it all for?"

"We're doing it to save the world," Verna said. "It is not a useless gesture."

Nathan forced a bright tone in his words. "If we can deflect that gigantic army, then we won't have to destroy the archive, and all the people can return home to a happy celebration."

Prelate Verna snorted. She joined the eight Sisters of the Light who pored over the segregated books of dangerous magic, hoping to learn new spells they could use to attack General Utros. They had already discovered several techniques they wanted to try, but time was running out.

Young Amber looked flushed and overwhelmed. She stared at several books spread out in front of her, but couldn't decide which one to read first. "Now I know what my brother felt when his commander left him behind to defend Renda Bay. He only had fifty soldiers, too."

"He had more than that, my dear," Nathan said, trying to calm her. "He had ingenuity, and the people of Renda Bay were motivated to fight back against the Norukai. We're also fighting back." He wrapped his new cape around his shoulders, feeling the fine fabric. "Admittedly, Utros's army is a lot larger than any raid the Norukai ever sent against Renda Bay. . . ."

Amber nodded. "If Norcross could do it, then so can I. I miss my brother. Do you think we'll ever see him again?"

Nathan gave her a reassuring smile. "Of course we will."

"Provided we survive the next two days," Verna corrected.

"Always the pessimist." Nathan sniffed.

She was not amused. "As I've said many times before, I am a realist. For today, our main effort is to ensure that all of these people get to safety. Only the fighters—the soldiers and the gifted—shall remain behind."

"We will make our best defense," Nathan said. "Do you need to study your Weeping Stone spell, or are you confident you have every aspect memorized?"

"I am confident, and I have the sorcerer's sand," Verna said. "If your defenses do fail, then—and only then—I will use the spell to bring down the cliffside." She gave him a hard smile. "I promise I will wait until the last moment, but if I do need to trigger the spell, I'll also be sure to wipe out as many of those soldiers as I can."

CHAPTER 47

The selka queen tore Chalk apart and discarded his body in a puddle of his internal organs.

King Grieve went berserk.

He became a glassy-eyed, rage-filled monster. He roared without words, a primal sound that would have made wolves shudder. Grieve swung his war axe in one hand and yanked out his gutting knife with the other. In one blow he cleaved the head of the nearest selka, and the queen sprang back like a graceful fish, splaying claws still dripping with Chalk's blood. Her long hiss might have been taunting laughter.

She landed nimbly on soft webbed feet out of the weapon's reach. Grieve charged at her like a mad bull, practically hurling the axe from side to side, but she dodged and slipped out of the way.

Bannon sometimes slipped into a red haze on the battlefield, which turned him into a fighting machine, a whirlwind of strength and sword. Afterward, he had no memory of what he had done, but when he did come back to himself he would see the bodies of his numerous victims, and he would be alive, although battered with a hundred injuries that he couldn't recall.

Now Grieve was in the same kind of frenzy.

Three selka closed in on the king to take him down, but in a fury he chopped off their limbs or heads. Grieve flung his gutting knife directly at the queen, but she bent backward in a flash. The blade slipped past, barely nicking her scaled chest, and embedded itself in the broad back of a Norukai who was fighting another selka. The Norukai reached behind him, pawed at the dagger as if wondering how it could possibly have appeared there, and his selka opponent used the opportunity to tear out his throat.

Amid the shouts, screams, and clashing swords on the deck of the Norukai ship, Bannon now stood free, his wrists unbound and the leg-iron chain loose around his ankle. He was ready to fight to the death, knowing he would likely not survive this massacre.

Lila barely took a moment to catch her breath. Eager to fight, she snatched a curved sword from a severed arm on the deck, wrenching it free from clenched fingers. She kicked the flopping limb away and raised the blade. She snapped at Bannon, "Arm yourself, boy! Even if the selka queen doesn't want to kill you, the Norukai do."

With the chain scraping behind him on the deck boards, Bannon ran to another dead raider in a pool of blood and relieved him of his sword. He swung the weapon to get the feel of it. "It's not Sturdy, but it'll do." He liked the weight of this steel in his hand, heard the swish of its edge cutting through the air.

Two hissing selka approached, ready to kill, but upon recognizing Bannon, they slunk away to attack different targets.

The other slaves whimpered, still tied to the deck and helpless. He made up his mind. "This isn't our fight,

Lila. Let the selka and Norukai slay each other. Guard me while I set the captives free so they can fight."

She took up her position by the slaves, holding her sword ready to fight any enemy who came at them. Bannon bent down and used his blade to cut their wrists free. Lila handed the slaves stout knives she had retrieved from dead Norukai on the deck. "Use these to dig out the bolts. Chop at the wood if you need to."

King Grieve's jaw dropped open with a roar, and his tongue flapped about like a flag of meat. "Chalk! Chalk was my protector." Even though the selka queen dodged among other fighters, Grieve closed in on her and raised his axe to hack down. "*Chalk was my friend!*" She dipped and dodged, and the axe blade only sliced her shoulder. The spotted frill on her head and back flared up like a saw blade, and blood oozed across her scaled skin.

He cornered the selka queen against the side of the serpent ship, but rather than let herself be trapped, she leaped over the side in a graceful arc down into the sea below, where the waves swallowed her. When the queen escaped, Grieve bellowed at the sky in a voice loud enough to crack the vault of heaven.

The sounds of fighting resonated from the other two ships nearby. Bannon knew that those slaves did not have his protection. As he swept his gaze across the deck, he guessed that at least fifty selka already lay dead, and many more hacked bodies had gone overboard along with Norukai victims. In the dark water below, countless selka swarmed in the waves. They feasted on the floating Norukai bodies, while others closed around the serpent ships and swarmed up the hull boards.

On the bloody deck, Lila turned from side to side,

holding up her sword. Her face was drawn, not at all afraid, and Bannon thought she looked beautiful. Violence brought out the true nature of the morazeth. He said to her in a quiet, hoarse voice, "I'm glad you're here."

Several selka threw themselves upon Gara the shipwright, clawing at her ropy gray braids. She punched one with her massive fist, stabbed another with her sword, but two other creatures chomped on her shoulder and side, fastening their needle teeth like a vise. Gara kept fighting as they tore hunks of flesh from her body. She staggered backward over the rail, and all three fell into the water below, where more selka closed around them and stripped Gara to the bones. The bloody water looked like dark wine in the night.

Unexpectedly, the sea people began to thrash in terror. Their loud hissing became a frantic splashing. From the waves, the selka queen let out a grating cry of challenge.

Something huge moved beneath the surface, a shadow in the dark water. It curved from below, and a long jagged fin broke the surface between the two lagging serpent ships. It glided like a serrated blade through the swarming selka. Some darted away, and flashes of scaled bodies disappeared below.

"Sweet Sea Mother!" Bannon said.

A huge frilled serpent head rose up, snapping its jaws, blasting out water and steam. The sea serpent towered as high as the masts of the Norukai ships. Its gills flared, its spiny fins flashed. It let out a thunderous bellow, darted down like reptilian lightning, and snatched up four of the selka in the water.

"Serpent god!" The Norukai began to cheer. "Serpent god!"

On deck, the raiders redoubled their fighting with a sudden surge of enthusiasm, and the selka retreated in primal terror as the monster loomed above them. Bannon thought that all the spilled blood and froth in the water must have drawn the underwater predator. Or was the blood sacrifice of the slave at sunset responsible?

The serpent god thrashed after its prey like a fox in a henhouse, boiling through the selka. On deck, the raiders drove back the remaining sea people, hacking them to pieces with wild abandon. The selka could not escape by diving overboard, where the serpent god would devour them. The desperate creatures killed a few more Norukai before the last of them lay slain on the deck. In the sea, the other selka had scattered and streaked away in all directions, fleeing the outraged serpent god.

Still filled with their battle frenzy, the Norukai heaved selka bodies overboard, and the sea serpent feasted. The Norukai believed that their people were also part of the serpent god, and they shared their blood with the serpent's blood. Without ceremony, they picked up their own dead and cast them into the waves to be devoured as well.

At the bow of the ship, near the carved figurehead, King Grieve ignored the victory. He dropped to his knees and picked up the gutted body of Chalk, holding the albino man against him as he sobbed, rocking back and forth. The blood smeared his muscular chest. "My Chalk, my friend!"

Whispering, the Norukai backed away in awe as the huge sea serpent rose above the bow, its giant head dripping water and blood. Its huge eyes fixed down on King Grieve, and the monster dropped open its jaws to show swordlike fangs interspersed with scraps of flesh from the bodies it had just eaten. Recognizing the king's despair, it made a clear offer.

Grieve clutched the dead shaman to his chest, torn with indecision. He looked up and met the eyes of the serpent god, then slowly nodded. "He is yours. Chalk is a part of you. Chalk is a part of us."

He gently laid the dead albino on the deck and stepped away. The serpent god bowed its flexible neck and dipped down to snatch Chalk's body in its jaws, as if in reverence. With a graceful motion, the serpent tossed the broken body in the air, caught it in a yawning mouth, and swallowed the albino whole.

After a long moment, during which the serpent lorded over the three Norukai ships, the huge monster dropped beneath the waves and glided away, deep under the surface.

The night held a collective sigh of relief as the Norukai counted their dead and tended their wounds. Down in the water where many bodies floated, sharks appeared, drawn by the blood to clean up the remains, now that the serpent god had departed.

Bannon and Lila still gripped their swords among the other captives, ready to defend themselves. The slaves huddled, numb with terror, though some were ready to fight with confiscated weapons. They clearly had no chance, however. As Bannon and Lila watched, the Norukai closed in on them, battered and in no mood for further resistance. King Grieve pushed the other raiders aside and glowered at Bannon and Lila. Something inside Grieve seemed to have broken. His face twisted as he spoke to Bannon. "Chalk liked you."

"I don't know why," Bannon said. "He told me about visions, but not what he saw."

Wrestling with his agony, Grieve squeezed the handle of his war axe. Bannon looked at Lila and knew she was calculating whether they would let themselves be captured again or fight to the death here and now with a handful of frightened slaves as their only allies. Even with so many raiders killed during the selka attack, the Norukai still outnumbered them many times over. Lila was ready to die to defend him, to kill King Grieve, but Bannon couldn't bear to see her throw her life away. He said in a harsh whisper, "Not now."

Grieve growled at her. "I am in no mood for more fighting, but I will kill you and be done with it, if you give me any reason."

Still tense, Lila looked at Bannon, then laid down her sword but without showing any hint of defeat. "I don't want them to kill you, boy. There will be another time."

As he surrendered his sword next to hers, shuddering with exhaustion and fear, Bannon hoped she was right.

CHAPTER 48

To make her preparations before General Utros's army arrived, Verna studied the sheer cliffs around the main alcove. She and Nathan had discussed the fine points of the Weeping Stone spell, interpreting the complex nuances of how to soften the rock and bury the entire archive like fossils in limestone. It was not surprising that the naive student Elbert had caused a disaster. Such magic was like a viper that could strike if not held properly.

"The knowledge here could change the world in countless ways." Nathan sounded forlorn. "The wizards in ancient times knew so much more than we do, and they had such great powers. In the right hands, the lore in Cliffwall could make so many lives better, heal terrible diseases, prevent disasters, bring food to starving villages. If only the right person used it for benevolent reasons . . ." He stroked his chin. "That is always the catch, isn't it? If General Utros and his sorceresses use the archive to dominate the world, the amount of suffering they would cause is inconceivable."

Verna shared his deep concern. "I will use the spell only as a last resort, if all our other defenses collapse.

But I am glad we have this option. Either way, General Utros will never possess this archive."

Nathan awkwardly placed a paternal arm around her shoulder. "I couldn't agree more, my dear, but I am worried about you."

She responded with a defiant smile. "I am no bumbling novice, Nathan. I can cast a protective web, and we will verify that all spell-forms are properly connected within the walls and tunnels. There is enough sorcerer's sand for us to lay down the boundaries and through-lines I will need."

She let out a quiet sigh and let him keep his hand on her shoulder. "You and I have often been at odds, but trust me in this. I know you and the other gifted defenders will do your best to block that army, and I would never underestimate your abilities. But if you and the D'Haran soldiers have to retreat, I need to be here to trigger the spell. Just in case."

Inside the great overhang, she and Nathan gazed out at the canyon below, which was now nearly empty except for Zimmer and his soldiers preparing their last stand. All the traps had been laid, the spells from the archive put in place; all the defenders had taken their positions.

Verna said, "I think I have the easy part."

Dangling by ropes, agile acolytes added a few grains of the prismatic sand at appropriate places around the high, sheltered archive. They found niches in the cliff or chipped out special gouges that would hold the grains in the right place to anchor the complex lines of magic. Verna had specified the correct placement deep within the tunnels as well. They had envisioned the three-dimensional complicated connections of the spell-form that wove through the entire library complex.

The teams used every last grain of sand that remained in the porcelain urn.

And now Verna was ready.

Astride his black stallion, General Utros stared ahead at the maze of high canyon walls that closed in around him and his army. The late-morning sun shone down through a dusty sky, driving the shadows against the cliffs. Next to him, Ruva smiled. Her body was covered with bright paint—black, crimson, white, all the significant markings she needed.

Following guidance from Ava's spirit to find Cliffwall, the army moved through the labyrinth. The high walls amplified the sound of hooves on the rocky ground, the jingle of tack, the men adjusting their armor, shields, and weapons. The murmur of excited voices echoed around him. They were almost to their destination.

Utros shifted his heavy helmet. "They know we are coming."

Ruva's smile hardened. "Even my magic cannot hide an army of so many troops, beloved Utros."

"Don't even try. I want them to see us. I want them to fear us."

Thanks to Ava, the general knew that they would find the hidden canyon, although Nathan Rahl or some other gifted person had cast enough distortion and confusion that even the spirit of the dead sorceress had not been able to learn as much as he had hoped. The details of the defenses were unknown to him.

Riding ahead, his scouts had located the secret entrance, the narrow stone bottleneck that led to the Cliffwall canyon and its towering archive. Six of the scouts had never returned, presumably captured or killed, but he had plenty of men to spare. Two intrepid scouts had returned with a report, and that was enough.

His vanguard marched forward in a wedge, the first thousand soldiers pressing down the canyon. They were prepared to fight through any defenses to reach the secret archive. No matter how many of them died, Utros could keep pouring in thousands more until they overwhelmed the cliff city. Even the most determined resistance could not stand up to that.

As they rode forward, Ava's spirit shimmered in front of Utros. "When you conquer Cliffwall, we will possess all that powerful lore, spells that no one can resist, maybe not even the Keeper himself! We will be invincible." She drifted close to her sister on the bay mare and overlapped Ruva with her insubstantial form. Again, the twins spoke in a harmonized double voice. "Together we will eradicate the last wizards of Ildakar, and then your army will sweep across the Old World with nothing to hinder us."

"Tell me if you learn anything about their plans," Utros said. Ava disappeared like a wisp of greenish steam.

The lead horses snorted and plodded along. Utros felt tense and excited, ready for what was sure to be a wholesale slaughter. Weapons ready, the first foot soldiers marched ahead in organized ranks. As the main canyon narrowed toward the bottleneck, the companies had to fall behind one another, becoming a human battering ram instead of a wave.

Ruva fidgeted in her saddle. "Let us go closer. We are almost at the entrance to the canyon."

Utros urged his black stallion forward. When the front ranks approached the high, sheer wall that was really a hidden crack leading into the main canyon, the soldiers stumbled to a halt, milling about, not sure where to go.

The general waited as word came back down the line, passed from company commander to company commander. "The wall is solid, General. There is no opening as we were told. It's a blind end to a box canyon."

"Not possible," he said.

Ruva interjected, "My sister saw the opening. It has to be there."

He and the sorceress worked their way forward among the armored men. From what Utros could see, the smooth stone wall did indeed look impenetrable. "Have they sealed it somehow? Closed this canyon?"

"If so, then we will blast through it." Ruva glared at the barrier. "But I sense something. . . ." She swept her gaze over the towering uneven surface, then extended a finger and traced lines through the air as she amplified her focus. "The people of Cliffwall are good at hiding. There is something here other than stone." Then she laughed. "It is not a solid barrier, my general! Just an illusion, a camouflage field."

She flung out both hands and released her gift, sending ripples through the air. A line of distortion washed across the cliff barricade as if a thousand spirit forms had been released. The curtain of imaginary rock buckled and faded under Ruva's onslaught, no more than a simple mirage. "Now we can enter."

The soldiers cheered, raised their swords, and prepared to attack.

The ground beneath them broke open and began to boil with movement. The sand and rocks of the canyon floor suddenly softened, and the soldiers stumbled backward, their boots slipping on the ground. The surface wasn't just unstable; it spewed forth innumerable scuttling creatures, an infestation of buried scorpions, each the size of a man's hand. The storm of stinging arachnids rushed out with sharp legs, hooked stingers, and snipping claws.

The soldiers let out a roar, colliding with one another, swatting, stomping, and slashing to get rid of the deadly bugs. The scorpions stung repeatedly and crawled all over them as they fell.

Undeterred by the distraction, Ruva continued to tear down the camouflage curtain until it vanished to reveal an entirely different sheer cliff with an offset opening, a crack wide enough for a flow of soldiers to enter. "There!"

As the swarming scorpions continued to pour out of the ground, Utros raised his sword and yelled, "That's the way in! Charge past the scorpions. Your boots and armor will protect you."

Though frightened and disorganized, the first terrified soldiers rushed ahead. Belying the general's promise, more than a hundred men already lay dead on the canyon floor, poisoned by scorpion venom.

"Ride!" Utros kicked his horse forward, with Ruva galloping beside him.

Needing no excuse to run, the vanguard charged to the canyon opening. After the camouflage fell away, the general looked up to see figures high on the cliff, several of them in wizard's robes. Utros spotted the ambush as the invading army pressed into the bottleneck, running from the scorpions.

The surviving wizards of Ildakar began their counterattack.

* * *

J ust inside the canyon, the D'Haran soldiers stood
ready to make their last stand, only a hundred against
a hundred thousand. The odds were breathtaking, and
impossible. Nathan stood beside General Zimmer, Olgya, Perri, and five Sisters of the Light. Stationed on the
outer wall were Oron and Leo for the initial defense,
in addition to all the traps they had established.

Using her expertise, Olgya had woven her camouflage spell, an impenetrable illusion that caused confusion and delay, but Nathan had never expected the
disguise to fool the enemy army for long. Nevertheless,
that challenge distracted the vanguard enough for the
scorpion trap to be effective.

Their plan would depend on numerous smaller victories instead of a single decisive blow, and the defenders had countless small and innovative attacks. General
Utros could not possibly stop them all. Still, a handful
of defenders against such an overwhelming horde . . .

Inside the main canyon from behind the towering
walls, they heard the initial attack begin as Leo and
Oron summoned their scorpions. Nathan turned to
Zimmer as if they were having a dinner conversation.
"I can't say how many times I've gone to battle against
impossible odds, sure that I was going to die." He gave a
rueful smile. "Yet here I am, still alive and still fighting."

"One of these days, Wizard, your fears are sure to
come true," Zimmer said.

"I might be a thousand years old, but I still have a
few things to do in my life." Nathan adjusted his blue
cape, resplendent in his ruffled shirt and new vest. He
also wore the ornate sword, just in case more traditional fighting might be required.

Oliver and Peretta fell back into the canyon, dodging
the sharp spikes that had been placed as a primitive

but effective line of defense against charging soldiers. "Here they come!"

Nathan smiled at the clever maliciousness. He had no doubt that the sorceress Ruva could strip away Olgya's camouflage curtain; in fact, they counted on it, because once the illusion faded, the army would plunge headlong, harried by all the scorpions—and they wouldn't expect a second camouflage field that hid the spiked spears.

The first enemy soldiers began to pour through the bottleneck into the Cliffwall canyon, but before they got far, the men stumbled into deep, hidden trenches. A thin layer of sand suspended by a levitation field covered the pits, looking like solid ground, but as soon as the soldiers stepped on the illusion, the sand and rocks collapsed. They fell screaming, impaled on buried spikes. The first hundred died without knowing what was happening, and such a nasty surprise demoralized the next ranks fleeing from the poisonous arachnids. They couldn't retreat or go forward.

But behind them, the invaders kept pushing ahead, running from scorpions, piling on by the thousands. Even when the soldiers saw the exposed trenches and spikes, they couldn't get out of the way, and more were forced forward and impaled.

Sheer numbers did what caution could not. Body after body fell upon the spikes, skewered on top of the hundreds of soldiers who had died before them. Within minutes the trenches were filled to the brim with victims, many still squirming and groaning. The next ranks of soldiers trampled them, packing down the countless bodies, to push into the canyon.

Outside the bottleneck, from the cliffs above, D'Haran ambushers hurled rocks down upon the soldiers below or fired a stream of arrows. It was a blood-bath. Leo, Oron, and two Sisters of the Light used their gift to call forth lightning and wind that slashed at the invaders. Though he was the former owner of yaxen slaughterhouses, Leo was skilled in winter weather magic. From his perch high up on the cliffs, he created sheets of sleet and ice, slapping down the ranks that had survived the scorpions and the spikes.

In a frenzy after she had dissolved the camouflage field, Ruva lashed out at the wizards above, retaliating with everything she had. Leo balanced on a high out-cropping near the top of the wall, and the sorceress blasted the rock beneath his feet. The outcropping crumpled. Gaping in astonishment, Leo tumbled down with a cascade of rock to the base of the canyon. Even as he plummeted, his wizard's robes flapping around him, Leo released wild bursts of magic. He smashed the opposite cliff and brought rocks down on the gathered soldiers, before he himself was buried in the avalanche. The raging winter winds and snow faded away.

Olgya summoned wisps of fog that built into a snarl of misty curtains that muffled visibility. The soldiers stumbled, running into one another, and the smoke screen tangled about, blinding many. Shapes appeared in the fog, ominous silhouettes, and the invaders at-tacked, striking down imaginary enemies, killing many of their own. The fog was only a distraction, though, and the army moved forward, blindly attacking.

Lord Oron and the Sisters continued their ambush from the outside of the bottleneck, but there was no stopping General Utros. The invaders marched over the corpses of thousands from the front lines. Wearing his horned helmet and his gold mask, the general looked like a demon as he urged them on.

Inside the canyon on the other side of the headwall, Zimmer rallied the line of defenders. "Prepare yourselves! We have to hold this opening."

Nathan summoned his gift to fight against the oncoming stampede of swords and men.

Outside the bottleneck, Ruva called up more magic and hurled explosive force that made the rock shudder. Twisted lightning cracked fissures in the cliff, flaking boulders away. With a resounding blow, the sorceress shattered the headwall and brought down a curtain of rock. When the roar quieted and the dust settled, she had tripled the size of the opening.

Ignoring the enormous number of casualties, thousands of howling soldiers surged into the hidden canyon with only Nathan and a handful of defenders poised to stand against them.

CHAPTER 49

Alone inside the evacuated main alcove, Prelate Verna watched the battle at the bottleneck mouth of the canyon where Nathan, General Zimmer, and their determined force stood ready to hold off the invading army. Verna admired their confidence, and Nathan often proved stronger than she ever imagined. He had escaped from the Palace of the Prophets after a thousand years, and he had removed his own iron collar, the Rada'Han, which should never have been possible. Since that time, he had done great works, achieved amazing success.

As she mused about her days long ago at the palace, Verna also thought of Warren, the studious and warm-hearted scholar who had captured her heart. She had loved him so much. She tried not to think of how he'd been killed fighting the armies of the Imperial Order. That loss had nearly destroyed her.

Once she and Warren had finally found each other, Verna wanted a lifetime with him, but their time as real lovers was tragically cut short. It was so unfair. She chose to savor the precious memories of what they actually had, rather than grieve for the time they didn't.

Even though years had passed, she still missed him. How different her life would have been, if only . . .

As the wind whistled along the cliffside, she stepped to the edge of the alcove and looked down to the stream running through the canyon, saw some scattered white sheep grazing aimlessly with no shepherds to tend them. Other cliff dwellings were empty, and she hoped the evacuated people would all be safe. If by some miracle Nathan and the defenders managed to hold the opening and drive away the invading army, perhaps the people could return.

She recalled that she, Renn, and a small group of people had succeeded in triggering the massive avalanches below Kol Adair, wiping out ten thousand of the ancient soldiers in a single sweep. Nathan, all the powerfully gifted men and women from Ildakar, her Sisters of the Light, as well as the trained scholars and D'Haran soldiers could do no less! Maybe they would succeed after all.

But Verna was too pragmatic to believe that, despite Nathan's confidence, they could hold the wall permanently against the army's assault. She knew what had to happen, and she was ready.

The deserted canyon was so empty and silent that Verna felt herself lulled into a brief moment of security. Swallows flitted about, tending their mud nests in small pockets in the rock, chirping and singing. She allowed herself a smile and relished the calm, but knew it wouldn't last.

From outside the canyon she heard the roar and shouts, the clang of weapons as General Utros slammed into the first line of defenses and traps. The D'Haran troops formed a solid barrier just inside the bottleneck. Nathan and his gifted companions spread out facing the wall. Even this far away, high up on the cliff face, Verna could feel the tension in the air.

When the first lines of enemy soldiers broke through the bottleneck, the magic was truly unleashed, on both sides. Shock waves rumbled through the narrow canyon opening, and the rock shuddered and splintered, sloughing down from both sides. The first ranks of invaders flowed through the gap like a pack of wolves.

Shading her eyes, Verna watched Nathan summon balls of wizard's fire, which he hurled into the oncoming enemy. The angry flames mowed down countless ancient warriors. Thorn and Lyesse raced about like stinging wasps, stabbing, ducking away, stabbing someone else.

The eight Sisters of the Light raised walls of air and bowled the soldiers back, impaling them on the swords of their own comrades. The gifted Cliffwall scholars, trained in only a few spells, broke more rock shards from the cliffs above and sent them raining down. Olgya summoned thick tendrils of mist, a shapeless mass of fog that blinded the soldiers as they charged forward, and she followed through with targeted lightning, wiping out dozens of the enemy. Perri transformed patches of the ground into quicksand, miring the first line of invaders.

But for every ten they killed, a hundred more broke through. The invaders were like an ocean wave that battered against the shore. The D'Haran soldiers met them with furious resistance. Zimmer bellowed commands and dove into the fray, not afraid to risk himself.

Isolated in the alcove high above, with all the silent archive buildings behind her, Verna clenched her fist and despaired at what she saw. The forces of General Utros kept coming, an endless stream through the blasted bottleneck, hundreds at a time. Even if most of the first wave died, they would eventually flood the canyon and overwhelm all resistance through sheer force of numbers.

She had known this would happen. She had warned Nathan, yet they still insisted on this last stand. It was good not to give up hope, but it was also good not to be foolish.

She knew it would be her turn soon. She listened to the echoing sounds of battle down below, the shouts of command, screams of pain, explosions and rockfall, the clash of blades. With a pang, she wished Warren could be here to help her. The two of them could have made a grand accounting of themselves.

Verna had memorized the Weeping Stone spell. Standing in front of the imposing structures crowded in the alcove, she looked at the ruin of the melted prophecy building. Now she meant to do the same to the entire cliffside and engulf the enemy army with a tidal wave of stone. But Nathan and the surviving defenders had to retreat to safety in time, as did she.

She got ready to do what needed to be done. With her gift she could trace the pattern of the spell-form laid down across the cliffside and in the tunnels, an intricate cat's cradle of connected webs, fields built upon collapsing fields, all waiting for her to tug on the first line of magic that would unravel the whole thing and set in motion a chain reaction to destroy the dangerous knowledge stored in the archive.

"You will never have this place, Utros," Verna vowed to herself. Once she triggered the spell, she would climb to safety at the top of the mesa above, using ladders and footholds installed for that purpose, and from there she would make her way to the rendezvous point. The others would also fall back to the highlands, where they would regroup.

Greasy black smoke mixed with a camouflage fog, rising from below after Nathan immolated more attackers with another round of wizard's fire. Ranks of the ancient army still hammered through the blasted bottleneck. Verna spotted the distinctive horned helmet of General Utros and the pale sorceress riding beside him as they emerged through the thick tendrils of mist. They let thousands of shock troops surge ahead of them, and the renewed surge broke the defensive lines, pushed the gifted fighters and the D'Haran troops back.

"It is time for you to go, Nathan," Verna whispered, as if she could communicate with him by mere thought. "Go! Now!"

Reaching the same conclusion, Zimmer raised his sword and called the retreat. Fortunately, he was a wise tactical commander and had planned for the inevitable. She heard his shout ring out as clearly as a sword strike. "Fall back to the far end of the canyon!"

The D'Haran soldiers fought for a few more moments, wanting to kill a last enemy warrior or two. The two morazeth each tried to increase their score of victims. But a dozen of the Cliffwall defenders had already fallen, and they couldn't afford more losses.

Giving them a chance to fall back, Nathan spread out a raging wall of wizard's fire, smearing his spell into an incandescent swath that incinerated the advancing enemy line. But as soon as the magical flames dissipated, the next wave rushed in, trampling the bodies of their fallen comrades.

Once the starving invaders saw the green valley enclosed by high rock walls, the orchards, the sheep, and the lush gardens, they raged forward, suddenly desperate in a different way. Nathan, General Zimmer, and the remaining defenders retreated in a straight line to the rear of the canyon and the steep trails up to the highlands. With nothing to stop them now, the enemy army flowed forward and spread out like an angry swarm of bees.

From her vantage, Verna watched the armed horde advance into the protected canyon. She knew that their last defenses had fallen, and even the faintest chance of victory was gone. It was time for her to do what she had known all along. She drew a deep breath to calm herself, let it out slowly, inhaled another. She imagined Warren's warm presence with her, giving her strength.

The prelate pressed her palm against the stone alcove wall. Though she had shown no hesitation in front of Nathan, she was indeed intimidated by the Weeping Stone spell. Thousands of years ago, the world's most powerful wizards had created it, experts much wiser and more adept than any prelate of the Sisters of the Light.

That spell now would be her final solution. Her gift allowed her to sense the prismatic grains of sorcerer's sand at the proper key points. She could feel the webs she had constructed throughout the archive, every anchor poised in the most delicate of balances. She didn't dare trigger the magic too soon, because she needed Nathan and the others to get away, and once the spell began to work, she would scramble up above the alcove and climb to safety.

She watched the defenders race along the canyon below, running for their lives. They spread out and darted into side canyons or ran up steep fissures, making their way to higher ground. They had all drilled exhaustively beforehand and knew exactly what to do. Some of the ancient soldiers pursued them, but the bulk of the attacking force swelled beneath the towering, inaccessible archive—their main goal. Like a conquering hero, General Utros rode on his black stallion through his own soldiers and turned his horned helmet to look up at the great alcove high up on the cliff.

Even from such a distance, Verna met his gaze, she was sure of it. "I will not let you have this place." She closed her eyes, touched her gift, tugged on the connected webs and lines of force that ran through the cliffs. "I weep for the stone to weep." Tears glistened in her eyes for all the knowledge that was about to be lost.

She ignited the sorcerer's sand, connected the nodes in her web, which sent streaks of fire through the rock and across the open air, which connected the points in the elaborate spell-form that she and Nathan had designed. Once she launched the spell, the power surged, bounced, ricocheted like a released spring. She smiled: the spell would complete its work now, no matter what happened.

When the hard stone of the alcove wall softened and turned to clay against her fingertips, she knew it was time to leave. Lines of transformation shot through the cliff, disassembling the mineral structure. Rumbling sounds came from deeper inside the mesa as tunnels collapsed and filled, but the main reshaping of stone happened here on the outer wall.

Verna ran to the wooden ladder that had been mounted against the cliff wall, leading to handholds and ledges above the alcove mouth. She heard a dripping, rumbling sound, and the glorious buildings inside the grotto wavered. Their foundations liquefied, and the structures themselves toppled over like huge trees felled by a woodcutter. The bricks and stone blocks broke apart and spat out into the air like broken teeth, tumbling into one another. The outer cliff wall began to flow like wax as the hard rock became mud, slumping down in tears of stone. The vaulted alcove opening began to droop down like a swollen eyelid.

Verna scrambled up the ladder, climbing above the overhang. The wooden rungs were still solid, unaffected by the spreading spell, but the end of the ladder sank into the buttery stone, making the steps slanted and unstable. The change was happening faster than she expected. The already-ruined prophecy building vanished entirely, buried as the roof of the alcove flowed over the top of it.

She pulled herself higher, above the mouth of the alcove, and paused to watch the canyon wall slump down below her. A stone wave flowed onto the first enemy soldiers, and the triumphant roar of the invading army turned into howls of dismay. They tried to flee, but could not escape the liquid rock that washed over them.

Reaching the top rung of the ladder, Verna stretched her arm and pulled herself up with the stone handholds dug into the cliff. She found a stable place for her foot. As she climbed toward the top of the plateau and safety, the spell continued building, cascading throughout the cliff. Inside the mesa, the numerous vaults of magical lore had filled in, and all the tunnels inside were erased. The countless shelves of books were now like ancient fossil bones embedded in stone.

Verna laughed with relief as the sloughing sound rose to a deafening roar. She had succeeded! It was enough. The swelling magic rang throughout her body and she pulled on the gift to find the connected webs, ready to pull the Weeping Stone spell to a halt. The sorcerer's sand anchored the key angles of the spell-form, but as the cliff collapsed, their positions shifted and swallowed the powerful grains, muffled by layers of stone. The precise pattern was disrupted.

The spell was like a monster that had broken loose.

Alarmed, Verna clenched her teeth and used her gift to strain against the unraveling webs like a rider trying to rein in a wild horse. In an odd displaced moment, she remembered how Richard Rahl had taught her to use a much kinder bit on her horse, which made the animal easier to control. Richard had cared about the horses as much as he cared about other people. She had learned so much from Richard. . . . But he wasn't here to help her now.

The Weeping Stone spell expanded rather than diminishing, as it was supposed to. Verna had acted as a catalyst and released the power pent up inside the ancient archive, and now the destructive magic grew like a conflagration.

As she held on and wrestled with the uncontrollable spell, a shimmering image swooped up in the air next to her, the sickly green form of the sorceress Ava. "I see your spell!" her hollow voice cried, rising to a shriek. "You will not stop the general."

Verna held on to the cliff handholds, knowing that the intangible spirit could do little to harm her directly. Ava hovered closer, intimidating, trying to terrify the prelate. "I cannot let you do this!"

But Verna was not easily terrified. As the spell continued to roar, bringing down the cliffside, she thrashed the air with her free hand, trying to drive the spirit away, but Ava filled her vision, disoriented her.

The Weeping Stone spell thrashed and writhed, and

Verna's attention slipped. Ava drew away her focus at a critical point.

Having climbed above the alcove to the stable rock, Verna thought she was safely away from the destruction, but to her dismay the cliffs above her began to collapse as well, far beyond what should have been the boundary of the spell. "No, this isn't possible!"

The cliff poured down to bury the ranks of the enemy army. A flood of stone paved over thousands of soldiers who rode through the canyon below.

Ava made one last brash attack in the prelate's face, a mirage with only a breath of tangible form. But as the walls collapsed in a wholesale disaster, the spirit cried out in dismay and vanished, swooping down toward General Utros.

Verna strained upward to reach a point where she could hold on and fight back, where she could stop the melting stone. She climbed several body lengths higher, but her foothold slipped away like a slurry of mud. The rocky knob in her hand became as soft as butter.

And she fell.

She dropped down the cliff face, clawing for a handhold in a mudslide. Her fingers caught in the soft stone, and she dug in up to her knuckles, but her weight dragged her down, and she gouged long furrows in the stone.

Verna attempted to use her gift to arrest her fall, still trying to dampen the overall spell. Despite all her reassurances to Nathan about being able to handle the power she unleashed, the connected webs and interlinked fields escaped her control. She sank and rolled in the liquefied rock.

With a last burst of magic, she deflected the fields and paused the spell so that the flowing rock hardened around her lower legs. But that did no good. She was trapped in a fist of stone, hanging upside down just above the canyon floor, where she watched more of the armored soldiers die.

She couldn't break free, but the cliff kept melting. Stone sloshed around her until finally Verna was buried in a wave that petrified around her.

Her last thoughts were filled with hope that her spirit would at last be reunited with Warren's beyond the veil, and they would have all eternity together.

CHAPTER 50

After the selka attack, the three battered serpent ships limped across the calm ocean toward the scattered Norukai islands. More than forty raiders had been killed by the selka before the serpent god arrived. Now the survivors licked their wounds, sewed up deep gashes, and admired their scars. Now they wanted to go home.

By now, only ten slaves remained alive on the main vessel. As a result, there were not enough captives to man the oars, and the Norukai were forced to work alongside the slaves, grumbling at having to row like the walking meat.

Devastated by the death of Chalk, though, King Grieve refused to tolerate complaints. He spoke little except to snarl orders, clearly in the mood to kill something. He slammed his iron-plated fist against the head of a man who objected too strenuously to the menial work, cracking his skull, and the other crew members quickly muted their complaints.

"Remember your king," Grieve roared, then lowered his voice. "Remember Chalk. We all grieve."

Bannon and Lila pulled to the sullen beat of oar master Bosko. Bannon muttered to Lila as they pulled the wooden oars, "We both could have died fighting that night. I hope the Norukai islands aren't worse than death."

Lila's expression darkened. "I chose to keep you alive, boy. Now we have to decide how best to spend the rest of our days." Her chains rattled as she strained against the oar. "I plan to make the Norukai pay a great debt of blood. We will have our chance."

Bannon agreed with her.

The serpent ships sailed for two more days until the lookout sighted the first of the islands. Stark and ominous, the hummocks of rock looked like rotten teeth rising from the water. After the mourning king's harsh discipline, the Norukai uttered a subdued cheer upon seeing their home again.

King Grieve stood at the prow, his large hand resting on the serpent god figurehead. He stared at the main island, a rough-edged black monstrosity with a narrow protected harbor. A looming fortress occupied the pinnacle of the main island, its sheer walls made of perfectly fitted black stone blocks, high above the crashing waves.

"The Bastion," Grieve said in a hollow voice.

Water foamed along hazardous reefs, but the Norukai expertly guided their three vessels toward the narrow harbor. Dozens of serpent ships were anchored in the water of the archipelago, while others were under construction in dry docks. Lila responded to the sight with a grim frown. "Nearly a hundred ships were destroyed at Ildakar, but he has at least as many more here."

Some of the anchored serpent ships were old and weathered, but many had new wood and fresh blue sails. Bannon's throat went dry. "They continued building their navy even after King Grieve and his fleet sailed off to conquer Ildakar." He knew that General Utros was already leading his army overland, and now this huge Norukai fleet looked ready to ransack the cities of the coast. He wished Nicci and Nathan were there to help them. "How will the Old World survive this, Lila? What can we do to stop them?"

"We'll find a way to break free," Lila said, keeping her hard voice low. "We can defeat them all."

On deck, Grieve stood in silence like a figure carved out of anger. He gripped his war axe and looked ready to cleave any person who gave him a reason to do so. The king's dark mood could not diminish the excitement of the other Norukai, though, and they rallied when they saw the large gathering of ships.

The three returning vessels pulled into the sheltered harbor of the main island. Some of the gruff raiders chattered, eager to see their wives and husbands. One Norukai woman pointed to other distinctive serpent ships in the main harbor. "Look, Lars is back!" When she gnashed her teeth, her scarred jaw rippled.

With disgust, Bannon remembered Lars, one of the three Norukai captains that came to Ildakar to sell their slaves. Egged on by his supposed friends Amos, Jed, and Brock, Bannon had brawled with Lars and his companions. "Sweet Sea Mother, I'd like a chance to kill him. He's the reason I was sentenced to the combat pits."

Lila laughed. "I understand why you hate that man, boy, but think of the unexpected reward you received. If not for your foolish street fight, you would never have become *my* trainee. Now you are skilled enough to kill many Norukai."

"I will put your training to good use, I promise," Bannon said. "As soon as we get the chance."

Looking up at the steep hills around the Bastion, he

saw garden terraces from which hanging clumps of succulent weeds draped down the sheer rock. The Norukai picked out an existence on the windswept island, growing what they could while raiding for anything else they required.

When the three ships tied up to the pier, the raiders detached the slaves' ankle chains, but kept their hands bound as they herded them off the ship. Grieve snarled, "Take them to the Bastion and add them to the workforce until they are broken." He grimaced with his scarred lips. "Or killed."

A woman with the physique of a bear marched toward them along the dock. Her treelike legs were bare except for boots that rose to her knees. She wore a leather skirt studded with brass knobs. A tight sharkskin wrap around her torso was strained to near the breaking point by her large breasts. Her square face was as lovely as a blacksmith's anvil, and ropy red hair was tied in five long braids that hung like tentacles. When she opened her mouth to yell a greeting, she looked even more like a serpent. "King Grieve, I was tired of waiting for you." Her voice was so loud that the chatter from the disembarking crew fell into a lull. "I am ready to be your lover again. Don't miss your chance!"

The woman stepped up to Grieve as if she intended to collide with him. Some Norukai chuckled, but the king's face was stormy. "Atta. I've given no thought to you since we departed."

"I haven't wasted time on you either," Atta barked. "I have taken other lovers, but they were inadequate. When I saw your ships return, I decided to give you another chance." She punched him hard on the shoulder as if it were a flirtation. When he punched her back and knocked her reeling, Atta just laughed.

Bannon recalled the name. In his many unwanted so-
liloquies, Chalk had rambled about someone named
Atta. Now, Bannon whispered to Lila, "Once, Grieve
was injured so badly that he had to miss a Norukai raid,
and Atta mocked him for it. Grieve broke her jaw so
that she had to remain behind too."

"Ah, and that is how they became lovers," Lila con-
cluded. She seemed to think there was nothing unusual
about that form of courtship.

Hearing Lila speak, Atta turned to sneer at her, regarding the lean morazeth as if she were a gutted fish
in the market. "And who are you?" She scowled at the
scant black leather garments Lila wore. "You think you
can seduce my Grieve? He would break you."

"If he tried, I would break something of his," Lila
said.

When the other Norukai snickered at the retort, the
beefy woman smashed Lila on her already bruised face.
Lila reeled, but managed to keep her feet. King Grieve
used the distraction to stalk away down the pier, ignoring the woman. Atta huffed and strode after him.

Bannon and the slaves were marched away from the
docks, dragged up steep paths until they reached the imposing stone foundation of the Bastion on the steep
slopes. Their way was blocked by a low barred gate
that led into the massive fortress. The iron bars swung
open on creaking hinges to reveal a Norukai guard
glowering at the slaves. "All of you will be taken to sta-
tions to help prepare the homecoming feast."

With their hands bound in front of them, the rest of
the slaves staggered behind Bannon and Lila into the
dank, cold passageway. Chill winds and the damp of the
sea rendered the corridor miserable. Water dripped
from salt encrustations on the ceiling, and slimy algae

made the floor slippery. Though her black leather covered little of her skin, Lila showed no sign of being uncomfortable, just razor sharp in her determination.

The guard led them along, ducking under the low ceiling. Other guards followed the line, shoving the slaves when they moved too slowly. They climbed twisting stairs and through passageways lit only by smoky torches.

Without any windows or sunlight, Bannon lost all sense of direction, but Lila silently marked and memorized every step. Finally they entered a cavernous, noisy chamber with fiery ovens, barrels of flour, large stone countertops, and gaunt workers preparing a huge meal. Fish roasted on grates over fires that roared into multiple chimneys. Fish stew simmered in large cauldrons.

The smells were as powerful as the clamor of the pots and pans. Bannon's hunger increased like a sudden wildfire. For many days he'd had nothing to eat but fish guts and slop, and now the aroma of baking bread and charred fish made him weak-kneed.

"Food!" cried one of the captives behind him, extending his bound wrists in an attempt to grab a knot of bread left on a counter.

A veteran kitchen slave lashed out, "Stop! Don't touch." He lifted his left arm to show the stump of his wrist. "Or they'll cut off your hand, then cook it and eat it as part of the feast." The newcomers quailed even as they drooled at the bounty around them.

An old man limped up to greet the Norukai guard. "New slaves? How many?" His face was so wrinkled he looked like a raisin dried in the sun. His eyes roamed over the new group. "Ten. That'll be helpful. King Grieve hasn't replaced the Bastion staff in a long time."

The guard merely grunted and tugged Bannon in

front of the wrinkled old slave, glad to be rid of his charges. This seemed to be a demeaning activity to him.

The old man took a kitchen knife and sawed the ropes that bound Bannon's wrists, then methodically lurched down the line, freeing the rest of the captives. He muttered to himself, "Twenty loaves of bread, three barrels of salted fish, five platters of pickled cliffweed, one for each table." As he cut the bonds of one female slave, she collapsed, but the old man grabbed her bloody raw wrists and hauled her to her feet again. "No time for that! All of us have work to do. If King Grieve is disappointed in the feast, he'll eat you instead."

Bannon did not think it was an idle threat. The old man continued his muttering. "Salted fish, smoked fish, and fresh fish for the king." He heaved a sigh. "Although the king hates fish. Doesn't like goat either." He addressed the new arrivals. "I am Emmett, and I'm here to help you—help you serve King Grieve. Most Bastion slaves do not last long, but I have been here for ten years, longer than any other captive. If you follow my instructions, I will see to it that you survive."

"Why would you do that?" Lila demanded.

"Because I need the help." Emmett lowered his voice, though there was only one Norukai near the far entrance to the kitchen, a husky woman who looked bored and disappointed. He pulled the new arrivals together and whispered in a conspiratorial, urgent voice. "I will help you stay alive, but you must listen to me. If you cause trouble, the king will break your bones and set them wrong, just so you remember." He looked down at his badly healed leg.

Lila flexed her fingers and frowned at her scabbed wrists. "My intent is to kill as many Norukai as possible. That's why I let myself be captured. I'm going to free Bannon, then I will escape." She looked at the other frightened slaves, thinking they were weak. "If you are useful, we may allow you all to join us when we leave here."

Emmett quailed. "That isn't how you stay alive! The Norukai will kill you. Trust me, I've seen it happen many times."

"You have not seen me," Lila said.

"Or me," Bannon added. "She's a morazeth, and I was trained in the combat pits of Ildakar. We may have a better chance than our predecessors."

Emmett groaned, deeply saddened. "Then I can't help you to stay alive." Back to business, he snapped his head up so abruptly that his gray ponytail bounced. "Right now, there's work to do here. Throw your lives away later, after the feast is over. No time to clean any of you up. No fresh clothes, but you—" He looked at Lila and her scant black leather outfit. "Yes, you in particular, I will give you an old, drab robe to cover yourself."

She was insulted. "I am proud of my body. This garment marks me as a morazeth."

"That garment marks you as an object of desire." Emmett looked frantic. "Do you want to be passed from table to table in a banquet hall full of lusty Norukai men? And women?"

"They can try," Lila said. "They will regret it."

Bannon remembered the mangled would-be rapist aboard the serpent ships after Lila had been captured, but he didn't want to test that again. He urged her, "Lila, it would be best not to call attention to yourself. Let's choose our own time to fight. Not now." Emmett brought forth a gray, tattered wool garment she could drape over herself, and Bannon pleaded with her. "Just wear it."

"You may have a point, boy," she admitted, and pulled the shapeless loose garment over her head to drape her body. "But I don't like it."

Emmett wrung his hands. "Come, we have to start serving. Captain Lars is already in the banquet hall, and King Grieve will arrive soon. You all must serve."

"I may be forced to bring them food," Lila said, "but I will not *serve*."

When the old man swallowed, the wrinkles puckered on his wattled neck. He shook his head. "It is my fervent hope that you all survive the meal."

CHAPTER 51

The kraken-hunter ship cut swiftly across the sea, heading north toward Tanimura. With her gift, Nicci summoned fair winds that stretched the patchwork sails, with the added advantage that the breeze diminished the foul smell that clung to the vessel.

The *Chaser* was mostly empty, now that the refugees had been off-loaded at Serrimundi, and the captain used the opportunity to have his crew patch and scrub the vessel. "Peel off at least a few layers of dried slime. I want to see some of the grain in the wood."

"Slime? You called it varnish before, Captain!" one of the shirtless men called back with a laugh. His voice whistled through missing front teeth.

"Indulge me." Jared smiled. "We'll cover it up with more kraken slime soon enough. If we see one of the beasts, I'm up for a hunt." The rest of the crew cheered.

Nicci did not want any delay. "We must reach Tanimura with all due haste, Captain. No time for hunting."

"We'll get there before you know it, Sorceress." Jared chuckled dismissively. "Remember, you were going to ride a smelly horse all this way." The rest of the crew snickered, finding the suggestion ridiculous.

That night, Nicci joined the captain in his cabin for

dinner, a slab of rubbery kraken meat. Jared devoured the meal with relish, and though Nicci found little about the food appealing, she ate anyway. "I've tasted worse," she said, and Jared took it as a compliment.

The krakener had a crew of fifteen who had been together for years, unlike many other ships, whose crews changed at every port. Kraken hunting was a hard, dirty, smelly job, and usually thankless. The men who worked such ships kept to themselves even in the dockside taverns, where they were considered a lower class than the crews of cargo ships. Nicci could tell that the lingering aroma of the slimy creatures would not wash away even after repeated trips to bathhouses, so these men accepted their lot and enjoyed their labors.

Jared was immensely proud of how many kraken kills he had made, how many cargo loads he had delivered to cities along the coast. "Those who like kraken meat look forward to my arrival. We are greeted with resounding cheers whenever we come to port." He gave his rakish smile.

"You are cheered by everyone who appreciates kraken meat?" she asked. "That can't be a very large number."

"They have discriminating tastes." He cut a chunk of the gray meat and chewed on it with a look of satisfaction. He washed down his meal with a gulp of ale. Nicci found herself taking more and more drinks of the bitter beer to counteract the taste. "I'll be glad to get back to kraken hunting, as soon as we defeat all these enemies you talk about."

"This war won't be over for a long time, and it's about to get much worse. That's why I need to get to Tanimura and rally the D'Haran garrison." She bit her lower lip. "I only hope that by now reinforcements have arrived from Lord Rahl. I dispatched an important message to him the last time I came here."

Nicci felt a pang to think that she was so far away from Richard, the man she truly loved. She and Nathan were doing this task for him, helping to spread the word of the D'Haran Empire, and now she needed Richard's help. If he sent a powerful military force marching south to Tanimura as a defense against the double threat, Nicci knew their victory was assured. Richard had never let her down.

"Just get me to Tanimura, Captain," she said, "and you will have done a great service for the war effort."

When the *Chaser* entered Tanimura Harbor, Nicci regarded the whitewashed buildings of the city she knew so well. Houses were crowded against one another, forming uneven lines of streets and alleys. Banners rippled from rooftops, showing the colors of D'Hara and the stylized "R" of Lord Rahl. Fishing boats and cargo ships crowded the harbor, but most importantly she saw dozens of large vessels that had been refitted as warships for the D'Haran navy. The sight satisfied her greatly, showing that General Linden had heeded her warning and begun to build up serious defenses.

Tanimura Harbor was much larger than Serrimundi's enclosed, sheltered harbor. Assisted by Nicci's directed breezes, the krakener cut a straight line toward the docks. The *Chaser* cruised past the flat expanse of Halsband Island, which was separate from the main city although it had been connected by graceful bridges.

The island once held the towering Palace of the Prophets, where Nicci had lived for many decades as a Sister of the Light and secretly as a Sister of the Dark. She had trained here and served here, and she had also served the Keeper of the underworld. Now the entire island was just rubble. By triggering the constructed spell that ran through the palace, Richard Rahl had brought down the gigantic structure.

Jared stood next to her, holding the ship's rail. "Ah, Tanimura! I love the smell of that harbor."

Nicci couldn't smell anything beyond the fishy slime of the krakener. "It is good to be home," she said, but her voice held no warmth. This place had too much darkness for her.

After the *Chaser* docked, Nicci disembarked quickly, intent on reaching the garrison. Captain Jared called after her as she walked down the gangplank, "My ship is at your disposal, should you ever need it again, Sorceress!"

"I'll remember that. It was a fast ship."

"With a good captain," he said.

She didn't reply as she worked her way through the bustle of dockside activity. Mules pulled wagons loaded with heavy crates; men stacked bales of hay and sacks of grain where merchants dickered over prices. Familiar sights and sounds brought back memories of when she had been an acolyte determined to serve the Imperial Order, because her mother had beaten those teachings into her. That upbringing had sent her down a dark path that had only worsened until Nicci finally reached a crossroads in her life in a man named Richard Rahl. . . .

Now, she moved through the streets toward the

D'Haran garrison. Several weeks ago, General Linden had dispatched a rider up to the People's Palace carrying her message and her request for help. Nicci knew Richard would believe her about the threat of General Utros. A large army of reinforcements might not have made the journey yet, but she expected they were on the way. She hoped Richard had at least sent a reply. She had not heard from him in such a long time.

Approaching the garrison, she was relieved to see soldiers patrolling the streets in chain mail and leather armor, with the officers wearing colorful capes. Word traveled swiftly as she walked at a deliberate pace, and by the time she reached the gates of the walled garrison, many soldiers had lined up, anxious to hear what she had to say.

"It's the sorceress!"

"Nicci's back."

"Death's Mistress!"

The anxious garrison soldiers parted as Nicci walked straight across the training yard and past the barracks to the two-story headquarters building. It had been built with fresh-sawn wood and only recently whitewashed to match the common architecture in Tanimura.

At their desks in the first offices, clerks looked up from writing notations in their ledgers, but she strode past them without a word. As she climbed the stairs to the second story, she had no doubt that General Linden would already be waiting for her.

Indeed, he sat at his desk, hands folded. Linden was a thin, thirtyish man, young for his high rank but promoted after so many officers had been killed in the previous war. A port-wine birthmark was prominent on his left cheek, and his crooked nose had obviously been broken more than once.

He gave her a serious nod of welcome. "I didn't expect you back so soon, Sorceress. We are working hard to increase the city's defenses. We built warships and refitted other vessels so we can secure the harbor. Our patrols have doubled on the water. Troop numbers have increased substantially, and we are getting stronger every day."

"Good," Nicci said. "General Utros is on the move, as I feared, and the Norukai are ravaging the cities on the coast. Serrimundi was attacked not long ago, as was Effren, and possibly Larrikan Shores. Things are about to get much worse."

"Yes, we've received reports." Linden tapped his finger on the desk. He had straightened the papers in front of him in anticipation of her arrival. "We dispatched aid down to Serrimundi after the last Norukai raid, and we are recruiting widely among the city people and the hill villages. I want to expand the army so that each large town has a well-armed defense force against other raids."

She stepped forward to grip the edge of his desk. "Make no mistake, General, these are not just raids. The ancient army of Utros forged an alliance with King Grieve of the Norukai. Together, they will overrun the Old World. Did my message reach D'Hara?" she asked, realizing that was the answer she most wanted to hear. "Will Lord Rahl send the D'Haran army to defend us? If your courier traveled as swiftly as I hope, the troops should already be on the way. We will need them soon."

Worry lines appeared on Linden's brow. Subconsciously, he rubbed his birthmark with his thumb. "Lord Rahl did send a response. He says he would like to aid Tanimura and the threatened cities, but . . . it is not possible at this time. He and D'Hara cannot help you."

CHAPTER 52

Exhausted and soaked with blood from all the enemy soldiers he killed, Nathan hauled himself up the rocks at the end of the dwindling side canyon. He climbed handhold after handhold, anxious to reach the highlands and the wilderness where they could shelter. Olgya climbed next to him, along with ten D'Haran soldiers who had retreated with their band. On General Zimmer's instructions, the defenders had separated into many different parties, all taking different routes.

One of the wounded soldiers with them, a cocky card player, was bleeding badly from a deep gash in his side. He spilled a trail of red as he plodded alongside the others, painstakingly working his way higher. Nathan wasn't certain the man would survive much longer. Though the wizard had little strength left, he could have used his gift to heal the deep cut, if they stopped for a while and rested. But that was not an option. Utros threw thousands upon thousands of warriors after the last surviving defenders of Cliffwall, and they kept closing in.

When Nathan finally reached a high point, he turned and watched Verna's Weeping Stone spell destroy Cliffwall. The roof of the archive grotto dripped down and closed over, sealing the tunnels and the library chambers forever. The rock walls melted and sagged like a mudslide, pouring down onto part of the army.

Even from his distant vantage, Nathan could feel the prelate's building magic that resonated through lines of force. The sheer walls began to run like wax, and as the destruction continued, he stared in disbelief. Verna had only planned to collapse the alcove opening and seal the books and scrolls in stone before she retreated. But the devastation continued to unfold. "Dear spirits, she is destroying the entire canyon!"

He saw Verna's tiny figure climbing above the slumping alcove, racing to get out of the way, but the stone itself shifted beneath her. Nathan sensed the exact point at which she lost control of the powerful spell. It was like a vicious dog that turned on its master.

Beside him, Olgya and the soldiers watched half of the Cliffwall canyon turn into liquid, and the flood of stone rolled down to engulf the countless ancient warriors. With a groan of dismay, Nathan watched Prelate Verna slip and plunge into the flowing rock. She tried to pull herself out, but sank down, engulfed.

The world went silent as the shock shut down his senses. His heart ached with a swell of memories. So much of his life had been bound up with the prelate. He had never loved Verna as he had come to love her predecessor, Prelate Ann, but now watching her die, he felt a tremendous blow. Tears glistened in his azure eyes and spilled down his cheeks.

Elsa had done a similar thing, unleashing enough magic to save them, even though she knew it would destroy her. Now both of those marvelous women were gone, sacrificing their lives in order to wound the army of General Utros.

After Verna died, her spell faded, and the lines of magic came untangled as fields collapsed and webs unraveled. The stone hardened again.

While the refugees stared in horror, though, they lost track of their pursuers. With an outcry, one of the gaunt enemy soldiers charged toward them with a notched sword. The wounded card player had sagged down on a rock to rest, bleeding heavily from his side, but now he lurched to his feet and used the last of his strength to deflect the attacker's sword. He drove his own dagger into the enemy's throat, but in the process he suffered another deep stab wound. Dying, the card player pushed himself over the edge of the drop-off so that both he and the ancient soldier tumbled down the steep canyon in a bloody tangle of arms and legs.

Although Nathan's party had finished the climb and worked their way into the high desert wilderness, enemy stragglers still pursued them up the canyon. Blocking off his grief, he found the strength to call up more wizard's fire, a sphere in each hand. With anger at Verna's death driving him, he hurled the searing fire toward the pursuers. They threw up their gauntleted arms to deflect the fire, but they could not block the unstoppable inferno that burned them to ashes.

Nathan dropped to his knees and wept. His long white hair was a tangled mess. His new vest and embroidered cape dripped with blood and human cinders. During the battle at the bottleneck in the headwall, he and his gifted companions had used every desperate trick, all the spells they knew. He had even killed five with his sword, and now his arm was sore from ringing blows.

Olgya stepped closer to him. She was compact and tough, wearing skirts and a wrap of her enhanced silk, which remained unfrayed even after all the abuse. Crimson droplets spattered her face. One of her tight braids had been severed by a knife stroke, and the ragged end hung down to her ear like a decapitated snake. Her expression was tight, as if all the gift had been wrung out of her, but she clung to life and determination. She nodded at the blackened stains in the wake of his wizard's fire. "We don't have to worry about pursuit anymore, Nathan. We can take care of any stragglers that managed to get through."

Nathan wiped his cheek and looked back down the canyon to where the flood of rock had rehardened, leaving innumerable bodies trapped within like flies in amber. "I know. Prelate Verna did what she needed to. Neither General Utros nor anyone else will get their hands on the dangerous knowledge from the archive. It is gone forever."

"It was necessary to protect the world," Olgya said. "We all agreed."

"That's true, but Verna is gone . . . just as Elsa is gone. With each victory like this, we lose a part of ourselves and a part of our heritage. What will be left of us when all is said and done?" He turned away so he no longer had to look at the ruins of the once peaceful canyon. He couldn't even feel satisfied to know how many of the enemy soldiers had been killed in the flood of stone. Thousands? Tens of thousands?

Verna was still dead, and the core of Utros's army was still out there. Even with Cliffwall destroyed, they would continue marching across the Old World.

"Let's get to the rendezvous point," Nathan growled, "and take stock of who we have left."

* * *

They followed a tangled route through the high canyons up and beyond Cliffwall, and they met up
with the other evacuating parties. Thorn and Lyesse
guided six soldiers, Rendell, and a handful of shaken
Cliffwall scholars. The two morazeth were covered with
gore and soot, their rune-marked skin laced with minor wounds, but they were charged with energy, as if
this were no more than an enjoyable game of Ja'La.

Thorn looked at her partner. "We killed so many that
we each lost track of our score."

Lyesse said, "Therefore we will consider it a tie and
start over. I look forward to the challenge."

The other woman nodded. "There will be more of
them to kill."

When all the groups gathered in their makeshift
camp, Oron was clearly relieved to see that Nathan, Olgya, and Perri had survived. "Good, we could not afford to lose more of our gifted."

"We've already lost too many," Nathan said.

"Who else is gone?" Olgya asked, looking around
and counting heads.

Oron described how the wizard Leo had fallen from
the outer cliff when Ruva blasted the stone. In addition
to many D'Haran soldiers, two of Captain Trevor's Ildakaran guards had been killed. Perri hunkered down
and shook her head. "Almost nothing remains of our
great city of Ildakar anymore."

"We remain," Lord Oron said.

"There won't be much left of the Old World once
General Utros is through with it," Nathan said. "Ah,
Verna . . . poor Verna."

The Sisters of the Light were deeply shaken by the
loss of their prelate. Sisters Rhoda and Eldine joined
Nathan by the small campfire. "After the star shift elim-

inated prophecy, our order's reason for existence suffered a terrible blow," Rhoda said. "But Verna didn't give up. She helped us try to find new purpose."

"No, Verna did not give up," Nathan said. "She made quite a difference for all of us, and for me in particular."

More Sisters joined him, and they all reminisced about the prelate. Nathan let out a bitter laugh, and when Mab looked at him in surprise, he said, "Considering all the resentments I held for the Sisters of the Light, the irony is deep that you should comfort me."

Amber also joined the group. "We should all comfort one another, because we've all been hurt, but we have to keep moving." She looked around for reassurance. "We are going to keep moving, aren't we? General Utros and his army will continue marching to the coast. My brother Norcross is at Renda Bay. He'll help us fight."

"Yes, my dear," Nathan said. "We must get to Renda Bay before that army does."

CHAPTER 53

The Norukai celebration for King Grieve and Captain Lars was loud, boisterous, and violent. Bannon found it sickening.

Caked with blood and covered with bruises and scabs from the selka attack, along with the daily abuse they suffered aboard the serpent ships, the new slaves were pressed into service in the Bastion kitchens. Overworked and terrified, old Emmett limped about loading platters with food, including a goat that still sizzled on the spit.

The head slave barked orders to his sullen kitchen crew, occasionally pausing for hurried explanations to the newcomers who didn't know what to do. "Take the roast goat! There's a rack behind the king's throne. He will slice off the meat himself, and I pray he doesn't complain that it's too bloody, if he is even willing to eat goat tonight. I don't dare tell him the banquet isn't ready." Emmett sighed, panting hard. "I have seen Grieve eat animals raw, and maybe he'll be in that sort of mood. I wish I had something other than goat or fish. . . ."

One of the kitchen slaves, a downcast man with a scar on his cheek, picked up an end of the spit while a new slave was shoved forward to take the other end. They shuffled off with their burden as a Norukai guard marched behind them. Whole fish were scraped from racks in the fiery ovens and placed on platters. Urns of pickled fish were carried off by slaves who staggered under the weight. When one such urn was thrust into Bannon's arms, he looked down into the hunks of gray meat preserved in salt water, vinegar, and lye. The stench reminded him of the horribly preserved fish that was a food staple during lean years on Chiriya Island. As the fumes roiled up, he held the urn as far out in front of him as possible and followed the roasted goat.

Emmett gave Lila a brass pitcher of wine, and she glared daggers at him. "I have no wish to pander to these vile creatures." She looked uncomfortable in the formless dress that covered her slender body.

"Neither do I, but my wish to live is stronger than my disgust, and if you want to survive, then you must cooperate." The old slave's voice had a pleading tone. "After the banquet is over, I can explain in detail how the Bastion functions and how you may be able to live another day, another month, and another year."

When the Norukai guards had left the kitchen to escort the servers, Lila slowly and deliberately dripped a mouthful of spit into the open pitcher of wine. The other slaves watched her, shocked but titillated.

Emmett was horrified. "They'll cut you into pieces and roast you in the fireplace if they find out!"

The morazeth faced him, defiant. "They didn't see me, and you aren't going to tell them."

On his way out the door with his pickled fish, Bannon saw what she had done. Mirroring her rebelliousness, he dredged up a lump of phlegm and spat it into the urn. "Sweet Sea Mother, we have to fight in any way we can."

The corridor beyond the kitchens led into a loud banquet hall. The walls were black stone, and smoke-stained timbers crossed the ceiling. Desiccated heads hung from hooks on the rafters, probably enemies that King Grieve had slain.

The banquet hall sounded like a battlefield, with boasting Norukai, pounding fists on tables, calls for food, and shouted insults. Six long tables were crowded with Norukai warriors who sported an array of hideous disfigurements on their faces, heads, and shoulders. The women raiders looked just as ugly as the men, and they growled at one another, striking and then being struck back in what Bannon realized was a brutal form of courtship.

At the front table, King Grieve slumped in a blocky throne that looked like a torture device. The bone spurs implanted in his shoulders poked out of his sharkskin vest like upthrust teeth. He hunched, brooding and bristling, deaf to the roar of conversation and the rowdy guests. He rested his clenched fists on the tabletop and just stared ahead. At the empty place beside him, Grieve had upturned a much smaller chair and smashed it on the table surface so that no one would ever sit there again. Bannon realized that must have been Chalk's seat.

The coarse woman Atta sat on the opposite side of the throne, as if she owned Grieve, but the king paid little attention to her. At the second table, the newly returned raider captain Lars sat like some kind of celebrity. Bannon recognized the man from Ildakar, and hated him. Lars was already half drunk, and Bannon wondered if the disgusting raider would remember him.

King Grieve suddenly sat up and pounded his fist on the table. "I gave you a death sentence, Lars." The conversation fell swiftly into uneven muttering.

The raider captain paused in midboast, set down his tankard, and turned to his king. "You told me to go out and die in battle, King Grieve. I launched raid after raid and killed at least a hundred weaklings by my own hand. I will die as you commanded, but I don't intend to die until I've killed a lot more."

The other Norukai cheered at his bravado, but Grieve did not seem amused. "You are still a coward for your failure at Renda Bay. You must atone to the serpent god for being defeated by mere walking meat."

Lars's cheeks flushed red with embarrassment. "I understand, my king, and I will make them pay. I would not have returned here had I not needed provisions and crew. Countless more serpent ships have been constructed, in preparation. If you want me to leave the entire coast in flames, then I require more ships." He lifted his tankard in a toast. The Norukai roared.

"We have more ships," Grieve said. "Chalk's visions promised we would have more ships." He stared down at his empty plate.

The servants carrying the steaming goat carcass hurried forward and settled the ends of the spit into the forked branches of the stand. The roasted animal wafted a savory aroma that filled the hall, briefly overwhelming the stench of so many unwashed and bloodstained warriors. Grieve grimaced.

Bannon carried his urn of preserved fish and purposely set it in front of Lars without comment. The Norukai captain leaned forward and inhaled deeply, then belched. "Perfect for the next course." He looked up at Bannon, met his eyes, and hesitated. The young man waited for him to explode with recognition, but Lars said only, "You are ugly."

Lars reached into the urn with his hand and scooped out the top gobbets of gelatinous fish. Bannon's wad of spit was indistinguishable from the mess, and Lars slurped it with a grunt of satisfaction.

Platters of fish were served at the head table, but King Grieve ignored them, apparently without an appetite. Atta hungrily regarded the goat carcass while everyone waited for the king to make the first move. Finally, Atta took the king's plate and stood. "It is my pleasure to serve you, Grieve. And you can service me with pleasure later." With her dagger, she stabbed the steaming haunch and carved out a portion of rare meat, which she added to the plate. She set it in front of him before she served herself a similar amount, then sat down and fell to eating beside him.

Grieve finally began eating, although he didn't seem to taste the meat, didn't enjoy the celebration. "Soon we go to war," he said, and by the tone of his voice, that was the only thing he looked forward to.

Lila entered with her pitcher of wine, unrecognizable in her loose wool dress. She walked with confidence, as if she had already defeated every single person in the room. She came stiffly forward and poured wine into Grieve's goblet. He dully drained half of the wine in a single gulp, ignoring her. As she turned to fill Atta's goblet, clearly resenting the effort, Grieve lashed out in his angry sorrow, shoving Lila away. He didn't even seem to know what he was doing in his red misery, but Lila lurched, and half of the wine pitcher poured down on Atta.

The Norukai woman exploded. Like a viper striking, she lurched to her feet, knocking her platter aside and dumping the goat meat on the floor. Lila reacted with morazeth reflexes to defend herself. She dropped the brass pitcher, which clanged on the flagstone floor and spilled the red wine like blood. Atta pulled back her fist, and the muscles in her meaty arm bulged.

Bannon pushed forward to help, frantic to save her, but Lila needed no help.

Her hand flashed up and caught Atta's fist as it slammed toward her. The Norukai woman strained, her muscles bulging as Lila thwarted her blow. Atta glowered, pressed, while Lila gritted her teeth and pushed back. She whispered through clenched teeth, "It was an accident." She flashed a glance at Grieve, who remained ignorant of what he had instinctively done. She turned back to Atta. "I am . . . sorry." It sounded as if the words were ripped from her throat.

With a heave of effort, Atta snatched her fist away. "An accident!"

Before Lila could move, the anvil-faced woman struck her across the cheek. Lila caught herself, coiled, but forced herself not to hit back. She said in an icy voice, "I am a morazeth. You have my apology, and that is all you will get."

Grieve finally took notice. He stood up and punched Lila on the side of the head so that she buckled to the floor. Atta loomed over her. "I give you a death sentence too, but just as Grieve did with Lars, I can take a long time to kill you."

"Do your best," Lila retorted.

At the entrance to the banquet hall, Emmett and several slaves hurried in with baskets of bread and trays of roasted and smoked fish as well as bowls of pickled saltweed. "Next course!" the old man said, distracting them. "There's more food to come, and countless desserts."

Emmett limped to the head table as the gathered raiders anticipated the second round of food. Moving deftly despite his limp, the old man maneuvered among the tables and took the stunned Lila by the elbow. "Come, don't just rest there! You have work to do in the kitchens." He also hooked Bannon's arm and escorted them both away. "Quick! We dare not make King Grieve wait."

While Atta continued her murderous stare, Emmett ushered the two into the shadowy corridors and whatever small safety the kitchens could offer.

O ver the next few days as the slave staff in the Bastion kept their heads down and continued their duties, Atta singled out Lila for torment. The Norukai woman found ways to confront her in the corridors and slam her against the wall in an attempt to provoke her. "Go on, fight me and I will kill you!"

Bannon tried to intercede. "Stop! We're just doing our tasks."

"This one's task is to die." Atta pressed her face closer to Lila. "Grieve is my lover. I know you want him."

"I want him dead," Lila said, "but if I have to kill you first, that would be fine with me."

Bannon whispered quickly, "If you kill Atta, the king will murder you himself."

Lila disagreed, and loudly. "If I kill her, then the king will laugh because she is weak." She challenged Atta directly. "Do you wish me to fight you? Give me a weapon and we'll see who walks away."

With a meaty hand Atta slammed her into the wall. "I will give you nothing, not even death. Not yet." The Norukai woman stalked off, but Lila remained standing.

She plucked at her loose woolen garment as if it offended her.

She and Bannon worked together whenever possible. Emmett helped them by giving them similar assignments, but when the Norukai realized the two were close companions, the workmasters forcibly separated them. Still, Lila managed to meet with Bannon often enough, and together they looked for any opportunity to escape the Bastion. But with so many armored and angry Norukai crowding the fortress, they found no possibilities.

"Old Emmett knows every corner of the Bastion," Bannon said. "He could help us escape."

Lila was skeptical. "After so much time here, he doesn't even remember freedom. He only remembers to be afraid for his own life." She shook her head. "I promised to rescue you, and I will find a way."

"And I promised to fight at your side. You trained me to face combat bears and sand panthers. I can handle a few Norukai in a fair fight."

Lila smiled. "You have potential after all, boy."

The next day, while Lila was tending a cauldron of boiling fish stew, Atta barged into the kitchens, raising her nose to the air. "It is midday. King Grieve is hungry." She stalked over to Lila at the large soup pot, sniffing loudly. "Something smells bad. I thought it was the cooking." She sniffed again. "But it's merely the stench of this vermin."

She grabbed the iron ladle, pulled up a brimming scoop, and slurped it while Lila glared. Then Atta purposefully poured the scalding liquid on Lila's shoulder where the bare skin showed from her garment's ragged neck hole. The morazeth flinched, but let out no sound of pain as the hot soup dripped down her arm. She just glared defiantly, enduring the burn.

Emmett hustled forward with his lurching gait. "Please, Atta! Don't kill my staff. King Grieve told you not to kill the staff."

"I didn't promise not to *damage* them." Atta looked at the healing bruises on Lila's face, the fresh red scald mark on her shoulder. Satisfied for the moment, she left the kitchens.

Bannon ran over to Lila with a washrag soaked in cool water and pressed it against her burned skin. Now that Atta was gone, she let herself wince.

Emmett shuffled his feet, and Bannon rounded on him. "This is why you must help us escape! We've got to find a way."

CHAPTER 54

Nicci was devastated to hear the news from General Linden. She realized only then how much she had been counting on Richard and the D'Haran army. "What do you mean he's not sending troops? Did I not convey the threat of the ancient army, of the Norukai fleet?"

"Yes, of course, Sorceress," Linden said as he nervously shuffled the papers in front of him. "Lord Rahl says he can't spare the army right now, and besides, such an army would never reach you in time."

Nicci paced off a short distance as she struggled to control her worry over how serious the situation was. She knew Richard. She knew him perhaps better than anyone other than Kahlan. Richard would know that she would ask for that kind of help only if she was desperate. And, she also knew that Richard wouldn't turn her down unless it was impossible for him to help her. Now, she had the added concern of what kind of problem Richard had on his hands, but she also realized that it was now her responsibility to defend Tanimura and the other cities in the south. Richard was putting his trust in her.

She turned back to Linden, her focus shifting.

"Richard wouldn't have left it at that. He must have said something else."

Linden nodded as he pulled open one of the drawers in his desk. He gave her a shaky smile. From the desk drawer, he retrieved a leather-wrapped parcel. "He did. He sent this." He placed the package on the desktop. "He said you would know what to do with it."

Nicci cautiously unfolded the leather, worried about what message she would find. To her surprise, instead of a message, she found only a bone box in the leather pouch, a cube barely an inch on a side.

As she turned the cube in her fingers, studying it more thoroughly, she realized that, despite its size, this was an object of great importance.

"We were afraid to open the box, Sorceress." Linden was intent and curious. "What is it?"

With her nail, she found a crack on the top edge and worked it open to reveal a cavity inside the box. The small cube held a floating, rotating orb of light no larger than a pea. The glowing sphere was lit from within by a network of faint lines and tiny sparks of light.

She recognized what it was, which only deepened her concentration. "It is a newly constructed spell."

Probing with her gift, she was able to recognize that this compact nugget had the same type of power as the original magic from the design of the Wizard's Keep, something that only Richard would understand. She realized that the spell was somehow keyed to the actual, ancient defensive nature of the Keep itself.

Linden looked on, his face full of questions.

"Whatever it is, Lord Rahl must mean for it to help defend us," Nicci said. "To help *me*." Still looking for answers, she felt inside the leather pouch again, but there was definitely no other message from Richard, no clue. She would have to figure this out for herself. The message must be on the bone box itself.

She closed the lid again, snapping it into place to hide the glowing pearl of the spell. The hard white sides of the cube bore fine etchings, lines, designs, and inscribed symbols. At first she couldn't read them, but then she recognized the language of Creation—which Richard understood, and he knew that Nicci also understood. Here was her message!

She knew that if General Linden or the courier had opened the pouch and looked at it, and she assumed they had, they wouldn't have known what those symbols were or what they could mean. Only those who could read the ancient language of Creation would be able to read those emblems and open such a box.

She also knew that only Richard could have made it, and Richard would know that no one but Nicci would be able to decipher those symbols. Until she could translate them, she could only wonder at the ancient power those symbols protected.

Richard would not have used spells in the language of Creation unless whatever was inside was both profoundly important and profoundly dangerous. This was personal, from Richard to no one else but Nicci. As she stared at the small bone box in her hand, she had to take a steadying breath at the connection to Richard she was holding. It was almost as if he was whispering a solution to her.

But what solution?

After long concentration and working through the symbols until she could read the markings, she still did not understand the answer. *Life to the living. Death to the dead.* How was she supposed to use that?

Nicci was mystified. With the stakes so high, why

didn't Richard just explain clearly? She had told him about the enormous threat of the reawakened army. She had counted on Richard, needed Richard's wisdom and strength, and now she was upset that he hadn't given her a plain answer.

Linden was smiling tentatively at her, hoping for good news. Distracted by the puzzle, she issued brusque orders for what she needed now. "I have to ignite a verification web to see what sort of constructed spell Richard created. I need space to work, an empty room where I won't be disturbed."

Linden jumped up from his desk and called soldiers. In only a few moments, they had pulled and scraped chairs from a meeting room down the hall. Nicci followed them into the empty chamber, preoccupied with her own investigation.

She knew she needed to do more than a standard verification web on this bone box, but rather an aspect analysis of a verification web from an interior perspective. That would allow her to examine the constructed spell down to its core element. She steeled herself, realizing that casting the web would require her to use Subtractive Magic. She had no other choice.

Nicci stood inside the large empty room in the garrison headquarters and looked around the whitewashed walls, the wooden floor. Linden and the soldiers waited eagerly just outside the door. "This place will do," she said, looking down at the tiny box. "Make sure I am not disturbed as I work. Much depends on what I learn here."

Fascinated by the enigma of the constructed spell, she paid no attention to the soldiers, who retreated farther from the door.

Using one of the daggers at her hip, she slashed her

palm, interested only in the blood that welled up. She would need a lot of it.

Standing in the middle of the wooden floor, she used the dripping blood to draw a careful Grace across the boards. The Grace was a powerful device, and drawn in blood under only the rarest of circumstances, but Nicci needed that power now. An inner and outer circle represented the underworld and the world of the living, separated by a square, and then at the center an eight-pointed star indicated the Creator's light, which radiated lines throughout the Grace. The entire process of drawing the complex symbol took her the better part of an hour.

When she was ready, Nicci stood in the center of the magic-infused emblem on the floor. Closing her eyes, she held the bone box in her intact palm, while she lifted the small lid with the other. Then she opened herself to her power.

Surrounded by her thoughts, keeping her eyes closed, Nicci felt nothing other than a kind of weightlessness. She drifted, searching, probing, and reached out with a verification web in search of answers.

Only when Nicci opened her eyes did she realize that she was floating upright and frozen in midair, drifting and slowly rotating several feet off the floor above the blood-drawn Grace. Through the open door to the room, she saw Linden and the curious soldiers watching her, astonished, but they were as still as statues. She heard not a whisper of air, couldn't even hear her own heartbeat in her ears. As she floated, life itself seemed to be suspended.

Extending her sight further, she saw that she was surrounded by lines of glowing green light that formed an intricate geometric framework tangled around her.

Nicci herself was the living core of a verification web for a constructed spell. Shifting her head, she also realized that one of her feet was suspended over the Grace's outer circle that represented the underworld.

Still not understanding, Nicci used her gift to ignite the verification web, as she had planned. She stretched out, studying all the glowing lines in the air rising from the Grace, ensnaring her own body and the glowing pearl inside the bone box.

But the web offered no answers. No matter how hard Nicci tried, the magic gave her only a blank response, and the constructed spell's mysterious purpose remained a complete cipher. Richard's intent was no clearer than it was before.

Frustrated, she withdrew her power and shut down the web, extinguishing the lines of light. They retracted back into the glowing orb inside the bone box. Gently, she drifted back down to the floor and felt solid wood beneath her feet, but her mind still seemed disconnected. She stood still, regaining her balance for a frozen moment.

Out in the corridor, Linden and the soldiers were too hesitant to offer help. After wiping her bleeding palm on her black dress, Nicci snapped the box closed again and pocketed it. She was profoundly heartbroken that whatever Richard had sent seemed useless, or at least incomprehensible. She had hoped for a miracle. Now she had to solve it herself.

General Linden cleared his throat. "What did you discover, Sorceress? Do you understand the weapon Lord Rahl sent for us?"

She turned her cold blue eyes toward him. "I fear we are doomed."

CHAPTER 55

The wave of rock was like a petrified tide that buried his front ranks, all those loyal fighters who had continued to follow him even though they had lost everything else. Utros stared at the fresh uneven rock that covered the canyon floor, searching for words. Finally, he said, "Our destiny is permanently wrapped in stone."

Ruva raged beside him, a roiling mass of barely constrained magic. "Those men gave their lives for you, beloved Utros. They know you will not falter. They know you will conquer the world, as you swore to do." She looked at the bodies partially imprisoned in stone. "And their sacrifice will help you achieve that goal."

"How?" Utros snarled at her. "*How* does this help me?" He looked at the devastation, the massacre.

The fallen canyon wall had hardened like a mudslide baked in the hot sun, studded with thousands of corpses like insects caught in pitch. His soldiers had worn the best armor; their swords were sharp, their training was excellent, and they could fight against any enemy—but how could they prepare for this? Arms thrust upward still clutching swords, gauntlets and booted feet protruding in the air with the rest of the bodies drowned under rock.

One man's head, his helmet askew, grimaced and gasped. The rest of his body was submerged in the stone; though he could still breathe, he was trapped, crushed. His mouth opened and closed, and his eyes bulged as he tried to sip air. The dying soldier couldn't even form words; he had no room left in his chest. His gaunt face turned blue as he suffocated, little by little.

Utros leaned over him. "I can do nothing to help you." His heart wrenched with vengeance and sadness. "I am grateful for your service and sorry for your sacrifice." He drew his sword. "This is all I can offer." He struck off the man's head, leaving a stump that spouted blood from the rim of stone.

He would order his soldiers to do the same to any other hopelessly trapped warriors. It was the right thing to do, but it made him sick.

Only by a miracle was he still alive. When the canyon first began to melt, Ruva and Ava had saved him, blocked him. After the defenders made their stand at the bottleneck, the general's soldiers had still pushed past the swarm of poisonous scorpions, the spike-filled pits, the camouflage curtain that hid the canyon itself. Nathan and the other gifted fighters had battled and retreated, battled and retreated, luring them farther inside.

Utros had been fooled, thinking that the rebels had only that one last line of defense. His army had believed in their victory as soon as they saw the cliff alcove filled with archive buildings, and Ruva had hissed with anticipation of all the powerful knowledge stored here.

His army had charged forward in a frenzy, and Utros could not have stopped them if he'd tried. They surged into the hidden canyon, like a rider giving free rein to a spirited horse. Though he wanted to be at the front of the troops, Ruva forced him to stay back. The starving soldiers fell upon the orchards and fields. They ran down the flocks of terrified sheep and tore them to pieces, eating the creatures raw. Before he could revel in his victory, Ruva sensed the resonance of an incredibly powerful spell . . . and then the cliffs flowed in a molten avalanche.

Ava's shimmering spirit had swooped in front of him, frantic. "Away! It is not safe! A massive spell! I tried to stop her, General!"

Ruva mirrored her twin's motions and used her gift to bowl Utros back against the rocks of the bottleneck as the wave of stone roared down on the front ranks of his army. Killing so many!

Now as he viewed the stark aftermath, the general tried to guess how many more of his soldiers were dead, additional numbers to add to the tally. Fortunately, the bulk of the ancient army had not even entered the hidden canyon and milled outside in the high desert, ninety thousand or more.

First Commander Enoch rode up, his face ashen as he stared across the rippled stone, countless embedded bodies, grasping hands, horrorstruck dead faces. He cleared his throat as if to spit out the harsh words he needed to say. "The Keeper claimed many more, sir. He knows us, and he wants us all."

"The Keeper will have to be satisfied for now," Utros said. "This is enough!"

Ava shimmered in front of them, her expression distraught. "He tugs me with greater strength. He wants my sister. He wants me!"

Ruva chimed in, "Thanks to our loyalty to you,

beloved Utros, we have the strength to resist him. Loyalty is stronger than love." She narrowed her eyes. "Loyalty is stronger than death."

Getting down to business, Enoch said, "We killed a sheep, sir, and we will roast it to feed all the prominent commanders, but the other soldiers still feel as if they're starving."

"Because they *are* starving," Utros said. "Even if they still move and march."

Ruva sounded defensive. "No! Our spell maintains them. They keep going even with the hunger inside. They will live until they are nothing more than walking bones!"

Utros watched in disgust as his soldiers spread out like scuttling beetles. They stripped the leaves and tender branches from the orchards, gobbling any fruit they found, ransacking gardens, breaking into the cliffside dwellings to scrounge even the smallest crumbs.

Far worse, though it did not surprise him knowing how desperate the preservation spell was, he watched the gaunt warriors race across the hardened stone, finding dead or dying soldiers that had been trapped. They did not try to rescue their comrades, did not look for survivors. Rather, they seized any hand or leg or face protruding from the rock and tore away strips of flesh, ripping the meat clean as they ate whatever remained of the bodies. They cracked the bones and sucked the marrow, lapped at the blood and gnawed any scrap of skin, muscle, or tendon, and moved on in search of more.

Ava shimmered before them and watched. "They need the nourishment. They will sustain themselves in any way they can. And they will continue to be your fighters."

Ruva explained that the preservation spell could hold the army for only so long. "Any food they find—" She paused and said in a harder voice to emphasize her point, "*Any* food will provide energy to keep them going."

Thinking of his legend, his honor, Utros felt sick. "What is becoming of my army? What is becoming of me?" He summoned his resolve, focused on the end goal, his reason for existence after so many centuries. "We will pay any price. We made that decision long ago, and it is too late to change now." He strode past the mangled remnants of his lost soldiers to look up at the sheer cliff that was now an impenetrable barrier. The Cliffwall archive was completely gone.

"They destroyed all that lore." He looked to the spirit of Ava. "Can you salvage anything? Pass through the rock in your spectral form and find a single scroll, a lone volume? Anything at all?"

Her intangible spirit flickered. "It is not possible. The books themselves are encased in stone. The scrolls are petrified." As she folded herself on top of Ruva, both twins said, "They eradicated the knowledge rather than let us have it."

Enoch said, "Such desperation shows how much they must fear us."

Utros nodded. "It was a wise tactical move. I would have liked for Ruva to have that magic as a powerful weapon for my cause, but we do not need it." He raised his voice so the other soldiers could hear him. "Don't ever believe we need a crutch like that! My army is sufficient."

A few vengeful soldiers picked their way to the far end of the canyon in hopes of catching the defenders who had fled into the highland wilderness, but Utros knew that Nathan and the others would be long gone.

"Tonight we feast on what we have," he said, "but we dare not rest for long. We must keep the army moving. Our goal is to reach the western sea and conquer any cities in between. The Norukai will already be ransacking the coast. King Grieve is engaged in the war." He turned so that the sunlight flashed on his golden half mask. "*My* war."

CHAPTER 56

The following day, the Bastion rang with excitement, and the Norukai rushed down to the sheltered harbor. "The war fleet has returned!" a guard shouted through the halls, causing the raiders to celebrate. The slaves received the news without enthusiasm.

From the upper tower, Bannon and Lila looked through an open window to see dozens of serpent ships sailing in. Bannon lost count after fifty.

Lila realized what they were. "They are the rest of the damaged raiding vessels from the river below Ildakar. The construction crews finished repairing them."

Bannon had not forgotten the battered vessels. The Norukai shipwrights would have worked the slaves day and night, until they were ready to set sail. Now in addition to Lars's raiding fleet and the hundred new serpent ships that had been constructed in King Grieve's absence, these vessels swelled the Norukai navy to an unstoppable force. They would ravage the entire coast.

"Sweet Sea Mother! We have to get away! It's more important than ever," Bannon said. "We've got to warn people that these attacks are coming. How will they be able to defend themselves?"

"It's now more important than ever, but our chances of escape are even worse," Lila said. "There will be twice as many Norukai in the Bastion, watching us every moment."

Bannon saw the newly repaired ships approach like a pack of wolves closing in on a wounded stag. Some vessels anchored at the outlying islands in the archipelago, while others docked directly below the Bastion. Those crews would be ready for wild revels and war preparations.

As he thought about it, he smiled slowly. "I disagree, Lila. Our chances just got better! Think of the drunken celebrations. The Bastion will be in complete chaos, and the slaves will be ordered about on countless tasks. Who will keep track of it all? Who will be watching us, in particular? Would even Atta bother harassing you?"

Frowning, Lila winced from her swollen bruises, the healing burn on her shoulder. "We might have our opportunity, but we don't have the resources. Where would we go?"

"If we could slip out of the Bastion, we will hide somewhere."

Lila was not convinced. "Then what? We would still be trapped on the island and surrounded by serpent ships."

"Emmett has to help us." Bannon knew it was the only answer.

As new arrivals piled into the Bastion, the old kitchen servant was paralyzed with the responsibility and fear of reprisal if the banquet wasn't perfect. The returning captains barged into the great fortress, filling the reception hall and throne chamber where Grieve received their reports.

The king remained sullen after the loss of Chalk, but

his rage had galvanized him. When the repaired ships returned from Ildakar, he was convinced that the only way to purge his sorrow was to devastate the Old World.

In the midst of the clamor in the kitchen, all ovens were stoked to bake bread, loaf after loaf that filled wooden handcarts. The larders were nearly emptied, but fortunately Lars had brought back supplies from his raids.

Emmett and his staff still had to prepare the food. Slaves hurried about, and the limping old veteran did his best to manage them. The well-trained slaves did their duties, but the newer recruits often dropped platters or spilled tureens.

With Lila beside him, Bannon cornered Emmett just outside the kitchen. "This is our chance. The Norukai will be drunk, loud, and unruly. You can help us escape."

The old man's blank stare melted into surprise, then horror. "You can't escape. They'll kill you!" He stuttered, "I-I can't lose two slaves. The Norukai need to be served. King Grieve has commanded it."

"King Grieve should not be your master," Lila said. "You saw the warships that just arrived, and you know the fleet he is building. We must get away to sound the alarm up and down the coast, and this may be our last chance."

"It isn't only so we can save ourselves," Bannon said. "Just get us a boat, even a small one, and we will sail away. We'll find the mainland, get the cities and villages to prepare their defenses. The people have to know that a war is coming their way. Think of how many innocents will be slaughtered."

Emmett looked distraught. "I know what King Grieve

intends to do. I've been here for a decade. Alas, I may be the only person from my village who remains alive."

"There will be countless villages like yours once those raids launch," Bannon said. "We can save some of them, but only if you help us get away."

"I . . . I don't know how. If I knew, I would have left here long ago." His thin voice cracked.

"Are you sure about that?" Lila said in a low voice. "Would you have been brave enough to escape on your own?"

Emmett fumbled with his ponytail, wrapping his fingers around the gray hair. "No, I-I don't think so."

"But you can help us!" Bannon insisted, then dropped his voice to a hush again. "It will be days before they realize we're gone, if they notice at all. King Grieve could never connect you to our escape. Sweet Sea Mother, please!"

Emmett struggled with his conscience, flexing and unflexing his fingers. His wrinkled face was seamed with sorrow, and as Bannon silently pleaded, he saw something break inside the old man. "I-I do know of a way down to the waterline. It's steep and rarely used, a small rock jetty, but I think you'll find a boat there. Some of the Norukai spearfish in the narrow coves."

"That's a start," Bannon said without thinking.

"We will make do," Lila agreed.

Perspiration sparkled on Emmett's forehead as he looked from side to side. He hunched his shoulders as he hobbled along a corridor, leaving the mayhem of the kitchens. "Come with me! We won't have much time."

They took a side corridor, then worked their way down a narrow set of stone steps that were slimy with moss. They descended steeply, running fingers along the wall to keep their balance. The veteran slave looked behind him often, stared longingly up the stairs as if desperate to get back to his duties. He winced with pain as he limped along on his poorly set leg.

Bannon would not turn down any chance to escape, but he realized that if he and Lila were going to sail off in a small boat, they had no water, no food, no clothing or blankets, not even any charts. They could rush back to the kitchens, grab some supplies. . . . No, he shook those thoughts away. This was their first opportunity to escape, and if he and Lila died out on the open water, at least they would die with some semblance of freedom.

The tortured staircase turned again and spilled them out onto a wider landing where daylight flooded through a small barred gate. Bannon drew in a deep breath of the fresh, salt air that replaced the dankness. Outside, he could hear waves crashing on the rocks.

He worked the gate's metal latch. Caked with salt and rust, the hinges groaned in protest, but he and Lila managed to swing the gate open, to freedom.

A stone jetty extended into the choppy surf, and two small boats were tied to the pilings. One was rotten and half full of water from the crashing spray, but the other was a fishing boat large enough to take two or three people and a haul of fish. It had a single mast and a roll of gray sailcloth tucked against the bow under the front gunwale. A pair of oars rested in the bottom of the boat.

Bannon controlled his disappointment. "I had hoped for something better, but I expected nothing less."

Lila said, "We will cross the ocean in a rowboat if we need to."

"You'll need to," Emmett said.

Bannon clung to a shred of optimism. "Two people can sail this boat. We will make it work."

Emmett squirmed, desperate to bolt back inside before the Norukai noticed his absence. Bannon looked at him, thought of the innumerable years of captivity the old man had suffered. "Come with us, Emmett. Escape! We'll all survive together."

The old man was taken aback by the suggestion. "N-No, I couldn't. I don't dare."

"You will never get away from King Grieve unless you come with us now," Lila said. In disgust, she yanked at the ragged neck of her wool garment, tore it, then flung the shapeless dress away. She stood proud, clad as a morazeth again.

The old slave struggled with his decision, but shook his head. "I can't! All of the other slaves . . ."

"All of the other slaves would also escape if they could. This is your chance! I'm begging you, Emmett," Bannon said.

But the old man was too frightened. "Go." He waved them off. "Don't waste your opportunity. I-I wasted mine long ago. Now I continue to serve." He swallowed hard. "Until I die."

"Until you die," Bannon said. It sounded like a prophecy.

Lila had no further patience. "Here's the boat, boy. The celebrations are getting louder. The Norukai are intoxicated, and night is falling. If we are to have any chance, it is now."

Bannon climbed aboard the battered fishing boat, giving a last glance back at the gate, but Emmett had already limped back inside, pulled the bars closed again, and vanished into the shadows.

Lila sprang into the boat with perfect grace. "You know how to sail, boy. Take us away from here."

Bannon undid the ropes on the piling and used one

of the oars to push them away from the jetty. Rowing carefully, he dodged the first line of rocks and spraying waves, then worked his way into the open water. He looked at the towering black Bastion behind them and shuddered as they headed out to the open sea.

CHAPTER 57

B ecause she would stay in Tanimura to help build the city's defenses, Nicci found temporary quarters in the main barracks at the garrison. It was only a small room with a narrow bunk and a writing desk, but it was sufficient for her needs.

General Linden stood at the door after escorting her to the room, still nervous after having seen her work with the Grace and the verification web. "I wish I had more appropriate accommodations, but the garrison has swelled with new arrivals, visiting commanders, and volunteers from the city guard." He fidgeted at the door. "Tomorrow, I will have my adjutant secure a more spacious room for you in one of the boardinghouses."

"I don't require extravagance, General. I just spent several days aboard a kraken-hunter ship." She inhaled deeply, smelled the fresh wood, the clean bedding. "This is a great improvement."

Linden wrinkled his nose. "I thought I smelled something a little off. Now I know what it was."

"I've had little rest since I first arrived in Serrimundi, and I will sleep well here." She felt disappointingly washed out, her strength diluted. Nicci's gift was her greatest weapon, and just as a soldier needed to sharpen his sword before going into battle, she needed to recover her strength.

General Linden gave a quick bow and closed the door, leaving her in the room. Alone and calm, Nicci allowed herself to relax, if only a little. She could never relax entirely, but she needed the rest and the strength.

Before attempting to sleep, knowing the questions would worry her throughout the night, Nicci again took out the small bone box from Richard. She opened the lid, probed it with her gift, but the answers still eluded her. Her sense of frustration increased. Why would Richard send such a cryptic message? Why not just a straightforward answer? This was not a time for games! She had been clear about the incredible threat they faced. If Utros and the Norukai raiders conquered the Old World, they would surely push northward into D'Hara.

Yet Richard's response had been . . . this?

She set the open bone box on the wool blanket and bent close to the rotating pearl of energy. She could smell the faint metallic crackle in the air. What did Richard want her to do with it? Why would he assume she could understand the message, even if she did read the language of Creation? After so many years of her being close to him, she and Richard were so tightly connected that Nicci knew his thoughts, his heart. She had been in love with him for a long time, but when she accepted his undying devotion to Kahlan, she resolved to become the second-most-important person in his life. Nicci believed she had achieved that.

Her powers were greater than those of any other sorceress. Along with Nathan, her vital mission was to tame the Old World in the name of the D'Haran Empire. But she *knew* Richard. She understood how his mind worked. She could often anticipate his thoughts and actions, and he understood Nicci with equal alacrity.

By sending this strange message, Richard knew that this was something she, and only she, would understand. It was a solution, if she could decipher it. "This object is all I need," she reminded herself, still perplexed. "It holds the key somehow." He was counting on her. She stared at the bone box, trying to find the missing piece, to understand how she could use this enigmatic constructed spell.

After about an hour, she gave up. Too exhausted to think about it anymore, Nicci knew her thoughts would be clearer after a good rest. She closed the box and pocketed it, then lay back on her bed, worried that her churning thoughts would keep her awake. But moments after closing her blue eyes, she fell into a deep slumber.

In the calm emptiness of a dream state, Nicci's thoughts stretched over vast distances, and she was surprised to connect with her sister panther again! She looked through Mrra's sharp feline eyes. Nicci had unwillingly been whisked away from the battle in Orogang, and now she was overjoyed to know the big cat was still alive. Considering the bloodthirsty ancient army in the abandoned capital, she feared that Mrra and the Hidden People had been massacred, though she knew they would have fought to the last. But her sand panther had escaped somehow.

Now, through her dream connection, Nicci knew that Mrra was running overland, loping along the hills and forests to get back to her. Because of the sliph, they were separated by a great distance. She could feel her sister panther's weariness, the sore pads of her enormous paws, but Mrra kept coming.

Through the animal's predatory senses, she realized that the big cat was not alone. Other panthers from her new pride accompanied her, and Nicci was overjoyed to know that some of the big cats had survived the battle at Orogang.

Even as Nicci slept in the Tanimura barracks, she and her sister panther ran along, linked together. Their bond was strong, and Mrra followed it like an implacable summons. Yes, the panthers were coming! No matter how long or arduous the journey, across the wilderness, over the mountains, Mrra would find her.

With her panther senses, though, Nicci detected something else, and she realized that the big cats were not alone. There were other fighters coming to Tanimura, moving at their best speed. Mrra's focus was not on them, so Nicci could not tell who or what they were, but she knew they were coming.

Armies were gathering. . . .

When Nicci awoke the next morning, not only was she well rested but she also felt a spark of hope, which refreshed her as much as the long rest had.

CHAPTER 58

While many refugees from Cliffwall scattered into the desert wilderness, Nathan and the surviving defenders headed directly westward, anxious to reach the coast in time to prepare the major cities for war. They pushed themselves hard, knowing they had to stay ahead of General Utros's army.

Their group passed small farming settlements, intrepid villagers who had come back to reclaim all the land that had once been drained by the Lifedrinker. Nathan's heart ached when their group paused one night to water their horses and beg food from a group of pioneer families. The settlers had established a foothold, tilling the land, planting crops, building a few homes and even a schoolhouse near a stream. Four milk cows were penned in a stockade, and the cattle lowed as their group approached. The villagers came out, suspicious of the large armed party of strangers.

Sitting tall on his own horse next to Nathan, Oron said in a low voice, "They think we are an army."

"They will not welcome the news we bring." Nathan stroked his chin.

The pioneer families gathered in the falling darkness

to face the riders. A bearded farmer in a wide-brimmed leather hat stepped forward. "We have little for you to take, if you mean to raid our lands."

General Zimmer pulled his horse to a halt at the head of the party. "We mean you no harm, though we bring you a warning. A large enemy army is marching behind us, a hundred thousand strong. They will take everything you have, and you can't stop them."

From his own horse, Nathan leaned forward and said, "Pack up your things and run to the hills if you value your lives."

The farmer families were dismayed. "But we can't abandon our homes! We just built this village, now that the Lifedrinker is dead."

Nathan straightened his rumpled cape. "I know. I saw what this valley was like before, but you can rebuild again. Please, heed what we have to say. Don't leave a scrap of food for the enemy. Go hide in the forests for a few days." He knew his words were hard. "When they are gone, you can start over, but at least you'll be alive."

The bearded farmer looked angry. "Who are you to tell us this? Why did you lure an army here?"

General Zimmer said, "The army will come, whether we are here or not. General Utros is on his way."

Thorn and Lyesse, who jogged along with the group, said, "We are killing as many as we can, but it will take a long time to wipe them all out."

The horses drank from the stream. Nathan knelt on the soft bank, cupped the running water, and brought it to his lips. The worried farmer families had little food to spare, and the retreating defenders took nothing more than was offered. General Zimmer led the party onward as the alarmed settlers scurried about, packing what they could.

As the group covered mile after mile, Nathan felt an eerie sense of familiarity to retrace his journey from when he, Bannon, and Nicci had traveled inland. Similarly, Oliver and Peretta rode together on their horse, pointing out landmarks they remembered from their own journey to Tanimura. Next to them, Amber looked ahead, wistful. "In a week we'll be in Renda Bay, won't we, General? My brother will help us. I'm sure he's made the town fully defensible."

Zimmer gave the young novice a sad look. "I don't doubt Captain Norcross has made remarkable progress, but I can't imagine what sort of defenses could stop the army of General Utros."

Oron snorted, "If all of Ildakar couldn't defeat them, what hope does a fishing town have?"

"What hope does any of us have?" asked Sister Rhoda. "Even after the prelate's sacrifice, they are still coming."

"I will not abide talk like that! The hope we have is the hope we make," Nathan said. "Gigantic armies have been defeated before, and invincible enemies have fallen. Think of Darken Rahl. Think of the Imperial Order and Emperor Jagang. Think of Sulachan and his hordes of half people. Utros is just another one to defeat, and we will do exactly that!"

Taking heart, the group rode onward.

Days later, when they crested the last line of hills before descending to the river valley that led to the ocean, the group stopped and looked back at the many miles they had traveled. Even from a distance they could see the dust and the trampled subjugated landscape from so many thousands of Utros's marching soldiers.

"They are keeping up with us," Captain Trevor said. "How can they move so fast?"

"How can they be alive at all, when they should have died centuries ago?" asked Sister Mab.

Nathan grimaced as sharp pain shuddered through his chest. His heart pounded as if it meant to burst out of the long scar, and he pressed his palm hard against his breastbone. "Leave me alone," he snapped under his breath, but Ivan's heart continued to pound with the eager anticipation of violence.

As the group followed the widening river toward the coast, they encountered trade roads and finally reached the outskirts and pasturelands of Renda Bay. The clear, sunny morning suggested that all was right with the world. A boy tending sheep and playful lambs greeted them, amazed to see General Zimmer and the battle-worn party. The shepherd boy had a mop of dark hair that looked as woolly as the sheep he tended. "Are you going to help us against the Norukai if they come back?"

Amber pushed her horse forward. "Have they come back?"

"Once." The boy's expression was troubled, then he grinned. "But we fought and we drove them away!"

Amber beamed. "I knew it!"

Nathan leaned down from his horse. "Be a good lad and run ahead. Find town leader Thaddeus and tell him we're coming. We have urgent news."

The boy awkwardly regarded his sheep. "I can't leave my flock. They're my responsibility."

"Your sheep will be fine for a little while. Now run along. Go! Fast as you can." The boom of command in the wizard's voice startled the boy, and he bolted off, racing down the road to the town.

Warm memories of Renda Bay filled Nathan's heart, enough to eclipse the shadow of Ivan for a time. He felt a fondness for this place, the first town they had discovered after he, Nicci, and Bannon were shipwrecked. The people of Renda Bay had welcomed the castaways, and the three of them had helped defend against a horrific Norukai raid.

Now, riding into the busy town, they wearily raised hands in greeting. The curious townspeople came forward to greet them. Resplendent in his D'Haran armor, Captain Norcross rushed through the streets and came up to present himself to General Zimmer. The voices and happy cheers rose to a loud clamor in the town square. It felt like a grand homecoming.

Thaddeus, a bearded, strong-backed fisherman, was soft-spoken but confident. Since the last time Nathan had seen him, the new town leader had grown into his role. "Welcome back after your long journey! The shepherd boy said you looked tired and hungry, and I have already ordered the inn kitchens to prepare food." He scratched his beard. "After all you've done to save this town, I won't scrimp on our hospitality." Thaddeus did a double take as he recognized Nathan. "Wizard! I never expected you to come back."

"Yes, I am truly a wizard again. My gift is back . . . and we are all going to need it."

"Where is Nicci?" The town leader looked around the dusty group of travelers. "And the young swordsman Bannon? He was a whirlwind with his blade. I think he killed twenty Norukai all by himself."

Nathan frowned. "We were separated." He gestured back to the group. "But we have several other powerfully gifted individuals with us, and we have much to tell."

No longer able to restrain herself, Amber rushed forward to embrace her brother, who seesawed between wanting to sweep her into a hug and trying to be formal in front of his commander. He managed to splutter, "I relinquish command to you, General. Renda Bay is yours."

Zimmer looked at Norcross. "And we have many preparations to make. I want to see what you've done while I was away."

Standing at rigid attention, the young officer delivered his report. "The town's defenses are in place, and they've already proved effective. Only a month ago we defeated a significant Norukai raid. The slavers ran away from here like beaten dogs." He allowed himself a smile. "They learned their lesson. I doubt the Norukai will come back."

"We have more to worry about than just the Norukai," said Nathan.

Oron rode forward with a sour expression and spoke without introducing himself. "We don't have much time, perhaps two or three days."

"If we are lucky," Lady Olgya added.

"Two or three days?" Thaddeus asked. "For what?" More townspeople came closer, dreading what they were about to hear.

"A gigantic army is on our heels," Nathan reported. "Nearly a hundred thousand warriors on a forced march, and Renda Bay is right in their path."

As the people gasped, Zimmer regarded the siege towers that rose on either side of the bay, the high walls built around the harbor, the impressive defenses that faced outward to protect against Norukai attacks. Out in the deeper water, three large sailing ships, the vessels that had delivered the D'Haran expeditionary force, were anchored and alert.

"You have done well to prepare for Norukai raids," he said, then lowered his voice, "but there's nothing we can do to save Renda Bay from Utros and his army."

CHAPTER 59

The stolen Norukai boat rocked on the open water as breezes gusted against the sail. Bannon's hands were sore and blistered from pulling the oars, and Lila worked just as hard while he rested, but they had both been toughened aboard the serpent ship, and now they rowed for their own salvation.

They had escaped the Norukai islands the day before, and they vanished into the thickening night before anyone in the Bastion noticed their absence. The drunken revelry faded behind them, along with poor Emmett, who had been brave enough to help them escape, but not brave enough to go with them.

Sailing off, Bannon didn't begin to feel hope until full night closed in. No Norukai ships could follow them in the pitch black. Even Bannon didn't know where they were going. Their small boat sailed off into the open ocean with no charts, no food or water. Bannon had only a vague notion of where the mainland might lie, but Lila did not doubt him for a moment.

When the sun rose the next morning, they searched for any sign of land, or for pursuing serpent ships. Together, they inventoried the items in the boat—a coil of rope, a net, and a bone-tipped spear for fishing.

Throughout the day, Lila stabbed into the water with the spear, and after nearly a hundred attempts, she skewered a fish and flopped it into the boat.

"Now we have dinner." She used the jagged spear to slice open the belly and carefully removed the entrails. "We need these for the moisture. We will split them."

Bannon grimaced at the memories it brought up, but accepted the offering. "We've eaten worse. Sweet Sea Mother, think of the lessons the Norukai taught us! Eating fish guts, rowing for hours on end. It may be the key to our survival."

Lila sneered as she lifted the spear. "I would show King Grieve my appreciation in person, along with that vile woman Atta."

Bannon forced a laugh. "I will not turn the boat around, even if you insist."

She gave him a perplexed frown. "I was not serious."

"Neither was I. Sometimes you are very difficult to understand."

"My thoughts are perfectly clear. You should make more of an effort." Lila's face was discolored with purple and yellow bruises, and Bannon suspected that he looked just as bad with his split lip and bashed eye. They had little time to look at mirrors in the Bastion.

They shared the moist raw fish, and Bannon began to row, while Lila perched with the spear again, looking for another target to skewer.

By the third day they were parched and sunburned, and they still had seen no sign of the mainland or any other island. That afternoon, the only small change to the monotony was a spreading dark patch in the water, which Bannon recognized as kelp fronds. He reached down to pull up some of the strands. "The bladders have liquid inside." He tugged hard on the slimy green ribbons. Rounded nodules in the stems were like buoys holding up the main plant.

"If you drink the salt water, it will eventually kill you," Lila warned. "Your thirst will only get worse."

"No, the water in the bladders is filtered through the kelp skin. It's strong and tastes terrible, but it is drinkable." Using his thumbnails, he pressed into the squishy sphere, cracked open the rind, and peeled it apart. The nodule contained only a spoonful or two of liquid, which he offered to Lila.

She frowned skeptically. "Are you certain?"

"Fishermen knew this on Chiriya Island."

"Then why are you giving it to me first? To see if it's poison?"

Bannon was disappointed. "No, because I was being nice."

"Thank you. Sometimes I don't recognize that." She drank, grimaced, then swallowed. "It is as acceptable as the fish guts."

"High praise indeed." Bannon pulled on the strands of kelp until he found another nodule, burst it open, and sucked on the liquid inside. It had a strong iodine tang, and he had to force himself to drink it, but his mouth and throat needed the water. Using the saw edge of the fishing spear, they cut the kelp stems and loaded the boat with twenty intact nodules while they drifted among the seaweed.

The kelp provided a habitat for fish, and Lila deftly caught six with her bare hands, scooping them out of the water and dropping them into the boat. Bannon relished the feast. "Thank you, Lila, for everything. You did promise to keep me alive."

"I have not saved you yet, boy."

"I'm alive so far. I count that as a temporary success."

When the waves grew choppy and the wind picked up, the gray clouds thickened into what looked like a smoke pudding. The fishing boat moved on at a swifter pace, but Bannon had no idea if they were even going in the right direction. He had seen many ocean storms from Chiriya Island, where he and his mother would huddle together in their cottage while his father would rage at the weather, which prevented him from going to the tavern.

The sail strained against the wind, and Bannon's long hair whipped about. When the clouds burst and rain sheeted down, he and Lila welcomed the first spattering of raindrops. As the rain increased, they turned their faces up to the sky, letting the droplets wash their salt-encrusted cheeks, opening their mouths to catch any of the moisture.

"We have no containers," he groaned. "All this rain will be wasted."

"Drink your fill," she said. Like a baby bird begging for a worm from its mother, she kept her mouth open and turned her face to the sky.

Bannon cupped his palms until he collected a few thimblefuls of water, which he slurped through cracked lips. He repeated the procedure again and again, but he was frantic to capture and store more rain. Puddles filled the bottom of the boat, but it was filthy water.

"We have no pots, no basins, nothing! And all this rain is coming down! Sweet Sea Mother."

"Your clothes," Lila said. "Take off your shirt and trousers."

"What?" He touched his already soaked cotton shirt.

"Take off your clothes now, boy." She began tugging at the fabric.

In a few moments he sat in only his smallclothes in the open boat. Lila spread out his shirt and trousers to be soaked by the rain; then she rolled them up in a loose wad. "That will hold some water, at least a few mouthfuls that will last for a day or two." She touched the black leather band across her breasts and around her waist. "I would do the same, but my garments are inappropriate." She frowned. "Maybe I shouldn't have thrown my other robe away."

When the winds grew so strong that Bannon feared the sail would rip or the single mast would snap in half, they took down the canvas. By folding the fabric, they were able to form pockets that also filled with rainwater.

As the storm increased, Bannon wound the rope around himself and Lila, lashing it to the gunwales. "If either of us is thrown overboard, we're dead. This will keep us in the boat."

"Unless we capsize," Lila said. Her spiky brown hair was plastered to her head, and rainwater ran down her bruised face.

"It's a chance we have to take."

The storm lasted for hours, and though Bannon was queasy from the churning waves, the stolen boat remained intact. And when the rain finally stopped, around midnight, the weather changed to a thick fog. Mist rolled in like a clammy blanket that obscured their view of the horizon, even though there was nothing to see.

He and Lila were drenched and cold, and as the temperature dropped, their sunburned skin made the deepening chill even more miserable. Bannon saw that Lila was shivering, and he began to shiver, too.

Downcast, she said, "I don't think we will ever make it to land, Bannon Farmer." When she intentionally used his name, he knew how serious she was. "I may not save you after all, but I did try."

They were isolated in the impenetrable fog, alone in the wilderness of waves. "I don't know where we are or how far we've come," Bannon said, "but I will not give up, and neither will you. Maybe it's my turn to save you."

"Our first order of business is to keep warm," she said, wrapping her arms around him and pulling him down to the bottom of the boat. As the collected rainwater sloshed around them, Bannon returned the embrace, drawing her close. Lila pressed as much of her body against his as she could, and Bannon held her tight.

"We can share warmth," he said. "I've heard it's very good for people suffering from extreme chills."

Lila tucked her bruised face against his bare chest. "Yes, I believe it is helping."

As they lay together, the sound and rocking of the waves soothed them like a lullaby. For a while, Bannon forgot that they were lost, and he fell asleep in Lila's arms.

The next morning he awoke to hear an odd and unexpected sound, a distant rushing and roaring. He blinked and sat up, disentangling himself from Lila. The morazeth snapped awake and sat up next to him.

"What is that sound?" she asked, as if they might be under attack.

The fog had thinned, leaving only a grayish veil that began to dissipate as the sun rose. Even before Bannon saw the coastline, he recognized the sound of waves crashing against a shore. "That's it! We found land." He stood up so quickly he rocked the boat. "I don't know how, but we found the coast. It's a miracle."

"It won't be a miracle unless we make it to land," Lila said.

Together they raised the sail and tacked into the breezes that drove them closer to the shore. He remembered being similarly lost and adrift in a small boat off of Chiriya long ago, the fog bank . . .

He gazed back out to sea, away from the shoreline. When he shaded his eyes in the bright morning light, he saw a flicker of humanlike figures on the waves, smooth heads with slitted eyes and wide fang-filled mouths. A flash of fear struck through him. If the selka attacked now, he and Lila could never fight them off!

But he realized that the selka wouldn't attack. They had *saved* him and Lila. Sometime during the night, the sea people must have taken the boat and dragged it close to shore.

Lila was too focused on the land to notice the selka. She sat on the gunwale and grabbed the oars, pulling as hard as she could. When Bannon glanced back again, the selka had disappeared beneath the waves.

As they approached the coast, Bannon saw the mouth of a river, a bay, and the buildings of a large town, as well as numerous fishing boats heading out into the morning. Bannon yelled and waved, though the harbor was still far away. "We're saved!"

Lila kept pulling on the oars. "We don't know where we are, but those people will help us. We will warn them about the Norukai fleet that is sure to come soon."

Bannon continued to watch the boats sailing out of the harbor, then scrutinized the buildings in the town. He saw the bridge that crossed the river to span the small bay. A flash of recognition suddenly struck him. "I know where we are, Lila."

Already one of the fishing boats had spotted them, and Bannon could see tiny figures waving. She pulled harder on the oars as the boat headed in their direction.

"That is Renda Bay," he said.

CHAPTER 60

The raucous festivities continued while the raiders prepared for full-scale war, but Chalk was dead. King Grieve sat on his imposing throne surrounded by wild Norukai, but he walled himself off with anger and grief.

Chalk was dead!

Lars kept feasting, drinking, and boasting, as if the success of his raids meant that he had been forgiven, but Grieve was not in a forgiving mood. As the revelry continued and the feasting tables were piled high with fish, bread, cliff tubers, and even hams and sausages brought in by recent raids, Grieve barely ate a morsel. His only movement was to clench and unclench his fists, feeling the squares of iron fused onto his knuckles. The scars on his cheeks rippled as he clenched his jaws. He exhaled a long hiss like the serpent god, but no one noticed the sound amid the pounding fists, laughter, and shouts.

Chalk was dead! His shaman, his advisor, his friend . . .

The repaired serpent ships had returned from Ildakar, fifty-one vessels remaining out of the hundred that had initially sailed, but they were as threatening as ever.

Those ships, along with Lars's raiding fleet and more than seventy new ships, gave the Norukai a powerful navy. If his ally General Utros fulfilled his promise with his vast army marching to the coast, the two forces would dominate the Old World. The Norukai people, having been driven off the mainland by Emperor Sulachan thousands of years ago, would now have the world again. Grieve's people would rip a gaping wound along the coast.

In normal times, he would have relished the thought of blood and violence, but *Chalk was dead.*

When the rage reached a boiling point, he lurched to his feet and let out a wordless roar that echoed across the room and brought the shouting and revelry to a stuttering halt. The rest of the Norukai looked at him, stunned; then Lars raised his fist and let out a similar roar, as did the other raiders, until the walls of the Bastion shook with their enthusiasm.

But Chalk was still dead.

Grieve trudged down the stone steps from his throne to meet the shouting Norukai. Misinterpreting his mood, some clapped him on the shoulder, pounded his back, but the king ignored them. At another time he might have punched them senseless, but now he did not consider them worth his time or his ire.

Two slaves brought in another roast goat, a scrawny one this time, because most of the island's flock had already been killed. Grieve didn't like goat anyway.

He needed to find a target for his annoyance, but he didn't know where to start. Prancing at his side, Chalk would have issued quirky and cryptic pronouncements, but why hadn't the shaman foreseen his own death? He could have saved himself! How could he not have envisioned the attack of the selka, how could he not have known their slimy queen would tear him open? He was a poor shaman not to have predicted something so vital!

Or had he seen something after all? Grieve remembered Chalk chattering during the sacrifice of the slave on the day before the selka attack: "Serpent god will save some of us. But I won't tell which ones!"

Had he known after all? Why hadn't he warned anyone?

Grieve wanted to smash a face. He realized that what he really wanted was to gut one of the slaves, so he could watch the victim writhe in agony in a pool of blood, just the way Chalk had died.

Looking up, he saw old Emmett, the wrinkled old man who had been a fixture at the Bastion even before Grieve had killed his own father. Chalk had encouraged him to slay King Stern and take the crown. The albino had foreseen it in a vision, and he had helped Grieve choose the perfect timing.

Why hadn't Chalk been able to avoid his own death? *The axe cleaves the wood. The sword cleaves the bone.* What did his pronouncements even mean? Could anyone make sense of them?

When Emmett presented a braided pastry filled with chopped nuts, Grieve realized that the limping old man seemed more frightened than usual, probably because he and his slaves had been bullied by so many visiting Norukai. Grieve glanced around the dining hall, still looking for a victim who could alleviate his sadness. He saw neither Bannon nor the morazeth Lila, and he realized he hadn't seen them for several days during the busy preparations for war.

He was surprised that Atta hadn't killed her supposed female rival by now. Grieve had no sexual interest in the scrawny morazeth, since he would certainly break her fragile body if he used her roughly, but now that sounded like a good idea. Yes, he would eviscerate Bannon, then knock Lila down onto the banquet table and have her there, right in front of all of his men. He could strangle her when he was finished, and that would also please Atta. Maybe that would finally cure him of his malaise.

He looked around at the serving slaves, but he didn't see them.

Old Emmett obsequiously offered the nut-filled pastry for him to eat. "You will find it delicious, my Grieve, a specialty of the kitchens for this celebration of your impending conquest."

The king knocked the tray out of the slave's hands and grabbed him by the long ponytail as if it were a leash, yanking Emmett's head back. "Where are Bannon and Lila? I want them here now."

The old man paled. "They are . . . they are on other duties, I'm sure, my Grieve."

Atta had been fawning over Lars, no doubt to make Grieve jealous, and now she shoved the disgraced captain aside and took her place next to King Grieve. "Yes, where is the skinny bitch? I fancy drowning her in a piss bucket after all these men have filled it." She let out a loud laugh.

"Bring them," Grieve demanded of Emmett. "Now!"

The old slave limped off like an injured deer fleeing an oncoming wildfire. He hid for the better part of an hour, but the impatient king sent several Norukai to drag him back into the banquet hall.

Bannon and Lila were nowhere to be found. Guards searched the Bastion and returned to the king with the infuriating report that they had interrogated every slave, but those two had not been seen in some time.

"I-I know nothing about it, my Grieve," Emmett whined, and the obvious terror on the man's face turned his words into a lie.

Grieve threw the crippled slave down on the table, flat on his back among the platters. Emmett's struggles inflamed the Norukai king's dominance, and he slammed the old man's head against the wood. With his right hand, he snatched the dagger at his waist and plunged it through the tendons of Emmett's shoulder, skewering him to the table. The wrinkled slave gasped with pain. "I don't know, my Grieve! I don't know."

The interrogation continued at length, and Grieve enjoyed the process, more joy than he had felt for many days. By the time he had cut off Emmett's left ear and two fingers at the second knuckle, another Norukai entered the hall to report. "A fishing boat is gone from the jetty, King Grieve. Someone took it!"

"No, no!" Emmett whimpered, bleeding from multiple wounds. "Maybe it broke loose and drifted away in a storm."

"Or maybe they stole it and escaped," Grieve growled.

Impatient, he slashed off the old man's other ear. He pinched the curved rind of flesh between his thumb and forefinger, waggling the ear in front of Emmett's face. "Tell me what I need to know, or I have many more bits I can slice off." He waved the dripping trophy again.

Finally Emmett broke down, sobbing. Grieve yanked out the knife that pinned the old slave to the table, releasing him. Emmett rolled forward, shuddering and bleeding, then babbled out a stream of words that coalesced into an explanation of how he had helped Bannon and Lila escape. The confession seemed cathartic for the old man, and he slid off the table, dropping to his knees and begging before King Grieve.

Grieve's mood hardened, and he summoned all the terrified slaves into the dining hall. "Our fleet is about to go to war! I command you to prepare an appropriate feast to celebrate our impending victory."

The Norukai let out a deafening cheer. When Grieve bellowed his instructions, the slaves quailed, and Emmett broke down into another flood of wordless sobs. The king realized that at last he was hungry again.

L ars and five other prominent Norukai captains sat at the main table, while Atta remained at King Grieve's side. She gave him a lascivious leer, blinking her cowlike eyes, but the king's attention was focused on the slaves who plodded into the banquet hall. On their shoulders, as if they carried a stretcher with a wounded warrior, they brought an enormous serving platter. The terrified slaves kept their gazes downcast as they placed the serving platter with its roasted meat in front of Grieve.

The shriveled blackened body of the old slave had curled up in a fetal position in the fires of the ovens. Emmett had been roasted alive, because the Norukai knew that terror and pain enhanced the flavor of the meat.

"He was old and tough," Grieve said. "I expect the meat will be stringy, barely edible."

Atta used her dagger to poke through the crisp skin, splitting open the black crust to reveal juicy flesh underneath. "I'll savor the feast just as I will savor our victory, King Grieve." She hacked a hunk of meat from Emmett's thigh and extended it to Grieve on the point of her knife.

He took the offering and chewed it. "Yes, it's good. This old man served the Bastion for many years, and now we serve him." He raised his armored fist. "Come, all of you—eat! This is our feast before war."

The Norukai rushed forward and tore into the roasted body of the old slave.

CHAPTER 61

The townspeople hurried to the docks to see the two castaways fished out of the sea, eager to hear their story. Nathan received the news with more joy than he had experienced in a long time. Bannon was alive!

The young man and Lila were sunburned and bedraggled from drifting alone for days, but they were feeling stronger by the time a small fishing boat called the *Daisy* brought them to Renda Bay. Kenneth, the *Daisy*'s pilot, clanged his bell as he arrived.

As Bannon stepped off the boat, he looked tough and determined, much different from the naive young man Nicci had rescued in a Tanimura alley long ago. His hazel eyes shone as he hurried down the dock and embraced Nathan. The wizard pounded him on the back. "Dear spirits, I never expected to see you again, my boy!"

Bannon stepped back, laughing. "Your wizard robes are gone! You look like an adventurer again."

"I never stopped being an adventurer, and now this war will require all of my skills, both with magic and with my sword." He embraced Bannon for a long moment, overjoyed. "You're back with us. That's the most important part for now! Dear spirits, it's good to see you."

Thorn and Lyesse used sharp elbows to clear a path through the townspeople crowded at the docks, wanting to see Lila. "We heard that a morazeth had been found floating in the sea," said Thorn. "It is good to have you here, Lila. We need more worthy fighters."

Lyesse said, "Thorn and I have been keeping score of our kills, but with the size of the army about to hit Renda Bay, you will quickly catch up with us."

"I will make a good accounting of myself," Lila said. Seagulls wheeled overhead, screaming like wounded victims on a battlefield.

"What army?" Bannon sounded more alarmed. "We came to warn you about the Norukai fleet. King Grieve will attack soon with hundreds of ships. He'll devastate the coast. You need to prepare."

Nathan recoiled. "A Norukai fleet is on its way? But the army of General Utros will be here in a day or two to ransack the town!"

Bannon paled. "The Norukai and Utros formed an alliance, but I thought the ancient army would take much longer to march across the land."

Lila cautioned, "We don't even know how much time has passed, boy. I have not been counting the days since Ildakar vanished."

Thorn inspected the healing bruises on her morazeth sister's face. "You are damaged. Have you two been sparring?"

"We damaged many Norukai as well," Lila said.

The people of Renda Bay crowded around, and General Zimmer strode up, accompanied by Norcross and

Trevor. "I want a full debriefing of what you know about the Norukai and their plans. I didn't expect to fight on two fronts so soon."

Thaddeus raised his hands. "We will share stories in my office in the town hall. We'll make our plans there."

Though Nathan could see how weary Bannon was, they couldn't afford to grant him or Lila a well-earned rest. He stepped forward with a reassuring smile. "There is one thing I can do for you, though." He touched the young man's bruised face, his puffy lip. Bannon winced when Nathan released his healing gift to repair the damage to the sunburned and freckled face, and within moments he stood whole again.

When the wizard attempted to heal the similar bruises on Lila's face, she shook her head. "The protective runes on my skin will block you. They guard me from magic, but they also thwart any efforts to use a healing spell." She drew a breath. "I will endure. It is nothing."

As they headed toward the town hall, the three morazeth walked together in perfect unison. Even after the healing spell, Bannon looked exhausted and battered, but now he had a spring in his step, glad to be back among friends.

In the town hall, Thaddeus dragged chairs around his sturdy wooden desk. Nathan shifted the ornate sword at his side and straightened his embroidered cape as he sat down. Zimmer did not sit, but paced near the wall.

Thaddeus ran a callused finger along the spines of ledgers on the shelves. "These books contain the names of people lost in Norukai raids over the past hundred years. We thought we had raised sufficient defenses, thanks to Captain Norcross. We believed we could drive the enemy away and keep Renda Bay strong, but all our efforts were in vain."

Bannon and Lila took turns telling the story of their ordeals among the Norukai. Lila gave a crisp, bare-bones report, but the young man's description of what had happened was agitated and emotional. "I wish we'd killed all of them! I wish I hadn't been captured by King Grieve. Then all of this would have been different."

"Nevertheless, we are back together," Nathan said with a wan smile. "Dear spirits, I am glad to have good news for a change. We have lost so much."

"And we're about to lose more," said Zimmer. "The army will be here within days."

Norcross was flushed and restless. "All of the town's defenses are in place, sir. The siege towers will guard the mouth of the harbor against the Norukai, and these people are determined to fight for their homes." His eyes were large with disbelief. "But if King Grieve has a navy of more than a hundred serpent ships, we can't possibly fight off that many. What are we going to do?"

Lady Olgya pointed out, "And General Utros will soon arrive with many thousands of soldiers. We'll be caught between the two forces."

Thaddeus swallowed hard and said in a small voice, "Renda Bay is doomed, isn't it?"

General Zimmer said, "Under other circumstances, we might be in a position to stand against the Norukai with all our gifted fighters, the D'Haran soldiers, and the determined townspeople. The siege towers are strong, and the traps in the harbor could sink several attacking ships. The catapults will do a great deal of damage." He sounded more grim. "But it will not be enough if we are pressed by two devastating enemies at the same time."

"I'm far less concerned about the Norukai than I am

about General Utros," said Oron, sitting in his borrowed wooden chair as if it were a throne. "The Norukai are unruly brutes, but Utros is the greater danger to our civilization."

"Both are threats," Nathan said, "especially if they have the same goal. We don't know when King Grieve's fleet will set sail, but we *know* those thousands of enemy soldiers are marching down the river road. They will be here soon. How are we to stand against them all?"

"If we had enough blood," Olgya said, "we could raise another shroud and seal Renda Bay off from the rest of the world."

Bannon looked queasy, knowing exactly what Olgya was suggesting. Nathan said, "We can't just hide like Ildakar. The rest of the world needs our help as well."

"My people are armed and ready to fight," said Thaddeus. "They've been trained ever since Captain Norcross and his soldiers were placed here. We aren't helpless, but we need to have some hope."

"And that is the catch," Nathan said, and his voice cracked. "We no longer have Prelate Verna. We have been whittling away at General Utros's forces, but not enough." When he looked up at Zimmer, he realized how haggard the commander looked. "General, is there a chance we can protect Renda Bay when the army arrives? Any chance at all?"

Zimmer pondered for a long moment before answering. "I've tried to imagine any realistic scenario that might lead to victory. Even though we inflicted terrible losses at Cliffwall, and Prelate Verna created great devastation, we still had to fall back. Renda Bay is smaller and far more vulnerable, so I'm afraid the answer is no. We must be realistic for our own survival." His expression sagged. "This town has to be evacuated. Everyone must pack up their belongings and leave."

Thaddeus groaned. "But we've been through so much! We fought off attacks and rebuilt our homes again and again. Now, to just abandon it all . . ."

"You have never faced anything like General Utros," Oron said.

"Alas, I have to agree," Nathan said. "Many villagers have already disappeared into the foothills because they've come to the same conclusion. You know it yourself, Thaddeus."

The town leader nodded somberly. "Hundreds of houses now stand empty after you brought your news. The people know what is coming."

"We must get the rest of the population to safety," said the sorceress Perri, "and we have to depart too. We can't just wait here and be overwhelmed."

Nathan stroked his chin. "We need to send word north as fast as we can and sound the alarm. The major cities have to be alerted. Nicci used the sliph to travel to Serrimundi and Tanimura, and I hope the Old World is already building up great defenses." His lips quirked in a smile. "She can be very persuasive."

"But that doesn't help Renda Bay," Thaddeus said.

Captain Norcross said, "We still have those three large sailing ships in the harbor and dozens of fishing boats. If we do abandon the town before Utros arrives, they could carry refugees to safety, save many lives."

Thaddeus rested his elbows on his scarred wooden desktop. "How am I going to tell my people? Some of them will insist on staying."

"Then they will die," Lila said.

Zimmer continued pacing with his hands locked behind his back. "There is simply no alternative."

Nathan remembered the gaunt and pale enemy soldiers that had attacked Cliffwall. "We have to do more than just empty Renda Bay. We cannot give aid and comfort to the enemy. They've been marching across the mountains and over the valleys, stripping the landscape clean in their wake, but they can't possibly have enough supplies to sustain them. They are starving. We dare not leave a bushel of corn, a chicken, a dried apple, or a grain of rice. We must deny that army any resources, any shelter." He stroked his long white hair and adjusted his cape. "You know what we have to do. We must destroy the town of Renda Bay—burn it down, leave nothing but scorched earth by the time General Utros arrives."

CHAPTER 62

After she inspected the Tanimura garrison, Nicci and General Linden worked for days strengthening the city guard and pressing countless new recruits into service, many of them drawn from the refugees that had flooded the city after the Norukai attacks.

Hundreds of battered survivors came up the coast road from the south, people displaced from Effren and Larrikan Shores. Many were weak and saddened, seeking only stability in their lives. Others could not forget the blood and fire, the nightmare of the ruthless raiders, and they wanted to fight back. With nothing but threadbare clothes on their backs and the scabs of healing wounds, they desperately needed aid, but Serrimundi could absorb only so many refugees, since that city had itself suffered significant damage in Kor's raid.

Up in Tanimura, Nicci listened to their stories, one after another. When she looked at the outraged survivors, she knew they could be forged into an army, which was exactly what the Old World needed. Calling upon her own determination, she rallied them in the Tanimura square. "Soon a full-fledged war will be upon us. Will you let the Norukai hunt you down and kill your families, or will you take up weapons and learn how to fight back?"

The resounding shouts nearly deafened her. She could see Linden's surprise as he looked at the unexpected and earnest recruits for the army. Nicci gestured to the refugees. "The D'Haran garrison here will give you what you need, and I intend to set up training bases in Serrimundi as well, rally the blacksmiths and armorers in every city. We don't have much time. Everyone needs to pull together. What happened in Effren must not happen again!"

She wanted to see the devastation for herself. With Linden's permission, Nicci gathered fifty soldiers and a dozen angry refugees, then set off on a swift military ship, sailing south to Effren.

Two days later, reaching the black scar of the town, they anchored the swift ship offshore because all of the docks had been burned to the waterline. Nicci accompanied her group of soldiers and pale survivors, who clung to spiderweb-thin threads of hope that they might recover something from the ruins. Others simply wanted to bury their dead or at least lay markers for fallen friends and family members.

As Nicci walked through the ruins, her boots crunched on charred wood and the cracked bones of victims. Though the fires had burned out weeks before, the smell of soot and ash hung in the seaside air. Nicci imagined she could hear the lingering echoes of screams. The imprint of pain, violence, and suffering would remain here for years to come.

"Sweet Sea Mother," muttered one of the guard recruits who had come from Serrimundi. "Those animals left nothing standing! Why would an army do this?" Soot smeared the side of his face where he had wiped away a tear. "If they meant to conquer Effren, why destroy it all? Why kill everyone? That is not how you win a war."

"The Norukai come to pillage, not to rule," she said. "You watched them attack Serrimundi Harbor. You know what they are."

The recruit looked around the dead, silent ruins, appalled. "If we hadn't stopped them, would they have done this to Serrimundi, too? To my city?"

"Without question. That is why we had to obliterate them. Captain Kor is dead, and not a single Norukai got away." Warm pride filled her chest. "But Lars is still out there. We will have to crush them again, and again, until they learn their lesson."

Nicci walked among the haunted forest of timbers, collapsed walls, charred rooftops of what had been a thriving town. She knew what Effren must have been like, a community of several thousand fishermen, boatbuilders, farmers, woodcutters, smiths, shopkeepers, traders. The town would have had taverns, inns, shops, stables, a marketplace. Now only ashes remained. The site was a dark stain, as if a bolt of lightning had erased the town from existence.

She and the soldiers walked slowly through the streets. Warm sun beat down through a hazy sky. The smoke was gone, but some of the recruits and refugees kept coughing, perhaps to hide their nausea and grief. She herself had helped defend the town of Renda Bay from another Norukai raid. In that instance, though, they had won.

Nicci remembered the Renda Bay cemetery, with many stone markers to indicate the dead who were buried there, as well as countless wooden posts bearing the names of those who had been taken by the Norukai. Nicci had learned to hate the scarred raiders then, and her opinion of them had not improved after she actually met Lars, Kor, and other Norukai traders who came to Ildakar to sell their pitiful slaves.

She entered the burned-out skeleton of what had been a tavern. One wall had collapsed, while two stone half walls remained intact. Nicci stepped gingerly through the rubble, absorbing the sense of the place and filling in details with her imagination. Blackened lumps had been tables and stools, a splintered counter. A sealed cask of ale had exploded when its contents boiled in the fire. Six skulls were readily visible, and she didn't doubt they could find others if they sifted through the ashes.

"What are we going to do here, Sorceress?" asked the anxious recruit, who had followed her.

"I wanted to see with my own eyes." She moved slowly, her black dress blending in with the burned ruins. Charcoal-encrusted beams had bent under the heat, looking like the bones of long-dead dragons. "And I wanted you all to remember that this is what the Norukai will do if we let them win." She inhaled deeply, smelling the death and agony around her.

The recruit nodded. Now he had a smear of soot on his opposite cheek from a second tear.

"Do we rebuild?" a long-faced refugee asked. "Once we are strong again, should we try? Should we start now?" He turned around in the destroyed tavern, and it was obvious he remembered the place. "Will we have the heart to make Effren our home again?"

"Not until after the war," Nicci said. "You would only be giving the Norukai something new to burn. For now, your best chance is to become fighters." If Utros and his army were on the way, and if the ancient general had indeed joined forces with the Norukai, then the Old World would be awash in blood. And soon.

In burned-out homes they discovered several ghost-like squatters, villagers who had fled into the hills and now came back to the remains of their town, shocked and numb. Two battlefield surgeons tended to their injuries. Nicci hoped to toughen and recruit them for the new military force she was building.

She would have preferred that Richard lead the D'Haran army to fight at her side and crush both Utros and King Grieve. But Richard was counting on her, and Nicci would not let him down. He had sent her down to the Old World to pave the way for a new golden age of peace and prosperity, relying on Nicci to crush any upstart dictator or ill-advised tyrant.

She had never dreamed of the threat she faced now, a gigantic army from centuries past, and a raiding fleet of countless attack ships.

How could Richard's small bone box be everything she needed? With a soot-stained hand, she slipped the little cube out of her pocket and looked at the etched letters in the language of Creation, felt the tingle in her fingers. Richard was a master of constructed spells and this one was tighter, more intricate than any she had seen. Through her gift, she could sense its potential, but not how it worked or what its purpose was. Nicci feared that its use was beyond her abilities, but Richard believed in her, so how could she do any less?

Who else could she ask? None of the other gifted in Tanimura had her breadth of knowledge, except perhaps some of the Sisters of the Light who remained in the city. The Sisters had eagerly scrutinized the artifact when Nicci asked their opinion, but despite their strong desire to help, none of the Sisters had offered any insight.

So it would have to be her. Opening the delicate lid, she studied the shimmering white sphere, the pulsing nugget of a constructed spell. "I can handle this," she said as an affirmation to herself. She would figure it out, when the proper time came.

Still, she had a hard time maintaining her confidence as she gazed across the wasteland that had been a thriving town.

Before the war was over, there would be many more devastated towns. The people were fighting for their lives, their homes, their families. This Norukai raid had killed hundreds, maybe thousands, but the Effren tragedy would be like a sharp stick poking a coiled rattlesnake. Nicci intended to inspire all the survivors to strike back with sharp fangs.

Effren, Serrimundi, Larrikan Shores, and all the coastal cities would recover and thrive again. Nicci just had to save the world first.

CHAPTER 63

With a sinking heart, Norcross followed his orders and worked to evacuate Renda Bay. The need to abandon the town had struck the people like a thunderclap, but their angry resolve to fight for their homes had crumbled in the face of reality. Even all of them together could never stand against nearly a hundred thousand armed warriors.

"This doesn't mean we are giving up," the wizard Nathan had insisted, "but even if every single person in Renda Bay killed a hundred enemies, General Utros and King Grieve would still have enough fighters to grind your town into dust. We'll still find a way to hurt them."

"I need to keep our people safe," Thaddeus agreed. "We will load the three sailing ships and every fishing boat we have, and others will flee into the hills and hide. We have to get our people out of here. We have to!"

Accompanied by squads of D'Haran soldiers, Norcross marched up and down the streets, pounding on doors. Criers shouted for all citizens to pack up their food and run for their lives. By the time General Utros arrived, Renda Bay would be a ghost town, stripped of any resources he could use.

Down by the docks, lines of men and women carried

satchels of their most precious belongings as they
boarded boats to get away. Wailing children clutched
their mothers' hands or tugged on their skirts; one pig-
tailed girl grinned as if this were a great adventure.

In order to make more room on the *Daisy*, Kenneth
had tossed any crates, barrels, and tools overboard.
Now loaded with people, the fishing boat rode so low
in the water that Kenneth looked concerned. He pulled
up the boarding plank. "Can't take any more people.
There are other boats."

Even though the relentless army was less than a day
away, according to scout reports, the villagers remained
mostly calm. They waited for more vessels to reach the
docks as the *Daisy* set sail and moved off past the stone
defensive towers. Once the heavily laden craft reached
open water, Kenneth turned north, followed by ten
other equally full vessels in a civilian flotilla. They sailed
away, hoping to be far out of sight before the armies
closed in.

As more boats took on passengers, one old woman
wrestled with two goats. She stamped her foot on the
dock boards, but the fisherman captain waved her away.
"You can't come aboard with the animals. There's no
room! We have to save the people."

"But Choo and Loo are like people. They're my children." She wrapped her bony arms around the goats.
"I won't leave them behind."

The passengers already aboard called out from the
deck, frightened and impatient, "Leave them, Maggs!
That army's coming."

"I know! And those soldiers will eat Choo and Loo."

Sensing the tension, Norcross hurried among the people. "Take your animals deep into the hills and hide,
ma'am. Turn the goats loose, and they'll be fine, but be

sure to go far enough away from the army. You can stay out there with them, or come back here to board a boat if you make it in time. We just don't have enough vessels to carry livestock!" The goats bleated pitifully, and Norcross frowned. "No matter how cute they are."

Old Maggs left in a huff, yanking the ropes and leading her goats through the crowds and out of town.

In small dinghies, sailors rowed load after load of people out to the three large cargo ships anchored outside the bay. After overseeing the evacuation, Norcross would join General Zimmer and Thaddeus, who were already aboard Captain Mills's ship, directing the movement and retreat.

Amber accompanied him, along with Sisters Rhoda and Eldine, while the other Sisters of the Light worked their way through the town with Nathan, Oron, and the remaining gifted defenders. They were preparing a surprise for the ancient army.

"We've been separate for so long," Amber said to him with a smile. "I want to stay with you."

"I missed you, too," he said. "When we're aboard our ship, we'll have plenty of time to catch up, but for now, all these people . . ." He sighed. "There must be a thousand left to evacuate!"

"I'll help however I can," she said, lifting her chin. "Prelate Verna was very patient in teaching me how to use my gift. She taught me amazing things." She looked away to hide her sad expression. "I really miss the prelate. She was so kind to me and so wise."

"She did meet a brave end."

Amber nodded. "Yes, but it was still an end. I'd rather she were still here."

Lila and Bannon came down to the docks, flushed from running. The young man looked upset. "That's a stubborn family! What do they expect to do? Throw clay pots at thousands of soldiers?"

Lila seemed equally annoyed. "It is a potter's shop, not a gold mine. We could not convince them." She glared at Bannon. "And you refused to let me knock them senseless and drag them here."

Norcross let out a heavy sigh, knowing that there were many families who simply refused to leave. "It might not be a gold mine, but it is their home. I only hope they're sensible enough to flee as soon as they see the army approaching."

Over the next hour, the last fishing vessels sailed away. The three cargo ships were nearly full after a constant succession of rowboats carried groups out to where the ships were anchored and came back to pick up more evacuees. When it was time, with the town mostly empty behind them, Bannon and Lila climbed aboard a dinghy so they, too, could take a place aboard Captain Mills's ship.

"This is a great improvement over our last boat," she remarked, and Bannon agreed.

Norcross and Amber remained behind to round up the last few boatloads. Thorn and Lyesse jogged down the streets, making a beeline toward the harbor as they sounded the alarm. "The first enemy soldiers are no more than an hour away!"

"We killed only four before we had to retreat," Lyesse added. "I don't think we slowed them much. They are more wary now."

Thorn frowned. "Nathan commanded us not to fight any more of the army for now, because it puts us at unnecessary risk." She sounded disappointed. "It seems wrong."

"Oron, Olgya, and Perri concurred." Lyesse sounded

equally downcast. "But since they are all that remains of the wizards' duma from Ildakar, we must obey them. They told us to go." The two morazeth watched the next dinghy come in, rowed by two muscular sailors.

"We all have to obey orders," Norcross said. Behind him, the town was empty. He could see the deserted wooden houses, shops, inns, town hall, and the open square. "There aren't many boats left for Nathan and the others. Are they almost finished?"

"Who can know about the work of wizards?" Lyesse asked with a snort. She sprang from the dock into the dinghy even before the sailors had tied it up. Her morazeth sister joined her.

Amber smiled at her brother. "Let's get out to the ships. It's our turn."

Norcross and Amber rode with the two morazeth and several other stragglers as more empty rowboats came to the docks for the last evacuees, which would include Nathan and his companions.

The burly sailors were weary at the oars, having gone back and forth several times already. Seeing this, Thorn and Lyesse moved them from their bench. "You require rest. Let us row."

Surprised, the muscular men relinquished the oars. The morazeth rowed with great vigor, pulling them toward the nearest three-masted sailing ship. As they passed beneath the tall siege towers at the mouth of the bay, Norcross looked up with a pang. He saw the catapults lined up, ready to hurl boulders at oncoming serpent ships. He had worked so hard on the town's defenses. "We were prepared to hurt the Norukai, but we won't get the chance."

"We'll get a chance." Amber clutched her brother's arm. "This is our chance to survive."

When the dinghy reached the sailing ship, Norcross and the passengers climbed up a slat ladder to the deck, which was already crowded with Renda Bay evacuees. Captain Mills stood at the stern shading his eyes, deeply worried. In the small boat below, the sailors prepared to set off again, glad for their brief rest while the morazeth rowed.

Norcross stared back at the deserted town. A gigantic army would swarm through those streets before long, ransacking empty buildings. He hoped Nathan and the others would make it back soon.

A lookout high on the mainmast used a spyglass peering southwest. "Confirmed, Captain! Sighting confirmed!"

Mills began clanging a brass bell mounted next to the wheel. He hammered the clapper back and forth for all he was worth. "Prepare yourselves! They're coming."

Norcross turned to look out at the open sea and saw a line of ominous ships just coming into view, all of them with midnight-blue sails.

Nathan went from building to building in Renda Bay, scribing spell-forms on bare walls, laying down protective webs, and adding anchor points. He fervently wished he had Prelate Verna there to help him, or Elsa with her transference magic. "Dear spirits, I don't normally use my gift for so much destruction, unless I absolutely have to."

"This time you absolutely have to," said Perri. The woman's gift was weaker than Leo's had been, but as a shaper Perri could use magic to shift wood and stone. She used her finger to embed gouges and spell-forms in the walls of town buildings, inscribing them swiftly and perfectly, whereas Nathan would have had to carve the designs more crudely with the point of his knife.

With great relish, Oron and Olgya went about setting booby traps. Lord Oron used paint to draw looping connective runes from one street to another, laying down what looked like an odd design but was actually a convoluted trap. This would become readily apparent as soon as the enemy soldiers triggered the small constructed spells in the doorways of major buildings and collapsed the interconnected webs. Olgya laid down magical trip wires across the main streets and inside the primary storehouses that were sure to attract the starving army.

Though he felt a chill about preparing such a cascade of powerful magic, Nathan knew this set of spells was not the same as Verna's Weeping Stone spell, which had slipped out of her control. This was far simpler, cleaner magic, and they all knew how to use it and master it.

Nathan had mapped the streets of Renda Bay and picked their targets. His gifted comrades listened intently as he described his strategy. "We have to lure the front ranks into the destructive zone. Only then can we let the magic be triggered, otherwise it'll be too soon."

Oron gritted his teeth, "So long as they are dead, I don't care where the magic strikes."

"We'll kill more of them if we let them reach the center of town before the trap is sprung," Sister Sharon pointed out. "The prelate killed thousands when she brought down the canyon wall. Let us do the same in Renda Bay."

"General Utros may be more cautious now," Nathan said. "The important part is that we deny them any supplies. His soldiers are already starving, marching along and half dead. They will drop from hunger and weariness soon."

"I'd rather they burn," Oron said.

Nathan and Perri worked together in the town hall for the last stage of their plan. Standing inside Thaddeus's office looking at the historic ledgers and books on the shelves, he felt sadness again. "More knowledge being wiped out. Again! I wonder how we will ever forgive ourselves."

Perri asked, "Would you rather keep your musty old tomes and let the world be conquered? Sacrificing a few books does not seem like such a great cost to defeat the army."

"I would rather survive and write new books."

Perri finished marking spell-forms on the walls of the town leader's office. "There, now the lines are connected from the tower down to the foundations. Renda Bay is evacuated, and everything is set. We should get to the ships."

"Yes, the army is close." Wearing his fine embroidered cape and vest, Nathan felt satisfied as he emerged from the town hall to meet his gifted companions. "Time to go. Everyone down to the harbor."

They hurried toward the docks, where the calm, blue waters of Renda Bay awaited them. The fishing boats had loaded up and already sailed away to the north. The three large cargo ships remained anchored, filled with passengers and ready to depart, with just a few rowboats ready to carry Nathan and his gifted saboteurs. He glanced one last time at the vacant town. Everyone seemed to be gone. The homes were empty, except for the booby traps of magic they had placed in strategic places.

He heard a sudden loud clamor from the sailing ships

out on the water, a bell ringing and ringing to sound the alarm.

Perri looked up. "What is that?"

"Nothing good." Oron hurried down the street to the waiting rowboats at the dock, where anxious sailors urged them to hurry. Nathan and the others ran faster.

From the dock he could see at least a hundred serpent ships on the horizon, sailing directly toward Renda Bay.

CHAPTER 64

General Utros had not smelled the sea in fifteen centuries. Long ago, one of his military marches had taken him to the coast, and he remembered how he had stared out at the sun on the open waves, observed the sailing ships and fishing settlements, and known he wanted to conquer them.

Now, the relentless march took his army along a river that flowed to the ocean. Approaching Renda Bay, he smelled the salt air again, which brought with it a tang of freedom. The soldiers marched nonstop, hour after hour, though they were gaunt and starving despite the spell that numbed the gnawing hunger in their bellies. Along the river, they grabbed fish, waterfowl, even weeds from the current, devouring whatever they could find. And they kept moving.

Utros, Enoch, and Ruva rode in the lead as they approached a significant town at the mouth of the river, the largest settlement they had encountered since crossing the mountains. Along the way, his army had overwhelmed smaller villages, mining towns, and crossroads settlements, which had offered only lean pickings. Renda Bay at last would offer supplies and materials.

"Tonight we will eat well," said First Commander Enoch, sitting high on his dark horse.

Utros considered making this fishing port his new base, where he could meet up with the Norukai fleet. After King Grieve and his serpent ships departed from Ildakar, the two great military forces had had no communication with each other, and their overall war plan was based on nothing more than crude maps and vague memories. During the long days of marching, Utros had pondered strategic possibilities about conquering the land, whether to use his army as a single battering ram to crush anything in the way, or to split the force into dozens of sub-armies dispatched in all directions. He would make his final decision once he conquered Renda Bay.

When the Norukai eventually joined with his army, the scarred raiders would inspire fear among their victims. Utros would let the reckless warriors bear the brunt of any resistance, suffering casualties so that his own men remained uninjured. That was his entire purpose for the alliance with them.

"Will King Grieve be here in Renda Bay? And his vile shaman?" Ruva's voice turned sour.

"We shall see. We don't need the Norukai, but we can use them." He urged his black stallion toward the town's outskirts. A ripple of excitement rolled through the ranks, an awareness that their destination was ahead at last, and the town would no doubt be filled with supplies and plunder.

They passed empty meadows, stripped orchards, abandoned farmhouses, vacant paddocks for goats, sheep, or cattle, but no livestock. Utros frowned. "The people have fled. Where are the animals?"

"That's no surprise, sir," Enoch said. "They must have seen our army coming for days. Who would dare to stand against us?"

Outriders broke into farmhouses and came out with blankets, some cook pots, and scraps of clothes, but they reported that the pantries were empty, every one of them. Even barrels in the root cellars were gone. More scouts ransacked the outlying buildings and issued similar reports. Seeing no food at hand, anywhere, the troops began to grow anxious.

Enoch's expression hardened. "Should I make a sortie into town, General? See what we can find?"

Annoyed, Utros urged his mount to a faster pace. "We will all go."

With a flicker in the air, Ava's shimmering spirit appeared. "I went ahead, beloved Utros. Renda Bay has been abandoned. The people fled." She drifted against her twin sister, and the green aura brightened, as if the two drew energy from each other. "The whole town is empty."

Ruva's voice echoed along with her twin's. "The wizard Nathan and his gadflies must have arrived first and warned them."

Ava separated. "We should have killed him and all those others at Cliffwall! That might have appeased the Keeper while we continue our war."

"Killing those people is of secondary importance," Utros said. "Even if the town is empty, we will occupy it as our base of operations. I need to plan our next move, with or without the Norukai."

He pressed his stallion into a gallop, and Enoch and Ruva rode beside him as if making a military charge. The soldiers in the vanguard let out a heroes' cry and charged ahead to attack a silent city.

At the edge of town, Utros noted stables, farm-houses, a smithy, a sawmill, a brickyard, a cooper's shop with half-finished barrels lying among piles of staves and iron hoops. At the center of Renda Bay they saw the main square, the large town hall. Everything was empty.

"Find them!" Utros pointed to the left and right. "Those are warehouses, grain silos. There must be some animals in the pens and stockyards. Report all food stockpiles you find. Our supply sergeants will divide up the spoils to best feed our men."

The encroaching army roared with excitement. Soldiers broke ranks and rushed into the streets, ransacking the buildings. They smashed doors and charged into warehouses, but they came back out perplexed, angry, and empty-handed.

"There's nothing, General," reported one of the first scout captains. "The barns and warehouses are vacant. We didn't find even a bale of hay for our horses."

Utros adjusted the horned helmet and stared ahead. "I have conquered an abandoned town." He pushed his stallion toward the central square. "There must be more here!"

Enoch gestured beyond the descending streets that led to the water and the open bay. "Down there, sir. Look at the docks—all the boats are gone."

Utros's leather gauntlet creaked as he clenched a fist. Beyond the mouth of the bay he spotted three large ships departing under full sail. Then he caught his breath as he saw more than a hundred serpent ships pursuing them like a pack of wolves. "The Norukai are coming. King Grieve hunts them down as they try to flee."

Ruva raised her fingers and traced invisible lines of

magic in the air. "I would be happier to kill those vermin ourselves, but I will rest easily just knowing they are dead."

"The fleeing people aren't our concern. They are already gone." Utros ran a finger over the smooth surface of his half mask. "We need to find what's left of this town. We need to feed our troops."

The streets were paved with cobblestones, and the horses' hoofbeats echoed loudly as they clattered forward. On the way to the central square, hungry vanguard soldiers rushed past the general and spread out to break into shops and homes. They smashed windows, battered down doors, and caused even more damage in their frustration. Utros expected they would find some stragglers barricaded behind doors, but Renda Bay was eerily silent.

Ava's spirit drifted about. "There's nothing . . . but also *some*thing. I sense danger here. Beware, General."

Ruva sat on her bay mare, shuddering. Gooseflesh covered her pale skin. "I can feel deadly lines of force. This isn't simply an empty town. Nathan and the others left something for us here." She sketched in the air with an extended fingertip. Ava faced her sister, touching her spectral fingertip against Ruva's, and together they opened a spiderweb of bright lines, identifying a pattern.

"It is a trap. These buildings are more than empty. They're waiting to be—"

As the scouts broke into prominent storehouses near the town hall, they triggered an activation web. Bright lights sizzled through the walls of the storehouse, and the shuttered windows overhead burst open with a flood of bright light, a flare of heat. Gouts of flame erupted through the roof. Covered with fire, soldiers staggered back out, trying to smother the flames on their smoldering leather armor. In seconds, the entire storehouse became an inferno, as if it had been built of straw and kindling.

On the opposite side of the square, another building ignited, then a third one with such a vigorous explosion that the wallboards shot deadly splinters in all directions.

Ruva raised both hands. "I feel the tingling everywhere, down that street, down this street, along that alley!" She looked in horror at the cobblestones, where she saw painted lines that some wizard had left behind. "We are caught in the middle of the web."

The town hall suddenly glowed with jagged cracks of orange heat, like lightning bolts within the stone blocks. A blast broke down the façade, and the debris crumbled toward them. The general's black stallion screamed, and he hunched over the saddle, holding on as he galloped away. Flames raged down the street as one spell triggered another.

Ava's spirit swooped along, leading him to safety. Other horses raced for the harbor and the open water. His soldiers scattered, charging at a full run down side streets, trying to stay ahead of the flame front. In doing so, they ignited one booby trap after another, setting off a cascade of magic.

The cobblestones cracked and shuddered. Lines of magic drew down into swirling patterns that connected building to building and square to square. The Renda Bay streets became molten, and all the adjacent buildings ignited from the connected tapestry of magic.

"Ride!" Utros roared.

The entire town became an inferno, incinerating countless soldiers. Summoning her gift, Ruva called a downpour to drench some of the fire and douse the lower streets. It was enough to keep Utros and the front ranks safe, but behind them the burning town cut off the rest of his army, engulfing many of the soldiers in flames.

Once he was safe by the waterfront, Utros turned away from the smoke and fire and looked angrily out to sea, where Norukai ships were approaching the fleeing cargo ships that carried the survivors of Renda Bay.

O ut beyond the harbor, the two big sailing ships commanded by Captains Straker and Donell sailed away from Renda Bay full of evacuees. As the last of the gifted defenders came aboard the third ship, Captain Mills rang the alarm bell again and again. The serpent ships closed in on Renda Bay.

Nathan took a position near the bow as they got underway, following the other two large vessels. A sudden ripple of dismay crossed the deck as the passengers watched orange flames blossom in the center of town. Smoke erupted in pillars. He smiled. "Looks like General Utros found our surprise."

Oron wore a grim expression as he stroked his thick, pale braid. "There is more to come."

Moments later, additional blazes surged, like storms of fire triggered by the unsuspecting invaders. The sky blackened as more smoke rose, and the inferno built upon itself. Before long, the entire town was engulfed in fire. The blazes leaped from building to building, raced down street after street.

Thaddeus and other evacuees from Renda Bay stared back at their receding homes, weeping. The freed slave Rendell placed a comforting hand on the town leader's shoulder.

Olgya was more intent on the countless serpent ships racing toward them across the sea. "How do we fight against the Norukai? They are closing in fast."

Captain Mills paced the deck, shouting orders to his sailors. Familiar with their ship, they used the complex interaction of rigging, rudder, and sails to catch breezes and steer the ship at the greatest possible speed. Some of the gifted passengers assisted by increasing the wind in the proper direction.

Norcross stood next to General Zimmer, who alternated his glare between the burning town and the fleet of pursuing serpent ships. "After attacking Utros so often, it should be a nice change of pace to fight the Norukai."

Nathan watched the receding siege towers at the mouth of the bay and felt a pang in his heart, which twisted as Ivan's presence plagued him, but he pushed back the darkness. He turned his attention to the oncoming Norukai fleet.

The serpent ships had the breezes at their backs, and they put on an additional burst of speed using oars manned by strong warriors. Ten Norukai vessels continued after the evacuating ships, while the rest of the enemy fleet slowed and diverted toward the burning town of Renda Bay. Increasing smoke rose into the sky.

Next to Nathan, Bannon watched the inevitable approach of the dark blue sails of the pursuing ships, his face flushed with anger. "Looks like I'll have another chance to kill some Norukai." He touched the sword at his hip, a standard blade that General Zimmer had provided from the D'Haran spares. "Any sword is good enough, but I miss Sturdy." He looked down at his unfamiliar weapon.

"You'll get practice soon enough, boy," Lila said. She

was armed with a dagger and a sword she had retrieved in Renda Bay, and she looked fierce. "Stay by me, and we will make a good accounting of ourselves."

Nathan knew how much the ungainly sword had meant to Bannon. Sturdy was a lot like the red-haired swordsman himself, unimposing and plain, but deceptively deadly. Nathan pondered the more ornate sword he had carried since leaving D'Hara. He had chosen it along with fine travel clothes to be part of his swashbuckling image. Nathan had considered the showy blade to be an important accessory for an adventurer, but now that he had his gift back, his real identity was that of a wizard. He could still fight with a sword whenever necessary, but the fancy, expensive weapon was not nearly as important to him—not as important as it would be to Bannon.

He undid the buckle and removed the scabbard. "My boy, you deserve this."

Bannon looked at him in surprise. "What do you mean?"

"Take my sword. It should be the best ever forged, considering how much I paid for it. The blade has served me well in many adventures, as you certainly know, but you would value it more than I." He extended the sword. "It is my gift to you."

Bannon was hesitant to accept it. "I've never used such a fancy blade."

"You stab with the point and cut with the edge," Lila said. "Nothing unusual about it."

Nathan pushed the pommel toward him. "You'd best take this before I change my mind."

Bannon accepted the sword from him. "Thank you, Nathan!" In wonder, he drew the blade out of its scabbard. Tears shone in his hazel eyes as he held the gleaming steel up to the sunlight. "Maybe King Grieve will see it and run away."

"I would prefer that he come closer, so you can stick it in his heart," Lila said.

Nathan felt warm satisfaction. "Give me your borrowed blade in exchange, so I'm not entirely unarmed."

Bannon handed over his sword, then proudly strapped on Nathan's belt and scabbard. "It is a sword more worthy of your skills," Lila said.

"I still miss Sturdy," he replied.

"*You* are the weapon, Bannon Farmer. A blade is just a blade."

The hounding Norukai kept closing the distance, and it was clear they would converge soon with their furious rowing. From the deck, Nathan could hear the shouts of angry warriors and the pounding beat of the oar master. "They are relentless. And a bit foolish."

One serpent ship pulled ahead of the other four, its oars moving like the blurred legs of a centipede. Standing behind the carved serpent figurehead, one Norukai roared out a challenge. He swung a spiked iron sphere on a chain.

Bannon recognized him. "That one is named Bosko. He forced Lila and me to row until we were ready to die."

"He thinks highly of himself," Lila said with a snort. "I can smell him from here."

Bannon looked at her with a hard grin. "His stench could be fierce enough to kill an enemy."

The foremost serpent ship raced ahead of the others as if Bosko wanted to capture them by himself.

Amber, Oliver, and Peretta huddled together in a quick conversation. "We can help," Amber said. "Watch this."

Oliver and Peretta stood beside her at the rail, shoulder-to-shoulder. They unleashed their gift and sent a joint wave of water and air that pushed across the sea and slammed the side of Bosko's ship. Aboard the vessel, the Norukai scrambled to hold themselves in place as the force shoved them sideways and snapped several oars. Some Norukai ran to the rigging, while others crowded the opposite side of the tilted ship, adding weight to bring it back level. The oars began moving again, but the wounded ship cruised erratically.

The three young friends cheered. "We did it. We stopped them!"

Captain Mills shouted, "Steady ahead! We can gain more distance."

Scrambling to gain purchase on his buffeted ship, Bosko held the carved figurehead as he swirled his spiked mace. He roared a challenge, calling them cowards.

Oron waited next to Nathan, his lips twisted in a frown. "It will not come to hand-to-hand fighting, not yet." Impatient, he lifted a hand, palm outward. "We can strike them from here."

Nathan smiled. "Those trainees did a good job, but we can put an end to this right now." Together, the two wizards summoned twin lightning bolts. Both jagged spears of energy struck at the same time, blasting the prow of the serpent ship and vaporizing Bosko in the blast of magic.

"Must be all the gas pent up inside him," Bannon said. Lila snickered.

The rest of the Norukai ships pressed closer, and Captain Mills looked grave. "Good thing those other fishing boats got enough of a head start. I hope they found coves and other places to hide, but those Norukai will keep after us for day after day."

Behind them the smoke of Renda Bay towered like an anvil in the sky. The passengers stared at it, knowing their homes were now obliterated. The rest of King Grieve's fleet clustered around the harbor town.

"We have to get ahead of them and sound the alarm to the other cities on the coast," Nathan said. "They will turn around soon enough once they know they can't catch us."

"There's another way I can help," Olgya said. "A trick I learned back in Ildakar, and I used it to some effect back at Cliffwall." Using her gift, she reached out to the water all around them and manipulated the weather to raise droplets. She summoned a fog bank as large as an island that spread out in a smoke screen behind them. White curls of vapor filled the air, hiding them from the Norukai captains. Soon, the evacuating ships disappeared entirely.

Nathan smiled as he saw the swirling fog. Olgya seemed in a trance as she thickened the wisps, weaving it like a great silken cloth of vapor. The serpent ships were quickly lost inside the smoke screen. "Most excellent. Now we can be on our way unimpeded."

Racing ahead of the wall of mist, the ships sailed under sunny skies, heading toward the large cities in the Old World.

CHAPTER 65

Renda Bay burned uncontrolled for two days before all the fires died out, leaving nothing more than ashes and foundation stones. The main Norukai fleet had closed in outside the harbor, while several of the vessels pursued the three sailing ships that had fled the destruction. Eventually, they returned.

Meanwhile, Utros ruled only ruins.

During the worst of the blaze, First Commander Enoch sent scouts back up the river, keeping to the water to make it through the fires to reconnect with the main body of the army, which was trapped on the other side of the conflagration. Thousands of troops rushed to cut firebreaks with axes and swords and formed lengthy bucket brigades from the river, but still the town burned.

Despite their best efforts and inexhaustible manpower, the army saved only a few dozen homes and shops, a pale victory since the buildings were empty anyway. Afterward, while ransacking the ruins in search of any scrap of food, they discovered more than two hundred charred bodies caught in the backwash of the fire, their bones mingled with ashes. More losses. . . .

Ruva combined her gift with Ava's spirit to clear some of the burned buildings in order to fashion a command camp, and General Utros used one of the intact houses as his base. He looked at the devastation and said in a low voice that only First Commander Enoch and the sorceresses could hear, "I had hoped to feed my soldiers here. Are they supposed to eat ashes?"

Ruva glided up against him. "My preservation spell will last. The soldiers can keep marching all the way to Tanimura."

Utros rounded on her, glaring through his gold half mask. "And what if they burn Tanimura to the ground, too? And every other town on the way? What if those people are willing to devastate every city in the Old World just to deny me a victory? How long can we last?"

Ruva gently stroked the skin on his intact cheek. "We will last as long as we need to, beloved Utros. We are loyal to you."

Shimmering in front of them, Ava said, "I stayed with you even through death, didn't I? Your soldiers are with you instead of in the underworld because they have sworn loyalty to you. This war will not end until *you* decide it ends. Victory is in your eyes, depending on how you define it."

Surrendering, he reached up to press Ruva's palm against his cheek. For just a moment he let himself remember Majel's delicate touch, the one time in his life that he had felt love and happiness, a time when he had believed in a perfect future for himself, for his lover, and for his emperor . . . a time when he hadn't needed to choose between loyalty and love. Now Utros made all choices for himself, to take from the Old World until there was nothing left.

The core of his huge army camped up the river road on the other side of the holocaust, because there was no place for them in the soot and ash. Waiting to receive orders from the general, Second Commanders Halders and Arros pressed Enoch for answers, and he told them to wait. The first commander presented himself in the general's makeshift command structure. "The soldiers are ready, sir. You need only issue orders. Do we continue our march? Do we leave Renda Bay behind and press on? What will we do with the Norukai ships?"

After a long moment, Utros said, "What I truly need are maps and scouts, and then I can decide where to go." He squeezed his hand into a fist.

"You are a legend to us all, sir," Enoch said. "Whatever you decide will be the correct tactical choice. We have lost many fighters in many skirmishes, and the enemy has proved to be far more troublesome than we expected, but your army can still overwhelm any city. Especially if the Norukai help."

Utros stepped out of the building and looked across the blackened city, where his people waited for his guidance. He looked toward the bay, where he saw many serpent ships gathered, including Grieve's flagship, he assumed.

He narrowed his eyes and nodded to himself. "Perhaps I need the Norukai more than I thought, at least right now. We can use their charts, their supplies, their manpower. Then King Grieve and I can plan our attack on the rest of the land. I need to speak with him."

Ava's spirit hovered in front of them. "In my spirit form, I can travel out to the ships and tell King Grieve that you request a meeting."

"Yes," Utros said, "but make certain he knows it is not a request."

The serpent ships dropped anchor outside of Renda Bay beyond the stone siege towers, as if wary that unseen defenders might still rain down projectiles and flaming arrows upon them.

After Ava had communicated with the king, the Norukai dispatched a landing boat to retrieve General Utros and Ruva. They waited together while four Norukai warriors rowed up to the intact dock. The men gruffly acknowledged Utros while leering at the slender, painted form of Ruva.

She responded to them with a cold look. "You may want to have me, but you should be afraid. The intense pleasure you would experience is bound to burst your hearts."

Two of the Norukai grunted, but one bold warrior guffawed. "That would not be a fighter's way to die, but it is a *man's* way to die."

The last of the men taunted her, "Or maybe the pleasure you receive from a Norukai would kill you first!"

Utros had no patience for the banter. "Enough! Take us to King Grieve. We have a war to win." These sub-human raiders appalled him, and he hated the fact that he needed them—for now—to accomplish his goals.

The raiders admired the burned remnants of Renda Bay. "You made your mark here already. We have left many villages like that ourselves."

One snickered, "You may have Norukai blood in you after all."

Utros snapped, "Just row us out to the ship!"

The landing boat reached the lead vessel, where a

group of brash Norukai greeted them on the deck above. King Grieve crossed his arms over his chest and received them. "So, our armies have joined together after all! I am eager for this war you promised me."

Utros climbed aboard. "We need to plan the best strategy for victory. Bring a meal, and we will talk in your cabin."

Grieve sniffed the air, relishing the stench of smoke that hung like a black fog over the harbor. "I enjoy the smell of a successful raid, and the destruction of a weak town. I hope you plundered Renda Bay of everything those people had before you burned it to the ground."

Utros was annoyed. "I did not burn it—I wouldn't have been so foolish as to destroy such a valuable asset. The people laid traps before they evacuated and turned the town into an inferno as soon as we arrived."

The Norukai king guffawed. "Then your men must still be very hungry!"

Utros clenched his fist at his side. He ground his teeth together so hard he could feel his half mask shifting.

The Norukai ships had full stores of salted and smoked fish, seaweed cakes, hard breads, and barrels of ale they had brought from the main islands. Utros wished he could distribute all that food to his soldiers, but he had already made such a request once, and if he asked King Grieve again, he would appear weak.

"It is merely a setback. My army can keep moving. Tell us about the other cities we will find up the coast. Which ones have the best plunder?" Utros said as they entered the king's cabin. "We need to pillage more. My soldiers must eat."

Sitting on a sturdy bench, Grieve gnawed on a haunch of some smoked meat. The animal didn't seem familiar. He didn't answer the question, preoccupied with eating.

Utros and Ruva each received a block of smoked fish on a pewter plate, which they found satisfactory. The sorceress chewed in silence until she finally asked, "Where is your shaman? Doesn't Chalk guide your decisions?"

"Chalk is dead." The expression on the king's horribly scarred face seemed to fall. "Now they all need to die. They all need to grieve."

"We still have to plan," Utros said, impatient. How could the loss of that simpering albino ape come close to the pain he felt upon losing Ava, his precious and beautiful sorceress? "Renda Bay was a disappointment. We need to march and resupply."

Through the half-open door to the cabin, they could hear the boisterous shouts and angry grumbles of the other Norukai on deck. A squarish, ugly woman named Atta entered the cabin as if she belonged there. She carried another meaty bone, which Utros thought resembled part of a human arm. She ripped off a hunk of flesh and chewed with wet sounds.

The hard bench squeaked under the big king's weight as he shifted his position. "My warriors are more than ready. Lars has already raided several towns and villages up there, and he can tell you which ones he left intact. There'll be little to scavenge from the ones he destroyed."

"The more he destroys, the more we will have to rebuild afterward. Tell him to restrain himself."

Grieve laughed as if the general had made a grand joke. "We will work together to conquer the Old World, but I still don't know how we share the land afterward."

"Let us see what remains," Utros said, "and then we divide it."

"Or we fight over it." The Norukai king focused his attention on the bone in his hand, gnawing another scrap of red meat and gristle.

Utros was glad that the gold mask hid half of his expression, and he struggled to keep his face blank. He set down his fork still bearing a hunk of smoked fish. "There is no need for that."

All the Norukai disgusted him, and he considered King Grieve to be even more foul than Emperor Kurgan. He planned on enfolding the entire Old World into his new empire, and in doing so he could use the Norukai for their strength and their penchant for destruction, but his mind and his honor could not encompass an empire that included such subjects as these. After the war was won, he would find a way to destroy King Grieve.

Ruva glanced at him with a hard smile, as if she read his thoughts.

"No need," Atta said, sitting her wide hips on the bench beside Grieve, "but it might be invigorating." She reached over to touch the gash across the king's cheek. "I am trying to decide whether I should be your queen, Grieve, or if I should have an empire of my own."

"You will have whatever I give you," he grunted.

She blew softly into his face. "I can get what I want from you, my Grieve."

With his iron-plated fist he punched her in the center of the chest. The blow rocked her off the bench, but she grabbed the edge of the table and kept her balance. She laughed and bashed him on the chin in return. Grieve lurched to his feet, dropping the bone as he spread his shoulders to flare the spiked spurs.

He held Atta's gaze for a long moment, then relaxed. "Later. When I bed down for the night, we will continue our wrestling."

She laughed. "It will have to be in your cabin, my Grieve. We broke my bunk last night!" With an unsettling flirtatious glance, the Norukai woman sauntered out of the king's cabin, still carrying her bone.

Utros was impatient, grim and serious. He would make his careful plans every step of the way, but this loathsome oaf did not seem to think ahead. "My army is ready to march. Renda Bay is burned, and we must move soon. With our forces united, King Grieve, we could accomplish exactly what we need."

Grieve scoffed. "I have more than one hundred forty ships. That's more than the coast can handle. Your army can march inland along the old imperial roads, while the Norukai prey upon the coastal towns."

"We need more of a plan than that!" Utros said. "This is a war, not a game."

Grieve tossed down his bone, which was now stripped of meat. He drained a tankard of ale while looking with displeasure at the general. "All war is a game, or else why bother?"

Utros tried to control his impatience. "We must agree on a target. Our main goal should be Tanimura, the heart of the Old World. That is the best way we can destroy the enemy."

Grieve crossed his massive arms over his chest. "Is there much to plunder in Tanimura? I've barely heard of it."

Utros's information was more than a thousand years out of date, but he remained confident. "Tanimura is filled with wealth and potential slaves, as many women as you want. Once we capture and destroy that city, we will have won the war."

King Grieve grunted. "That is all the plan I need. We will each make our way north. After we strike Tanimura, we can take our time and pick clean the carcass of the Old World."

CHAPTER 66

When Nicci left the ruins of Effren, she directed the fast military ship to stop at Serrimundi so she could check on their defense preparations. From the tension in the air, she knew they all took the threat seriously. Harborlord Otto had dispatched swift patrol ships beyond the rocky mouth of the harbor, and lookouts remained on top of the bluff above the Sea Mother carving. Inside its sheltered harbor, the city remained watchful and safe.

The lookouts had developed a simple but effective means of signaling at great distance, to spread any warning more swiftly. If any patrol ship spotted the Norukai fleet, they could drop and ignite rafts piled high with kindling, pitch, and green wood. The floating fires would produce greasy smoke visible from far away, and the watchers on the bluff could sound the alarm to the city. Norukai raiders would never surprise Serrimundi again.

When her expedition returned from Effren, they brought more refugees to join the crowds that already strained Serrimundi's resources. Nicci intended to head back up to Tanimura as soon as possible, but she would verify that Serrimundi was secure before she left.

The sheltered harbor remained a blur of activity. By now many of the sunken wrecks had been dismantled to clear a passage for larger trading ships. Rowboats and fishing vessels dodged the burned masts that still protruded from the water. Salvage crews continued to restore the docks while also building up the city's defenses.

Nicci walked along the harborside in a new black dress, since her old one had been patched and cleaned so many times it had fallen to tatters. The dress fit her well, and she drew the attention of observers as she walked past. Now that her blond hair was growing out again, the strands tickled her neck.

On the new wharf, she found Otto talking with Captain Ganley of the *Mist Maiden,* which had been too large to sail out safely through the sunken ships. Five other large ships remained at anchor, waiting for their chance to leave, but they were not idle. Salvage crews affixed sheets of beaten metal to the hulls as armor.

The harborlord and Ganley stood beside a stack of crates taller than their heads. Both men turned as Nicci approached. "Thanks to you, Sorceress, my *Mist Maiden* will be a warship now," said Ganley, "though I prefer peaceful trading from port to port."

"Every ship needs to be a warship until the war is over," Nicci said.

Otto tugged on his wide-brimmed hat, shading his eyes. "By the end of the day, we'll have a passage clear so the larger ships can leave the harbor." He sighed. "Part of me just wants Ganley to take my daughter and her children away to safety, so I can focus on guarding my city."

"They might be safe, but the rest of you wouldn't be," Ganley said. "I have my part to play, as do we all."

"The *Mist Maiden* is too useful as a warship," Nicci said. "It will serve as an important defense at the mouth of the harbor if the Norukai make their way past the protective reefs."

She was pleased to see that hundreds of the initial Effren refugees were now armed and practicing maneuvers in an open area where two warehouses had burned down during Kor's raid. The men and women, still dressed in rags, wore hodgepodge armor, chain mail, leather, even some plate. They fumbled through their training, clumsily wielding swords, but getting better, hour by hour.

Nicci nodded toward the recruits. "Their sheer numbers will help build a defense force if the Norukai come ashore here again."

"I intend to stop that from happening in the first place," Harborlord Otto said. "With our new armored warships we will block the mouth of the harbor. They will never get past the Sea Mother into the city proper."

Ganley set his jaw. "A line of five large vessels will prevent any invaders from entering the harbor."

Nicci was impressed. "A significant improvement from how lax you were when I brought my first warning."

Leaving the two men, she walked to the next pier, where she saw an old man in a loincloth, his head shaved clean and his skin so tanned it looked like hardened leather. With unexpected flexibility, he sat crosslegged on the end of the dock. Four young men dove underwater in front of him. Stone weights of various sizes rested on the dock beside the old man, and the young divers each took one and plunged deep, as if they were intentionally drowning themselves. After a remarkably long time, they would swim back up to the surface, struggling to carry the weights. The old man gave a nod of appreciation when they returned the stones to the dock, but he offered little praise as their teacher.

Nicci saw that his bare chest was covered with line after line of tattooed circles, more than she could count. Her lips twisted in an instinctive frown. "You are wishpearl divers."

When he raised his head, ropelike tendons stood out on the old man's neck. "I am the best wishpearl diver. My name is Loren, and it is my burden to train these whelps and find out which ones have the lungs to follow in my path. Some of them die." He shrugged. "Then I have to go down to retrieve the stone weights myself so the next trainees can use them. It's quite a bother."

With an outburst of exhaled air, a young diver splashed back to the surface and slammed the stone weight on the boards in front of the old teacher. Loren said, "Obviously that was too easy. Try a heavy one next." He handed the young diver an impossibly large stone, which instantly dragged him under.

Nicci frowned at the rippling water. "I have had dealings with wishpearl divers before, not all of them positive. I am Nicci."

Loren snorted. "Everyone in Serrimundi knows who you are, Sorceress. Not all of my dealings with the divers are pleasant either. None of the trainees comes close to my ability yet, so they have no reason to be arrogant."

"You sound overly proud of your own achievements," she said.

"Pride is perfectly acceptable when it is based on true accomplishment."

All five divers pulled themselves to the surface and

hung on the end of the dock, looking at their trainer. "We did every task you set for us, Loren," said a broad-faced young man. He looked up at Nicci with a predatory grin that reminded her of a shark. She gave him a similar grin in return, and he flinched.

"Then I will set you more tasks," Loren said. "You aren't exhausted enough."

Nicci turned to the old trainer. "Why don't you tell them to work on the sunken wrecks? Have them do something useful for their city."

One of the young men treading water said, "Wishpearl divers don't do menial labor!"

Loren's darkening expression instantly showed that the young man had given the wrong answer. "You will do whatever labor I tell you!" He pointed to his tattooed chest. "You are not wishpearl divers until I say you are. You still have baby lungs! Inhale a bit of humility."

During the previous Norukai attack on Serrimundi, Nicci had shamed four wishpearl divers into helping her. They had carried shielded bottles of wizard's fire, which sank several serpent ships. It almost made up for her despicable first encounter with the arrogant men aboard the *Wavewalker*, when they had poisoned her and tried to rape her.

Loren leaned over the end of the pier and barked down at his students, "Listen to the sorceress. Go help with the work in the harbor. You will serve Serrimundi."

"Why should we do that?" sneered the arrogant diver. He kept glancing hungrily at Nicci.

She said, "Because you will receive something better than riches. You will prove you are useful." The trainees scowled at her as if that were the last thing that interested them. "And if the Norukai overwhelm

Serrimundi, they will not be inclined to buy wish-pearls . . . if any of you survive."

"Go, clear the sunken wrecks!" Loren commanded. "And when you are finished, I may let you have women again."

Treading water, the divers scoffed at their trainer, "We are wishpearl divers! Women throw themselves at us."

Loren glared back. "Not if I spread the word that you all have the scabby disease."

Appalled, the divers swam off toward the nearest sunken wreck in a rush to join the dismantling crews.

The brass alarm gong rang out from the bluff above the Sea Mother, cutting through the harbor activity. Even with the pounding of wooden mallets and the clang of armor plate, a hush fell across the waterfront. Nicci stared toward the lookout on the top of the bluff, who was waving his arms. "Is it the Norukai? Do we have to fight again?"

"No, not Norukai." Loren cocked his head to listen. A percussive beat rang out three times, then paused, then three times more. "Just cargo ships. Three of them."

"Three? Why would merchants sail together?" Nicci asked. "They are competitors."

Loren still sat cross-legged on the dock, baking in the sun. "I have not seen it before. This must be something unusual."

Before long, as the ships sailed through the narrow mouth into the sheltered harbor, Nicci learned that they had come up the Phantom Coast all the way from Renda Bay.

And that they carried Nathan, Bannon, and others from Ildakar.

* * *

Captains Mills, Straker, and Donell anchored the ships near the tall carving of the Sea Mother and dispatched rowboats to bring representatives to the docks.

Though she covered it well, Nicci felt as astonished as a little girl when she saw the erudite wizard with long white hair aboard the first boat. He wore a ruffled shirt, long cape, and vest. Behind him sat the ginger-haired swordsman Bannon Farmer and the morazeth Lila in her distinctive black leather. Nicci had never expected to see them again. She couldn't guess how they had come to Serrimundi, on the other side of the Old World from where she had last seen them.

Nicci could see that Nathan had never expected to see her either. As the rowboat pulled up to the dock, Bannon lurched to his feet, rocking the boat and waving vigorously. "Nicci! I can't believe you're here."

Lila grabbed the young man's wrist to steady him. "I would be angry if you fell overboard and drowned now, boy. I've worked too hard to keep you alive."

When the boat was tied up, Bannon sprang onto the dock, unable to stop himself from giving her an enthusiastic hug. "I missed you, Nicci! We've been through so much. I know you were worried about me."

"Not overmuch." Despite her words, Nicci was glad to see him, too. Her voice caught in her throat, and then she let herself embrace him, a hug that he gladly returned. "I am pleased that you're alive, but I've been otherwise occupied building defenses, fighting Norukai, even clashing with General Utros."

She extricated herself from the hug, but had only a moment of relief before Nathan also swept her into an embrace. "So have we!" the wizard said. "Much has happened, and the war is right on our heels! I am so glad we're reunited. We have a world to save."

"And with all of us together again, we have a much better chance of doing it!" Bannon said.

Nicci's stern resolve melted with relief, and she stopped fighting it. "I was indeed concerned about you both. I thought we were separated forever. I was sure you must be dead by now, or at least trapped beneath the shroud of eternity."

"We thought you might be dead, too. I'm so glad you're alive!" Bannon grinned at her, and Lila gave him an annoyed sidelong glance.

"I see we have many stories to tell," Nathan said. "Renda Bay is destroyed, and so is Cliffwall. General Utros and his army marched across the land from Ilda-kar, and we couldn't stop them."

Bannon blurted out, "The Norukai fleet struck Renda Bay at the same time, more than a hundred ships. They are sailing northward to ransack the coast, and General Utros will be marching along the imperial roads. I'd wager they all intend to strike Tanimura."

The observers crowded around them reacted with alarm and dismay. "How can we possibly fight them?" asked Harborlord Otto.

Nicci realized that Nathan, with his scholarly experience and his knowledge of the language of Creation, might be able to help her with Richard's mysterious bone box. She felt the cold grow more intense in her heart. "This is what I've been waiting for all along."

CHAPTER 67

Rowboats brought the gifted passengers from the three ships to the Serrimundi docks, but the Renda Bay refugees remained aboard, waiting to find a new home. Harborlord Otto sent boats loaded with supplies, water barrels, and provisions, but his city simply couldn't absorb thousands more refugees.

While Nicci and Otto planned a public meeting to discuss the alarming new information, Bannon took Lila to explore the edge of the harbor and the headlands. Past the docks, they walked along a gravel path toward the high bluff at the mouth of the harbor. He stared at the towering stone carving of the Sea Mother that loomed high above the sea at the mouth of the sheltered harbor.

"This figure is famous even on Chiriya Island," Bannon said to her with a grin. "I never thought I would see the great Sea Mother of Serrimundi with my own eyes."

He turned to Lila, hoping she would share his sense of wonder. Her facial bruises had faded now and she looked beautiful . . . in the way a finely honed knife was beautiful. Ever since their escape from the Bastion, she had remained close to him, never letting the young man out of her sight. She insisted on protecting Bannon even as they slept together in a narrow cabin aboard Captain Mills's ship, although when he held her, Lila was hard rather than soft. Regardless, he would not have wanted any other companion.

"You often speak of the Sea Mother, usually when you intend to swear," Lila said.

Standing beneath the imposing carved figure, Bannon craned his neck up the bluffside. He tried to imagine sculptors hammering away at the dark sea rock to reshape the natural formation into the beautiful and intimidating woman. "I've never seen the actual Sea Mother myself, but it was said in times long past that she appeared like a goddess in a silvery form."

"She is beautiful," Lila admitted grudgingly. Her tone carried more resentment than admiration.

The giant feminine face looked benevolent, and the huge blank eyes stared beyond the harbor toward the sea. The Sea Mother was there to protect Serrimundi against all enemies, although she had not batted an eyelash when the Norukai came. Bannon knew that Nicci was the one who had saved the city.

Walking along, he was pleased to rest his hand on the finely tooled leather scabbard and the ornate sword that Nathan had given him. Never in his life had he imagined owning such a magnificent weapon. He had been so proud of Sturdy, which he'd purchased with his own coins. He had trained hard, holding the leather-wrapped hilt in his hand. He doubted that any other weapon would ever feel so natural, but he had to admit that Nathan's sword seemed nearly as perfect.

Happy for this respite before the next horrific battle, whenever it might come, he was glad to walk with lovely Lila. He felt like a different person, no longer a young cabbage farmer who had escaped from a dreary existence on a backwater island, someone whose father had beaten him and murdered his mother . . . someone whose best friend had been abducted by Norukai slavers.

No, that was the old Bannon. Now he had traveled widely and fought in great battles; he was filled with wonder and hardened by experience. Now he had clean clothes, a full stomach, a fine sword that was worth a fortune, and a beautiful woman, his trainer, his lover, who refused to leave his side. He could barely believe it himself. Bannon looked up at the majestic carving and muttered, "Sweet Sea Mother." He smiled at his own words.

Lila interrupted him with a bitter undertone, "You consider her too beautiful, boy, just like you fawn over Nicci."

"What?" Bannon blinked at her. "I fawn over Nicci?"

"I have seen you. Your heart beats faster when you look at her. She is attractive, I admit, but so am I. Is my hair not blond enough? Her breasts are larger than mine. Is that what you desire?" She tensed as if ready to attack him.

Bannon didn't know what to say. A long time ago, he had indeed been smitten with Nicci. He flirted with her, even brought her flowers in hopes of winning her heart—only to learn that those flowers were poisonous. Nicci had scoffed at his intentions, and when he didn't forget his silly crush, she had threatened to kill him. He chuckled at the memory. "Nicci? She terrifies me!"

Lila drew the sword from her hip and with her other hand she took out the agile knife. Bannon knew full well how it could deliver surges of impossible pain. "Do

I not terrify you, boy? Defend yourself, and maybe you'll learn your lesson."

She lunged with her long blade, and it was all he could do to yank Nathan's ornate sword out of its scabbard in time to counteract her blow. Steel crashed against steel. Previously, Bannon had practiced with the new sword, fought in a shadow dance against imaginary opponents, but now Lila was serious. She struck again, backed away, then slashed hard across his abdomen. She would have gutted him, but he leaped back at the last instant. The swish of the blade's point kissed the fabric of his shirt. "Lila! What are you doing?"

He defended himself with every bit of his skill. The fancy sword felt different in his hand, and the balance was a little off. He adjusted his grip and brought the blade up in time to catch the shorter sword that Lila wielded. His wrist vibrated with the blow.

They continued to fight beneath the looming Sea Mother. Bannon's boots slipped on the gravel path, and Lila pounced. She snapped, "You make me angry when you lust after other women."

"I wasn't!" Bannon cried. She hacked at him twice more, but he successfully blocked her. The sword felt better now, and his movements were smoother. "I've thought of no one but you!"

"Prove it," she said, and struck again.

Bannon barely blocked severe injuries, and Lila was relentless. He didn't know what she meant. As he continued fighting, however, the sword became a natural extension of his arm. He studied Lila's fighting technique, but he already knew her so well. He anticipated her strikes and counterstrikes. He panted heavily and his arm was sore, although she had barely broken a sweat.

He pushed himself harder until he finally saw the tiniest opening as her blade dipped. Bannon raised his sword to strike her head, but he turned the flat of the blade just enough to land a resounding blow on her skull.

Lila staggered back and pressed her palm against the stinging pain. At a safe distance, she lowered her sword and turned to face him. Instead of seeing the expected flash of anger in her eyes, Bannon saw admiration. "You fought well, boy, because I taught you well. I wanted you to prove yourself with that new sword. You need to realize that a weapon is just a weapon. You keep moping because you lost Sturdy, but this blade will kill an enemy just as well. Now you know it in your bones."

Bannon looked down at the sword. "You were doing that for *practice*? Just pretending to be jealous?"

"I do not pretend," Lila said. "Our bodies moved perfectly together while we sparred, though I prefer how our bodies move when we are in bed. You have now convinced me that I am the center of your attention. That is enough fighting between the two of us." She turned him away from the stone Sea Mother and led him back down the gravel path away from the headlands. "I want to leave this woman who watches us. We will not need to fight like that again."

The public meeting with ship captains, guard commanders, and city leaders took place that afternoon in a vacant warehouse. The wood and brick walls were scorched from Kor's recent Norukai raid. Benches were brought in for seats, and crates were lined up to provide a makeshift speaking platform.

As representatives gathered to discuss the situation,

Nathan took stock of the crowd. General Zimmer and Captain Norcross represented the D'Haran expeditionary force that had originally marched down from Tanimura. Sisters Eldine, Rhoda, and Mab jointly represented the Sisters of the Light, since they had not yet chosen a new prelate. Nathan doubted they would ever find a woman who could replace Verna.

As she stood on the raised platform waiting for the audience to settle down, Nicci crackled with power and confidence. Perri, Olgya, and Oron, the gifted fighters from Ildakar, were also a force to be reckoned with. Townspeople from Serrimundi gathered in the doorways and lined the walls of the warehouse, listening to what might be the most important meeting of their lives.

Otto pounded a mallet against the wooden wall, and the resounding boom dropped the crowd into silence. When they spoke to the audience, Nathan, Nicci, and General Zimmer described the situation as they saw it. Oron and Olgya interjected with their own experiences, and Bannon also joined in, talking at length about the awful Norukai. As misery dripped from his voice, town leader Thaddeus told how Renda Bay had been burned to the ground in order to stall General Utros and kill as many of his soldiers as possible.

Jared, the cocky krakener captain, called out, "So how soon will the Norukai come for us? If they followed you after Renda Bay, they could be here any day now."

"The pursuit broke off swiftly," said Captain Mills, sounding proud. "The wizards sank their lead ship, and Olgya hid our ships in a fog bank. The rest of the serpent ships withdrew to Renda Bay, as far as we could tell. Our fishing boats found refuge in coves and smaller towns up the coast, but we sailed here at top speed to sound a warning."

Zimmer scratched the side of his cheek. "The Norukai are in no hurry. They will attack and ransack other villages along the coast as they make their way north, and General Utros's army will take some time to march across the land."

Otto said, "If the army travels along the old imperial roads to reach Tanimura, they may well bypass Serrimundi, because the roads swing inland. That's one reason why our city remained mostly independent from the Imperial Order. We were out of the way. Maybe we don't need to worry about General Utros."

"Oh, good," Jared chimed in sarcastically. "More than a hundred serpent ships should give us no trouble at all."

"We have enough to worry about," Nicci said. "I believe Tanimura is their primary target. Up there General Linden is building defenses with the D'Haran army, the Tanimura militia, and countless vengeful refugees. He has formed a significant navy to guard the harbor as well as a large army. Tanimura is prepared to put up a strong resistance."

Zimmer nodded. "Linden is a good commander, but I'm still anxious to get back to my garrison and consolidate our armed forces."

Captain Donell said, "My ship is full of people from Renda Bay, and supplies won't last forever. If we can't unload the refugees here in Serrimundi, I'll need to move on to Tanimura, and soon."

Captain Mills said, "I'll take my ship up there as well."

"The *Mist Maiden* is armored and I can use it to guard the mouth of Serrimundi Harbor," said Captain

Ganley. "We have several vessels in place, but we could use another large ship to form a blockade and hold off an invasion if it comes."

Captain Straker said, "I'll stay here. My sister lives in Serrimundi."

Oron and Perri looked at each other, and then Oron called out, "The two of us will ride with Captain Mills and join the defense of Tanimura."

"Then I will stay here and help protect Serrimundi," Olgya offered. "This is not Ildakar, but it seems a fine city."

Nervous, Harborlord Otto looked to Nicci. "You are a powerful ally, Sorceress. Please stay. Serrimundi needs you."

"That's not why I'm staying," Nicci said. "I want to intercept King Grieve as soon as possible. I'm ready to fight."

Bannon piped up, "I'll be with Nicci." He blushed and glanced quickly at Lila. "Both of us will."

The morazeth woman said in a firm voice, "I am staying with Bannon Farmer."

"I would hate to break up our group of companions again," Nathan said. "But before we can truly prepare, we have to know where the Norukai fleet is, how fast they are coming, how far they have sailed."

Nicci called to all the gathered captains and townspeople. "I want to sail south in the swiftest ship until we encounter the raiders. Who will take me directly to the Norukai fleet? We need to know where they are." Her smile became hard. "We will harass them, provoke them, and get them to bypass Serrimundi, maybe lure them all the way to Tanimura where the real defenses lie. We can crush them, once and for all."

The people from Serrimundi let out sighs of relief and hope.

The krakener captain stood up from his bench. "The *Chaser* is at your disposal, Sorceress. You know how fast my ship is, and my crew knows those waters well. We often hunt krakens there. We can sail from Serrimundi as soon as you wish." He grinned. "Or as soon as we clean up a little for our guests."

"That won't help a bit," Otto muttered.

CHAPTER 68

Thousands upon thousands of weary soldiers marched onward, creating a low rumble across the land. The army's progress did not pause, mile after desperate mile. Individual men faltered, but the main group, the single-minded ancient fighting force, moved on. After crossing the continent, the soles of their boots were worn to ribbons, their feet bloody. Their skin was sunburned and stretched tight against their bones from malnourishment. They stripped the land of any edible shred.

General Utros looked back at the dust cloud raised by the endless ranks. He saw the hollow yet stony expressions on their faces, sunken eyes staring ahead, intent on their goal, intent on their leader. They did not complain, partly because of the numbing preservation spell, but primarily because they still believed in Utros. They would march all the way to Tanimura and capture the great city, which would allow him to anchor his empire from Orogang across the continent and up to the New World.

Utros held his head high even under the weight of the helmet. He would not let his men down. Fifteen centuries ago, they had laid siege to Ildakar, and after reawakening they had battled their way over the mountains, across the valleys, and all the way to the sea. That in itself was a victory, but General Utros wanted more. They marched north along the imperial road toward their real prize.

Ruva rode beside Utros on her bay mare, but she seemed in a trance. Although he insisted that she eat well, the sorceress seemed gaunt, even wasted. Her voice was quiet above the plodding hooves of the horses. "Do you think Ava will be in Tanimura? I miss my sister."

Utros frowned. "Ava's spirit appears whenever she wishes."

"I haven't seen her in so long." The vibrant paint that marked Ruva's body was smeared and flaked off in patches, which disrupted the arcane loops of the spell-forms the twins had so carefully painted on each other.

More disturbingly, he saw a faint fuzz of hair, tufts of stubble that showed how Ruva had not maintained the exquisitely careful shaving of her body. Her eyes had a distant and disturbing hint of madness. "Will Emperor Kurgan be in Tanimura, I wonder? I will help you defeat him, beloved Utros."

"Iron Fang is no longer our enemy. We have others to conquer," Utros said, then added an edge to his voice. "I need you, Ruva. You are my sorceress, the only one left."

Her disturbed eyes flicked back and forth. "No . . . no. We are both here. Ava will come back. The Keeper doesn't have her yet."

He clenched his jaw, grinding his molars together as if to crush any unwise words before they came out. The scarred half of his face stretched tight. "I need your focus. I need your magic." He softened his tone. "And I need your companionship."

Ruva blinked and came back to herself. She shook her head. "You shall have it. I feel stretched thin without my sister. She is here and yet not here. Part of my Han is frayed, but she will make me whole again if she comes back." Ruva lifted her head and shouted out in a raw voice, beseeching the sky, "Ava, where are you? The Keeper cannot have you yet. He can't have either of us."

After finding no respite in Renda Bay, the ancient soldiers had leveled what remained of the town, sifted fruitlessly through the ashes, and then watched the fleet of serpent ships gather again and set off. The Norukai could offer little assistance to the landbound troops, nor did they have much interest in doing so.

King Grieve would revel in his newfound war, raiding town after town as he moved northward. Utros's soldiers would take much longer to reach Tanimura. They needed to move at a forced march and hope to reach that great city by the time the Norukai raiders arrived.

Rather than working their way along the rugged coast, they moved inland, where they found a direct but long-abandoned imperial road. Utros was glad to find it still existed. Such roads were not meant to be trade routes, but straight-line thoroughfares by which Sulachan had led his armies up to the New World and his war with the wizards there.

The old roads were overgrown, the paving stones buckled and shifted with time, but the route was plain, a direct way to Tanimura. "It has been a long time since a conquering army passed this way," he mused.

Behind him the army trampled everything in their path as they moved on and on.

Finally, in response to Ruva's summons, a flickering

shape appeared in the air. The green-limned spirit of Ava drifted in front of the horses. "I am here," she said in her hollow voice, "but it grows more difficult to hang on each day."

Ruva opened her arms to her twin as she sat in the saddle. The spectral form intensified even as Ruva weakened; then Ava's form dimmed and Ruva drew strength in return. "We are connected, sweet sister."

"We are being torn apart," Ava said. "The Keeper wants us both, and the more I deny him, the harder he pulls."

"The Keeper wants us all," Ruva said.

The spirit separated again and hovered before Utros. She extended a slender arm and pointed back toward the endless lines of troops. "The Keeper calls them. He knows them. They can't forget that their place is in the underworld."

"Their place is with their general. And they will keep marching."

Behind them the troops plodded onward in uneven ranks. Weak and exhausted, some of them collapsed, falling to the flattened road. The dazed comrades behind them trampled the bodies, while others, ravenous, fell upon them, tearing off the ancient leather armor and devouring the flesh down to the bones.

Ruva laughed with an irrational edge in her voice. "See, the Keeper claims his own!"

"The Keeper will have to be satisfied for now." Utros lowered his voice. "He already has Emperor Kurgan, and he has Majel, but I have this world for now, and I swore to conquer it. I need my army. My place is here." He raised a fist to the sky. "I will hold on until I have accomplished my task!"

Ava's spirit let out a strained laugh that was eerily

echoed by her twin sister. "The Keeper pulls us all closer to the veil. He will wait, but he will not be denied forever." Her faint spirit stretched and pulled, and she reached a yearning arm toward Ruva. Her twin tried to grasp her, tried to hold on, but Ava wavered like an image imprinted on smoke. Her spirit vanished.

Utros and Ruva rode on alone. Under his breath, he promised the Keeper, "I will bring you many more souls, if you will just wait . . . wait."

CHAPTER 69

True to his word, Captain Jared readied the *Chaser* for departure within the hour. In recent weeks, the ship had ferried many refugees up to Tanimura, rescuing survivors from ruined towns, and delivering emergency supplies. This time, Jared would sail south on a reconnaissance mission until they encountered the Norukai fleet, and then the *Chaser* would race back with a report.

While docked in Serrimundi Harbor, the captain had added armor plating to his ship. The krakener was dirty and stained, nothing much to look at, but the new copper plates made the ship look gaudy.

As they sailed out of the harbor and past the line of reefs, Nicci remained on deck, letting the evening breezes ruffle her hair. Even brisk winds didn't entirely drive away the ever-present fishy smell. Nathan, Bannon, and Lila joined her, staring into the deepening darkness.

Nathan, always confident and pleased with himself, was even more so now that he was back with his companions. Even aboard the dingy ship, he wore a fine shirt, new vest, and embroidered cape. His long white hair drifted about as he faced the breeze.

"Though the future is dire, I am glad to be with you again, Sorceress. Richard made me promise to take care of you, and I would hate to disappoint him."

Nicci raised her eyebrows. "He sent *me* to keep *you* out of trouble, and now we've got an entire war on our hands."

"It is not a war that we started, dear Sorceress, but it is a war we will finish."

Bannon patted the scabbard at his hip. "And I'll fight at your side. They will be no match for us."

Nicci recognized the ornate blade that Nathan had carried from D'Hara. "You gave him your sword?"

"The boy needed a new weapon, so I accommodated him."

Bannon's expression sagged. "King Grieve threw Sturdy overboard. I loved that sword, and now it's at the bottom of a river." He drew his new blade and looked down at the gleaming steel. "But I love this one just as much! It is a wizard's sword."

"The boy has earned a decent weapon after all he's done," Nathan said. "Now that I have my gift back, I can make do with an ordinary sword." He patted the standard military blade at his side.

Lila managed to place herself between Bannon and Nicci. "The blade is what kills the enemy, not its appearance." She glanced at Nathan. "Nor its cost."

When full darkness set in and the *Chaser* cruised through open water, Captain Jared rang the bell to get the attention of the crew. "We will serve dinner, fine kraken meat to impress our esteemed guests!"

One of the crew members joked, "I thought we were going to use that meat to kill the Norukai when we found them."

Jared took mock offense, and the rest of the crew laughed. He presented platters of the meat in grayish puddles of "special" sauce, which he explained was a recipe that his mother had concocted to make the kraken meat taste delicious. "You mean palatable," yelled another one of the crewmen. They laughed again.

Nathan tasted the dish with trepidation, while Lila and Nicci ate their meals without comment. "Better than fish guts," Bannon observed, as if it were a compliment, and then he spoke at length about how his mother used to cook kraken meat with cabbage on Chiriya Island.

Jared sat on a crate on the open deck and grew serious as he leaned forward, meeting Nicci's eyes. "My crew and I are glad to have this important mission. Krakeners put up with a lot of ribbing from other sailors. We know that our ship smells. We know that fancy cargo vessels are cleaner and more comfortable, and we even know that some people don't like the taste of kraken meat. But we are loyal citizens, and we will fight to defend our land."

Later that night, after the crew had quieted, Nicci took Nathan aside. "On my previous visit, I did dispatch a message up to the People's Palace to inform Richard about this terrible war. I asked him to send help, but apparently he's involved in some crisis of his own up in D'Hara. He didn't explain." Her expression darkened. "He is, however, confident that I can handle any problems here in the Old World."

Nathan's nostrils flared. "You mean that *we* can handle any problems."

Nicci produced the small bone box and extended it to him. "Richard told me this is all I would need. I cast a verification web, poked and prodded with my gift, but I still don't know what it is. Maybe you can help me figure it out."

Curious, the wizard took the bone box and inspected each side. "These markings are the language of Creation. 'Life to the living. Death to the dead.'" Cautiously, he pried open the lid and let out a whistle of amazement when he saw the glowing pearl of magic that twisted and rolled and rippled. "It is . . . hmmm, I believe it's a constructed spell."

Nicci nodded. "But I don't know what it does or how to trigger it. I am missing the key. Richard thinks I will understand what I'm supposed to do."

"Given time, I might be able to decipher it. I have some familiarity with constructed spells."

"As do I, but so far this has baffled me."

Nathan turned the bone box back and forth in his hand, then handed it back to her. "We can work on the puzzle together, but if Richard says this is all you need, then I'm sure you are up to the task. Meanwhile, we have other ways to fight the enemy." He gazed ahead of them across the dark sea. "As soon as we find those serpent ships."

For the next few days, Nicci and Nathan augmented the southerly winds, which doubled the speed of the *Chaser*. Jared's crew kept a sharp lookout for the raider fleet, but the ocean remained quiet. Nicci and Nathan scrutinized Richard's complex constructed spell, but came up empty-handed.

By the third day, the crew aboard the ship became anxious, and the captain's aloof demeanor grew tense. To burn off their restlessness, Lila and Bannon sparred across the deck, while Nathan stared toward the watery horizon.

Nicci stepped up to him. "I'm anxious to find the Norukai, but every mile we go without encountering them means they are that much farther away. Serrimundi and Tanimura have extra time to build their defenses."

"Sweet Sea Mother, we're ready to fight!" Bannon said, resting his sword tip on the deck. "Right now."

The shirtless lookout dangled from high on the mainmast. He called out, "Smooth water ahead, Captain! Mirror water!" The crew suddenly became energized, and the captain grinned with anticipation.

Nicci followed the lookout's urgently pointing hand, where an unusual and unnatural smooth patch of water looked like glass. "What does it mean, Captain?"

"That's a sure sign a kraken is just below the surface!" He barked orders to the crew while he himself ran to the captain's wheel, altering course. "We can't miss an opportunity like this. It's right in front of us." His chest swelled as he inhaled a deep breath. "It's time we remembered we're krakeners!"

The crew gathered ropes, harpoons, and weighted nets, moving with the efficiency of long practice. Excited, they shifted their weapons from one hand to another and flexed their muscles.

As the *Chaser* approached the oddly smooth water, a smooth green tentacle broke the surface and curled upward, then sank again, cresting barely a ripple. The kraken hunters howled out a challenge. One overeager man hurled his harpoon, which fell far short, and he promptly reeled in the rope hand over hand to get his weapon back.

The tentacle was smooth and covered with slime,

mottled with leopard spots. Another tentacle glided out of the water, and then four more tentacles arose, each one covered with suckers. Their movements were languid, as if the creature were merely stretching in the ocean air.

"Will it attack?" Nathan asked.

The crew laughed at the suggestion, and Jared rolled his eyes. "Krakens are docile beasts that graze on seaweed. They squirm a lot when you kill them, but they're not the monsters people think they are."

As the *Chaser* closed in, the crew gathered at the rail, cocking their arms and readying their harpoons. Other crew members held ropes and nets. It was a coordinated effort, as if they were soldiers about to go into battle.

"I count seven tentacles," Bannon said. "How many does a kraken have?"

Jared waved his hand. "However many it likes, and the more tentacles they have, the more meat we can harvest."

"We're in range, Captain!" the lookout called.

The sailors needed no more encouragement. Like archers launching a volley of arrows, they hurled their harpoons into the glassy water. Seven of the jagged spears splashed uselessly in the sea, while four sank into tentacles.

The thing was like a spider startled in the center of its web. One of the laughing sailors wrapped his rope around his waist, and the kraken's reflexive jerk nearly pulled him overboard, but two of the man's friends grabbed him in time and pulled him back.

More harpoons struck as the *Chaser* closed the distance. The sailors pulled on the ropes, while the struggling kraken yanked back. The ship's hull strained and creaked against the monster's mighty tug. Two of the new armor sheets popped loose with a clang.

A forest of tentacles flailed upward, dripping slime. As it rose to the surface, Nicci could see that the kraken's body core was a sphere with a hard shell like a crab's, and the tentacles extended outward like the spokes of a wheel. Several harpoons struck the shell and bounced off.

One tentacle quested forward, trying to grasp the people on deck. Bannon ducked as the sucker-rimmed tip barely missed him. Nathan chuckled, but didn't notice a second tentacle that slashed sideways. The rubbery arm caught him a resounding blow and sent him sprawling. He smashed against a large crate and cracked his head, leaving him stunned. The wizard's long white hair was matted with kraken slime as well as a blossom of blood.

Bannon hurried over to help. Nathan groaned and picked himself up, pressing a palm to his head. "I assure you I'm all right. Just a little rattled." He struggled to his hands and knees on the deck, barely conscious. "I think I'll rest a bit."

The tentacles writhed around the ship, and the hunters continued to disable their prey. They hacked off any appendages that came close, leaving the creature with several stumps.

Jared grinned at Nicci. "Feel free to use your gift, Sorceress. Couldn't you stop its heart with a blast of magic?"

"I would not wish to deprive you of your amusement," Nicci said in a dry voice. "I will save my magic for fighting the real enemy."

The harpoon hooks embedded themselves in the rubbery hide. The sailors strained against the ropes, pulling the wounded beast closer to the *Chaser*. They lashed the ends around stanchions, holding the kraken in place. It struggled in its death throes, flailing amputated tentacles. The crew would soon haul the carcass aboard and spend hours butchering it and storing the meat.

Suddenly, the kraken jerked hard and vanished beneath the surface, straining the ropes and the hooks as it submerged.

"It's getting away!" one of the sailors bellowed.

"That's not possible," Jared said. "Something is pulling it down!"

The men doubled up to haul harder on the ropes, but the kraken was dragged under as if caught in a tug of war. "There's something deep underwater."

Bannon held his sword, looking over the side, with Lila beside him ready to fight. Nathan huddled on deck, groaning as he held his bleeding head.

Jared ordered, "More harpoons! I don't want to lose our prize!"

The hunters grabbed spears, but the kraken sank out of view with an even sharper jerk. Harpoon hooks tore free, ripping out chunks of the slimy hide. Ropes snapped and spun loose of the stanchions. A gush of blood blossomed around the submerged kraken, and the mirror water began to churn. The crew cried out in unison as the waves exploded.

The frilled head of an enormous sea serpent rose up, as large as a dinghy and as fearsome as a dragon. Its giant jaws clamped down on the squirming kraken, and tentacles flopped about like worms in its mouth. When the sea serpent crunched down on the armored body core, green fluid spurted out.

Bannon backed away, bumping into Lila. "It's the serpent god!"

Lila drew her short sword and stood next to him, ready to fight. "Perhaps King Grieve sent it here."

The monster opened its jaws, tossed the dying kraken up into the air, then gulped the morsel down before turning its slitted eyes down toward the *Chaser*.

The krakener crew scrambled about, but they had no place to hide.

The monster flared its spiked frills and let out a bellowing hiss. The spray drenched everyone on the ship, and the lookout tumbled from his perch on the mast, barely catching himself on a rigging rope.

"I've fought dragons before," Nicci said, looking up at the enormous sea serpent. "This is no different."

Nathan struggled to his feet, bleeding from the blow to his head. "I'll offer what assistance I can, Sorceress."

The serpent god wheezed out as it loomed over the *Chaser*. Nicci summoned a lightning bolt that scorched a smoking line down its sinuous body. With a roar, the serpent god lunged down and bit the side of the ship, splintering wood. The crew threw their harpoons, but their spears did little damage to the scaled hide.

Nicci recalled when she had fought the dragon Brom, using the Subtractive side of magic. Now she extended her gift and easily found the serpent god's heart near the top of its long neck. The heart was as large as a barrel, beating hard. She unleashed her gift, caused the muscle to swell and darken . . . then burst. The serpent writhed backward, arching its jaws toward the sky in agony.

But even after Nicci had exploded its heart, the monster struck again, sweeping its great neck sideways to snatch a panicked crewman in its jaws. With one chomp, it bit the man in two and tossed the pieces into the water.

Nicci couldn't believe the creature still lived. "I stopped its heart!" She reached out with her magic again, then realized to her surprise that this creature had more than one heart.

Once she concentrated, she discovered six hearts down the length of its body, each one independent, each beating to keep the underwater monster alive. "Then my work has just begun." She lashed out with her destructive magic, finding another heart and stopping it. She burned a third heart to a lump of internal charcoal.

Each time Nicci hurt it, the creature recoiled and smashed into the ship, causing even more damage. The *Chaser* would not last long.

Groaning and still dazed, Nathan managed to summon a ball of wizard's fire and hurl it at the serpent god's head. The searing magic flames burned between the creature's jaws and roasted its tongue.

Nicci didn't stop her attack. With methodical intensity, she destroyed all of the monster's remaining hearts, one by one. At last, the giant serpent collapsed onto the water, causing waves that rocked the kraken-hunter ship. The dead serpent god floated in the sea, longer than two or three ships.

Jared and his crew stared in dismay. The captain dropped to his knees and touched the bloodstain on the deck where his crewman had been killed. Bannon and Lila stood shaken, holding their swords ready as if some other monster might emerge from the deep.

Unsteady on his feet, Nathan placed a hand on Nicci's shoulder. She knew it was meant to be reassuring, but he seemed to be steadying himself. "Sorry I couldn't be of more assistance."

"The serpent god is dead, Nathan. We killed it."

High up on the mast, the bedraggled lookout squawked, "Ships! Norukai ships on the horizon!"

Far out on the water, Nicci saw more than a hundred ominous vessels sailing toward them. From afar, the raiders had seen Nicci kill their serpent god, and even at a distance she could hear their howls of outrage. All the oars were extended, churning the water, so the serpent ships approached at great speed.

Nicci crossed her arms over her chest. "We have found them at last." She felt a deep chill upon seeing the size of the fleet. "Turn your ship about, Captain. Quickly! Back to Serrimundi with all possible speed."

Still unsteady, Jared shouted for the crew to reset the sails as he spun the wheel to turn the rudder. Though exhausted from battling the sea serpent, Nicci called up her gift, and Nathan assisted her as best he could. Together, they created a wind as strong as a storm to help the ship flee. The *Chaser* raced away with the Norukai fleet in pursuit.

CHAPTER 70

When his ships came upon the floating carcass of the serpent god, King Grieve stared down into the water, sickened and enraged. This fresh agony felt as strong as the pain he had experienced upon seeing his beloved Chalk murdered.

From the prow of his flagship, Grieve had watched the ugly kraken-hunter vessel with its gray sails and metal-plated hull, and he would never forget that ship. He had seen the sorceress strike down their serpent god. He would hunt it to the end of the world, if necessary.

But he could not simply sail past the body of their fallen serpent god. "Drop anchor! All ships. We halt here."

Drums pounded, and shouted orders ricocheted across the water. The Norukai ships sailed close enough together that the staccato commands passed from ship to ship. With oars extended, Grieve's ship maneuvered close to the drifting dead monster, where they dropped anchor stones and tied up the sails to keep the vessels in position.

Grieve had sacrificed to the serpent god many times. Now, he squeezed his massive hands against the rail until the wood creaked with the strain. The spikes in his shoulders protruded. He opened his jaws wide and roared with all the air in his lungs, all the power in his voice, a loud inhuman cry, much like the sound made by the serpent god.

The rest of the Norukai did the same, and the din was like a thunderclap that went on and on as one crew after another took up the howl. Grieve wanted blood, needed blood. He would find the sorceress and tear out her throat with his own teeth. First, though, he and his raiders would repay the serpent god for the grace and strength it had given them.

The monster's body floated motionless just off the bow. Grieve looked down at its magnificent head, the frilled fin, the triangular jaw that was now a burned horror from wizard's fire. One milky eye stared upward, half closed.

"The serpent god is dead," moaned one of the raiders beside Grieve.

The king bashed him on the side of the head, and the man reeled away, clutching the blood that streamed down his face. Grieve snarled, "The serpent god is always here. The serpent god is *us*."

He drew the long gutting knife from its sheath, swung himself overboard, and dropped down into the water. He plunged into the waves near the dead sea serpent.

As the raiders peered down from above with dismay and curiosity, the king swam to the scaled form and wrapped his muscular arm around it, holding on like a lover's embrace. The pale underbelly turned upward as the body drifted on the sloshing waves.

Grieve hauled himself along its length, using the scales and fins for handholds. In all of history, no one else had been so close, so intimate with the serpent god except for the blessed victims whose flesh it incorporated. But he was *Grieve,* King Grieve of the Norukai! He was part of the serpent god, just as the serpent god was part of all of them.

He pressed down on the scales, then rested his scarred cheek against the wet form. He closed his eyes and tried to draw the power into himself, absorbing what he could from the magnificent creature. "I am the serpent god. We all are the serpent god," he whispered to the dead form.

The countless serpent ships had fallen eerily silent as the raiders watched him.

Grieve plunged his long knife into the belly of the sea serpent. Aboard the ships, the Norukai gasped and groaned, but he glared up at them. "This is what we must do!" He sawed farther, cutting a long incision. Entrails spilled out in wet ropes that drifted in the water. With so much blood, he knew that sharks would come soon to feed, but Grieve and the Norukai would take what they required first.

He kept cutting until he found the first of the reptilian hearts. It was large, round, and purplish red. He hacked a chunk of the tough heart meat, which he stuffed into his mouth. He opened his scarred jaws wide to take in as much as he could. Chewing, he tasted the tar of burned blood. The flavor was exquisite, but the power was even more remarkable.

He knew that Chalk was a part of the serpent god, too. The serpent god had fed on the shaman, and now that strength was flowing into the Norukai king.

"I am the heart of the serpent god," he yelled. "All my people must join me." He cut off another piece of the meat and raised it out of the water. "All Norukai must *be* the heart of the serpent god."

Three raiders leaped overboard without further encouragement. Once they understood what Grieve meant, others also jumped into the water and swam to the serpent god. With their own knives, they sliced the belly down its length to find the other hearts.

Atta was the first. The hefty woman swam up to Grieve and hacked off a piece of the heart for herself. After she chewed and swallowed, she turned her blood-smeared face to him and offered him another piece, which he accepted.

More Norukai swarmed around the floating body, butchering the creature. They removed the multiple hearts, some of which were charred and blackened, others still fresh and filled with blood. Every morsel contained the essence of the great deity. When the hearts were consumed, the raiders stripped the meat from the serpent's bones. This was a feast unlike any they had ever experienced. The Norukai had pillaged towns, stolen their food, raped their women, but nothing could compare to this thrill.

The water became a froth of red. The circling sharks were wary, unwilling to approach the fierce Norukai.

As the feast continued, Grieve's shock was replaced with an intense confidence. The great serpent god might have been slain, but it was not a cause for sadness. This was a transformation, and he felt it swell within him. Around him, hundreds of raiders stripped the carcass and squabbled over the last morsels. Every Norukai wanted to partake, though he knew that was not possible with the tens of thousands of bloodthirsty warriors aboard their fleet.

"You have eaten the heart of the serpent god," Atta said as she floated next to him, caressing the scar on his cheek with one bloody finger. "You are King Grieve. You are all of us."

"Yes, I am all of the Norukai. I have fed on the heart of our god, and now I myself am its living manifestation."

He and Atta swam back to their ship as the Norukai continued to work on the carcass like seagulls tearing apart a bloated whale. When he climbed aboard his ship again, he caressed the carved figurehead. He raised his fists into the air and shouted, "I am the serpent god now. We are the serpent god, and we will strike and kill."

He inhaled until his lungs were so full he felt his chest would burst, and then he exhaled a gigantic roar that rippled across the masts. All the Norukai resounded with their response.

One serpent god might be dead, Grieve knew, but now there were many more serpent gods—elsewhere in the sea, and also in human form—and they were far more deadly.

Yes, the world would grieve.

CHAPTER 71

Driven by the enhanced wind, the *Chaser* practically flew across the waves toward Serrimundi. The krakener pulled far ahead of the Norukai fleet, and the crew made makeshift repairs from the sea serpent attack along the way.

They could not reach Serrimundi fast enough to please Nicci. After seeing the number of serpent ships, she was convinced that even Serrimundi's new defenses could not withstand such an attack. The much larger city of Tanimura might stand a chance, with its full navy and strengthened army, but not Serrimundi. Effren and Larrikan Shores had already been wiped out by a much smaller Norukai raiding fleet.

Serrimundi was more than ten times larger than Renda Bay, however, and such a city simply could not be evacuated in only a few days. It seemed an impossible situation.

She stood at the bow of the *Chaser* with Nathan, Bannon, and Lila, discussing options. Even with their speed and significant head start, Nicci doubted they would have enough time to make the necessary preparations—whatever those might be. Together, they tried to develop a plan that would give Serrimundi the best chance of survival.

Just before the *Chaser* approached the line of reefs beyond the harbor mouth, they encountered one of the patrol boats. As they raced past, Nicci cupped her hands around her mouth and shouted, "Light your signal rafts. The Norukai are on their way!"

The patrol boat's crew dropped the floating platform overboard and lit the pile of green kindling to raise a column of smoke that could be seen for many miles. Other widely separated scout boats spotted the signal and replied in kind, lighting their own rafts to pass the message along and notify everyone in the city. The lookout on top of the Sea Mother bluff hammered on her gong to sound the alarm.

Serrimundi was on full alert by the time the *Chaser* sailed past the *Mist Maiden* and four other armored cargo ships that defended the mouth of the harbor, just beyond the towering stone carving. When the krakener pulled up to one of the repaired piers, Harborlord Otto, Lady Olgya, Captains Ganley and Straker, and other city representatives hurried to meet them.

"The Norukai are maybe two days behind us," Bannon blurted out. "We have to get the whole city on high alert."

Otto nodded soberly. "We are as ready as can be. Everyone is armed and trained, the ships are reinforced with metal plates. We knew this might happen."

"You have made an admirable effort here, but alas we are convinced it will not be enough to save Serrimundi," Nathan said.

Captain Ganley looked indignant. "Don't underestimate us. Our people know this is their only chance to save their homes. They will not give up without a fight."

"It will be a battle such as the Norukai have never seen." The harborlord crossed his arms over his chest.

"But you will still lose. Even if you inflict numerous casualties on the raiders, they will still burn your city to the ground," Nicci said. "Tanimura's defenses are ten times stronger. They have built up a whole fleet of warships ready to defend the sea, and their standing army includes a garrison from D'Hara, thousands from the city guard, and countless refugee recruits. Oron, Perri, and the other gifted are already there with General Zimmer. Our best chance is to lure the Norukai fleet directly to Tanimura, where they will be wiped out."

"But what about Serrimundi?" Otto asked, his voice cracking. "What are we to do?"

"You may not need to fight at all," Nathan said, touching a finger to his chin. "We have an idea to protect your city. Lady Olgya's actions gave us the idea, in fact."

The gifted woman from Ildakar was surprised. Her hair hung loose now, rather than in the familiar braids, with a ragged hunk where an enemy soldier had cut one off. "I inspired you? I am intrigued."

Otto looked from Nathan to Nicci. "I like the sound of that, but I don't understand what you mean."

Leaving the krakener, Nicci walked down the dock, all business. She regarded the rolling hills, the sections of the city that spread inland from the neat, protected bowl of the harbor. Her memory and her imagination had not failed her. "Yes, it is possible."

Otto and the others followed her as she walked the length of the pier, anxious to hear what she would suggest. In front of the first line of warehouses Nicci turned and looked back at the harbor, the headlands, and the opening to the sea. "The Norukai islands are far to the south, and this is new territory for them. Before Captain Kor's raid, Serrimundi had never before been attacked, so the Norukai know very little about your distant city. None of Kor's raiders escaped alive, so no one was able to bring a report to King Grieve. He isn't aware of the exact location of Serrimundi."

Nathan brushed the front of his new vest and adjusted his embroidered cape, as if he were about to step onto a stage. "If fate treats us favorably, we may be able to distract the Norukai and trick them into sailing right past Serrimundi."

"We want to hide your city," Lila said, with as much inflection as if she were merely remarking on the weather.

Ganley gasped. "Hide Serrimundi? Where would you put it?"

Nicci lifted her chin. "If we time it right, the Norukai might not see the harbor at all. Because we killed their serpent god, King Grieve is pursuing the *Chaser*. He wants his vengeance on *us*. If we can provoke them, taunt them, and make them keep chasing us, we might get the entire fleet to sail past Serrimundi . . . if they don't see the harbor in the night."

"How could they not see an entire city?" Otto removed his wide-brimmed hat and wiped perspiration from his brow. "I still don't understand this."

But Olgya began to smile. Nicci looked to Captains Ganley and Straker, both of whom stood ready to follow her instructions. "If other armored ships join us as we race away, King Grieve will keep following us."

"He wants to kill me, too," Bannon said. "And Lila. We just have to keep the Norukai too preoccupied to look for Serrimundi. That's why we can't let them see the city."

"We must camouflage it," Lila said, as if impatient for the discussion to come to the point.

Amid the surprised gasps, Nathan held up a finger. "A sufficiently gifted person such as yourself, my dear"—he turned toward Olgya—"could summon a thick mist to blanket the mouth of the harbor, just as you hid our ships from the Norukai after Renda Bay, and outside the Cliffwall canyon before that. If the raiders don't know to look for Serrimundi, then the diversion should be straightforward enough. Before that, we need to stall and harass the raider fleet, make sure they arrive at night and sail past this part of the coast. . . ."

Nicci turned to Otto. "Harborlord, you'll need to darken the city tomorrow and each night until the Norukai pass. No one can light fires or lanterns after sunset. Serrimundi must be pitch black when the serpent ships come after us."

"But my city wants to fight too!" Otto said. "Are you suggesting that we hide here in the fog and let Tanimura handle the war for us?" The lines in his face deepened. "Sorceress, you gave a grand speech that all the cities of the Old World must pull together against our overwhelming enemy. Serrimundi can't just sit by and let Tanimura face it themselves! We are not cowards."

"I'm not suggesting that you do nothing." Nicci's lips took on a hard smile.

Bannon rested a hand on the ornate pommel of his new sword, and his grin was enthusiastic. "After the Norukai chase after us in the dark, the rest of Serrimundi's warships can follow all the way to Tanimura. When the battle begins there, you can strike them from behind."

Lila added with a grim smile, "If you stay far enough back, King Grieve will never expect you."

"A large curtain of mist . . ." Olgya twisted her long hair in her fingers. "While you lead them away like a fox on a hunt, I can create a thick fog bank to hide Serrimundi." She looked out to the towering figure of the Sea Mother on the bluff. "And that is just to start. . . ."

The following day, knowing the Norukai fleet was fast approaching, the kraken hunter sailed away from Serrimundi followed by four armored cargo ships. Serrimundi scout boats ranged farther south, prepared to light their signal rafts as soon as they spotted King Grieve and his raiders.

Left behind, Olgya watched them go, vowing to do her part to save the city.

Harborlord Otto had dispatched runners throughout the city, issuing a complete ban on fires, lanterns, not even a candle behind a shutter for the coming night. When darkness fell, Serrimundi had to be invisible, swallowed up in darkness and fog. Olgya had practiced her spell to call up the mists in the sea.

Near sunset, the lookout on the bluff spotted a curl of signal smoke to the south, which meant the raiders would be here within hours. Ready to intercept, the *Chaser* and the four sailing ships angled swiftly toward the smoke to provoke the oncoming Norukai fleet. They would taunt the serpent ships and bolt away, sailing north, leading them toward Tanimura for the final battle.

More than an hour later, near full darkness, the provocateurs sailed back past the harbor, pushed by magically enhanced winds. As deepening night blanketed the harbor and city with gloom, Olgya got to work before the Norukai could heave into view in hot pursuit. Waiting beneath the Sea Mother carving at the headlands, she used her gift to touch countless droplets of water, raising a mist from the calm waves beyond the mouth of the harbor. At first it was like faint steam rising from a pot of water about to boil, then it thickened into lacy wisps of fog that coalesced with other strands into a low-lying blanket.

The mist rolled up and into the harbor, blanketing the hills, flowing along the coast, and extending out to sea. Even as the darkness thickened, no lights twinkled from any homes in the crowded city. Olgya thought of families huddled together in the dark, comforting one another. The night had an unnatural hush.

Back at Ildakar, she had watched her glorious city vanish behind the shroud of eternity; now she had to make another city disappear, but in a different way. Olgya thickened the mist around the mouth of the harbor so the Norukai would see nothing but a blurred coastline, if they could make out anything in the darkness. As the last gloom faded into deep night, she spotted the blue sails of more than a hundred serpent ships racing after the *Chaser* and the four armored cargo ships. The enemy fleet was dizzying in its size, but Olgya had seen it before, at Renda Bay. She now saw the sense in Nicci's plan; no matter how hard the people might fight back, these ships would have destroyed all of Serrimundi's defenses, filled the harbor, and burned the city to the ground.

Even if the trick worked, however, Olgya intended to make her mark here.

As the thick fog spread and settled, Olgya took a dinghy and rowed out of the mouth of the harbor. The

currents were erratic, but she used her gift to steady the
boat as she made her way out to the long line of dangerous reefs beyond the harbor.

Rowing hard, she picked her way along the foamy
line until she chose a place to lay down another deadly
trap. She created a small shimmering ball of light, flickering cold flames that were tightly layered like the petals in a rosebud. She laid the glowing kernel among the
reef rocks, ducking from the spray hitting the rocks.
Her little spark glimmered there, immune to the water
that tried to douse it. This wasn't normal fire, but would
become a beacon bright enough that she hoped it would
lure some of the oncoming Norukai ships right to the
Keeper.

Finished, she rowed back to the sheltered harbor,
confident the trick would work.

Out on the reefs, her enigmatic light grew brighter
in the fog.

L ars stood at the bow and howled into the night,
shouting a challenge at the fleeing ships. The *Chaser*
sailed ahead into the darkness.

He remembered Nicci from Ildakar. Now the blond
sorceress kept provoking the raider fleet by lashing out
at them with bolts of lightning. King Grieve drove his
fleet after them in a headlong charge. Groaning at the
benches, the muscular Norukai pulled on the oars, driving the serpent ships faster than any wind.

The small krakener and four large warships fled
north with all possible speed, which told Lars that the
sorceress could not sustain her attacks. She and other
gifted provocateurs had struck and harassed the serpent
ships at sunset, but then they turned and fled. Obvi-

ously, they feared King Grieve's mighty navy! Nicci's lightning had been nothing more than a sting to enrage the wild bear of the Norukai fleet, and the serpent ships swooped after her, closing in for the kill.

Lars commanded his crew, "Pull at the oars. You are not weaklings!" The muscular raiders, both men and women, sat at the benches and gritted their teeth, groaning with the effort. The oars dipped into the water, cut deep, and pulled back. He did not want his ships to lose their quarry in the darkness as thickening fog rose all around them.

While Grieve and his fleet sailed forward like a battering ram, Lars and his ten ships hugged closer to the shore. This was farther north than he had ever explored, even on their recent destructive raids. Just like his comrade Kor had been, Lars was under a death sentence, obligated to fight until he died. He would keep attacking these scared little people for as long as he could, but he didn't expect they would manage to kill him anytime soon.

Now his raiding ships sailed through the black night and suffocating fog, but Lars could hear waves rushing against the nearby coast. "Row faster! The sorceress is out there somewhere. We must be the first to catch her."

"Will King Grieve feed her to the serpent god?" asked one of the warriors.

"There is no serpent god," said Ura, a muscular woman who was too ugly even for Lars. She'd shaved her head to make herself nearly indistinguishable from a male, although she could not hide her heavy breasts. "*We* are the serpent god, and we take the sacrifices ourselves."

Lars said, "First we have to catch them."

The oar master pounded on the drums, and the

serpent ships plunged into the impenetrable fog. Near the serpent figurehead, one sailor cried out in surprise and pointed forward. "Lars, look! Some kind of beacon."

A bright light sparked upward from the veils of white mist, like a full moon. It glowed and pulsed at the waterline, tempting, dazzling.

"What could it be?" asked Ura.

"It is magic," one of the raiders muttered.

"Of course it is magic—we are hunting a sorceress!" Lars said. "That is where she must be! Adjust course. We will follow that light and run it down."

The sailors pulled hard on the oars, and the serpent ships cut through the water like vipers ready to strike. The tantalizing beacon glowed through the fog, calling them. It lifted higher in the sky then dropped low again.

"Prepare your weapons," Lars said.

The Norukai seized their assortment of blades and clubs and rushed to the front of the ship, ready to swing themselves overboard as soon as they cornered their prey. The glow brightened, and Lars had to shade his eyes. He still didn't know what it was, but the beacon seemed to be retreating. "Faster!"

Just as the first serpent ships approached the dazzling orb, he heard the crash of breakers—far too close. He had only a moment to think before his ship ran aground.

"Reefs!" Ura screamed just before she was hurled overboard by the impact. Jagged rocks ripped open the lower hull, smashed the keel.

Lars slammed against the rail. Many of his sailors bowled into one another and tumbled over the side, yelling in rage. Hulls cracked and crunched as more of his serpent ships smashed against unseen reefs. The glowing beacon hovered mockingly overhead, brightened to a flare, then winked out, leaving them in mist-shrouded darkness.

Another serpent ship careened into Lars's vessel from the starboard side, crushing the hull, snapping off the oars like twigs. The impact shattered his ribs and his left arm, and Lars fell over the side as his ship tilted. Water gushed into the open gap in its hull.

He plunged into the roiling water and flailed with his useless broken arm. His bare chest scraped against the sharp reef rocks. He saw dozens of his crew scrambling for purchase against the heavy waves, holding on to the wreckage.

At least seven of his vessels had run up onto the reefs, and Lars realized that the glowing orb had lured them into treacherous waters. A trick! Hundreds of wounded Norukai were swept out to sea or caught up in the churning foam and pulped against the rocks.

The fog grew even thicker, hiding them from the rest of the receding fleet. Lars could only hear the resounding crashes as more serpent ships plowed into the reefs and other vessels. When he tried to shout, a curl of seawater gushed into his mouth. He coughed, his shattered ribs stabbing like knives. He tried to pull himself onto the questionable safety of the reef.

Ura climbed up on the rocks that were slick with green seaweed, reaching for a handhold. She cried out as something grabbed her. She clawed at her leg, trying to break free, but she was jerked into the water. Nearby, Lars heard more screams, not just anger and surprise from the wrecks. His people were being attacked! The Norukai clawed for shelter on the reefs, but more were swept under, seized by something beneath the water.

Lars squirmed about, looking for an enemy. "Who are you?" He had lost his sword during the fall, and his arm was broken, but he bunched his other first. "Where are you?"

Humanlike forms glided up out of the water, sleek and gray, covered with scales and with mouths full of needle teeth. They slithered onto the reef rocks to fall upon their helpless prey.

The selka had pursued the Norukai fleet, waiting for their chance, and now they rose from the foamy water. Three of them grabbed Lars. He struggled, but they tore him to shreds before dragging his body in pieces under the waves.

CHAPTER 72

The imperial road rolled ahead of them, mile after mile, unwinding in lazy curves along the foothills. Tens of thousands of trampling boots left a much wider swath behind them as they crossed the land.

Utros dispatched scout parties and procurement armies along offshoot tracks, but only a few of the parties were successful in bringing back enough food for him, Ruva, and his primary commanders. Meanwhile, the main body of his army pushed onward like a slow stampede.

The general shaded his eyes to look ahead down the endless road that eventually led to Tanimura—or so he hoped. Hovering nearby, Ava's spirit let out a brittle laugh. "We have only to walk forever, beloved Utros, and then we will be there!"

He tried to squeeze greater speed from his stallion, but the animal was exhausted and hungry, plodding along with no more energy than the shambling soldiers behind them.

Utros had conquered many cities in the past, and he remembered every victory. Numerous town leaders or self-proclaimed kings had fallen under his sword. Back then, his army was invincible, and his success was guaranteed in each engagement. He had never imagined that Iron Fang's entire empire would fall, but Utros still intended to complete his mission.

The endless string of soldiers marched through the low hills until they formed a sprawling camp that stretched throughout the woods. The soldiers didn't bother with cook fires, for they had nothing to eat except a few rabbits, squirrels, or other wild game they had scrounged. By now, his warriors were so ferociously hungry that they devoured any animals they killed without bothering to cook the raw meat, while their starving comrades licked any smears of blood left behind.

As darkness fell in the sparse forest, Utros lay back on the ground and drowsed while listening to the rustle of the camp. He had vowed to conquer the Old World, and his men had followed him for so long. He would not let it all be a fool's chase.

Ruva lay beside him, curling her naked body against his, but not in an erotic way. She drew strength and comfort and gave it back to him. Without speaking, she just pressed her back and shoulders against his chest. He wrapped his muscular arm around her. "Tell me you can keep them alive, Ruva. Tell me your spell is strong enough."

"Strong enough?" Her body shook, and he realized she was laughing. "You think I am stronger than the Keeper?"

"Keep him at bay for a little while longer. It is to his advantage to let me continue my war, because we will send him many more souls." Utros felt a shiver and opened his eyes to see Ava's glimmering form above them, as if jealous that her sister could touch his solid form and she could not.

"The Keeper wants what he wants. The Keeper wants me." Ava drifted closer, extended her flickering arms. "He wants Ruva, both of us." Her image strained like a flame in a wind. When her sister reached out for her, Ava vanished. Ruva slumped back down, sobbing, curled up in a fetal ball.

When sleep still eluded Utros after an hour, he rose and walked among his soldiers, speaking quiet encouragement to anyone who remained awake. He walked to the perimeter of the camp, where the forest grew darker and thicker. He heard rustling in the underbrush, saw shadows of movement, and he tensed, ready to fight whatever might be out there. When he dropped a hand to his side, he realized he had left his sword back with Ruva.

Tawny shapes drifted among the shadowy trees. For a moment he thought they were stags, in which case he would send out hunters to shoot them down, but when several of the wild forms glided toward him, Utros saw they were not deer, but feline, predatory.

Sand panthers whispered through the woods, their large paws barely crackling the forest debris. Catching him alone, easy prey, a massive female bounded toward him and let out a roar. The other cats streaked forward into the camp.

Though unarmed, Utros swung his fists as the panther crashed into his chest and bore him down. With a grunt of effort, he heaved the big cat aside, only peripherally noticing that the tan hide was covered with branded runes such as he had seen on the combat beasts from Ildakar. Claws raked across his upper arm, cutting deep into the thick muscle before his metal bracer caught the claws. In the brawl, he punched the snarling panther under the chin.

Roused by the noise, other soldiers came running, and more big cats fell upon them. The lead female, though, targeted Utros specifically. Something was driving the animal; this was not just some mindless predator making a convenient kill.

As more soldiers rushed to defend the general, he heard another round of shouted alarms in the extended camp. A clash of swords rang out into the damp night air. As he battled the sand panther, he couldn't let his attention waver, but he saw human forms darting in, barely visible in the forest gloom. With a swift, dispersed strike, they attacked the groggy soldiers, killing hundreds before they melted back into the trees, never becoming fully visible.

Utros continued to wrestle with the panther. Her claws ripped through his leather armor and tore open his side. The cat's eyes shone in the starlight, full of murder, and when she roared, he could feel her hot breath on his face.

"Utros! No!" Running up, Ruva raised her hands and summoned her gift. A crackle of magic swept through the air, flames that licked out to slam the panther, but to the general's astonishment, Ruva's fire merely rippled around the spell markings on the tan hide, causing no harm.

The bright flash of impotent fire was enough to startle the cat, though. The animal leaped back, snarled, then pounced on Utros again. With the sweep of a paw, she knocked off the gold mask, which clattered to the ground. Ruva struck out again with her magic, buffeting the panther, and as Utros rallied, the big cat retreated, snarled one more time, and melted back into the trees.

With their general under attack, hundreds of his soldiers grabbed their weapons and came running to the rescue. More than a dozen sand panthers were attacking his army in a concerted effort, but when so many soldiers rallied against them, the cats snarled, slashed a few more times, and bolted into the forest. They vanished into the night.

Hungry for revenge, some soldiers rushed into the forest in pursuit of the mysterious attackers, but their battle cries turned into screams as they died out in the darkness.

Utros stood, bleeding from where the panther had mauled him. Sobbing, Ruva pressed herself against him. "You're hurt. You're bleeding, so much blood!" Then she smiled oddly at him. "Blood . . . has magic."

The sorceress clasped the deep cut in his biceps, squeezed, and unleashed her gift. He felt a tingling warmth as his muscles and skin knitted under her healing spell. He had rarely asked either of the twins to heal him, because battle injuries were worth savoring. Even the pain counted for something.

But Utros could not afford to be weak. He needed the full use of his body. As Ruva patched his worst wounds, he stared into the forest where the panthers had disappeared. What had driven them here? What guided them?

Now alert and on edge, the soldiers in the camp gathered up the bodies of the men who had been slain by the panthers and the mysterious attackers in the forest. Under normal circumstances, his warriors would prepare the fallen for a respectful burial or funeral pyres, but these were not normal circumstances.

Utros did not want to think about what they did with the corpses.

* * *

Sleeping on the *Chaser*'s deck as it raced away from Serrimundi with the Norukai fleet in hot pursuit, Nicci fell deeper into herself, and her dream presence connected with her sister panther.

Mrra moved with twenty other sand panthers, pacing the army of General Utros. The panthers had no maps, but Nicci had a clear sense of where they were from the strength of her connection. The spell bond was growing stronger as they came together after being widely separated. Mrra continued to lope toward Nicci, day after day, closing the distance and trying to help.

Nicci tasted blood as she dreamed. Seeing through feline eyes and feeling her claws and muscles, she crashed out of the forest and attacked the enemy soldiers. Connected to Mrra, Nicci guided the cat to find a singular target, the most important victim in the entire army. General Utros.

She and Mrra attacked the commander, wounded him, tore off his golden mask, but even though the branded runes protected her from direct damage by magic, Ruva's powers were dangerous. And the general and his soldiers could kill the panthers. Nicci urged them to withdraw.

Licking blood from her whiskers, Mrra bounded off into the forest, and Nicci smiled in her sleep.

The ships sailed into the night, heading toward Tanimura with the serpent ships behind them. Knowing that Mrra was on her way with a new pride of sand panthers brought joy to Nicci's heart.

But now she also knew that General Utros and his army were marching closer and closer.

CHAPTER 73

While waiting for Nicci to return with her reconnaissance of the Norukai fleet, Tanimura prepared for war. General Zimmer knew that the fate of the D'Haran Empire rested on whether or not the forces under his command could stand against the crushing blow coming their way. They had to be ready.

Arriving at Tanimura aboard Captain Mills's ship, which had sailed directly up from Serrimundi, he felt great satisfaction to see fifty significant ships protecting the harbor and patrolling the waters. They ranged in size from fishing boats to three-masted vessels capable of long sea voyages. Nicci's earlier warning had sunk in. This city could mount formidable defenses, and Zimmer was glad to see it.

After disembarking from the cargo ship that had been anchored for months as a guardian of Renda Bay, he marched through the city with the remnants of his expeditionary force. Insisting on discipline, Zimmer forced his returning soldiers to walk in steady ranks to demonstrate they had not forgotten they served in the D'Haran army. After all the hardships they had suffered since leaving Tanimura, their uniforms were tattered and their boots were worn and cracked. Their skin was weathered, their muscles toughened through hardship. He said, "We must try to look as impressive on our return as when we departed." The troops moved at a brisk pace up the city streets back to the garrison, glad to be home.

At the garrison, recruits were drilling in the town square, and they turned to look at the returning troops in surprise. Zimmer strode into the courtyard with squared shoulders and entered the main headquarters building.

When he reunited with General Linden, the other man rose from behind his desk to greet him, dismayed by the weathered condition of Zimmer's armor, the tattered cape of rank, the hardened look in his eyes. "You look as if you fought a war just this morning!"

"I've fought several wars, Linden, and saved the biggest one for last. The battle is coming here, sooner than you might expect."

Linden called for a hearty meal, the best food Zimmer had tasted in some time. While the weary general ate, Linden opened a ledger and dipped a quill in an inkpot so he could scribble notes as his companion described their adventures and the threat of the Norukai fleet as well as the army of General Utros.

"I am happy to report that we're aware of it. Nicci warned us, and we have been making constant preparations." Linden closed his ledger, then rattled off his own summary. "Lord Rahl understands our need, but he is occupied with another crisis in D'Hara. This war is ours to handle, and he has complete faith in us. He sent Nicci a powerful constructed spell, which he says is all she needs."

Zimmer nodded. "I have seen what Nicci can do." He tore another hunk of meat from the roast chicken on the platter in front of him. "But I have also seen the Norukai raiders, as well as the ancient army. Utros and his soldiers marched across an entire continent and they mean to conquer Tanimura. From there, they will move on to the New World. Unless we stop them."

Linden set his jaw. "And we will form defenses they have never seen either. Tanimura is strong."

Zimmer finished the entire chicken, ate a cluster of sweet grapes, and drank a goblet of water. "That's what I am here to help you with."

For the next several days he and his weary but energized troops whipped the Tanimura militia into shape. Zimmer wore fresh D'Haran armor, feeling resplendent as a general again. He inspected the city armories, watched the frantic work of swordsmiths, tanners, armorers, shield makers. Even though blacksmiths had worked all day and night, many new recruits did not have blades of their own, so they made do with clubs, axes, long-handled mallets. Crude weapons required less finesse and training to use, only anger and strength, and the fighters had plenty of that.

Tanimura was already a populous city, one of the main trading centers on the continent. The many citizens, as well as countless new refugees, were prepared to defend their homes. Fletchers produced arrows by the thousands, and archers practiced for hour after hour. Workers squatted on barrels and covered the arrow tips with pitch, rolling balls that could be lit on fire for an even more deadly barrage.

Captains Mills and Donell had delivered the displaced population of Renda Bay, and those thousands of angry people expanded the fighting force. Many families offered to share spare rooms so that the new refugees had places to stay and food to eat.

Zimmer rode down the streets, rallying everyone. In the practice yards he saw townspeople fitted with leather vests and helmets. They sparred with one another, flinging sweat out of their hair as they learned the basics of swordplay.

Attached to the lower part of the harbor, Halsband Island—where the Palace of the Prophets had once stood—was just a flat area of crushed rubble, perfect for use as a training field. Militia members marched back and forth, learning how to fall into ranks and clashing in mock battles.

As he walked the streets to the waterfront, Zimmer came upon Oron and Perri. Lord Oron's expression was dour as usual. He had rebraided his pale hair and restored his haughty expression. Perri followed him, younger and meeker, but her eyes also had a hardness after what she'd been through. Together they looked out at the multiple ships gathered to defend the waters around Tanimura. Every ship carried spears, bows, and fire arrows to be used for naval battles.

"We might just be able to hold off the Norukai fleet," Zimmer said. "Tanimura has never seen such a powerful navy."

Oron ran a finger along his lower lip. "Ildakar taught us many ways to fight, but this city also has plenty of gifted, including the Sisters of the Light. Many of us will man the ships in the harbor to face the Norukai fleet, but others will remain in the city to assist your large army. You have thousands of defenders ready to fight against a land invasion." He gazed at the hills behind Tanimura. "There's no telling when General Utros will arrive."

"We'll be ready for him," Perri said. "And the Norukai."

Zimmer mentally reviewed the other times he had faced impossible odds. He himself had led guerrilla teams to harass Old World towns that supported the Imperial Order. Back then, he had been forced to accept the new dictum that there were no innocents in that war, that even women and children who aided enemy soldiers were enemies in their own way. Zimmer had not been proud of that work, but Lord Rahl's forces had won.

Across the harbor, smoke signals rose into the sky, and a succession of brightly colored pennants waved to signal the arrival of ships. The *Chaser,* the *Mist Maiden,* and two other large sailing ships had just arrived from Serrimundi, putting the rest of the harbor on high alert.

When the swift krakener pulled ahead of the larger ships and reached the main piers first, Zimmer, Oron, and Perri hurried to meet them. Nicci and Nathan were the first to disembark, both of them looking exhausted from a great expenditure of their gift.

"We pressed these ships as fast as we could," Nathan said.

Nicci added, "The Norukai fleet is on its way, right behind us."

"Has Serrimundi been attacked?" Zimmer asked. "What happened?"

Oron interrupted, "How much damage did Lady Olgya cause? I hope she wrecked dozens of serpent ships."

"If our plan worked, then Serrimundi is safe. Olgya disguised the harbor with a great fog bank at night, while we lured the ships onward. They pursued us through the darkness." Nicci looked around impatiently.

"King Grieve's ships will arrive in less than a day. All of Tanimura must be ready to battle them."

Zimmer clenched his fists. "We'll be on high alert. As you can see, we have prepared significant defenses."

"Tanimura is our best hope of stopping them," Nathan said.

Bannon and Lila joined them. "We have a score to settle with the Norukai. I'm ready to fight them again, any time."

"It's more than just the Norukai," Nicci said. "Last night, I dreamed through my sand panther's eyes. The army of General Utros is closing in, and then we will be fighting on two fronts."

CHAPTER 74

T he *Chaser* sailed out to the edge of the harbor in the morning sunlight. Standing on the deck of the krakener, Bannon wrapped his palm around the hilt of Nathan's sword, *his* sword, and kept watch for the Norukai serpent ships, sure that soon enough they would see countless dark blue sails. Nathan had decided to stay with him and Lila aboard the *Chaser*, where they could face the first clash with the vile raiders. Captain Jared's vessel was a scrappy little warship prepared for battle.

Bannon's long ginger hair was loose, just like Nathan's. Lila looked at them both. "You should cut your hair so no enemy can grab it."

"I am rather fond of my hair," Nathan said. "It makes me look dashing. One cannot sacrifice everything."

Lila sniffed, but didn't argue with him. Wearing only her morazeth leather, she planted her feet on the deck and stood ready. The studded soles of her high battle sandals would give her good traction even if the deck were tilted or covered with spilled blood.

Bannon looked across the sparkling waves, then turned to the wizard. "Thank you again for giving me the sword. I never wanted a better blade than Sturdy, but I will make you proud with this one." He slid the weapon from its scabbard, and sunshine gleamed on the smooth steel.

"Use it well, my boy, and that will be thanks enough."

Bannon turned back toward the city. "I bought Sturdy here in Tanimura after those thugs nearly killed me. I'm not so destitute anymore. I can't believe Nicci rescued me instead of just leaving me to my fate. It was my own foolishness!"

Nathan mused, "The sorceress likes others to think she has an icy heart, but Richard taught her to help those in need. She can see the value of an investment. She made the effort to save you, and how many enemies have you slain to repay her for that one kindness?"

"Not enough," Lila said. "But we will make up for it as soon as King Grieve arrives."

Pounding drums and ringing bells set up a racket across the ships. Farther out to sea, patrol boats lit their smoky signals.

"Norukai are coming!" shouted Captain Jared. His grin showed the gap between his front teeth. "Set the sails! What are we waiting for?"

Bannon braced himself, and Lila stood beside him, wearing a satisfied smile. "Maybe the stink of this ship will kill the first line of attackers," she said.

Jared brushed aside the teasing insult and stared ahead at the oncoming ships.

King Grieve stood behind the carved serpent figure-head and stared at the great city as it came into view. He let out a hissing roar when he saw the count-less armored ships arrayed in a defensive line, blocking the harbor.

But they couldn't stop him. Grieve was the serpent god. Every fighter in his fleet also carried the blood of the serpent god. His warriors had the energy and soul of their deity surging through their veins.

In the previous day, as they sailed with all possible speed toward Tanimura in pursuit of their prey, his warriors had seen a great omen that added fire to their veins. One of the lookouts had shouted, pointing off to the horizon where another huge snakelike form curled in the waves. Grieve had felt his heart swell to see another manifestation of the serpent god, and he let out a bellow that echoed across the choppy sea. The other Norukai joined in a resounding roar as the new serpent god swam off.

Grieve and his people would engage in this battle themselves, but they all carried its presence inside them. Their victory was now assured.

Grieve didn't know where General Utros's army was, nor did he care. Though they were supposedly allies, the pompous commander was worthless, and the Norukai would do what they already did so well. His raiders would smash Tanimura and claim all the surrounding lands by the time Utros and his exhausted army marched up the imperial road. By then, the Norukai might be ready for another fight and wipe them out.

The raider ships cut through the water like sea serpents. Warriors strained at the oars, pulling in perfect unison. The oar masters pounded their drums as hard and fast as the heartbeat of an angry fighter. Grieve's fleet raced headlong toward the Tanimuran ships lined up to block him. They would all sink. He would smash them. Burn them.

Atta strode up behind him. "I fight at your side,

Grieve. They will all grieve, while we laugh and feast. Afterward, we will make love like two animals in heat."

Grieve let out a low rumble in his chest. Atta was a vigorous and exhausting lover, just what he needed to burn off the bloodlust from a good battle. Right now, he had to concentrate on killing instead of lust.

A sullen mood crossed him. He missed Chalk's amusing antics and his chatter. The shaman could have foretold how this battle would end. Then again, Grieve often could not understand the albino's confusing pronouncements. "The axe cleaves the wood, the sword cleaves the bone."

As she looked toward the defensive ships braced outside of Tanimura, Atta snorted, "It is a trap. They lured us here."

"We see their trap, but we will not be deterred." Grieve's raiders would career like a battering ram into those warships. "The sharks will feed well tonight."

"We all will," Atta replied. Other crew members added their cheers.

As the ships approached, Grieve recognized a small gray vessel pulling ahead of the other Tanimuran ships. The krakener. "There, that ship! We will destroy every vessel that stands against us, but first . . ." He ground his teeth together, rippling his scarred jaws. "That ship is first. That ship is mine."

CHAPTER 75

The widely dispersed Tanimuran navy was a motley collection of large and small ships, some heavily armored and riding low in the water, others more nimble. Hardened fishermen and veteran traders knew how to combat storms and big fish on the high seas, but they had never battled anything like the Norukai.

More than a hundred serpent ships sailed toward them. Nathan stood at the bow of the *Chaser,* feeling his pulse race. He found that he quite looked forward to the encounter.

The foremost Norukai ship pressed directly toward the krakener, oars churning the water. "Sweet Sea Mother, here they come!" Bannon said.

Across the defensive line, the fighters prepared for the clash, soldiers, sailors, and archers. There were also gifted men and women, including Oron, Perri, several Sisters of the Light, trained scholars from Cliffwall, and other gifted Tanimura residents who offered their abilities.

Captain Jared grew more serious than Nathan had seen him before. "I didn't know the Norukai had so many ships!"

Impressed, Nathan smiled. "King Grieve likes to prey upon helpless villages. Today, he will learn we are different."

Nicci had stayed on land along with Zimmer and Linden, joining the D'Haran troops that patrolled the waterfront. They were ready to fight in the streets if the Norukai broke through the naval blockade and tried to pillage the city. Nathan knew the sorceress could stop them, but he didn't intend to let any of the serpent ships break through.

As the attackers approached, the scarred warriors crowded the decks, raising swords and axes. Clutching the serpent figurehead, King Grieve thundered out his primal challenge.

Bannon roared back at the top of his lungs, "We will kill you, Grieve! Come and get us, you ugly bastard!"

Looking at him, Lila cocked an eyebrow. "Impressive, boy."

Nathan directed his sharp focus toward the Norukai king, who was the most hideous of them all. A repulsive blocky woman beside him pumped a fist into the air with a meaty arm.

Nathan felt the dangerous magic build inside him. "Come and meet your fate."

He had first seen the Norukai after he, Nicci, and Bannon had been shipwrecked near Renda Bay. During the attack on that town, the Norukai had mowed down so many helpless people. . . .

As if Bannon was recalling that same night, his expression hardened. He held his sword in a death grip, and sweat prickled his forehead. "There'll be a big fight ahead. I may go into my blood rage and I won't know what's happening." He looked at Lila. "So many of them to kill."

The pounding of Norukai drums echoed across the harbor, and the shouts of challenge grew louder. Inside his chest, Nathan felt his heart twist with anger, not entirely caused by the lingering shadow of Chief Handler Ivan. He whispered to the dark presence inside him, "You will soon have as much violence as you desire. Make yourself useful."

The serpent ships came closer and closer. The raiders pulled on their oars in a final charge.

At the *Chaser*'s bow, Nathan raised his hands, spread his fingers. "It's about time." As a crackle of magic infused the air, the breezes picked up, and his cape snapped about like a flag in the wind. On other nearby ships he saw Sisters of the Light standing at the bow, and they all summoned their magic as well.

All along the defensive line, the gifted fighters stirred the water, tugged on the waves, stretched the sea. Froth swirled in front of the *Chaser*, and Nathan drew upon his gift to fashion new waves like a baker stretching dough. Exhaling with the effort, he pushed his hands down, using the unseen force to create a trough in the water. The blow sent successive ripples, each one building upon the last, and waves began to coalesce into whitecaps that rolled toward the Norukai fleet.

Nathan shoved more power into the water, churning bigger waves and pushing a storm into the sea. His fellow gifted fighters on other ships used similar magic to form waves and unleash surging currents into the normally placid harbor. As the enemy fleet advanced, high waves rocked the vessels from side to side like flotsam in a squall, throwing several Norukai overboard. One man slipped down into the sweeping oars, which battered him under the water.

Nathan saw Oron aboard Captain Straker's ship,

slashing his fists sideways to whip up towering waves, which capsized a serpent vessel. Seawater sloshed over the deck and swept away a dozen angry raiders.

Nathan resonated his waves with Oron's, which built them to twice the force. Hammer-walls of water crashed the Norukai ships together like toys, breaking open hulls and snapping masts.

But the raiders kept coming. King Grieve demanded more speed from his crew, and they pulled relentlessly on the oars. From the prow of each Norukai vessel, a carved serpent stared with jaws wide, ready to ram.

Nathan pushed a wave against one of the flanking serpent ships, raised it high, then instantly withdrew the water so that it plummeted back down and splintered in the sea. Waves threw two raider ships against each other, shattering both like eggs.

Dozens more plowed through the wreckage of their own ships. The Sisters of the Light worked together to raise a concerted shield of water that doused more Norukai ships and pushed several vessels back, but the raiders only rowed harder.

The *Chaser*'s crew held on for dear life in the back-wash of the waves. Bannon stabilized himself against the rail, while Lila planted her feet and kept her balance, glaring murder at the oncoming attackers.

King Grieve somehow managed to keep his rowers pushing the lead ship forward. With surprising speed, his vessel plowed toward the krakener. Even with half of its oars snapped, the king's flagship came forward like a snarling beast. Nathan tried to slam it with a wave, but the enemy ship kept coming.

Beside Grieve at the bow of the vessel, the ugly Norukai woman waved a sword of her own. The king raised his war axe.

Nathan called wind to try to drive away the oncoming ship, but the flagship crashed ahead in a suicidal push. He shoved his wall of air with such force that he cracked the mainmast, but the enemy vessel could not be stopped. The ship rammed the krakener with an impact like a thunderclap that shuddered through the hull and deck. As it slammed into them, the serpent figurehead shattered into pieces. Boards shivered and cracked.

Bannon was flung down the deck as the *Chaser* tilted, and Lila snatched his shirt to keep him from falling.

But Nathan had been concentrating on his gift, shaping the wind and moving the waves. He could not catch himself fast enough and lost his footing. Thrown off balance, he tumbled into the rail, tried to grab it, but slipped. He fell overboard and into the churning water filled with broken wood and bleeding bodies.

CHAPTER 76

Although the initial clash took place out on the water, Nicci and the ranks of D'Haran soldiers took their positions along the docks, ready to drive back any raiders that managed to break through the line of ships. With Grieve's reckless navy, at least some of the vessels might make it to the city and wreak havoc.

Many Sisters of the Light were out in the harbor, but Nicci remained on shore with Sisters Eldine, Rhoda, Mab, and Arabella. She was armed with her two daggers, as well as her gift. She still carried the small bone box Richard had given her, even if she had not yet deciphered its purpose. Richard knew there was something special about Nicci's background, her knowledge, her gift. In the meantime, she had plenty of other ways to fight a war.

Linden had dispatched scouts to ride into the hills above Tanimura, looking for any sign of General Utros's army, but the scouts had not yet returned. Meanwhile, the Norukai were attacking *now*. The soldiers lined up, ready to protect the city.

In front of a group of waterfront warehouses, General Zimmer sat high on his warhorse, surveying the tremendous naval battle under way out on the water. His mount snorted and shifted from side to side, sensing the violence in the air. Along the extended wharves, all the piers were empty, every ship dispatched to fight the Norukai. His men moved restlessly in ranks, hands on the hilts of their swords, anxious to cut down any raiders that made it to shore.

The serpent ships plowed into the Tanimuran blockade. The gifted fighters summoned great waves to disrupt the Norukai advance, and even from the docks Nicci could hear the distant clamor of raider ships smashing into one another. Thunderclouds gathered as the wizards lashed out with storms.

At the forefront, King Grieve's ship rammed into the *Chaser*, causing tremendous damage. Nicci watched two Norukai vessels flank Captain Mills's ship and throw grappling hooks so the raiders could swarm aboard. Though many serpent ships crashed into one another, hammered by waves and driven back by the gifted defenders, others succeeded in breaking through the blockade and pushed directly toward the city. Dozens of enemy vessels had already sunk, and yet they kept coming.

Angry, Nicci longed to be on the front lines using her gift to destroy the Norukai. She did not like to feel safe while others were dying, but she would not leave Tanimura so vulnerable. "We will have our time soon enough," she muttered under her breath.

Waiting on dry land, the soldiers sent up a cheer, hurling angry insults out toward the enemy. General Zimmer shook his head in disbelief. "The Norukai are insane. Look at them! They do not value their own lives. They sacrifice five or ten for every one that gets through."

The Norukai plowed forward despite the storm winds and crashing waves. Thirty raider ships penetrated the blockade, leaving many more behind as they charged straight toward the docks.

Nicci turned to the Sisters. "Nathan and the others will do their best on the water. Now it is our turn to mop up the rest."

"I'm glad to fight beside you again, Sister Nicci," said Eldine. "It is good that you came back to the Sisters of the Light."

Nicci's eyes hardened. "I did not come back. I'm not a Sister of the Dark, nor am I a member of your order. I serve Lord Rahl, and I serve myself." She flashed a glance at the gathered women. "But we are Sisters in our own way, against a common enemy."

As the handful of serpent ships careened toward the docks, Zimmer dispatched armed companies up and down the waterfront to meet them. Their boots created a staccato thunder as they ran along. Vengeful refugees from Renda Bay and Effren joined the D'Haran army to help fight, but the professional soldiers would bear the brunt of the first onslaught. Zimmer spurred his horse, and the soldiers yelled as they charged.

Several raider vessels also approached the shores of flattened Halsband Island and the new connecting bridges to the main city. Sister Rhoda looked at where the Palace of the Prophets had once towered above the city and flashed a hungry smile. "Maybe Halsband Island will grow green again if we drench it with enough Norukai blood."

Nicci smiled. "I like that kind of thinking, but these nearer ships will cause a problem first."

A trio of battered raiders headed for a patch of

open shore at the far end of the main piers. One hull bore burn scars from where lightning had scorched the wood. The dark sails showed gaping holes, but a few intact oars pushed the ships along on a drunkard's path until they ran aground on the stony shingle. Scarred raiders boiled off the decks and dropped onto land.

Two more serpent ships slammed into one of the empty docks, grinding against the pilings. Muscular slavers leaped over the rail and bounded toward the city, weapons drawn and ready for mayhem.

Nicci and the D'Haran soldiers were there to stop them. The Sisters of the Light lashed out with icy rain and sharp projectiles of hail, but the Norukai hunched down and charged ahead with their axes, spiked maces, chained balls. Opening their scarred mouths, they howled.

One of the new D'Haran soldiers was terrified. "They're monsters."

Nicci said, "They bleed like humans and they die like humans."

To demonstrate what she meant, she summoned wizard's fire in her palm. As raiders stormed toward her, their screams changed when Nicci's flaming ball exploded in the first man's chest and spurted out his back. The unstoppable fire roasted three other Norukai close behind him.

She summoned a second sphere and hurled it higher, so that the fireball dropped down into the ranks behind. Though many died screaming, the Norukai did not halt their charge for an instant. Even as their comrades fell dead, waves of raiders stomped over the charred bodies and kept running.

"Shields!" Zimmer shouted, and his soldiers held their shields edge-to-edge to form a solid barrier. They advanced slowly, swords extended to meet the enemy with a resounding slam of leather, wood, and metal.

Nicci lobbed another fireball high over their heads, and it exploded on the nearest serpent ship, igniting the deck and mast and killing the last few Norukai trying to disembark.

The disciplined D'Haran soldiers held a firm line, but the Norukai were in a mindless battle rage. Many angry refugees broke ranks and ran into the fray, throwing themselves upon the wild raiders who had destroyed their homes and killed their loved ones. Town leader Thaddeus leaped in, swinging a boat hook. He bashed skulls and stabbed faces with the pointed spar. Renda Bay survivors followed his example with enough fury to stall the initial Norukai charge. Zimmer's men regrouped and moved forward.

From the roofs of waterfront warehouses, D'Haran archers fired volley after volley into the swarm of raiders. Soon the streets were piled high with Norukai bodies, and blood ran through the gutters. But the raiders kept coming.

Ten more serpent ships crashed against the empty piers and disgorged a thousand yelling warriors. Heedless of their own safety, raiders rammed into the lines of D'Haran defenders, plowing past the shields and running to the warehouses, which they set on fire. As flames caught on the wooden walls, bales of fabric, and stored sacks of grain, thick smoke curled upward. The archers on the rooftops had to leap for their lives.

With twin bolts of lightning, Nicci blasted several attackers into red mist and blackened meat. Every Norukai that ran onto shore seemed to expect death, and they meant to cause as much destruction as they could before they died.

One warrior with a face like a misshapen potato stalked toward General Zimmer, who was engaged in mortal combat with another opponent. Seeing that he needed help, Nicci extended her gift, found the ugly raider's heart, and made it explode. The Norukai man dropped like a felled ox. Four of his comrades looked at him, unable to understand what had happened. Nicci released her gift again and stopped their hearts as well.

Out in the water, the naval battle continued. At least forty serpent ships had already been wrecked or sunk.

As Nicci worked to create more wizard's fire, a Noru-kai woman swung a spiked club at her head. Nicci ducked and plunged her dagger into the woman's heart. Even with the blade stuck in her chest, the woman still pressed the weight of her heavy body against Nicci. While Nicci was distracted, the wizard's fire flickered in her hand, but she slapped the remnants into the woman's face, and her head burst into flame. Nicci shoved the weight aside and turned to face her next victim.

Then, in the heat of the battle, the sound of the clamor changed. Nicci heard loud shouts from the outskirts of the city, a banging of drums, a howl of alarm. Scouts galloped along the hill roads and raced into Tanimura, shouting in panic.

Though their voices were diminished by the distance and the chaos of the battle at the waterfront, Nicci recognized the scouts. Ice formed in her gut as she saw a long line of soldiers coming behind them at a fast march. They wore armor and carried standards that she had seen before, the mark of an emperor who had died fifteen centuries earlier.

Nearly a hundred thousand strong, the army of General Utros rolled over the hills toward Tanimura.

CHAPTER 77

When King Grieve's ship collided with the *Chaser*, the impact threw Bannon against a crate on the deck so hard his head rang. He smashed his elbow, but managed to keep his grip on the ornate sword.

But he couldn't react in time to save Nathan from being thrown overboard.

"No!" Bannon lunged, but the deck boards were slippery with spray and covered with a hard varnish of kraken slime. He sprawled on his back and rolled. Lila seized his wrist before he, too, fell overboard.

"The wizard can take care of himself." Lila pushed his shoulder, turning him. "No time. Look!"

Bannon reeled backward as dozens of barbaric raiders leaped across the gap. The Norukai were a storm of bladed weapons, bulging muscles, and scarred faces. Their battle cries made them sound like hungry beasts.

"Hold together!" Jared yelled. With a hard, out-of-place laugh, the krakener captain wielded a long-handled hatchet designed for lopping off tentacles. With a sideways sweep, he caught one of the overconfident Norukai by surprise, proving that the hatchet could slice off a human head as easily as it severed kraken appendages.

Bannon braced himself with his sword, while Lila stood at his side with her sword in one hand, a dagger in the other. Her hungry grin looked more intimidating than any of the Norukai did.

King Grieve crashed onto the deck of the *Chaser*. His heavy boots thudded on the boards, and he swept his war axe back and forth with one hand as if it were a toy. Recognizing Bannon, he laughed aloud. His snort sounded like a loud belch. "Walking meat." He strode forward. "Dead meat." The blade of the war axe was as broad as the king's head. The sharpened crescent edge gleamed like a silver smile.

The ugly and uncouth Atta thumped beside Grieve, and Lila hissed at her own nemesis.

The *Chaser*'s crew ran forward armed with boat hooks and clubs. They were strong from hard work and brave from wrestling kraken. The ten D'Haran soldiers aboard the ship also threw themselves into the fray.

Ignoring the other raiders on the deck, Bannon stepped up to face King Grieve with his fancy sword raised. "Of all these enemies, you're the one I want to kill the most."

Grieve charged like an Ildakaran bull, and the studs of his boots dug into the layers of hardened slime. He swung his axe with both hands, putting all of his effort into the blow.

The weapon would have shattered Bannon's chest, but he twisted his body out of the way, calling upon instinctive training. He dodged the axe and twirled like a dancer, dropped, bent, and came up again. Keeping his sword low, he struck hard and sideways.

Grieve turned his thick torso so that the sharp steel

clanged against the iron links of the chain around his waist, striking sparks rather than drawing blood.

Attacking him from the opposite side, Lila sprang upon the king with her dagger and short sword, slashing with a blur of sharp edges. "We'll both kill him, boy."

Then, like an avalanche, Atta slammed into her with crippling force, knocking her away from Grieve. Lila rolled on the deck and turned on her new foe, shifting focus without the slightest hesitation. While sprawled and scrambling to her feet, Lila swung at Atta's lower legs and stabbed her dagger point deep into the woman's meaty calf. Bellowing in pain, Atta smashed a hard fist down on Lila's head, but Lila sprang to her feet and crouched, coiled to fight.

Grieve swung his war axe again with enough force to chop down a mast, and Bannon barely avoided evisceration. "Chalk talked with you. You twisted him. You tricked him. My Chalk!" He swung the axe again. This time Bannon met the blow with the sword. The steel was strong, but the vibration of impact shuddered all the way to the young man's shoulder.

"Chalk was mad," Bannon taunted. "You should have let the razorfish eat him down to his bones the first time."

As expected, the comment sent the king into a blind rage. Bursting with sorrow and hungry for revenge, Grieve snapped his mouth open so that his face looked like a yawning, wet hole. "You will die for that!"

As he fought, Bannon felt a red haze rising around his vision. "A lot of people tried to kill me, and I am still here." He became stronger, faster, every movement fueled by instinct and adrenaline. The deafening sounds of hand-to-hand combat all around him became more distinct.

Bannon hacked with the sword and carved a bright red furrow across Grieve's chest. The king didn't seem to realize he had been cut. He twirled the battle-axe and chopped down again, driving Bannon backward. The young man parried with the sword, slashed low, and nicked Grieve's thigh, but the king continued pressing.

In the harbor around them, the gifted defenders maintained the turbulence, swamping or crushing serpent ships, slamming wooden hulls against one another. Even with the blockade, dozens of the serpent ships had broken through and headed for the inner harbor, where they smashed into the docks and disgorged wild Norukai. They swarmed into the city, which had already started to burn.

Bannon couldn't help them, though. He had enough trouble just trying to survive here. He would have to leave the rest of Tanimura to Nicci, Zimmer, and the others.

As if trying to cut down an oak with a single blow, Grieve swung his huge axe again. Bannon lurched to the side and collided with Atta just as she brought down her curved sword at Lila. If he hadn't dislodged her, she would have severed Lila's arm. With a snarl, the Norukai woman spun to lash out at him, but Bannon blocked her blade with his own and turned back just as King Grieve followed through with his axe.

Using the moment of distraction, Lila threw herself upon Atta, hacking deep into the woman's right arm. The Norukai clacked her teeth together as blood spouted from mangled muscle, but she effortlessly switched her blade to the other hand and attacked Lila again. The air around them was filled with a mist of blood.

Grieve struck at Bannon again and again, each blow

powerful enough to cleave a man in two. The young man dodged and recovered his balance. He was not afraid of King Grieve, and he did not want to back away. He wanted to kill the awful man. He met each blow with Nathan's fine sword, striking back as hard as he could.

By now, though, his muscles ached from the effort, and his bones rattled from the abuse. As the red haze crowded in and tunneled his vision, he breathed harder; his pulse accelerated, his muscles tightened. His throat went dry. Every fiber of muscle, every drop of blood, every bead of sweat, every strand of his long hair became consumed with defeating the Norukai king.

Bannon never knew what caused his blood rage. Maybe it was some angry flaw he had inherited from his brutal father. When the mindless fury consumed him, he became a killing machine with no thought or awareness other than his opponent. He couldn't remember every blow or even every victim.

As he hacked at King Grieve and his vision blurred into that fugue of murderous energy, Bannon fought to hold on to himself and push back the haze. He wanted to *remember* this! He slashed hard and up, barely missing Grieve's throat.

"Sweet Sea Mother!" Bannon said, grinding his teeth. "I'll slay you, and I will remember every instant of this fight."

The king flung his shoulders back to avoid the sword tip, then lunged toward Bannon. Grieve's face turned ruddy. "You cannot kill me. I am the serpent god!"

Bannon made a scoffing noise. "I've already seen the serpent god killed."

With a shout as loud and as violent as the king's, he collided with Grieve, swung, chopped, stabbed. The king defended himself, using the metal cuff around his wrist to deflect a blow, turning to let his sharkskin vest catch the glancing blade.

Bannon did not relent. He thrust and swung and hacked at the big man's shoulder, chopping loose an implanted bone spike. Grieve yowled as blood sprayed from the gouge, but the pain triggered additional energy. "I am King Grieve. *I* am the serpent god!" Bannon dodged another vicious sweep of the war axe. "You'll all grieve!"

The explosive strength of his attack was unstoppable. The king drove Bannon backward, pressing him against a crate near the rail. Grieve raised his war axe over his head and brought it down with enough strength to split his victim from head to waist. Bannon evaded death by a hairsbreadth, and the axe embedded itself deep into the wood. The blade wedged into the rail and stuck in the thick layers of adhesive slime. King Grieve grasped the handle, tugged, twisted, tried to break the axe loose.

As King Grieve struggled to wrench his weapon free, Bannon seized the instant. Putting all the strength of his back and shoulders and arms behind his sword strike, he chopped down on King Grieve's neck.

The sharp blade cut all the way through the king's spine. Grieve's head rolled off, held by just a scrap of skin. His jaw yawned open and his tongue dangled out as blood spouted. Stretched by the weight, the thin ribbon of tissue snapped, and Grieve's head dropped over the side of the ship and into the churning water.

Bannon collapsed to his knees and felt a sudden indrawn breath of silence. He seemed to hear Chalk's voice, the shaman calling out gibberish again and again. And now Bannon understood.

The axe cleaves the wood. The sword cleaves the bone.

A scream loud enough to shatter glass rolled out behind him. Atta looked as if her heart had just been torn beating from her chest. "My Grieve!" She thundered toward him with all the fury of a combat bear.

Grieve's headless body collapsed to the deck. Some of the krakener crew cheered, then threw themselves on the other Norukai with redoubled force.

Atta came at Bannon like a rabid dog, and he raised his sword to block her. Everything seemed to move slowly, and his weary muscles were cold sludge. When Atta was one step from him, her sword raised for the killing blow, Lila appeared behind her and thrust her blade directly through the other woman's back. She shoved hard with both hands, pushing the blade through Atta's heart, and the point sprang out like a sharpened sapling between her breasts.

Dying, Atta flailed her arms, then let her curved sword fall with a clatter to the deck. She pawed at the steel point that had sprouted from her chest, slicing her palms. Though Atta was much heftier than her slender opponent, Lila held the big woman up with the sword. Dark blood flowed in puddles.

Finally, Atta slid down along the cutting blade, and Lila let the body fall onto the deck.

CHAPTER 78

A ripple of dismay passed through Zimmer's standing army as they wheeled about to face the horde of ancient soldiers that appeared on the outskirts of the city. Battle horns sounded, and a roar of voices rose like a thunderclap from Utros and his warriors.

Zimmer rallied his fighters, "We are the D'Haran army! We stand against all enemies!"

"We are more than that," Nicci said. "We also have thousands of refugees armed and hungry for vengeance. Now they have their chance."

Meanwhile, the Norukai raiders fought their way deeper into the streets of Tanimura, yowling like crazed beasts. They let out a resounding cheer upon seeing their allies arrive, which virtually assured their victory. They burned and ransacked whatever they touched. The two enemy armies closed in on the city like flames fanned by a stiff breeze.

Nearby, a Norukai warrior tilted his head back and laughed at the sky, twirling a club in his hand. Annoyed, Nicci burned him to ash with wizard's fire, and his club clattered to the ground, still clutched by smoking fingers.

Spurring his warhorse, Zimmer led a charge through the chaotic Norukai, trying to get closer to Nicci. She shoved with a wall of hardened air to clear the way for him. Sweat dripped down the general's face, and his right cheek was splattered with blood. He glanced at Utros's enormous army outside the city, his expression grim. "Now I see the wisdom in your insistence on keeping so many troops on land. I don't know if our entire army will be enough to stop General Utros from conquering the city."

Out on the water, the Tanimuran navy had smashed and sunk many serpent ships, but along the waterfront dozens of Norukai vessels had plowed into the piers and disgorged more and more bloodthirsty barbarians. Meanwhile, Utros directed tens of thousands of ancient soldiers toward Tanimura from the opposite side, broken into several enormous divisions to engulf the city. Countless defenders and innocent citizens would be slaughtered in the coming hours.

Nicci didn't underestimate the mayhem the Norukai would cause, but Utros was a *conqueror*. She feared him more. "I need to mount a strong defense against the ancient marching army. I leave you to stop these raiders, General. Are you capable?"

He let out a loud chuckle. "Am I capable? Lord Rahl would be ashamed of me if one of his generals couldn't stop a crowd of ugly raiders. We will show them how we fight for D'Hara. Take the militia members with you and stop Utros."

At Zimmer's signal, one of his adjutants blew a war horn to signal the vengeful militia members, most of whom had only a few days of training. With her gift, Nicci amplified her voice to reach all the way to the rear ranks of people from Renda Bay, from Effren, from

Larrikan Shores, from other destroyed towns. "To the hills! We have to cut off General Utros and his army."

Yet another serpent ship slammed into the piers, and Zimmer rallied his soldiers for a forward charge. Hundreds of blades flashed as the D'Haran army ran to meet the Norukai. He called over his shoulder, "Go, Sorceress!"

Thaddeus raised his borrowed sword and called on his people from Renda Bay, while the freed slave Rendell adjusted a leather helmet that sat askew on his head and shouted to his own squad. A hundred armed refugees under his command ran along with him.

Utros's army carried tattered pennants with Kurgan's ancient flame emblem, as well as new flags with an even larger symbolic fire. At the forefront of the enemy ranks Nicci could identify the general by his distinctive horned helmet and a glint of gold from his mask. He seemed to regard the city below as if it were a fat calf to be slaughtered. His sorceress rode beside him, crackling with magic as she called a storm cloud above her.

Separated into broad divisions to attack the city, tens of thousands marched across the forested hills. One division curled around to the northern end of Tanimura, while General Utros and Ruva directed the bulk of the army. The division nearest Nicci and her militia entered the dark expanse of the Hagen Woods just above the flattened ruins of Halsband Island. They plodded relentlessly forward, and once through the thick woods they would trample the lowtown and outlying residential areas to overwhelm the core of Tanimura.

That was also the area Nicci knew best because of her time among the Sisters. She shouted to her fighters as she led them in that direction, "To the woods! We will use the forest to our advantage."

The Hagen Woods had long been a sinister place. The Sisters of the Dark had performed their bloody sacrifices and horrific initiation rituals here. The place was already soaked with blood, and now she would give the soil more.

Thousands of eager militia members followed her. Rendell and Thaddeus seemed to be competing with each other, racing ahead to fight back. On their way, the fighters crossed the city district nearest the bridges to Halsband Island, where countless clothiers, food merchants, craftsmen, candlemakers, weavers, and stonecutters had once thrived by serving the Palace of the Prophets, along with taverns, gambling dens, and whorehouses that were patronized by the trainees of the Sisters. After the destruction of the palace, though, the district had fallen on hard times, and many of the homes were abandoned.

As her refugee fighters ran through the empty streets to intercept the army division, they passed a few families who huddled in their homes, mothers and fathers holding crude weapons ready to fight if the war came to them. Nicci called back a warning: "We'll try to hold them off, but if the soldiers break through from the Hagen Woods, then you must flee. You can't hope to stop them."

The ancient army had already flooded into the thick forest on their way to the lowtown, but Nicci paused at the edge of the dark pines and tangled oaks. "These dense woods will work to our advantage. The enemy soldiers will have to break ranks as they move through the trees. We'll attack them and kill them. We cannot let them reach the city."

Exuding confidence for the benefit of her ragtag fighters, Nicci marched into the woods ready with her gift and with her dagger. The twisted branches and thick underbrush made running impossible, but her fighters worked their way closer to where they could hear the clamor of the approaching army. Disappointingly, General Utros was not with this division, but she knew she would have her moment to face him.

She pulled in front of the others, intending to keep them safe. Not far ahead, she heard thousands of enemy soldiers crashing through the woods. She saw the first line of warriors shoving aside branches and underbrush, and they spotted her at the same time. Even though she wore a dark dress, her pale skin and blond hair made her visible in the gloom of the Hagen Woods.

But thousands of them came yelling through the forest, eager to wipe out the refugee militia. The ancient warriors were flesh and blood again, but they were gaunt, hollow-eyed, their cracked lips drawn back. Desperation clung to them like a tight garment.

As ten bloodthirsty men rushed to cut her down, Nicci extended her gift, found two large trees near the clump of soldiers. As she had done before, she heated the sap and flash-boiled the moisture inside the thick trunks. The liquid expanded, exploded, and the shattered trees hurled sharp wooden stakes in all directions. Just in time, she raised a shield to protect her own fighters, but the flying splinters killed dozens of the enemy in an instant. The shattered tree collapsed and toppled onto even more ancient soldiers.

Nicci detonated another towering oak, which wiped out another group of opponents, while additional ranks of the enemy division collided with her militia. Minimally trained but full of angry energy, the refugee fighters engaged in battle under the dark branches.

Nicci flung out walls of air like battering rams to flatten lines of armored warriors. She burst the hearts of some, when she could focus her pinpoint concentration, she struck out with wizard's fire, and when all else failed, she used her dagger to cut throats and stab hearts.

The ancient soldiers kept coming, plowing into the woods and driving back the outnumbered militia. The enemy sacrificed themselves without even counting their losses. General Utros had given them orders to push forward and sweep into the city, and they would not be deterred.

Overwhelmed, Nicci's refugees began to falter. Rendell had a deep gash in his arm, and his leather helmet had been knocked off. Thaddeus pulled him to safety as two attackers closed in on him.

Even Nicci couldn't stop them all, and she felt the tide turning. "Hold the line! We can't let them get through to Tanimura." She lashed out with every trick she could think of, but her gift wasn't infinite. The militia began to stumble back.

But as her fighters faltered and retreated, a tan panther bounded in and mauled one of the ancient soldiers. Mrra flattened the man and tore out his throat. With a roar, the big cat turned her bloody muzzle toward Nicci and thrashed her tail. Nicci felt a surge of delight. "My sister panther!"

More big cats dashed through the thick trees, dozens of them hidden by the forest shadows. As they struck, the ancient soldiers recoiled in primal fear evoked by the feline predators. Mrra's new pride of cats was not large enough to thwart that many soldiers, but the terrified reaction was effective enough to make them waver for a moment. Mrra bounded close enough to brush against Nicci, and then she sprang away to attack more victims.

Nicci held her ground. Parts of the Hagen Woods were burning after her wizard's fire, and many trees had fallen, shattered from within. The militia stiffened their resistance and fought harder.

Then more forms flowed through the thick forest like human shadows, a large fighting force of figures cloaked in gray. They attacked the ancient army from its flank, causing a sudden uproar as Utros's soldiers found themselves fighting on two fronts. The gray-robed people fell upon the enemy division, using antique swords to hack leather and chain mail, severing arms and heads, thrusting through ribs. The unexpected support gave Nicci's militia another surge of enthusiasm, and they pressed back, regaining the ground they had lost.

Nicci recognized the unexpected reinforcements—the Hidden People! As they fought in a shadowy blur, she saw a young woman with thin hair tied in a ponytail. Her gray hood had fallen back. "Asha! How did you all get here?"

"We came to fight for you, Nicci." The girl slashed with her sword, catching an enemy soldier in the back. "You freed us from the zhiss, and now it is only fair that we help you."

Nicci was amazed. When the sliph had whisked her away from Orogang, General Utros's expeditionary force had filled the square, an overwhelming army. She had thought sure the Hidden People would be massacred. "How did you escape from the soldiers in Orogang?"

Asha laughed. "Escape? We killed them all. We have far more people than you guessed! And we knew where you were going, since you showed us Tanimura on the relief map in the speaking chamber. We knew all the mountain passes, the rivers, and the cities, and we decided we had to come here. We followed your sand panther."

Nicci felt an optimism that would have made even Bannon proud. "Good. Now we can eradicate this division."

They fought with redoubled fury and decimated the invaders. Nicci was sad to see how many brave refugees also died in the forest, but over the next few hours they succeeded in wiping out the entire division.

Nicci stood exhausted, her black dress stained and tattered from countless slashes. The forest was a blood-soaked bog, and dead bodies lay piled several deep. Her surviving militia members rallied around her, proud that they had managed to hold the Hagen Woods, but an even larger battle was still taking place in the main city.

Suddenly the branches in the nearby trees whipped about, leaves crackled, and a shimmering feminine form appeared in the air, the green-haloed outline of Ava. She looked outraged. "Utros will send you to the Keeper!"

Nicci summoned the remnants of her gift to tear at the wavering spirit. "I killed you once already."

The spirit recoalesced from the onslaught and swooped among Nicci's militia, causing fear but little harm. "Our army is many times stronger! Our forces will crush you all."

Nicci said smugly, "And yet you will still be dead."

Screaming with frustration, Ava rattled the trees

again. Nicci shoved with her gift, and the spirit swirled away. "I will tell General Utros where you are. He wants to be the one to kill you."

After Ava vanished, Nicci looked into the empty air. Her defenders muttered in fear, but she scoffed. "Let him try."

CHAPTER 79

The ships of the Serrimundi navy sailed north, following the Norukai fleet. The serpent ships raced along toward Tanimura, completely unaware of the armored vessels in pursuit. Olgya had summoned just enough mist to create a veil that hid them from the Norukai lookouts.

Harborlord Otto rode at the front of the *Mist Maiden,* wrapping his hands around the rail. Captain Ganley stood beside him, shading his eyes. "Are you tense? Or eager?"

"They are ahead of us, and I don't want to miss the battle," Otto said. "I'm glad we saved Serrimundi from destruction, but we're still part of this war. Imagine how much harm a whole Norukai fleet will inflict on Tanimura! A small raiding party nearly wrecked Serrimundi harbor!"

Chuckling, Ganley stroked his beard. "But this time we know how to fight back. And when we come at them unexpectedly, it will be like a knife in their backs. It is what they deserve."

Otto looked down to the water where the prow cut the waves into white foam. He was startled to see sleek figures swimming beside the *Mist Maiden.* At first he thought they were dolphins, but he recoiled when he recognized the human forms, the scaly skin, jagged fins. "Selka! Those are selka swimming beside our ship."

Ganley watched hundreds of the sleek forms streak toward Tanimura, like escorts for the Serrimundi navy. "I don't think we need to worry about them. The selka and the Norukai are mortal enemies. Ours is not the flesh they wish to devour."

"We will feed them plenty after today's battle," Otto said.

All of the Serrimundi vessels had been armored with metal plating at Nicci's insistence, and now their crews were trained with swords, spears, and boat hooks. Dozens of expert archers were aboard each ship, ready with baskets of pitch-wrapped fire arrows.

Olgya joined them at the bow, her hair undone from her usual braids, the strands uneven. She had used her gift to summon wind, pushing the metal-clad ships at greater speed and closing the distance to the Norukai. Now that they approached, she stretched out her fingers and relaxed, undoing the mist spell that had created a blurring veil around their ships. The fog dissipated, revealing them . . . but the Norukai were looking forward, expecting nothing from the open sea behind them.

Ahead, Otto could see Tanimura with its great harbor ten times the size of Serrimundi's. The tremendous battle had already begun, and he heard the shouts and screams, the clang of metal, the hulls splintering as ships collided with the harbor blockade. The Norukai rowed furiously, slamming into the line of defensive ships.

"Nathan is there," Olgya said, nodding to herself, "as well as Oron and Perri. They are putting up a strong gifted defense."

Otto could see many wrecked serpent ships sinking after being battered by a succession of huge waves. "They've done good work already."

"And we'll do more." Olgya spread her arms wide and brought them together with a resounding clap. With the release of her gift, she sent a shock wave through the water, creating a line that was at first a ripple, building higher and higher into a great rolling wave that hurtled toward the rear of the attacking serpent ships. "Our first blow will get their attention."

In the smooth wake behind Olgya's wave, the harborlord saw streaking scaled figures, hundreds of the muscular selka as they raced forward to join the attack. The rolling wave crashed into the rear line of serpent ships.

On their decks, the Norukai fighters whirled and screamed in outrage at the surprise attack. Then the selka surged up the hulls.

Otto laughed, and Captain Ganley shouted for his archers. Within moments, a blizzard of flaming arrows arced through the sky and pelted the wood and sails of the raider ships.

But that was only the beginning. Closing in like the jaws of a trap, the Serrimundi ships joined the battle.

Nathan fought to keep his head above the blood-churned water. Grieve's damaged ship creaked against the weathered krakener, scraping the new armor plates with a flurry of sparks. When the waves buffeted him, he was nearly crushed between the two hulls, but he used his gift to shove the ships apart and just barely save himself. He sprayed water between his lips. "That would have been an embarrassing end for a great wizard."

On the *Chaser*'s deck above, he could hear the fighting, the clash of metal and battering clubs. A dying Norukai splashed into the water beside him, clawing at the gaping wound in his chest.

Nathan's boots and soaked cape weighed him down, but he kept himself afloat in the rough waves and worked his way along the side of the *Chaser*. He yelled up, "Someone throw me a rope! I can help if I get up there." Since they were fighting for their lives, though, no one paid attention to the man in the water.

Nathan knew Bannon and Lila were skilled fighters, but the Norukai were nearly inhuman. Frustrated, he dug in with his nails, trying to climb the wet and slimy hull boards. His boot found purchase on a clump of old barnacles, and he pulled himself higher, reaching up until he caught the frame of a porthole above the waterline. He grasped the lip of wood with his fingertips and used it for purchase, straining to climb just a little higher until he was out of the water, dripping like a waterlogged dog.

Partway up the hull, he found himself stuck. He couldn't reach the rail still two feet above his extended arm. He clawed for a higher grip, struggled to keep his footing, but the leather soles of his boots were smooth, and they slipped on the boards. He tried to hold on to the porthole frame, but found himself falling backward. Instinctively, he used the gift to create a wall of wind. Under normal circumstances, he would have used the push of air against an enemy, but now he used the same magic to form a cushion beneath him. With a hard shove, he used the burst of air to throw his body higher until he tumbled over the rail. He sprawled across the deck, which was slippery with blood and old slime.

He rolled to his feet, ready to fight. Bannon and Lila

faced him, panting hard to catch their breath, both covered in blood. The headless corpse of King Grieve lay on the deck, with an apelike Norukai woman sprawled next to him.

Captain Jared and his men quickly cornered the few remaining Norukai aboard the *Chaser*. Feeling left out, Nathan called a carefully directed bolt of lightning to blast the last raider standing.

Bedraggled and drenched, Nathan stepped up to Bannon and clasped his shoulder. "Are you all right, my boy?"

The young swordsman stared at the headless body of the Norukai king, and a smile slowly dawned on his face. "Yes, I'm just fine."

When Nathan shook his head, clumps of white hair flopped from side to side. With a sniff, he summoned his gift, evaporated the water, and refreshed his clothes. "If we are going to have even a small victory, then my appearance should appropriately reflect it."

Bannon looked at the blood on his sword, Grieve's blood. "Thank you again for this fine blade, Nathan. I would have killed as many with Sturdy, but your sword was perfectly acceptable."

"Glad you enjoyed it, my boy, but this little tussle is just a tiny ripple in the overall battle for Tanimura." He looked toward the shore. "We have much more to do." The momentum of the Norukai navy had been broken, but many serpent ships had slipped past the blockade and pressed to shore, where the raiders were now ransacking the waterfront district. Fires rose from the city.

Then Nathan stared in disbelief as General Utros's army appeared in the hills above Tanimura!

"Dear spirits, we—" Before he could get the words out, Nathan felt a black surge inside, pain that echoed through his chest and entire body. The remnants of Ivan seized his heart, and Nathan dropped to his knees on the deck, gasping, unable to scream. His heart fought to keep beating.

Thump, thump. Thump, thump.

He had struggled to keep control of his new heart ever since Fleshmancer Andre had finished his work, but all of Nathan's good deeds had not cleansed the corruption of that evil, violent man. He grimaced, curled back his lips. "No! You are dead. You . . . cannot . . . have your . . . heart."

Thump, thump. Thump, thump!

Sparkles of pain drifted like black snowflakes inside his eyes. He clawed at his chest, but Ivan's heart twisted as if turning itself inside out to punish Nathan. "You are not there!" he wheezed through clenched teeth. "You're not real!"

Lila and Bannon both grabbed his shoulders. "Nathan, what is it? How can we help?"

He struggled against the spirit of Ivan.

Thump, thump.

Thump, thump.

Thump.

Nothing.

Nathan's eyes went wide as he felt his heart stop. He couldn't breathe, and he fell forward onto the deck. He could sense nothing, only a void surrounding him like a cocoon. He twitched, trying to reassert control over his body, over his heart.

Bannon and Lila were shaking him, and the krakener crew was shouting. He screamed silently inside his head as darkness suffocated him. Flickers of green mist gathered around him, and he heard a tempting call, a whisper, then a demand. *"You are dead. You are mine."*

Was it the Keeper? Or Ivan?

I am not, he thought, but his lips could not form words. His anger increased. The last vestiges of his gift tightened around him, and Nathan used every scrap of energy and determination he had. *You cannot have your heart back.*

With a surge of his gift, he pushed his heart, made it beat, tore the black presence to tatters. Ivan retreated into his bloodstream, but still lurked inside him. The greenish veil faded from his vision.

Thump, thump.

Thump, thump. Thump, thump.

He heaved a great gasp of air. Bannon pulled him upright, pounded his back. "Nathan, are you all right?"

"I'm alive. I just had a . . . disagreement with a visitor inside me." He dragged himself to his feet, but wobbled. "I am all right." He brushed aside their concerns and turned to watch the enormous army of General Utros encroach on the outskirts of Tanimura. He knew he needed to be there, to stay alive so he could help Nicci and the others with the grand fight.

At the waterfront, many buildings were on fire, and he could see the furious clash as General Zimmer and the D'Haran army tried to hold the harbor district from the rampaging Norukai. But the enormous army of General Utros was a far larger threat.

Out in the water there were at least forty serpent ships still intact. Nathan climbed to the krakener's raised deck next to a disheveled Captain Jared, and they both gazed past the naval battle to the open sea beyond the harbor, where an unexpected group of warships was closing from behind. Nathan let out a cheer.

Covered with blood, Bannon shaded his eyes. "Look! We have reinforcements!"

Lila gave a nod of appreciation. "The navy from Ser-rimundi, of course. They followed, fully armed. They have come to join the fight."

An outcry of dismay rose from the remaining serpent ships, as the crews realized they would be crushed between two groups of attackers.

Nathan smiled. "That should take care of King Grieve's navy."

"Do not count a victory just yet." Lila turned to look at the city, where the breathtaking forces of General Utros were closing in. "We still have to defeat that army, too."

Nathan realized their skills would be more vital for the battle inside the main city. He shook his head. "No, I do not believe we can count on a victory anytime soon. Captain Jared, we need you to take us to shore—posthaste!"

CHAPTER 80

The smell of blood, sweat, and dust combined into a powerful and, for Zimmer, all-too-familiar odor. Though sickening, the smell also fired the blood in his veins. It served as the fuel that kept him fighting.

Tanimura's waterfront warehouses burned behind him, and the blaze had already spread to another block of large buildings. Bitter smoke mixed with the reek of burning goods from the dockside market.

As Zimmer squeezed his thighs to control his horse amid the mayhem, he could not count all the fallen D'Haran soldiers in the streets. A few more serpent ships ground up to the docks and released a new horde of wild barbarians. But Zimmer called the D'Haran army to shift their offensive. As a well-trained tactical commander, he knew that the ancient army of General Utros was a far greater threat than these chaotic Noru-kai. He directed his charge instead to meet the first lines of the invading ancient army.

He raised his sword and yelled from the saddle, "All cavalry! Bear the brunt of the enemy advance, break their momentum. After that, archers, foot soldiers, it will be your turn."

The horse hooves clattered on the paved streets as they rushed toward the first division of the Utros army. One large force curved along the hills toward the Hagen Woods and the lower city, and Nicci and her enthusiastic militia fighters had gone to cut off the advance there. Another segment of the army, ten thousand or more under the banner of the veteran First Commander Enoch, marched directly toward the heart of the city.

Utros's strategy was clear. They would overwhelm and hold the center of Tanimura, then spread conquering forces throughout the districts, while the Norukai continued to ravage the harbor and the waterfront.

Thorn and Lyesse sprinted just behind Zimmer. Even on foot, the two morazeth easily kept up with the cavalry riders. Thorn wasn't even breathing hard as she called out, "Today is a day for much killing, General."

Lyesse chuckled. "I am glad we do not have to hide in the bushes anymore. I much prefer a full fight!"

Gripping the hilt of his sword as he rode, Zimmer nodded to the two women. "You are welcome to cause as much mayhem as you like."

On the other side of the city, General Linden had marched his large portion of the D'Haran army to meet another division of the ancient army. He remembered a dictum he had pounded into his soldiers when they faced impossible odds. "Every war is a succession of battles. Each battle is won after many fights, hand to hand, sword to sword, life to life."

The D'Haran cavalry did not slow their charge as they careened into the ancient army. The enemy soldiers fought with an odd mixture of precision and abandon, and Zimmer recognized that something was not right about them. They seemed gaunter than the enemy he had fought at Cliffwall, more spent.

His foot soldiers and archers jogged behind the cavalry, maintaining the general shape of their ranks. Just ahead, Zimmer could see First Commander Enoch, a tall hardened veteran whose scarred face held the burden of countless battles. From his dappled mount, Enoch's icy eyes locked on Zimmer's and knew his true foe. Although Zimmer was young for his rank, he carried the weight of many battles as well.

As if their minds were connected, both commanders yelled a challenge at the same time, and the two men crashed together. Zimmer's horse reared up, giving him height as he hacked down with his sword. His blade struck against the veteran's chain mail, but Enoch parried, clashed his sword against his opponent's. The older man surprised Zimmer by releasing the reins and grabbing a dagger in his other hand. He caught Zimmer in the side, cut into his leather armor, but only enough to scratch his ribs.

The screams, the impact of steel, the terrified snorts of horses, and the pounding of hooves swirled around him like tangible thing. Zimmer's horse skittered sideways, and Enoch pressed in, his face filled with pinpoint concentration for the battle at hand. Zimmer wheeled his mount and used the saddle as a fulcrum for his attack. The two horses were like equine battering rams.

The line of D'Haran archers arrived behind the cavalry, nocking their arrows and launching a fusillade of projectiles over the heads of the front lines to shower down upon the ranks behind Enoch. Hundreds of enemy soldiers dropped, and the archers let fly as fast as they could nock and draw. D'Haran foot soldiers came behind the archers, hacking at any encroaching enemy warriors to protect the bowmen.

Oliver and Peretta each carried a large hunting knife,

which was easier to wield than a sword. Never straying far from her two friends, Amber did her own fighting. The gifted young novices were not strong enough to unleash sweeping devastation like Nicci or Nathan, but they were clever and effective with their strikes. Together, they used their gift to work small, effective spells. With flickers of fire, they heated the hilts of the enemy swords, which made the yelping soldiers drop them in pain.

Peretta called out to her friends, "Intense fire is difficult to make, but we can use bright light instead. That's easy. Blind them!"

Oliver grinned. "Yes, the flash spell!" He twisted his fingers and muttered the words he needed for focus. A burst of light blossomed directly before the eyes of an attacking soldier like an erupting star. The man slapped a hand to his eyes and stumbled into another soldier. Unable to see, he swung instinctively and stabbed his own comrade.

Triumphant, Oliver, Peretta, and Amber repeated their flash spell in the faces of other warriors.

Arabella and Mab, the only two Sisters of the Light still with Zimmer's troops, were more formidable opponents. They rode on each flank of the main cavalry and hurled buffeting winds strong enough to stagger the enemy ranks.

"By the Creator, we have our work cut out for us," Mab said.

A glowing female form swooped in over the advancing army, the pale shade of Utros's dead sorceress. Shrieking with mad laughter, Ava's spirit joined First Commander Enoch. Though intangible, Ava could still use the remnants of her gift to send disruptive waves through the D'Haran soldiers and spook their horses.

Ava swooped directly through the mounts, terrifying them, and the panicked horses pawed at the air, wheeling sideways and colliding into one another.

Ava's features transformed into the face of a gaunt demon with a wide, fang-filled mouth, her eyes sunken into dark hollows. The D'Haran soldiers slashed the air, their swords cutting harmlessly through her wispy form.

First Commander Enoch kicked his horse in the ribs and charged forward. Zimmer brought up his sword to parry the blow, but Enoch struck with all the might of his battle-hardened muscles. Suddenly a bright flash like a solar flare burst in front of Enoch's face, blinding him. He grabbed at his eyes, too late to shield them from the dazzling burst.

Oliver, Peretta, and Amber cheered, then turned their unique attack upon other enemy soldiers.

Zimmer's horse slammed into his opponent's, hurling the old veteran from his saddle. Enoch landed and rolled before stumbling back to his feet, unable to see but sweeping his sword from side to side. Knowing that First Commander Enoch was his main foe, Zimmer swung out of his saddle and dropped to the ground. Enoch stabbed at the air as he struggled to see.

Nearby, Thorn and Lyesse fought with wild abandon, grinning wolfishly with a weapon in each hand. Spatters of blood flecked their skin. The scant black leather garments provided little protection, but neither morazeth needed it. They hacked from victim to victim, moving on to the next target even before the last one fell to the ground.

"Fourteen!" Thorn cried as she stabbed another man through the ribs.

"Sixteen for me," Lyesse said. "You better catch up, sister."

"We will take stock when the day is done."

A giant-statured warrior loomed in front of Lyesse. Each of his biceps was larger than her head as he lifted a two-handed sword, but Lyesse slashed him across the stomach, then slid her blade through the gap in his thigh armor and into his groin. She dodged out of the way as the giant bleated like a sheep in the slaughter pen and crashed to the ground.

Ava's spirit swooped in to terrorize Thorn and Lyesse, but when the intangible spirit tried to pass through their bodies with a disruptive tingle, the protective runes blocked her, and she ricocheted off of them. Flustered, the dead sorceress whirled off to attack someone else.

As his horse galloped away, Zimmer regained his balance on the ground. For the moment, he would face First Commander Enoch on foot. He shouted, "My name is General Zimmer, and I command the D'Haran army. I want you to know the name of the man who will defeat you."

The veteran was still blinking the dazzling colors from his eyes, but he sensed Zimmer close to him. He raised his sword and struck out, poking the air and yelling. "You haven't defeated me yet!" Enoch drove forward in a flurry, chasing the other man's voice. Each time his sword struck Zimmer's, his aim grew better. "You have seen our army, Zimmer. Why bother fighting? Surrender and join the conquerors. Your bodies don't have to litter this entire city."

"The Keeper will take me when he wishes," Zimmer said. He was impressed at how well the man fought.

They clashed again. Enoch squinted, blinking furiously as his vision began to return. Two riderless horses charged by, nearly trampling them, and Zimmer jumped out of the way. With foam flying from the bits in their mouths, the frightened horses ran away.

Zimmer spun to defend himself as Ava's shimmering spirit rose in front of him, laughing. She swooped toward him like a vulture, harrying him, and he instinctively tried to block her with his sword. The green glow intensified with her anger. As her intangible form engulfed him, he felt her dark, twisted power oozing inside his body like an appalling violation, a filthy finger probing into his heart.

Ava's spirit had spied for General Utros, exposed the hidden Cliffwall archive. Because of her, Utros had attacked Cliffwall, which brought about the destruction of the archive and the death of Prelate Verna. This spirit had caused so much misery, so much death!

As Ava swirled around him, flickering, Zimmer hacked in the air with his sword. Her mocking laughter taunted him, and he tried to stab her, even though he knew he could never kill a spirit. The green glow flared brighter.

With all his strength, he thrust his sword through the dead sorceress's chest, but the killing thrust passed through her as if she were no more than smoke. Instead, he felt the hard impact of something solid crunch against the blade. He thrust harder, shoving the point all the way through leather and chain mail, and then a solid chest.

Shrieking, Ava swirled away to reveal to Zimmer that he had skewered First Commander Enoch through the heart. The old veteran had lurched up to him, hidden by the dead sorceress's flickering form.

Impaled on the sword, Enoch coughed blood. His sword slipped out of his limp fingers and dropped with a clang to the ground. He touched the steel, blinking in wonder. "This is . . . death. At last." His body fell as gravity pulled him off of Zimmer's sword. "There you are, Camille . . . my love."

Ava flickered away, furious. Enoch dropped onto his side with blood bubbling from the wound in his chest. The veteran stretched out a gauntlet, reaching for something that only he could see.

Though the furious battle continued around him, Zimmer stared. Time seemed to stop, and he gave his enemy a chance to die. Enoch gasped, "Alex and Aaron, my sons . . ." He smiled. "You no longer have to beg for me. The Keeper can have what he wants."

He slumped back and died. Zimmer's vision was uncertain, but he thought he saw faint forms rising from the ground, arms outstretched and pulling another dim outline down with them.

But even with the first commander dead, the invading army came forward, unstoppable.

CHAPTER 81

Even with as much harm as they had done to the Norukai fleet and the army of General Utros, Nicci could see that Tanimura was about to fall. She had not seen a battle so overwhelming since the armies of Emperor Jagang besieged the People's Palace.

The surviving members of her militia withdrew from the Hagen Woods, leaving a bloodbath behind them, but as they crossed into the city, they encountered waves of constant fighting. Utros's main force pushed toward the center of Tanimura, while other contingents spilled into every street, where they ransacked buildings and battled their way through makeshift barricades the defenders had erected. The fighting took place in houses, alleys, rooftops, and streets, and the city's outnumbered defenders used that to their advantage.

In an open public square ahead, Nicci spotted the banners of General Linden and his D'Haran soldiers, and they were fighting in what looked like a last stand. She led her militia there to join them in the fight; she could see they needed her.

The Hidden People accompanied her, racing along in their gray robes. Many had fallen in the Hagen Woods, but they did not count their dead. Breathing hard, young Asha had a knife-edged smile. "We traveled across the continent for you, Nicci. We will fight for you now."

The rest of the Hidden People were just as determined, carrying swords from the weapons stockpile they had stewarded in Orogang. For more than a thousand years, they had waited for General Utros to return, but their hero had cruelly turned against them. Now the deadly people, and the pride of ferocious sand panthers, might shift the balance here and save Linden and his troops.

Fighting their way through city streets, Nicci's followers slew hundreds more as they drove like a wedge through the invaders, cutting off an entire group and killing them down to the last man.

Ahead, Linden's regiments had taken up a defensive position in a square enclosed by high buildings. His D'Haran soldiers stood several ranks deep, with an outer line of shields as a barricade. Archers in the rear launched volleys of arrows into the enemy army, but the invaders crashed into them like waves against a rocky shore. Linden shouted ever-more-desperate commands, and a standard-bearer beside him raised a flag showing the colors of D'Hara and the stylized letter "R" for the House of Rahl.

The defensive line held firm until an unexpected part of the flank began to crumble. Under the constant barrage, the shield line buckled and dozens of enemy warriors raged through as if it were a hemorrhaging wound. They ran past the shield line, which then closed behind them and re-formed, stronger than before. Nicci smiled at the clever trick. Thirty enemy warriors, now trapped inside the line, were all cut down, one by one.

Amid the great ground battle, unexpected lightning

drew a zigzag line in the air, and the energy struck an ancient subcommander and his adjutant at the front of the enemy charge. The blast shattered the victims into smoking pieces.

Looking for the source of the surprising attack, Nicci was amazed to see a wizard with long white hair dressed in a fine cape and vest. "Nathan!" He couldn't hear her over the sounds of battle, but when she extended her fingers to the sky and brought them down, Nicci drew her own lightning bolt to incinerate three more soldiers next to the ones he himself had killed.

That got the wizard's attention. Nathan waved, and beside him Bannon and the morazeth Lila also shouted, glad to see her.

Using a battering ram of wind to clear the way, Nicci led her surviving militia members to reinforce Linden's troops, disrupting the ancient army and causing a panic. The prowling sand panthers tore at the enemy soldiers, but Mrra herself was reluctant to leave Nicci's side, now that they were reunited at last.

Nicci fought her way close to General Linden and his beleaguered troops. She unleashed another bolt of branched lightning, which strafed the front lines of enemy fighters, and still more of them flooded into the city. Already exhausted, Nicci dug deep into her reserves of energy.

Knowing the stakes, she resorted to a darker form of destruction, pulling upon dangerous Subtractive Magic. She called upon that side of the gift only when it was absolutely necessary, for those were the skills she had learned when she was a Sister of the Dark. Now she served the D'Haran Empire, and she served Richard. Her heart was strong enough to handle it.

She opened herself, stretched out her gift in both the

positive and negative directions to draw another bolt of lightning, but this time she joined it with an infinitely dark crack in the sky, like a mirror image entangled with the white bolt. The zigzagging blast killed more than a hundred in a single strike. The fury of her lightning stunned the front ranks of the enemy division, driving back their charge and giving Nicci's militia the window they needed to surge forward and reinforce Linden's troops.

"Thank you, Sorceress." Linden looked ready to drop from exhaustion and blood loss. His shield was splintered, and his leather armor and chain mail were ragged from many blows.

Nathan strode up to her, grinning. "Dear spirits, I'm glad to see you! I know you rarely use Subtractive Magic, but that was sorely needed." He watched the Hidden People join the defensive line and raised his eyebrows. "Oh, I see you found some friends."

Bannon's ginger hair was matted with blood and sweat, but his hazel eyes shone. "Now we can all fight together! The Norukai are mostly defeated, and Captain Jared took us to the docks so we could help here in the city." Barely able to contain his own news, he blurted out, "At least King Grieve is dead."

That got Nicci's attention. "How did he die? Badly, I hope."

"The boy killed him," Lila answered with clear pride. "Cut off his head."

Nicci rewarded the young swordsman with a gratified nod. "Well deserved."

"We broke the backbone of the Norukai fleet out there on the water, and the Serrimundi navy arrived just in time to attack them from behind." Nathan looked beyond the square to the sweeping harbor, where innumerable serpent ships were sunk or burning in the water. But the Norukai did not go quietly. The fighting continued to rage on the water, and many of the landed raiders still pillaged the streets.

Worse, though, General Utros's army continued to ransack Tanimura, and several divisions were closing in from all sides. From the defended square, Nicci could see Utros in his distinctive horned helmet surveying the attack from high ground. The general sat on his black stallion, directing his troops with the painted sorceress at his side. Given time, his army could simply trample Tanimura to dust, leaving only a flat expanse of rubble, just like Halsband Island.

Smoke rolled into the sky from the burning buildings, and the air resounded with battle. Screaming seagulls wheeled overhead, anxious for the feast they would have with all the dead bodies piled in the streets.

Nathan looked ashen as he caught his breath. "I have used so much of my magic already today that I'm afraid I have little left." He regarded her with relief. "At least you can still draw on Subtractive Magic, which is something the rest of us cannot do."

"If that is what's necessary," Nicci answered with a frown. "We promised Richard we would protect D'Hara, and he knows my abilities. I'll do anything to stop Utros from marching north into the New World. Richard has his own problems there. He left this to me."

She had to stop the enemy here and now, because she loved Richard too much. She longed to see him one last time, though she had long ago accepted that she would never have his love in return. Nevertheless, his respect, his friendship, his complete confidence gave Nicci strength she didn't know she had. He *believed* in her . . . and he said he'd given her everything she needed. Richard would never abandon her.

She thought of the small bone box and the glowing constructed spell. Despite her best efforts, she had been unable to decipher what Richard meant. *Life to the living. Death to the dead.* What did that mean? And how could she use it?

So many brave fighters were already dead, and Utros's ancient army kept coming. The great military force should have been dead many centuries ago, but the petrification spell from the wizards of Ildakar had thwarted the Keeper. Every single fighter wearing the flame symbol should have gone to the underworld long, long ago.

Death to the dead. . . .

With a sudden idea, she snatched out the bone box from her pocket and held it in her bloodstained palm. When the blood touched the bone, the energy of spilled life affected the delicate container and the scratched symbols. The markings intensified, glowed.

Life to the living. Death to the dead.

Thoughts clicked together in her mind, and she suddenly understood what was necessary, the missing piece she had forgotten. The answer had been there, but she hadn't looked for it in the right way. She hadn't thought the way Richard would think.

When trying to analyze the glowing, rotating sphere, she had performed a test she knew well. An obvious test. But while she had used Subtractive Magic to ignite a verification web, she had not used it on the *constructed spell* itself.

It was a form of constructed spell that contained a bit of original magic from the design of the Wizard's

Keep, from a time when wizards also possessed Subtractive Magic. Such a defensive spell from the Keep, she realized, had to contain Subtractive elements. Richard would have known that. Why hadn't she seen it right away? No wonder Nathan, the Cliffwall scholars, and the Sisters of the Light had not been able to help her.

Her pulse raced faster as the answers came to her in the din of the surrounding battle. Without Subtractive Magic, the spell would be sterile! That was why Nicci could not find anything meaningful when she had initially tried to decipher the contents by touching the tiny sphere with her power.

It would not be meaningful without the direct injection of the Subtractive element! That was the missing piece.

Now she knew what to do, and it was indeed everything she needed, just as Richard said.

Nicci snapped shut the bone box again, covering the glowing spell. A hard smile crossed her face. She saw General Utros on higher ground outside the city, but he was far away, with an entire army between himself and Nicci. She had to get closer.

"I need to get a message to Utros," she said. "An ultimatum."

Hidden People slipped in among the attacking soldiers, killing many and then darting away. They were used to moving in the shadows. They crowded in among General Linden's armed warriors, and Nicci called to get their attention. "Asha! I need you. I have a task for the Hidden People, and the war may depend on it."

Asha killed another enemy soldier and withdrew, still holding her bloody knife. Five more Hidden People heard the call and fell back to present themselves. "We are ready to do whatever you need, Nicci."

She leaned closer to the few eager volunteers. "No matter what it takes, I need you to get a message to General Utros. Go around the army or go through them, hide, dodge, but get to him by any means necessary." She pointed to the distant figure high above the storm of battle. "Tell the general that I demand to speak to him. Have him meet me on Halsband Island." She paused, and then added with a hard smile, "Tell him it is Nicci—the one who killed his sorceress Ava. He will come."

Nathan's eyes went wide. "Dear spirits, do you know what you're doing?"

She felt the bone box in her pocket. "I'm absolutely certain. Richard told me this is all I need. General Utros has to come face me."

Young Asha nodded and looked to her fellow Hidden People. "We will go for you, Nicci. At least one of us will deliver the message, at all costs."

They flitted away through the streets, where their shadowy cloaks made them invisible in the raging battle.

As the fight continued and the ancient soldiers swept through the streets of Tanimura, Oliver struggled not to feel dismay. For every soldier that fell, ten more swept in behind him. It was like trying to empty the sea with a bucket.

Fearless, Peretta stood holding up her hands and curling her fingers to summon bright flashes of light she could throw into the faces of the enemy. The ancient soldiers saw what she was doing, though, and that made Peretta a target.

Oliver watched an archer draw an arrow and aim

toward her, pulling back the string. "Peretta!" Oliver screamed, but she couldn't move in time as the archer let fly. Instead, he remembered the training and pushed a gust of wind, creating a burst of air that deflected the arrow's trajectory just enough so that it barely scratched the young woman's shoulder as it streaked past.

Peretta ducked, wincing at the fresh wound, then grinned at him. "Thank you, Oliver."

In retaliation, she blinded the archer with a flash of light, and Oliver summoned a small burst of heat that snapped the bowstring. Released, the bow sprang back, smacking the soldier in the head.

Amber joined them. "We have to find a better way to fight. These spells, one at a time, can't defeat such a huge army."

"We're fighting as best we can," Peretta said.

Amber's face was flushed. "But everything we studied at Cliffwall, all that we learned—there must be something we can use!"

Oliver shook his head. "We found the magic to summon all those poisonous scorpions from beneath the ground. That proved to be quite effective." He sighed. "But there are no scorpions here in the city."

"Not scorpions . . . but what else does a city have?" Amber asked. Her lips quirked in an eager smile, waiting for them to answer.

Oliver didn't know what she meant. He had very little experience with cities. Cliffwall was clean and compact, and he had rarely been elsewhere. Cities like Tanimura seemed dirty to him, crowded and unpleasant. Peretta also shook her head.

Amber's eyes gleamed. "Rats! Beneath any city there are thousands of rats."

"Oh! We could use the same summoning magic,"

Peretta said, understanding what she meant. "Call up the rats from the sewers, from the alleys, gutters, and midden heaps."

A D'Haran captain with his group of beleaguered defenders shouted a cry of defiance as they were surrounded by overwhelming enemies. Raising his sword, the captain yelled for the others to join him in a fight to the death. He led a hundred soldiers against a wall of ancient warriors marching through a square.

"Quickly!" Amber knelt and placed her hands against the flagstones of the square. Peretta and Oliver joined her, shoulder-to-shoulder. "Remember what we used for the scorpions. Call them—call them all! Can you feel them?"

Oliver sensed the tingling in his fingers. "Yes, I think so. Little and furry, but with sharp teeth."

"And hungry," Peretta added. "They are very hungry."

With their combined gift, they reached out, sent a call. While the minds of the scorpions had been tiny and susceptible, the rats were more intelligent. But the three young companions were able to convince the rodents that this was what they *wanted* to do.

Oliver could sense scurrying feet, furry bodies rising up from the sewers, running through the gutters. The creatures swirled out of Tanimura's underbelly, all claws and teeth, naked pink tails and red eyes.

The D'Haran captain's sortie slowed, defeated by a horde of enemy soldiers that surrounded them. Blood sprayed as ten enemies fought against every defender, hacking them down one by one, until the brave captain himself was dragged to the ground.

As the defenders fell, though, the rats boiled up from the streets in a brown wave of death, just like all the scorpions that had erupted from the desert floor back at Cliffwall. They were dirty vermin that lived beneath the moist and noisome shadows of the streets, but they also defended their city.

The invaders howled and flailed as they suddenly faced this ravenous wave that fell upon them, thousands of furry bodies that crawled up their legs and gnawed their skin, tore through chinks in their armor. Though they thrashed their weapons and clawed with their gauntleted hands, the enemy soldiers could not fight against it. Their voices became a panicked outcry, and their disciplined, regimented advance across the square broke apart.

Oliver, Peretta, and Amber watched, shaking with fear and awe, as innumerable rats fed upon the enemy.

CHAPTER 82

Tanimura had already fallen. General Utros knew he had won.

From his high vantage above the city, he could watch the ebb and flow of the fighting. He had encountered setbacks, as in every war. One entire division led by Second Commander Halders had entered the thick forest in a flanking move, and had never emerged. Something in that dark woods had defeated them.

But Utros had more soldiers, many more. King Grieve's Norukai had caused great carnage in the harbor and on the waterfront, but they were mostly broken. He had never relied on those brutish allies for this conquest, though he was happy to let them bear the brunt of so many casualties. He would mop up the rest of them as soon as he quelled the other fighting, but that wouldn't take long.

First Commander Enoch had taken five thousand men in a central prong straight into Tanimura. Second Commander Arros drove another division of five thousand along the western hills and into the rich nobles' district. More of his soldiers, tens of thousands, were still on the outskirts waiting to surge in and plunder. Tanimura could do nothing to stop his victory.

But he couldn't understand what Nicci was up to. What did her brash message mean? She was in no position to make demands.

As Utros stood pondering, the pale young captive struggled in his grip. He squeezed his gauntleted hand around the girl's throat and lifted her off the ground. Her small feet jittered and twitched, trying to touch the dirt, but Utros raised her higher, squeezed tighter. With minimal effort he could crush her larynx and snap her neck, but he needed the girl to speak first. "Tell me again what Nicci said. Every word."

"Meet her," the captive gurgled. "Nicci demands it. On Halsband Island." The girl flailed her hand toward the barren island connected to the main city by new, rickety bridges.

Ruva chuckled. "Each of the messengers said the same words."

"Why? What does she want?" Utros pressed his face closer to the dying girl, who showed no fear. Her mouth gaped like that of a fish left to bake in the sun, but she couldn't speak any words. He paused, furrowing his brow. "I recognize your garments, your pale skin. You are one of the worms hiding in our sacred capital of Orogang. You attacked my men."

The young woman clutched uselessly at his hand, trying to draw a breath. "You attacked *us*! Orogang has always been ours."

"Orogang is *mine*—my capital." Utros squeezed tighter, and her eyes bulged. "Why does Nicci want me to come to that island? *Why?*" Forgetting himself, he squeezed too hard, and her neck cracked. The girl fell limp.

Disgusted, Utros tossed her body to the ground, discarding her beside the other four Hidden People who had delivered exactly the same message. Through his golden half mask, he frowned at all the broken corpses, turned to Ruva, then to the open island. "Is it a trap?"

Ruva's eyes carried an edge of madness. "It may be a trap, but it will not work. Never! We are stronger!" The sorceress had grown more violent, more volatile than he had seen her before. She claimed that the Keeper called to both her and her sister through the veil, but Utros would not release them to the underworld. Not yet.

Ruva suddenly calmed, considered, then shrugged. "How could Nicci possibly lay an ambush there? It is open, indefensible." She smiled. "No, she wants to surrender, beloved Utros. There is no other explanation."

Utros shook his head in consternation. "Why would she do that? Even if we come to terms, Nicci thinks that I can snap my fingers and stop the army? They're starving, and now at last they have their victory. I can't control them, nor would I want to. After today they will all eat well even if they have to pick Tanimura clean." He swelled his chest. "Afterward, my army will be strong and ready to march again, the way they were meant to be."

"If Nicci wants to surrender, let her do it," Ruva said, sounding hungry. "Then we can kill her."

Ava's spirit shimmered before them, pale and insubstantial, more diluted than he had ever seen her. "Kill Nicci the way she killed me!" Ava folded herself on top of her twin sister, and they both laughed. "You must confront her. She creates her own doom."

"Yes, beloved Utros. You must do this. We want her, my sister and I. And you want her. Nicci opens her arms to embrace death, and we will kill her." Ruva was ready to explode with eagerness.

Utros remained wary, but he allowed himself to be convinced. He also wanted to crush the sorceress who had taken his precious Ava from him. "Yes, you deserve your revenge, and I will grant it. I wanted to face Nicci on the battleground, but this saves me the trouble of finding her." He turned away from the dead messengers, thinking no more of them. "Bring a hundred troops as an escort. We will meet her on the island and put an end to this." He bunched his fists. "She is a fool."

The joy in Thorn's voice was palpable, and she showed her exuberance by decapitating her opponent. "That's seventy for me, sister." The ancient warrior's neck stump spouted blood, and the lumbering body took two staggering steps before it slumped forward. "Seventy! Can you beat that?"

"Only sixty-five for me," Lyesse said. With greater intensity, she spun about and dove into two armored soldiers who closed in on her. She stabbed one in the stomach, whirled and kicked the other back, knocking him off balance so that the edge of his sword missed her. She withdrew her blade from the already dying man, stabbed again to kill him, and turned to dispatch the first man she had knocked off balance. "Sixty-six and sixty-seven! I will catch up with you."

Thorn laughed. "You may try." She turned, determined, leaping forward—

And ran directly into a serrated spear point.

A broad-shouldered man gritted his teeth and shoved the spear harder. He grinned as he skewered the lean morazeth on his weapon, pushing the spear all the way through her abdomen and out her back.

Thorn coughed blood. Her knees went weak, and she

could barely stand, but the spear itself held her up. She grabbed the shaft, tried to hold on.

Lyesse screamed and hacked at another warrior in her way, wounding him. She didn't bother to follow through as she leaped toward her sister morazeth.

The spear wielder wrenched his weapon, tried to yank the blade back so he could defend himself against Lyesse's furious attack, but Thorn clutched the shaft and refused to let it go, even as she died. She prevented him from having his weapon back.

Lyesse screamed again and struck down with such fury that she amputated both of the warrior's hands that gripped the weapon. Her blade splintered the shaft itself. The spear wielder stared in horror at his bleeding wrists, and she stabbed him in the throat. He had killed her companion, her sister morazeth!

Without the spear to hold her up, Thorn crumpled to the ground.

Lyesse was deaf to all of the battlefield sounds. Thorn was breathing heavily. Her words came out in liquid, bubbly chokes. "Seventy killed in one day," she gasped. "Seventy." She reached out to clasp the hand of her sister.

Lyesse cradled the dying woman. "A good number, one that any morazeth would admire."

Thorn gripped her with red, wet fingers. "My score . . . is yours. I grant you all my kills."

"I accept them, and I will add many more in your name."

Lyesse sensed the instant when the Keeper claimed Thorn's spirit. Though time seemed to stop for an infinitely long moment, she held the other morazeth while the battle continued to rage. Lyesse gently set her sister's body aside.

As she saw countless soldiers continuing to crash into Tanimura, she knew that she had more than enough targets to reach the greatest score any morazeth had ever achieved.

CHAPTER 83

U neasy but trying not to second-guess Nicci's plan, Nathan followed the sorceress as she made her way across the new wooden bridge that connected the lowtown to Halsband Island. The flattened expanse had served as a practice field for the Tanimuran soldiers and the refugee militia as they prepared for war, but the rubble gave the island a haunted, abandoned air. Nicci seemed to think it was perfect for her needs now.

If only General Utros would come. Nicci had no doubts at all.

Bannon and Lila walked in tandem as their small group made their way to the meeting point. The young man carried Nathan's ornate sword, and it seemed a part of him now.

After killing King Grieve, Bannon was hardened and also restored. Even so, Nathan feared that the bright, hopeful young man would never get back his foolish optimism. For a long time he had clung to a positive façade as a defense against the cruelties he had experienced in life, but now Bannon was strong and whole, with an iron will. He was not a victim and he did not complain about all the times he'd been beaten down.

Instead, he drew strength and built bonds where others would only have sought vengeance.

His surprising relationship with Lila, for example, was a partnership that made both of them stronger. Nathan didn't know if he himself would have been so strong or so forgiving of a woman who had been his captor and harsh trainer.

He realized that for his own part, after the Sisters of the Light had locked him up in the palace for so long, Nathan had come to love Prelate Ann, and he had also respected and admired Prelate Verna. Those women had been his captors, yet he had managed to resolve his differences with them. In a way, he understood Bannon.

As they prepared for their desperate gambit, battles raged across the city, and hundreds if not thousands of Norukai continued to pillage and burn down the harbor district. Even if Nicci defeated General Utros here, the ancient army would keep devastating the city. He believed that Tanimura was doomed, no matter what happened here on Halsband Island.

But Nathan trusted Nicci, and he held on to hope. He saw her rigid back, the muscles that rippled beneath the black fabric of her dress. He could sense her building up her strength for a final confrontation. Mrra prowled alongside them, inseparable from Nicci.

They followed crushed pathways where military maneuvers had packed down the rubble. Nathan tried to make out the foundations of the fallen Palace of the Prophets, the remnants of the immense towers that had imprisoned him for ten centuries. "Once I escaped, I hoped never to return here," he said aloud. "With the whole world to explore, why would I go back to a place with such sour memories?"

"You are here with us," Bannon said.

"And we are about to face the commander of an army that intends to conquer the world," Lila added.

Nathan stroked his chin. "For a reason like that, I can come back to Halsband Island one more time."

Nicci found an acceptable spot and stopped. Nathan realized this was where the arched entrance of the palace had stood. Through the stones beneath his boots and the shimmering silence that resonated with power, he felt a calm like the eye of the storm.

Nicci stood silent with the big sand panther at her side. Mrra's whiskers twitched with anticipation. Bannon and Lila held their swords and tried to look intimidating, as if they were Nicci's elite guard. Nathan's embroidered cape waved in the breeze.

Finally, they watched a large party of mounted soldiers come riding over the bridge toward them, led by a standard-bearer with the flame banner of the ancient empire. General Utros rode at the fore. The slender sorceress paced beside him on her horse. The general's retinue consisted of more than a hundred soldiers, but Nicci did not seem intimidated by the numbers. Nathan had never seen her look so confident.

Nathan stood ready to fight for the sake of D'Hara. As the thought calmed him, centered him, he suddenly felt a surge of hot poison through his chest. His heart hammered as the dark spirit of Ivan tried to take over again, but Nathan grimaced, clenched his fists, and hissed in a harsh whisper, "Why won't you die?" He pounded his sternum, and the dark presence swirled away.

Utros and his escort soldiers looked bloodied and weary, but their faces shone with anticipation. Nothing matched the madness of Ruva's expression. Her eyes were like fractured gems that held remnants of lightning. Utros sat tall in his saddle like a predatory beast as he pulled his horse to a halt and glared at Nicci.

Nathan kept his voice low. "I hope you know what you're doing, Sorceress."

Nicci just smiled. "I am not worried." She touched the pocket of her dress. "It is my job to take care of the entire enemy army."

CHAPTER 84

Although she could see only half of his face, Nicci could tell that General Utros already believed he was victorious. Resplendent in his leather armor, he rode toward her like a supreme conqueror. His escort soldiers clustered close, ready to defend their general, and his standard-bearers raised Iron Fang's ancient flame symbol, which he now claimed as his own.

Nicci faced him in only a bloodstained black dress. She lifted her soft chin, and her blond hair flowed freely around her head. She ignored the rest of the soldiers, didn't even acknowledge the painted sorceress at his side. "I wasn't certain you would be brave enough to face me, General Utros."

The horses shifted on the broken stones, but the escort riders forced them into rigid ranks. The men looked gaunt, their skin pale except where it was streaked with blood, particularly around their mouths.

Utros tilted his horned helmet down at her, and she could see his eye blazing through the hole in the gold half mask. "It takes little courage to face the vanquished." He gestured expansively behind him. "The city has already fallen. There is nothing you can do but surrender. I am glad you realize that."

Nicci remained silent.

Mrra growled low in her throat. Nathan, Bannon, and Lila stood ready to protect Nicci, but they looked insignificant surrounded by Utros's escort guard. Even in the isolation of Halsband Island, the sounds of continuing battles wafted from the main city, but Nicci heard only the blood rushing in her ears, felt her strength rising.

Ruva glared from her bay horse. Much of the pale sorceress's carefully applied paint had flaked off, leaving only muddled messages. Her shoulders jerked with anticipation. "I want her, beloved Utros."

A flitting spirit appeared in the air, Ava's glowing shadow. "*We* want her!"

Ruva laughed. "Send her to the Keeper, and then maybe he will leave us alone! My sister can stay with me."

Ava's shimmering form swirled close, overlapping with her twin. "We will stay together. Always together."

General Utros swung out of his saddle and dropped to the ground in front of Nicci. His boots crunched on the loose stones of the Palace of the Prophets. The escort guard sat motionless, as if they had turned to statues again.

Still she said nothing, merely faced him with a stony expression.

Utros loomed over Nicci. "Nothing you say will change the outcome of this day. No concessions you make will alter my victory. I came here to destroy you. There will be no surrender terms. My army will enslave any people still alive in Tanimura. We will rest in this city and rebuild, and when I have restored my army to its full strength with thousands of new recruits, we will march north and conquer all of D'Hara. I will achieve even more than what Emperor Kurgan demanded of me. I will rule both the Old World and the New."

Nathan stepped closer to the implacable Nicci and defied the general. "Emperor Kurgan is long dead, just as you should be."

Utros looked at the wizard as if he were an annoying distraction. "Iron Fang is the past. I am the new emperor."

"Your allies are defeated," Bannon blurted out. "Look out at the harbor! The Norukai navy is destroyed. King Grieve is dead—I killed him myself."

Utros showed little surprise. "That saves me the trouble of doing it. Grieve was unruly and uncontrollable. I would have had to be rid of him sooner or later."

Knowing that people were dying every moment, Nicci snapped, "Enough talk, Utros! I brought you here to end this."

The general glared at her. "It is already ended. I will accept your surrender, but my army will continue to ransack Tanimura. You have lost, Sorceress. Your Old World has lost. There is nothing you can do."

Still in the saddle, Ruva pulled her lips back to expose her teeth. "We must have Nicci. She needs to die. My sister and I will accept no other terms. She is ours!"

Ava's mocking spirit flickered in an invisible wind. "You can rip out her heart, dear sister, and I will rip out her soul."

Utros looked to the twin sorceresses, then back at Nicci, and he smiled with half a face. "Agreed. That is our only demand. Your life is forfeit, and if I watch you die with enough pain, then I might call off some of my troops. That is what true surrender looks like." He nodded. "Are you a leader, Sorceress? Will you give your life to save all those people in the city? Choose now!"

Bannon crouched in a fighting stance, and Lila stood beside him with her sword raised. Nathan extended his hands, ready to call on his gift.

Nicci felt glad for their loyalty, although she didn't need it. She touched the coldness in her heart, and her voice came out as hard as black ice. "You misunderstand, General. I did not call you here to give my surrender. I came to defeat you. I came to send all of you to the underworld, where you are long overdue."

The escort troops shifted in their saddles, amused by her bravado. Standing in front of his stallion, Utros cocked his head back. Her comments seemed like braggadocio, but Nicci was deadly serious. She could feel the bone box in her pocket.

General Utros drew his sword and advanced on Nicci, ready to strike her down where she stood. Ruva slithered out of her saddle and approached, while the pale remnant of her sister hovered beside her, glowering. Because Nicci's demeanor was so completely confident, the twins showed a flicker of uneasiness.

Nicci said, "Thanks to Lord Rahl, the only war wizard born in many centuries, the underworld was sealed forever and the veil was made impenetrable. The dead could no longer return to the world of the living."

"We know this," Ruva sneered.

"You and all of your soldiers should have been dead fifteen centuries ago. Your souls have been on the wrong side of the veil for all this time." Nicci looked beyond Utros to the escort soldiers. "When you were petrified, the Keeper did not know he had lost you, but now you are flesh again . . . and your souls are forfeit."

"We are here," Ava snapped. "I am with my sister."

From the general's troubled expression, Nicci could see that her words were no surprise to him. She said, "You know this in your heart, General Utros. You should be long dead."

"My empire is here in this world," Utros said. "To-day we have sent enough souls to the underworld to satisfy the Keeper."

"But they are not the correct souls. I was once a Sister of the Dark, and I was allied with the Keeper." Her expression hardened. "I no longer serve him. He is no friend of mine, but I will happily give him what he is owed." Her gaze traveled out to the city of Tanimura, where countless ancient soldiers continued fighting. "All of your souls. Life to the living. Death to the dead."

Utros did not seem amused. "You are arrogant and powerless."

Nicci snatched the bone box from her dress and slid aside the delicate lid, which was now stained with blood from her hand. Inside, the small glowing pearl rotated, shone brighter.

Seeing it, the twin sorceresses recoiled. Ava's spirit shrieked, and Ruva lunged forward, realizing the danger even if she did not understand what the object was.

Utros raised his sword to kill Nicci, but Bannon and Lila both dove in to drive the big general back a step. Knowing he had to give Nicci whatever time she needed, Nathan shoved with both hands, palms outward. The blast of solidified air ripped harmlessly through the spirit of Ava but slammed Ruva backward, disrupting the spell she was trying to work.

Nicci had finally realized what Richard's constructed spell truly was—that Subtractive Magic, *her* Subtractive Magic, was the necessary component to unleash the devastation. Nicci herself was the key, the foundation. Richard had known she would figure it out.

Life to the living. Death to the dead, written in the language of Creation. This spell would heal the frayed threads in the veil. What had once unraveled would be tied up again.

She called upon both sides of her gift. Holding the bone box in her palm, she summoned lightning, and an arcing bolt of pure white energy, braided with an opposite bolt of black Subtractive power, struck the bone box and vaporized it in a blinding flash of pure elemental power. The dual elements twisted together and struck the glowing orb, delivering the required element to ignite the internal protocols of Richard's constructed spell. The magic began to unfold around her and run toward its terminal objective.

As Nicci ignited the spell, the backwash levitated her into the air. Glowing lines grew and lengthened, crisscrossing to form a cylinder around her, as if a two-dimensional spell-form had become three-dimensional in order to be viable in such an extreme circumstance. With a roaring sound that reverberated across the flat expanse of the island, those patterns of lines, angles, and arcs continued to grow outward, extending away from the cylindrical spell-form. Lines of light raced through the air to support triangles and intersections. While orange light spiraled outward, the lines of power braced complex angles of pure white.

Nathan staggered backward, shielding his eyes with the sleeve of his frayed ruffled shirt. The lightning bolt had been powerful, but it was no more than a whisper compared to the constructed spell she had just triggered. The magic continued to grow.

As the lines expanded and branched ever outward, thorns of light sprouted in needle-sharp points. Their patterns and flow interacted and connected, giving the entire web of lines their intended purpose—to open the torn veil wide enough so the Keeper could seize all the long-overdue souls and drag them to where they belonged.

Life to the living. Death to the dead.

After Nicci set the constructed spell in motion, the routines continued to grow through a rhythm of intersections and routes that arced out in all directions. Suspended within the web, lifted off the ground, she felt each new line as if some cosmic needle were taking a stitch through her soul to draw the thread of light out of her and into the fabric of the spell. She experienced profound pain and pleasure at the same time.

The spell would encompass General Utros and the entire ancient army.

Nathan watched the unfolding, increasing lines of power, knowing that this was beyond anything he could do. Richard had created the spell, but Nicci was the engine driving all the destruction. Encased in her web of expanding, invincible magic, the beautiful sorceress wheeled in the air.

Utros's escort soldiers screamed and backed away. Their horses reared in panic. Ava and Ruva cried out in challenge and terror, trying to defend against what

Nicci had unleashed. The general strained to stagger forward, struggling to lift his sword so he could kill Nicci, but the weapon seemed as heavy as a mountain.

Bannon and Lila were buffeted by the surging power. They tried to stand their ground, holding their swords to defend against powers they could not imagine. Halsband Island shook and shuddered, and the settling rubble underfoot made the ground unsteady, while Nicci hung suspended in the air as light showered around her.

With impossible speed, the dazzling lines spiraled across the landscape and rolled past the island, beyond the bridges to the lowtown, then across the harbor. The spell raced like an ill wind through all the districts of the city to the outlying hills and beyond. Unstoppable, it swept up tens of thousands of the invading army. The underworld was now open and ravenous, demanding to have these souls.

Men in ancient armor screamed as the glowing green lines overran them, netting some, while impaling others on the thorns of orange light, slicing others with razor black energy.

Tendrils flew out beyond Tanimura, far down the coast, racing across the Old World to reclaim all the souls of the ancient army, wherever they had been dispatched. The very line between life and death was at stake, now torn open.

As the veil to the underworld tore to allow passage of all those souls, Nathan felt his heart rip as well. The darkness within him hammered outward, struggling, trying to hold on. He clutched his chest as pain exploded like a battering ram inside him. He had not experienced agony like this since Fleshmancer Andre had split open his breastbone to pull out his old, weak heart.

Now the remnants of Ivan strained and struggled. That evil man's spirit resisted, but the raging constructed spell demanded every scrap of his tainted soul as well. Searing green light blazed around Nathan's eyes, inside his mind, and he used his own gift to *push* the hated presence out of him.

With a last dull saw blade of pain, the poisonous vestige of Ivan slipped out of him and fluttered away like scattered raven's wings. The chief handler's spirit was sucked down with all the other screaming souls as the world and the underworld yawned open.

Nathan realized he was at last free.

Green mist swirled like a sudden fog, rising from a world that did not belong to the living. Across the battlefield in the hills and the city streets, the ground shuddered open. Countless ancient soldiers were yanked screaming into the underworld, their souls reclaimed, their centuries-old bodies crumbling to dust.

From the center of the storm of magic, Nicci realized that elements of the spell patterns were themselves in the language of Creation, a design that transitioned into an elemental language that hummed with the rhythm of life itself and also called to the dead.

Ava's shimmering spirit tried to flee, pulling against the invisible claws of destiny. Her intangible form stretched and tangled, then was whisked away with a fading shriek. Leaping after her dead sister, trying to catch her, Ruva struggled with the limitations of her physical form. Their connection was too strong, and the Keeper demanded them both. Ruva's soul tore away, inexorably following her twin to the underworld. Empty, her body dropped lifeless, disintegrating into grains of dust and fragments of yellowed bones.

Suspended in the air as the magical holocaust continued, Nicci knew that this spell-form was complex beyond her comprehension. She gazed in awe at the network of light woven into a fabric of forms around her, motifs and unfathomable emblems. She was not surprised that Richard had been able to conceive such power. Caught in her own web and also shielded by it, she watched the very stuff of creation and annihilation.

By using the interior perspective of the constructed spell, by being the initiating element, Nicci was more than an observer, but also a participant. It was her very will, her fury, her nature that became an empowering element to annihilate the vast invading force in one stroke. It was Nicci herself who laid waste to the ancient army and cast them tumbling into the world of the dead.

Strong and defiant, General Utros resisted until the last minute, but even the legendary commander could not withstand the call of the Keeper, the obdurate demands of mortality. As he shuddered and struggled against the pull of the constructed spell, the gold mask fell off to show his stripped face.

Knowing he could not win, Utros raised one gauntleted fist, shouting a final vow. "Now I can conquer the whole underworld!" His massive body disintegrated as his spirit vanished into the whirlwind of green mist.

As the spell finally wound through to its terminus, its task accomplished, Nicci felt more alive than she had ever been. Embraced by Richard's spell, she had dealt out death, once again becoming Death's Mistress. Richard had written the message for her in the language of Creation on the bone box. In that moment, neither world—the world of the living nor the world of the dead—seemed entirely real to her. She was the Grace. She was life. She was death.

Only then was Nicci released from her prison of light, exhausted and exhilarated by the experience. She drifted back to the ground and slumped in the rubble of the Palace of the Prophets.

More than ever, she ached for Richard. It was bliss to have been held in the embrace of his spell, but now it was gone. That moment of love and protection evaporated as the last few lines of light went dark.

CHAPTER 85

The ravaged city reeled as the world itself cracked open. Misty veils rippled through the streets as the ancient warriors were swept away to where they should have gone centuries before. With howls of despair louder than the roar of battle, the soldiers collapsed in full armor, falling to dust. Tanimura became a literal city of the dead.

The D'Haran fighters, the city militia, the ragtag refugee army, and the everyday citizens were left amazed as the seemingly hopeless battle simply ended before their eyes. The overwhelming enemy was vanquished by an ally no one had expected—the Keeper himself.

Among his weary and wounded soldiers, General Zimmer stood wrung-out and shuddering. His hand trembled as he gripped the hilt of his sword. For hours he had lived in a mechanical process of defending himself, cutting down one opponent after another. They were all faceless to him. Surely he had slain more than a hundred by his own hand.

Lyesse, her bare skin painted red with blood, turned with angry disappointment at all the opponents who had dropped dead in front of her; she clearly wasn't finished getting revenge for Thorn.

Sisters Arabella and Mab staggered up to General Zimmer, dragging with every step. Mab bled from a deep cut in her upper arm and another in her ribs, and Arabella held her up. Now that she had a moment when she wasn't fighting for her life, Sister Arabella healed her companion's injuries, strengthening Mab enough so that she could stand upright again.

Oliver, Peretta, and Amber joined them. All the rats they had summoned had fled back into the sewers and grates, gorged with fresh meat and matted with blood, but no one understood why the entire ancient army had just crumbled to dust in a hurricane of inexplicable magic.

"What do we do now, General?" Oliver looked around, but none of the others even spoke questions aloud.

At the far side of the blood-strewn square, where so many ancient soldiers had vanished into death, twenty fierce Norukai stood with their mouths wide, suddenly finding themselves alone and vastly outnumbered. Now that the tables were turned, they bellowed their defiance and raised their axes, clubs, and swords to keep fighting.

Though battered, the D'Haran soldiers were rejuvenated by the sudden reprieve, and their battle cry was ten times as loud as the scarred raiders'. General Zimmer led the charge. "Now we clear the streets of Tanimura, wipe out every last Norukai, and dump their bodies into the sea."

Fueled by the prospect of certain victory, his army ran after the burly raiders, who turned to flee.

* * *

Bannon was horrified to watch the underworld open up and reclaim all the lost souls in a nightmarish storm. In the aftermath, it took him a long moment to realize that the defenders of Tanimura had somehow won.

After the astonishing play of lights, forms, and tangled lines, Nicci had collapsed in the rubble of the Palace of the Prophets. Nathan squatted next to the sorceress, cradling her in a tender gesture. "Dear spirits, I don't know when I've ever endured the like. You saved us. You saved us all!"

Her voice was ragged. "Not just me. You all helped. I could not have done this without you." Nicci looked at him, then at Bannon and Lila, nodding in gratitude. "But this was also Richard's doing. He made that constructed spell and said it was all I needed. Even though I didn't understand what he meant, I believed him. He had faith in me, and that faith made me stronger than I've ever been before."

An uncomfortable silence settled over Halsband Island and extended throughout Tanimura. Now that General Utros had turned to dust, his gold mask lay facedown on the broken stones. Only a few bits of his horned helmet remained, mostly decayed, next to bone splinters. Of the escort soldiers, only a few scraps of metal, rusted buckles, and broken links of chain mail lay on the ground.

Diminished sounds of fighting came from the city as new skirmishes erupted. With his sharp vision, Bannon could see knots of Norukai warriors trying to fend off a surge from the overjoyed D'Haran defenders. Lila flashed an eager glance at Bannon. "Sounds like the fun isn't over yet, boy. Would you like to join me? If we run, we might get there before someone else slays them all."

Bannon looked at his ornate sword. The hilt now felt perfect in his hand, entirely his. The edge was notched from the recent fighting, but any good swordsmith could restore its razor edge. "I do want to see all the Norukai dead, but sweet Sea Mother, I have done enough killing for today."

In the main city, the vengeful militia members, Tanimuran city guards, and D'Haran soldiers surrounded the last Norukai. A few raiders managed to get back to two of the grounded serpent ships and shoved off into the harbor, but they found no safety in the water either. The ships of the Tanimuran navy as well as the reinforcements from Serrimundi still remained to fight them. A rain of fire arrows dropped down on the serpent ships before they could get out of the harbor. Before long every last raider vessel was engulfed in flames and burned to the waterline.

A short while later, General Linden rode to Halsband Island with a handful of soldiers, followed by several Hidden People in bloodstained gray cloaks. Zimmer followed soon after with his own bedraggled escort. "We are mopping up throughout the city," Zimmer said.

Linden added, "By standing together, we might have withstood the Norukai, but we had no chance against the army of General Utros." He shook his head, looked at the dust and bone fragments scattered amid the rubble, the trivial remnants of so many ancient soldiers. "I can't believe it."

Nicci said, "With Richard's help I found a power even greater than an invincible army—the power of life and death."

Life to the living. Death to the dead.

"The power of destiny," Nathan said, raising his eyebrows. "Never forget that she was indeed Death's Mistress."

More Sisters of the Light made their way to Halsband Island, their former home. During the battles in the city, Sisters Sharon, Lucia, and Heather had been slain, and now the remaining Sisters marked their passing. Sisters Rhoda, Eldine, Mab, and Arabella greeted Nicci and Nathan, relieved. "It seems fitting that the last battle took place on the very foundations of the Palace of the Prophets," Rhoda said.

"So much magic was entwined through the structure of that building, maybe some of it remained," Arabella said.

"I am glad the palace is no more," Nathan said with sniff. "It no longer had a purpose."

Nicci said, "With prophecy gone and gifted young men no longer suffering, your entire order has no purpose."

"Prelate Verna wrestled with the same question," said Eldine. "She tried to find a new reason because our old ways were gone. By helping at Cliffwall, the Sisters worked to understand and guide the use of magical lore."

"But now Cliffwall is also gone," Mab said, "buried in stone."

Nathan mused, "The world still has many central sites filled with mysterious and dangerous books. Those archives have to be tended and watched—and protected. That could be your order's new purpose."

The Sisters looked at one another. Amber kicked a few broken pebbles at her feet. "We came to Tanimura because this is where the Palace of the Prophets was.

That is why I joined the order in the first place. I want to do something significant. I need some important task. Prelate Verna told me not to give up hope. My parents are already proud of my brother, and they'll be even happier after they learn how brave Norcross was today, how many Norukai ships he fought." She sighed. "I wanted to be important too."

"You will be," said Sister Mab. "We'll rebuild our order. Without the prelate, we have traveled together and fought together as equals, but as Sisters of the Light we must have a new leader. Who will be our prelate?"

Eldine looked at Mab, and Mab looked at Arabella, then slowly all of them turned to Nicci. "You were once a Sister of the Light," said Rhoda. "You betrayed us by becoming a Sister of the Dark, but we know you have come back to the sacred cause. You are stronger now than ever, stronger than any of us."

Mab said, "Stronger than any Sister of the Light that ever existed, stronger than any prelate we have had before." Her eyes shone. "Working together with all the resources of Tanimura, we could rebuild the Palace of the Prophets!" She looked up to the skies as she imagined towers there.

Nicci scowled. "I'm no longer a Sister of the Dark, that is true, but neither am I a Sister of the Light. I am Nicci, a sorceress, companion to Lord Richard Rahl. He gave me a mission for the D'Haran Empire, and I do not intend to be sidetracked."

Nathan felt more disturbed. "If you mean to rebuild the palace, if you raise even one foundation stone on top of another, I want nothing to do with that." He shuddered. "I have things to accomplish in my life."

Nicci actually smiled at him. "We all do."

CHAPTER 86

The survivors of Tanimura spent the next two days extinguishing fires and killing the last of the enemies. They tracked down the Norukai stragglers, who proved to be cowards after all when they fought alone. Knowing they were hunted, they crawled into storage buildings and fishing shacks; some even hid under the damaged piers, holding on to pilings in the water and trying to remain unseen. When the cornered raiders were discovered, angry city people used harpoons and boat hooks to impale them in the water. Nicci didn't consider it torture, merely justice.

Leaving Halsband Island, she and Nathan reunited with many other gifted men and women from Tanimura. Together they used their magic to douse fires with rain they squeezed out of the air. Many of the larger buildings, including twenty noble villas in the hill district, had been burned down to skeletons.

And there were thousands of wounded to be tended. Volunteers from Tanimura, as well as earnest refugees from Effren and Renda Bay, formed triage teams. The merchants of the garment district boiled fabric and tore it into strips to make bandages. Oliver and Peretta, along with Scholar-Archivist Franklin, Chief Memmer

Gloria, and their Cliffwall followers, used the knowledge they had learned in the archive. They called upon any scraps of the gift they could use to help heal the wounded, saving thousands of lives.

While Bannon had only rudimentary first-aid training, the morazeth had a great deal of experience in tending combat wounds, even amputations. Lila knelt beside a man whose hand had been chopped off by a Norukai axe. His bleeding had clotted in the hours since he had fallen, but he was weak and sickened. Lila cleaned the stump and wrapped it in a damp bandage, gritting her teeth as she pulled the knot tight.

"That will keep him alive for now," she said to Bannon. "We'll need the healers and herb women to make vats of salve, or else the wounds will get infected, and more will die in the coming weeks."

The victim groaned, "My hand! How can I do anything without my hand?"

Lila spoke more to Bannon than to the moaning patient. "A warrior usually dies when he falls in the combat arena, but we remember the story of a champion named Kalef, a slave brought from afar, who reigned in the arena until an opponent hacked off his hand at the wrist. Even as he bled, Kalef kept fighting until he collapsed to his knees, but still he wouldn't yield. Normally, the challenger would strike a death blow and become the new champion, but the crowd was so enthusiastic that Kalef was allowed to live. Healers nursed him back to health, and when he regained his strength, he returned to the arena with a modified sword, fighting with a blade screwed directly onto his wrist. He killed his next opponent and became champion again."

Now, Lila looked down at the wounded man who

stared in shock at the bloody bandages around his wrist. "That one will never be a champion, but he will learn to be useful. There is much work to do in Tanimura."

Though tending to the injured was the first priority, the numerous corpses also had to be dealt with. Every one of General Utros's soldiers had disintegrated, but more than ten thousand other people had died in the fighting, and their bodies were strewn along the streets and piled in the market squares where they had made their last stands.

After several days in the hot and humid Tanimura air, the bloated corpses began to stink. Seagulls swarmed over the city, feasting on any cadavers they found, pecking out the eyes and flying off when the body-handling teams shooed them away. Out in the harbor, larger flocks of the birds landed on the floating dead. Predatory fish picked the bones clean.

Generals Zimmer and Linden assigned soldiers to mortuary detail. Porters who had previously worked at the docks now loaded their carts with bodies and dragged them out of the city. The desolate expanse of Halsband Island became the perfect site for enormous funeral pyres that burned constantly, fed with wood and corpses.

Plumes of greasy black smoke hung like a pall in the air, and the smell of roasting meat was so pervasive that no one had much of an appetite. Even butcher shops closed their doors, because they had no business. The funeral pyres created a layer of ash over the ruins of the Palace of the Prophets, which would become a new foundation of soil. One day, the island might come alive again.

While all of the slain D'Haran soldiers, militia members, and innocent citizens deserved to be burned in the cleansing pyres, no dead Norukai would receive that honor. During the cleanup, when the body handlers gathered the bodies, the raider corpses were separated out and dealt with last. Wearing looks of disgust, D'Haran soldiers hauled carts piled with dead Norukai wearing sharkskin armor, metal adornments, spikes implanted in their skulls or shoulders. By now, all the bodies showed signs of decay, their skin discolored, the flesh swollen. They looked even uglier than usual.

Captain Jared reluctantly offered the *Chaser* as a corpse ship, piling his deck with the hideous raiders. Nicci and Zimmer watched as soldiers pushed stinking cartloads along the pier, and even the krakeners held their noses in disgust as they lifted the bodies aboard.

The *Chaser* made repeated trips, sailing out beyond the edge of the harbor to the deep water, where Jared and his crew threw the dead Norukai overboard, one body at a time. Some sank, some bobbed. They would all drift away in the currents to be eaten by fishes and erased from memory.

Jared had even reported, with a shiver and a thrill, that on his last run, when the sharks feasted on all the bodies, the circling triangular fins had scattered. Among the Norukai corpses, other figures surfaced, selka reveling in the abundance of dead enemies. They tore at the meaty flesh as if they couldn't contain their malicious joy. The krakener crew had stared, horrified, but not frightened. The selka looked up at them with slitted eyes, but made no move to attack. They satisfied themselves with the Norukai corpses and swam away.

Captain Jared's once-cocky outlook had been replaced with a sad shadow, and beard stubble covered his cleft chin. As he took on another load for disposal, he crossed his arms over his chest and looked at Nicci, who had come to see him on the docks. "It's loathsome work, Sorceress, but nobody else would do it," he scoffed. "Once again my krakeners prove their worth."

Nicci said, "Your ship smelled foul before, but this is intolerable."

"Oh, I will tolerate it, Sorceress, though this is fouler cargo than any tentacled beast. I can't wait to dump the last of these bodies." Jared brightened. "My crews are eager to hunt krakens again. We'll bring back delicious meat to feed this city while it recovers."

"Thank you, Captain," said Zimmer, but without enthusiasm.

As Tanimura made plans to rebuild, they were only one city of many that had been damaged in the war. As the survivors of Renda Bay, Effren, and other devastated towns helped clear the burned-down warehouses, sawmill operators cut fresh lumber, and armies of carpenters worked to restore the city. Bricklayers formed foundations, clay handlers added stucco to walls, whitewashers used buckets of lime to finish the new structures.

Thaddeus and Rendell, who had become fast friends after saving each other's lives more than once, worked to erect new homes and shops at the waterfront. Thaddeus said, "Now that we no longer have to worry about the Norukai, someday I would like to take my people back to Renda Bay and rebuild our own town."

"I will go with you." Rendell had sad eyes, but he managed a smile. "My Ildakar will never return, and I want a fresh start. I liked Renda Bay."

"There's still a great deal of work ahead of us," Thaddeus said, "but we'll have our freedom and our homes."

Hearing them, Nicci stepped closer. "You will determine your own destiny, your own rule. You'll be responsible for your actions, but you also have a strong conscience. Then you'll truly be a part of the D'Haran Empire."

Four of the Hidden People, moving quietly in the daylight that was still a blessing to them, came to Nicci, looking concerned and lost. Free of their ancient responsibilities, they had trekked across the land so they could fight for Nicci, but now they didn't know what to do, since all the battles were ended and they were far from home.

"The bustle of this city confounds us," said one man with deep lines of concern on his pale face. "Nearly six hundred of us still survive. General Utros is defeated, but what will become of Orogang? That city is still our home."

"And it is quiet!" said another man.

"Then make it your home," Nicci said. "Go back there and live in the sunlight. By now, the zhiss are all dead. You no longer need to hide in the shadows. Smash open all the bricked-up windows, let in the air. Orogang can become a grand capital again."

"But we will be all alone," said a woman, tugging on her gray hood.

"Not for long. Traders will come to Orogang. You will be one of the key cities in the mountains." Nicci smiled. "And I'll make certain Lord Rahl knows about you. He may even set up a satellite capital in Orogang. Would you like that?"

The Hidden People beamed, and it seemed as if light had returned to their features. It was just one more of the many pieces coming together after the defeat of General Utros and the Norukai scourge.

As the most urgent tasks were completed in the aftermath of the war, the refugees began to reassess their future. Scholar-Archivist Franklin, along with his rival and companion Gloria, gathered with the Sisters of the Light. "Cliffwall is destroyed, and all those books are lost. We have to re-create them as best we can."

Gloria tapped a finger to her temple. "They are not lost if my memmers still know them. We can reproduce thousands of volumes, but it will take time."

Because funeral pyres still covered Halsband Island, the Sisters had taken up residence in an empty inn whose owners had been killed in the attack. There in the common room, at long tables once used for boisterous crowds with tankards of ale, the scholars sat beside volunteer scribes. They used stacks of paper, ledger books from the harbormaster's offices, any scrap that could capture words. The memmers sat back with their eyes half closed, muttering line after line as they recited the books preserved in their gifted memories.

The Cliffwall scholars had devoted their lives to learning, to poring over every word in those ancient books, and now they participated in writing them down. By day, they wrote in sunlit rooms, and at night they lit lanterns to continue scribing. The memmers' voices grew hoarse as they dictated, but they didn't stop. It would take many years to recapture most of the lost knowledge, but they would keep remembering and keep writing.

CHAPTER 87

After a brief squall the night before, the Tanimura harbor smelled of clean salt air rather than death, blood, and decay. Nathan inhaled deeply as he sat at the end of the dock and looked down at the last page in his life book, considering how he would wrap up his story.

A gray splat struck the boards beside him, and a seagull spun overhead with a shriek that sounded like mocking laughter. Nathan glanced up with an annoyed snort. "I could blast you out of the sky with a tiny ball of fire, you miserable bird." The gull was not intimidated by the threat and flew away under the bright blue sky.

Out in the harbor, most of the wrecked ships had been dismantled to clear passage for trade. Two large cargo ships remained sunk in the shallows, their hulls tilted underwater, masts protruding like drowned trees. The people of Tanimura would leave those hulks as a memorial, so that anyone who came to the city would be reminded of the battle.

Nathan had nearly filled the life book with adventures, and that fact gave him pause, even stymied his creative efforts. If he'd had plenty of pages left, the words would flow. He would have described every thought, every setback, every victory. How could he sum up so many grand events on the single remaining page? He considered simply purchasing another blank book so he could keep writing, but this precious volume wasn't just a book from a stationer. This was his *life book,* given to him by the witch woman Red, in the Dark Lands. The first volume had been written in ink made of his own burned blood, chronicling the first part of his life. He had filled this second book by his own hand, but the leather-bound volume was a special gift nonetheless.

With his boots dangling over the end of the dock, he reread the last pages he had written the night before while he sat on the barracks steps in the Tanimura garrison. Nathan knew he would need to find finer rooms eventually, provided he and Nicci remained here in the city. He already felt restless.

He looked down at his descriptions of the wizards of Ildakar, Mirrormask and the slave uprising, the awakening of the enormous stone army. His eyes stung when he read about dear Elsa, her transference magic, and how she had died. His brief workmanlike lines were sadly inadequate, not because he meant to give her short shrift, but because he didn't have the heart to write what Elsa deserved.

He had tried to do better chronicling the end of Prelate Verna and the destruction of Cliffwall. His descriptions of the final battles in Tanimura were merely vignettes, but he simply didn't have the room. Each event deserved a full chapter of its own, if not an entire volume. Still, what he wrote was the truth, and that was what mattered most.

Knowing the importance of his work, he forced

himself to keep writing, to finish the job in the paper he had available. With tiny letters and succinct prose, he addressed the brave sacrifices of so many soldiers, Bannon's victory over King Grieve, and the cataclysmic end of Utros's ancient army when the underworld reclaimed them.

He had so much more to say, but he reached the bottom of the last page. His final lines were cramped and dense, and when there was no more room he simply wrote, "And thus was the Old World saved."

The dock boards creaked with approaching footsteps, and he turned to see Nicci walking toward him in her black dress. The big sand panther padded along beside her, her tan fur clean and brushed, as if she were no more than a contented, groomed pet. Nicci stopped beside him at the end of the pier. "If this is how you spend your days, Wizard, you will grow fat and lazy."

A seagull flew overhead, scolding Mrra. The panther roared, and the bird flew away.

"It is a well-deserved rest." Nathan looked down at the last page. "Writing an objective and thorough chronicle is a different kind of battle, but just as hard. I'm afraid I didn't have enough paper." He closed the book.

Nicci's lips tightened in a smile. "I'm certain you found room to include your own exploits."

"Oh, not all of them. Dear spirits, that would take an entire library."

She didn't react to his humor. "When you tell your stories in taverns and banquets, I'm sure you will provide excruciating detail."

"I am wounded by your attitude." Placing a palm to

his chest, Nathan felt the lumpy scar and his steady heartbeat, and realized that it truly did feel like *his* heart after all. The heart of a wizard.

Mrra let out a low growl and turned back toward the shore, her tail thrashing. Nicci spun, suddenly wary.

An unexpected form stepped out onto the pier, a slender woman in a gray shift that clung tightly to her body. Her skin was pale, her face gaunt to the point of being cadaverous. Her scalp was a tangle of red locks like ropy twisted snakes, and she smiled at them with unnatural black lips. She strolled forward, ominous, confident as if no one else existed except for the three of them. At her side walked a strange creature with spotted russet fur, pointed ears, and a long muzzle—not a cat, not a wolf, but some other species entirely. Mrra bristled and prepared to protect her sister panther.

Nathan felt a chill. "Dear spirits! It's Red."

The witch woman glided up to them. Nathan couldn't imagine how she had passed through the hills and the entire city of Tanimura without causing an uproar. He climbed to his feet and stood at the end of the dock, still clutching the life book.

Nicci was instantly defensive. "I had hoped never to see you again."

The witch woman's laughter was a musical sound, but not music Nathan wanted to hear. "Our hopes are not always rewarded." She cast an offhand glance back at the city. "That battle left enough skulls and bodies to properly decorate Tanimura. It's a shame you feel the need to clean them all up." Red's forested hills and the sheltered glen of her cottage were strewn with the bones of those who had died when they came to seek the witch woman's services.

"It was only as much death as we needed to assure victory," Nicci said.

Hunter, the strange russet animal at her side, sat on his haunches and stared at Mrra, eye-to-eye. The sand panther's whiskers twitched.

Red turned to Nathan, as if she expected him to know why she had come. "You have something for me." It was not a question. "I doubted you would return to the Dark Lands and deliver your life book to me, so I came in person. You should have known that's what I expected." Her black lips formed a smile.

Nathan was surprised. "I only finished writing no more than a few minutes ago. How did you know?"

"I'm a witch woman. I foresee things. You read the first lines in your book."

Nathan turned to the words that had been inscribed there even before Red gave the book to him:

Future and Fate depend on both the journey and the destination. Kol Adair lies far to the south in the Old World. From there, the Wizard will behold what he needs to make himself whole again. And the Sorceress must save the world.

He sniffed. "Those words drove us across the Old World and guided me where I needed to go. You did indeed set many things in motion by writing that." He pursed his lips. "Prophecy is not usually so clear and direct."

Red let out a full-throated laugh. "Nathan Rahl, you know better than anyone! That was no prophecy, no premonition. It was just an idea, and you followed it however you wished, interpreted the words the way you wanted. You set your own events in motion." She extended her hands, waiting for him to hand her the book. "I can't wait to read the entire chronicle."

Nathan reeled from what she had just said. He had followed those words on a quest to restore his gift. Because of what Red had written, he, Nicci, and Bannon had traveled over Kol Adair and all the way to Ildakar. Those words had driven them so far, but had he just been chasing a mirage?

No, not a mirage, he realized. His own destiny. As a former prophet, Nathan Rahl knew that people would do what they were meant to do, no matter what words were written. He had made his own fate.

Red's furry companion sniffed Mrra. Both animals remained ready to pounce, but Nicci and the witch woman kept them under control.

When Nathan surrendered the life book to her, he felt a profound sense of loss, as if a part of his story had ended. Did this mean his adventures were over now? That he would just retire in Tanimura? He certainly didn't intend to do that.

A moment later Red produced another book, though she had not noticed her carrying anything. She held out a fresh volume bound in pale doeskin. He accepted it in wonder and opened it to find the volume full of blank pages.

The witch woman said, "It took you a thousand years to fill the first book and barely a year for the second. I wonder when you will make me come back and retrieve this volume. That is up to you."

Without further farewell, Red walked back down the creaking dock with her shaggy pet following. Nathan ran his thumb along the smooth leather of his new life book and pressed it close to his chest.

* * *

At the edge of the thick Hagen Woods, the pines and oaks created dense shadows. Nicci could still smell blood from the recent battle. This place carried so much dark history, but now it was nothing more than a normal forest. The hush that had hung over the tangled branches was replaced by birdsong.

Mrra peered into the forest with golden eyes. The underbrush rustled, and muscular feline forms glided toward them, the survivors of the sand panther pride that Mrra had led overland to fight against General Utros.

Nicci stroked Mrra's head, scratched behind her ears, and the panther purred contentedly. Her pelt was covered with branded symbols from Ildakar, but Mrra was the only member of her new pride to bear such markings. The other big cats had roamed the wild all their lives, and Nicci knew that was what she wanted.

Mrra twitched her tail and stared into the forest, but she refused to leave her sister panther. Nicci wrapped her arms around Mrra's neck, pulling the cat close. She held tight and stroked her fur for a long moment. "Thank you, my loyal companion. Run with your pride. You deserve it."

Mrra let out a rumble in her chest, and Nicci felt the vibrations against her cheek as she held more tightly. "Our spell bond will never be broken. I will always be your sister panther." She felt a thickening in her throat as she swallowed hard and continued. "But this is your *pride*. Roam the world with them, live your life, hunt, find a mate, have cubs of your own . . . and be free. That is all I ask of you. I will let you know if ever I need your help. Thank you for the new sisters and brothers you have shared with me." Mrra looked up with golden feline eyes, and Nicci stroked the cat's head again. "Go!"

Mrra let out a roar and turned to the other cats waiting in the forest. She bounded into the tree shadows until Nicci could no longer see her, but she would always feel the sand panther in her heart.

CHAPTER 88

The sword's edge had been sharpened to a thin steel razor, erasing the nicks and notches from all the blows Bannon had struck during the fight.

"Good as new," said Mandon, the swordsmith. "After you've killed a hundred more enemies, come back to me and I'll fix it again."

Bannon was pleased with the ornate blade and doubly pleased to know that the swordsmith remembered selling him Sturdy, so long ago. "That was my first sword and a good one. I wish I still had it." Pushing back the sadness in his voice, he turned Nathan's fine weapon from side to side, watching how sunlight flowed like liquid down the polished steel. "But this one will do."

Mandon chuckled. "I still have that chopping post in the back if you'd like to test it."

Bannon remembered when he had first purchased Sturdy. So full of the pain and tragedy that he hid every day, he had hacked the post to splinters. Now, he was much more controlled. Not only was he a better swordsman, but his inner hurts were hardened and healed. His optimism was more than a false façade—it was a real part of him.

The other swords in the smith's shop had been picked over for the defense of Tanimura, and many notched and bloody weapons had been retrieved from the streets, pried from dead hands. Mandon would have years of work cleaning and resharpening them all.

Bannon sheathed his sword with a satisfying click in the scabbard. "It's just fine as it is. I don't need to hack at a wooden post." He paused to smile. "I prefer opponents who fight back, but I think we've done away with all of them for now." He added cryptically, "The sword cleaves the bone."

"I'll fight you, boy, if that's what you want." He turned to see Lila standing outside the shop, clad in her scant black leather. Though they had been lovers many times, she still intimidated him in certain ways. It was another sort of battle that Lila intended to win, but it was one he did enjoy. Bannon liked to think he had softened her as much as a morazeth could be softened.

"I don't need any swordplay for today," Bannon said to her. "But I'd be happy for your company otherwise."

"Good. I came to retrieve you." She crossed her arms over her chest. "The kraken-hunter captain asked for you. He says he knows what you want."

"Captain Jared?" He frowned, puzzled. "What is it he thinks I want?"

Lila gave him an impatient sniff. "You made it quite clear that you wish to leave Tanimura." She seemed disappointed in him.

He remained curious. "Then let's go talk with him and see what he has to say."

Down by the docks, crew members loaded crates of supplies on board the *Chaser*. From the foredeck, Jared directed the workers in a loud voice to emphasize that he was in charge, but they ignored him and did what they already knew how to do.

Jared saw them approach along the dock and waved. "I thought you'd come running, Bannon Farmer! This is your chance. The *Chaser* sails out with the evening tide if you want to go along. We're heading to Chiriya Island."

"Chiriya Island? Back home?" He hesitated, uncertain. "I haven't entirely made up my mind yet." He looked at Lila.

"Yes, you have," she said, with frown lines appearing on her brow. "Though I'm surprised you'd want to go back to that island. You've had few kind words to say about it."

With a bright flush, Bannon looked down at his boots. "I have no kind things to say about my horrible father, and he is dead. I couldn't save my mother, and she was what anchored me there. My friend Ian was gone, so I had no reason to stay. But now I am a much braver man, and I realize that there's also nothing to fear about going home." After so much death and mayhem, after all he had been through with the Norukai slavers, the selka attack, and the defeat of the ancient army, he was weary to the bone, and in his heart he just wanted some peace. "I don't know what that place holds for me anymore. I'm not convinced I've any reason to go back."

Jared crossed his arms over his chest and he called down to them. "I've just had disturbing word, too—enough to make me reconsider the destination, if you didn't want to go there so badly."

"Wait, I never said—" Bannon spluttered, then paused. "What disturbing word? Has something happened to Chiriya Island?"

The krakener captain grimaced. "More Norukai ships seen in the vicinity." He paused only a moment for the news to sink in. "We broke the back of King Grieve's fleet, that's for sure, but there are more serpent ships plying the seas. Raiders with their own mind for destruction. And now that we've conquered and strengthened the major coastal cities, they'll be forced to attack softer outlying targets. Like Chiriya Island."

"Then we have to go there!" Bannon said. "Some-body has to help protect them. They don't know how to fight. How will they—?" He looked at Lila. "You and I can show them."

She still seemed to hold a grudge. "I thought you were trying to get away from me, since you wanted to leave so badly."

He was shocked. "I never said that. I . . . Sweet Sea Mother, I never thought it through! I contemplated go-ing home, just as a daydream. I was just thinking of those poor villagers. Even with all my bad memories of Chiriya, there are still a lot of good people who don't deserve to be slaughtered by the Norukai."

"You didn't even know about the new Norukai threat until just now." Lila sniffed. "That wasn't part of your decision."

Jared grinned at them from the side of the ship, show-ing the gap in his teeth. "She's got you there, lad." After two of his crew members trudged up the gangplank, each with a keg of ale balanced on his shoulder, Jared bounded down to meet them on the docks.

"Wait . . ." Bannon hesitated again, his thoughts whirling. "Would it bother you if I go somewhere? You sound hurt."

Lila stiffened. "You have seen me fight. It takes much more than that to hurt a morazeth. And would you not want me at your side if it comes to fighting more Noru-kai? Although why you would bother to help such weak-lings instead of getting your revenge is beyond me."

He squared his shoulders. "Because that island is full of people just like I was, and *I* didn't deserve what hap-pened to me. People just like Ian, and he didn't deserve it. I want to save them, if I can. I, uh, assumed you would go with me."

"You did not think to ask?"

"Would you go with me to Chiriya Island? And wher-ever else I might go?"

She nodded. "I accept your reasons. I will accompany you." Lila adjusted her black leather skirt. "You always manage to find circumstances in which you need pro-tection. I don't dare let you go alone."

Though Nicci tried not to show any emotion, saying farewell to Bannon turned out to be more difficult than she expected. As they stood in the large square above the harbor, the young man came forward and hugged her for a long moment, much longer than was necessary, and she allowed it. She even embraced him back.

"I will miss you, Nicci. I've grown much in strength and wisdom during my time with you." When he finally let go, Bannon turned to Nathan.

The wizard clearly felt proud of his protégé. Tears welled in his azure eyes. "My boy, you are a brave fighter and a fine companion. You were naive and gullible when we first met, but now you are a man, stronger, braver, and more accomplished than I ever expected."

"I admit, I am impressed," Nicci said. "When I saved you from your own stupidity in that Tanimura alley, I was certain you were a lost cause. You created your own problems, and I vowed never to rescue you again."

Bannon's voice quavered with emotion. "I didn't need any more rescuing, did I?"

"Yes, you did," Nicci said with a laugh, "but no more than all of us did. You fought beside us, and we fought beside you. Go home, Bannon Farmer. You deserve it."

Nathan looked closely at Lila. "You swear to protect him? As a morazeth?"

"Always. You should not need to ask."

Offended, Bannon touched the sword Nathan had given him. "I thought you said I could take care of myself!"

Nicci and Nathan looked at each other with an amused expression.

Lila repeated, "You have nothing to worry about. I've already given my word."

They lingered for a long moment as the sun set, then Bannon and Lila made their way down to the kraken ship that was ready to depart.

Nicci turned back to look at the streets of Tanimura and around the harbor. The flat expanse of Halsband Island was still blackened with the ashes of funeral pyres, but the flames had finally gone out, and the brisk ocean winds had scoured the air clean of the stink of death.

Now that they stood together in the square, Nathan asked her, "So, what is to become of us? Are you also going to rest on the knowledge that the world is safe, thanks to us?"

"The world is never safe. And our promise to Richard is never over." Her brow furrowed with concern. "We know he is embroiled in a great crisis of his own up in D'Hara. If the danger is so great that he could not

spare troops when I asked, then perhaps we should return to the People's Palace and help him."

Nathan's lips quirked in a small smile. "I knew dear
Richard couldn't survive without us for long. You think
we should ride north, off to the rescue?"

"I believe he needs us." She wanted nothing more
than to fight at Richard's side again, to see his handsome face, feel his presence. But she had left D'Hara for
a reason, knowing that his heart belonged entirely and
unconditionally to Kahlan. Nicci accepted that, so she
had gone far away to keep serving him, but at a safe
distance where the ache in her heart would gradually
fade.

Wrestling with her decision, she looked around the
square, felt the weight of all that had occurred here.
Though the people in Tanimura were battered and emotionally drained, they knew they had won, and victory
gave a brightness to their mood.

The messenger who rode into the main square from
Altur'Rang, however, had a hard and twisted look on
his face, flinty eyes, and a sneer that was haughty and
superior. He raised his voice and demanded the attention of the crowd as they finished their work for the day.
"I bring word from the new capital of our restored empire!"

Nicci was instantly alert. "New empire?"

The man looked down from his horse and gave them
a withering look, as if they were beneath his notice. He
adjusted his helmet. "Your ignorance does not diminish the glory of Emperor Argus. Altur'Rang has been
under attack by an ancient army, and yet I bring word
to you that the foolish enemy warriors have been vanquished."

Nathan stepped closer. "Dear spirits! Was it the army of General Utros?"

"An expeditionary force of thousands of armed men," said the messenger as others gathered around. "But they were doomed to failure once they encountered the might of Emperor Argus. We offered them the chance to swear allegiance to the New Imperial Order, but they declined." His lips twisted in a smile. "Our fearless troops would have massacred them, but the Keeper himself intervened. The ground opened up and their souls were swept away to the underworld."

Nicci stepped forward to face him. "The Imperial Order is destroyed, and Emperor Jagang is dead." She didn't add that she herself had assassinated the horrible man.

"Emperor Jagang was no longer relevant," said the messenger. "The Imperial Order has returned under a new and stronger man, a ruler who would make Jagang quiver with awe."

Nicci couldn't imagine that anything would make Jagang quiver, but she merely assessed the arrogant messenger. She knew his type. She glanced at Nathan, whose eyes were wide and whose face was drawn.

"Dear spirits, a new Imperial Order?" he whispered.

Nicci knew what they had to do. "I had thought our duty was to go and assist Richard, but just as he was confident we could handle this war ourselves, we must be confident that Richard can deal with his own crisis." She narrowed her eyes. "If there is a New Imperial Order, if there is a man who claims Jagang's throne, then you and I have to go see this Emperor Argus ourselves."

"Indeed we do," Nathan said, his face flushed with anger. "Indeed we do."

Nicci raised her voice to the messenger. "We will accompany you to Altur'Rang. We would meet this Emperor Argus."

The man turned to them, assessing them. High in the saddle, he ran his eyes up and down Nicci's body, her blue eyes, her blond hair. She hoped she wouldn't have to kill him before they reached the grand capital city. "I cannot guarantee he will see you. Argus is an important man."

"I'm sure he is," Nathan said.

The messenger nudged his horse forward, slowly leaving them behind as he rode through the square to continue spreading his news. He called over his shoulder, "I will depart in the morning. You may follow me, but I will not pamper you."

Nathan chuckled. "Oh, young man, we do not need pampering."

Nicci's expression tightened. She felt hardened inside and knew that her work here in the Old World was not done. Richard had dispatched her and Nathan to spread the word of the D'Haran Empire, to let the world know that tyrants and despots and slavery would no longer be tolerated. Richard counted on her to crush them before they became too great a threat.

"We still have work to do, Nathan," she told him. "And you have a whole new life book to fill."

He nodded. "You are indeed correct, Sorceress." They watched the haughty messenger depart, already making their plans. "We should prepare for another journey."

"And another fight."

The wizard hesitated as he looked down to the harbor. They could see the krakener ship setting sails, ready to drift out to sea with the evening tide. "I planned ahead, my dear Sorceress." He reached into the vest that covered his ruffled shirt and pulled out a folded sheaf of papers. "I wrote a lengthy letter to Richard, and General Zimmer promised to dispatch a courier to ride north and deliver it to the People's Palace. It tells Richard everything he needs to know about what we've been up to." He arched his eyebrows. "Would you like to read it?"

Nicci accepted the letter, along with a lead stylus in case she needed to make notes. She skimmed the pages of stories that Nathan had written about their adventures, expecting that he would make himself into a legendary hero while portraying Nicci and Bannon as his faithful companions. Instead, she was surprised to see that the focus was on her own actions, making Nicci out to be the savior of the Old World.

Nicci handed the letter back to him. "It seems adequate. Remember, I came with you in the first place because Richard was sure you needed watching."

Nathan made a noncommittal sound as he scribbled a note at the very end before sealing the letter packet.

"What was that?" Nicci asked.

"A mere postscript to reassure Richard."

"Reassure him in what way?"

He tucked the letter back into his vest. "Merely a promise that I will keep watch over you, because no matter what you think, you still need watching . . . with or without the New Imperial Order. You can't save the world on your own."

"I am not alone," Nicci said, and realized it was true. The idea was suddenly strange to her, given her past, her time under the thumb of her stern mother, serving the Keeper as a Sister of the Dark or crusading for the Imperial Order. All of that was behind her forever. Nicci was stronger, better, braver. Those who wished to harm the world didn't have a chance.

She looked at Nathan, then drew her gaze across the bustling city of Tanimura, the forested hills, and the entire Old World beyond. She had no idea what sort of threat Emperor Argus or the New Imperial Order would pose, but she—they—would deal with it, no matter what.

"No," she repeated, "I am not alone."

THE WORLD OF
TERRY GOODKIND

DISCOVER THE SWORD OF TRUTH

THE NICCI CHRONICLES

In the world of Terry Goodkind's *New York Times* bestselling Sword of Truth saga, the warrior Nicci and her travel companion, the wizard Nathan, explore new and fantastical realms, encountering familiar allies, dangerous magic, and creatures forged by twisted sorcery.